MODERN MAGIC
Tales of Fantasy and Horror

Edited by
W. H. Horner

Illustrated by
David Seidman

Wilmington, Delaware

This book contains works of fiction. All names, characters, places, and events are either products of the authors' imaginations, or are used fictitiously. Any resemblance to actual events, locales, or persons—living or dead—is entirely coincidental. All trademarks and registered trademarks are the property of their respective owners.

All rights reserved, including the right to reproduce this book, or portions thereof, except in the case of brief quotations embodied in critical articles or reviews.

Fantasist Enterprises
PO Box 9381
Wilmington, DE 19809
www.fantasistent.com

Designed by W. H. Horner
Cover designed by W. H. Horner and David Seidman

Modern Magic: Tales of Fantasy and Horror
Copyright © 2006 by Fantasist Enterprises
ISBN 10: 0-9713608-4-7
ISBN 13: 978-0-9713608-4-6

First printing: April 2006

9 8 7 6 5 4 3 2 1

This book is available for wholesale through the publisher and through Ingram Book Group. It can be ordered for retail at most booksellers, both online and off, and is available from the publisher's website.

Fantasist Enterprises grants a discount on the purchase of three or more copies of single titles. For further details, please send an e-mail to bulkorders@fantasistent.com, or write to the publisher at the address above, care of "Bulk Orders."

Gadzooks!

Copyright Acknowledgments

Here be Dragons © 2006 by Kelley Armstrong

Stock Management © 2006 by Sarah A. Hoyt
Kindled Morphogenesis © 2006 by Alexa Grave
Salvation in a Plastic Bag © 2006 by P. Kirby
Joy, Unbottled © 2006 by Ron Horsley
Souls of Living Wood © 2006 by Eugie Foster
Peter I am Lost © 2006 by Kelly Hale
Zaubererkrieg © 2006 by Stephen D. Rogers
The Apprentice © 2006 by Joy Marchand
Office Magic © 2006 by Jon Sprunk
Raven © 2006 by Elaine Cunningham
Beauty, Sleeping © 2006 by Melissa Frederick
Unsung Hero © 2006 by Michael A. Pignatella
Swan Dive © 2006 by Christe M. Callabro
Feast of Clowns © 2006 by Robert Guffey
Subversion Clause © 2006 Richard Parks
Love's Consequence © 2006 Rhonda Mason
The Healer's Line © 2006 Jill Knowles
The Lamia © 2006 James S. Dorr
Midnight Snack © 2006 Ken Brady
Pavlov's Breast © 2006 Steve Verge
Golden Rule © 2006 Donna Munro
Wishbone © 2006 Erin MacKay
No Worries, Partner © 2006 Jim C. Hines
Pentacle on His Forehead, Lizard on His Breath © 2006 James Maxey
Undead Air © 2006 John Passarella
The Woman Who Walked with Dogs © 2006 Mary Rosenblum

Cover & Interior Illustrations © 2006 by David Seidman

To those who dare the dark alleys of the world, despite the goblins we instintually know exist.

-W. H. H.

For my muse, Cessie, who continues to inspire me every day.

-D. G.

Contents

Introduction
Here be Dragons — ix
Kelley Armstrong

Prelude
Stock Management — 1
Sarah A. Hoyt

The Fae
Kindled Morphogenesis — 11
Alexa Grave

Salvation in a Plastic Bag — 17
P. Kirby

Joy, Unbottled — 23
Ron Horsley

Souls of Living Wood — 37
Eugie Foster

Peter I am Lost — 43
Kelly Hale

Magic Users
Zaubererkrieg — 51
Stephen D. Rogers

The Apprentice — 53
Joy Marchand

Office Magic — 57
Jon Sprunk

Raven — 65
Elaine Cunningham

Beauty, Sleeping — 79
Melissa Frederick

Unsung Hero — 89
Michael A. Pignatella

Infernal Encounters
Swan Dive — 101
Christe M. Callabro

Contents

Feast of Clowns *Robert Guffey*	107
Subversion Clause *Richard Parks*	125
Love's Consequence *Rhonda Mason*	143

Monsters

The Healer's Line *Jill Knowles*	161
The Lamia *James S. Dorr*	169
Midnight Snack *Ken Brady*	181
Pavlov's Breast *Steve Verge*	187
Golden Rule *Donna Munro*	191

The Undead

Wishbone *Erin MacKay*	201
No Worries, Partner *Jim C. Hines*	207
Pentacle on His Forehead, Lizard on His Breath *James Maxey*	219
Undead Air *John Passarella*	227

Epilogue

The Woman Who Walked with Dogs *Mary Rosenblum*	247
About the Contributors	256

Introduction:
Here be Dragons
Kelley Armstrong

Even in this most modern of ages, our children grow up believing in magic. We tell them that an elf can travel the world in a night, riding the sky in a reindeer sleigh. That an ordinary rabbit can, for one day, do the same, and zip around the world hiding jewel-toned eggs. That a fairy can sneak to our bedside and ease the loss of a tooth with a silver coin.

From there, it's an easy leap for a child's mind to see magic everywhere. That golden glimmer in the shadow-choked forest? Not a stray sunbeam, but a leprechaun's pot of gold. Those tiny tracks around the dew-damp flowers? Not scampering mice, but the vestiges of midnight pixie dance. Those lumps of gray at the bottom of the ravine? Not a line of boulders, but a sleeping dragon, resplendent wings tucked under his dull gray form.

Our parents try to tell us there are no leprechauns, no pixies, no dragons, but we know better. If an elf can travel the world in a night, surely there must be sleeping dragons in that deep ravine. Then comes the day the magic is shattered, when we overhear a misspoken word or a schoolmate sets us straight. There is no jolly elf, no magical rabbit, no generous fairy. And so, we admit, that line of boulders in the ravine is probably just that: a row of rocks.

Yet some of us are reluctant to give up the magic. Even as adults, knowing there are no elves, no dragons, no vampires, no shape-shifters, we are drawn to the places where they still live: in art, in film, in stories. Especially in stories.

Yet having grown beyond stories of friendly ghosts and harmless pixies, our tastes have changed, and we find ourselves hungering for darker, sharper, harder fantasy, something that better reflects our adult lives. There's still room for the lighter side of magic, but we now look for that shadowy underside as well, a vicarious outlet for darker fears and urges. And when we do, we turn to the sort of fantasy we find in the stories in this collection, not snuggled into cozy bygone worlds of dragons and castles and knights, but set in our own, often harsher, modern world. Here we see our own universe, complete with all of our hungers and fears and dreams, coexisting with the fancies and monsters of our childhood.

As we read these stories, for those few minutes, lost in the words, we enter a place where magic is everywhere. Here is a place where something ancient can lie, dormant and waiting, in the murky water of a discarded bathtub. Where a ballet diva can deny the devil his share of her successes. Where werewolves, vampires and dragons can meet in plush hotel rooms to battle over the future of humankind. Where cubicle workers can wage war against office ignominy with words of corporate magic. Where a reluctant vegetarian can find unexpected relief hunting the monsters of the night. All this takes place in a universe very much like our own . . . and yet not like it. Recognizable, yet fantastical. Through these stories, the magical world of our childhood rises, like the fiery phoenix, consuming our imaginations and obliterating our doubts.

Kelley Armstrong

As a writer, and one who spends far too much of her adult life living in the world of magic, I'm always astounded by this process, how we can, with a few simple words, pull readers back into that long-lost world. Even though I, better than most, can see behind Oz's mask and understand how the illusion is constructed, as I read these stories, I was still transported. I searched for the explanation, and recalled the story of my son and the Komodo Dragon.

My youngest son is fascinated by dragons. His favorite toy belongs to his older sister, but there's no place she can hide it that he can't find it and drag it out, giggling with glee, treasure clutched in both arms. It's a dragon, of course, a two-foot tall stuffed dragon with shimmering iridescent skin, scaly batwings and huge silver talons and teeth. A toy both terrible and wondrous, as all the best monsters are.

When we were planning a trip to the zoo last year, he and his brother were pestering their sister for details, she who's been there countless times before. His brother asked the normal questions. Will I see lions and tigers and bears? Giraffes and elephants and rhinos? The youngest asked only one: will there be dragons?

Before I could intercept, his sister said, "Yes," and proceeded to explain that he would see a giant lizard called a Komodo Dragon. He was ecstatic. I was concerned. I tried to stave off disappointment, showing him pictures of a Komodo Dragon, and explaining that it didn't have wings or horns or breathe fire. He didn't seem to care.

That day at the zoo, I approached the Komodo Dragon enclosure with trepidation, certain I was about to have a very distraught three-year-old. I showed him the dragon . . . and held my breath. He stared . . . and said nothing, just stared. He continued to stare long after his brother, sister and father had wandered off, and we stood there together, watching this motionless gray log until the others returned and, even then, I had to pull him away.

When we left that building, he couldn't stop smiling. Somehow, where we saw only a giant lizard, he'd seen a dragon, maybe envisioning its beautiful wings tucked under its sleeping form, its glistening teeth and eyes hidden as it dozed, and surely, at night, after everyone was gone, it would come to life in all its fire-breathing glory and soar above the city with its brethren.

That's the magic of a child's mind, and that's the magic we find in these pages. We don't see dull, black words on a dull, white page. The words, like that sleeping lizard, are only the portal to our imagination. Once it opens, the world beyond becomes clear. We see fairies and werewolves and ghosts and sorcerers and, yes, sometimes even dragons.

PRELUDE

Stock Management
SARAH A. HOYT

Look, detective, my name is George Drake. My parents had a sense of humor, which—I see, from your blank expression—you don't appreciate.

You stare at me, from the side of your beat-up grey desk. Your eyes peek, menacing and dark above your reports. How can you stand to eat your greasy fish sandwich and drink that bitter, acid-smelling coffee?

You're not here to answer any questions.

True. But what good is my answering yours?

Oh, you saw the scene in that hotel as well as I did.

No, maybe you saw it better since I was busy fighting with all my might, with open mouth and flashing tooth and furled wings. . . .

But do you remember what you saw?

You don't think so.

Your little ape-brain, working in the way your ancestors learned when they peeked out of their dark caves and saw something that defied their reason—your little ape-brain, I say, has erased all traces of what you saw.

You and your trained investigators will have collected charred bodies, and bitten bodies and bloodless bodies, and people in inexplicable comatose states.

Yet you're treating this as a typical gangland killing.

Oh, you lean back and snicker at me, your best mocking ape-laughter, exposing those ridiculous stubby teeth of yours that are not good for chewing anything except cooked meat, and you tell me, "Try me, just try me."

Oh. I'll try you all right, because otherwise *they* will win and if they do—

What did you scribble on that pad? *Paranoid delusions?*

The paranoid part is true, I suppose. I do feel I'm being persecuted. So would you. So *should* you, because both of us are being chased down a blind alley—herded into death. Both of us and humanity, besides.

But the only deluded ones are you and your kind, thinking you're safe, and the night terrors banished forever, even while they control your every move.

I suppose your granny didn't tell you about dragons, or werewolves, fairies, vampires. . . . No, she wouldn't have.

Grannies aren't what they used to be.

But you must have heard about those creatures. In comic books, cheap novels, late-night movies—

I'm sure you think all those creatures are imaginary, dreamed up by your ape-ancestors, with their little ape-brains—

Evolution, yes, of course I believe in evolution. Most of your science is on target—if incomplete. It's not that evolution isn't true, just woefully narrow. Scientists sifting through bones and digs, choose the evidence they think makes sense, ignoring all other: the human footprint on a million-year-old rock; the five-hundred-thousand-year-old *Homo sapiens* skeleton.

They don't fit the picture and so off they go, treated as so much white noise in the beautiful music of evolution.

Only suppose, detective, suppose, for a moment that this wasn't true. Suppose that humans—not necessarily *Homo sapiens*—came from the stars, long ago, while nothing but a few pathetic mammals skittered about sucking dinosaur eggs. Suppose they then created *Homo sapiens*—

No, I don't read the *Enquirer*, either.

Last night's events. Ah. Last night's events. It will be hard to explain without telling you what came before.

My—uh—in your terms—my *family* got a summons, six months or so back. A summons to a summit.

This was important, because my family has had the ruling of human history these last two hundred years.

How, you ask? Oh, nothing illegal. Patient scouting out of opportunities, patient waiting, like a cat by a mouse hole. It is said that of all of . . . the families, ours is the most patient, the most articulate. It probably doesn't hurt that we're not inclined to eat human flesh—yes, I mean that literally—and that we live long. Very long. Longer than any other sentient.

So, when we—the Drakes—got the summons, it came as an unpleasant shock. For obvious reasons, when one family assumes prominence, it tries to sweep the other ones from positions of power, to drive them to the dark never-never of half-legality and mythical existence. There are several ways to do this, among them assassination. The Lupus clan ruled the middle ages. The burning pyres of the inquisition were their last attempt at keeping power, but they'd lost the battle long before it came to that. They'd lost it when people started reading about Greece and Rome and rediscovering an age before the sword and blood were the mightier—

Yes, the summons came from the Lupus and, in your blessedly enlightened age—thanks to us Drakes—it came by fax.

Our. . . . My father . . . our ruler, looked it over and evaluated it. It was his opinion—and how right it was—that it was a trap and therefore he decided to put as many of our people as he could around the location of the meeting.

I didn't know exactly where our people were—you understand—I'm the hundredth son—no, such profuse spawning isn't rare—and as such I have no need to be informed of all decisions.

In fact, it was decided I shouldn't know, just in case something went wrong and I was captured by the other side.

We had reason to suspect the Puck family might be in with the Lupus, as might the Vlads—they've long ago shed the other name, that confused them with us.

Anyway, I was expendable, I was sent to the meeting as my father's representative. The other side has trouble telling us apart and would never be able to distinguish me from my older brother, the heir, or even, maybe, from my father. As I said, we age slower than the other races.

Mind if I smoke? A cigarette, I mean. Thank you. It is a comfort. My mouth still tastes foul from the flaming last night. And tell me, detective, have you never found it odd that on the Internet the term *flaming* was so widely used for destructive attacks? Our fingerprint, if only you could see it.

The meeting took place at the Garth-Nemes. Owned by a relative of mine. We do own most of the wealth in the world. And create most of it. Wealth is our sustenance and we've learned to accumulate it.

You'd never think it, to look at him, but a computer tycoon who surprised the world with his meteoric rise to success in recent years—and some drake's hoard he's accumulated—is, of course, one of us, as are others—others you'd be shocked should I disclose their identities.

No, I don't intend to. No use challenging me. Not because it's such a secret, but because you wouldn't believe it any more than you believe anything else.

I went confidently to the meeting, knowing our people would be in the area and, besides, my father had assured me that there wasn't much the damn wolves could do to bring us down.

Our fortresses are secure, the prominent members of our race well-sheltered and guarded. And we are, physically, larger than any of the werewolves, or the fairies, or even the damn vampires.

Yes, of course, that's the families I alluded to. Those are their natures and their family names: Lupus, Puck, Vlad.

Although, understand, very few of them go under those names in the real world. And very few of them can be spotted, when in human form.

Certainly no one in the lobby of that expensive hotel looked other than human.

The valets and maids slid around on the high-pile white carpeting like ships across a smooth sea. And none of them—not one—*smelled*.

And right at the entrance, as I asked the help where room 3F was, where I was supposed to meet the others, the lack of smell bothered me.

When one of the valets—a small, blond young man—smiled at me, I noticed he had sharp, small teeth. Not enough for it to deviate alarmingly from pattern human but . . . it scared me, made me feel uneasy.

None of them seemed to see anything wrong with me. No. I wasn't naked. I only lost my clothes when I shifted shape.

When I went into the hotel, I wore a jade-green suit. Our family wears jade-green a lot. Look at the cover of computer magazines and you'll see that he, too, wears it.

I walked down an unexceptional corridor, to an unexceptional hotel meeting room.

Furniture, of the massive and pseudo-Mediterranean type—dressers and chairs in pickled oak—cluttered the hallway.

The meeting room was also massive: a salon with oatmeal-colored, textured-fabric walls, oatmeal-colored Berber carpeting, an oval golden-oak table, and oatmeal-upholstered arm chairs around it.

On the chairs sat what were definitely not your average people—although your eye might not have spotted their strangeness.

I knew I had trouble the moment I saw them.

Unlike us—the Drakes being egg-spawned and therefore running in similar-looking groups as you can tell if you look at any computer-company in the country—werewolves have a definite hierarchy that can be gauged on sight. Their rulers are always the largest of the pack.

The werewolf present . . . well, he stood at least six-eight, perhaps six-nine. He had sharp vulpine features, a mass of black hair that grew not only on his head but also on his arms, and across the backs of his hands. Tufts of black hair burst between the barely-joined-together front halves of his shirt. His gold watch band just showed amid the black forest.

He grinned at me as I entered, a wolf-grin displaying his prominent canines.

Beside him, the Vlad—no one you'd know, they avoid the limelight. . . . Listen to me! They

Sarah A. Hoyt

avoid all light, of course. She was a mousy woman, with dark hair caught up in a bun, and spectacles. She looked at me and smiled, displaying her fangs.

I didn't like the smiles, but what I liked even less was the representative of the Puck family. You'd recognize him instantly. His amiable face has gazed at you from a thousand photographs in a thousand magazine covers—his winsome smile has graced supermarket-checkout scandal sheets and serious publications dealing with policy. Particularly after his recent marital difficulties.

Oh, your eyes widen. You didn't recognize his corpse, then?

He was one of the first I flamed, but perhaps I flamed him too thoroughly. I'm amazed, though, that his disappearance hasn't been noted yet. But then, the Pucks, too, tend to be born in large pods, and perhaps one of his brothers has taken his place. Or perhaps this was one of his pod-brothers who died.

Anyway, when I saw him, I knew I was in trouble. This was not a meeting to challenge my family's supremacy. It was a meeting to inform us that we'd already lost the battle.

I started sweating and my change-reflexes attempted to take over.

I swear I'd never guessed the Pucks were in any way making a bid for power. Of their own accord, they can't organize anything, not even themselves. For most of humanity's history, the power balance has gone between our family and the Lupus, with the other two families shifting alliances as needed.

The French Revolution was probably the only bid the Vlads ever made for power, and though they weren't exactly our allies, their eruption allowed us to overturn the werewolves once and for all.

They did rule the countries behind the iron curtain, too, but only for seventy years, a flick of a finger on the eternal dial and the long life-spans of our families.

So . . . I didn't suspect the Pucks of ruling ambitions and I never recognized *him* for one of them. Though I suppose only the glamoury of which his kind is capable can explain his survival in power this long, particularly given the lack of organization that is also typical of his kind.

As I said, they all stood and smiled at me.

I was sweating and shaking, but I managed to say, "I am Drake. You have summoned me."

The werewolf smiled and said, "Yes. We have summoned you to give you a chance to cut a deal. As you can see, we have allies in high places." He gestured towards the Puck, who smiled his slickly persuasive smile in my direction.

"Wait," I said. "Wait." My skin had started beading with the peculiar ichor sweat that lubricated the way for the scales that would follow my transformation. My incipient stump of a tail twitched impatiently within my well-tailored pants. Stumps of wings beat at the back of my shirt, between my shoulders.

They had the highest political offices. I took deep breaths, trying to calm myself, trying to avert panic, trying not to show my fear. "Wait, you can't be so sure of your position. Yes, you might have the politics, but we have business and in this dual world we live in, politics are no longer the hinge of it all. It's not like your benighted middle ages when taking the king meant taking it all. The chess game has changed a little, Lupus, my friend."

He laughed. It is something awful to see one of them laugh. "Oh, yes, you have the business. But do you, now? Your people might hold the high offices and rake in the money, but aren't they dependent on hundreds of humbler servants?" He smiled at the Vlad. "Drake, while your people took over the computer industry and built your vaunted Internet and started talking of taking humanity out of the planet and into space, we have been working. We, and our allies." He smiled at the Vlad, who smiled back, her little black eyes twinkling behind pince-nez glasses. "One by one, at our request, the Vlads have penetrated, subverted, taken over offices everywhere. They abandoned their blood banks to join forces with us. You even find them all over your computer companies. Not every office worker is a Vlad, only the influential ones. And influence and power isn't always where you expect them. They're secretaries, humble file clerks, bureaucrats. And they hold the real power." He grinned at me. "If you don't believe me, think why else office buildings would be forests of little cubicles, lit only by artificial light. In how many office buildings have you seen partitions blocking out daylight from the broad windows? All the work of the Vlads.

"They've worked in other ways, too, promoting the political power of the Pucks. The Pucks started infiltrating politics in the beginning of the twentieth century. Now they dominate all countries and most parties. We haven't changed much. The wolves remain the military might of the world. Some of us might have made inroads in politics and religion. You'll recognize us, if you think about it, by the hairiness and the disposition, but mostly we stayed in the shadow. This time we're working through our allies. And we're ready to give you an ultimatum." He grinned wolfishly.

"We only demand a share of the stock management." His beetling eyebrows rose and fell. "The livestock management. You are the smart ones, the clever ones, cook us up a war or a rebellion, a confusion large enough to create many corpses on which the rest of us can feed, unseen. It is a lamentable thing that my race needs human blood to survive, as do the Vlads. Oh, they have their blood banks, for everyday sustenance, but they still crave and need the living blood." He shrugged, apologetically, huge shoulders rising and falling and causing the hair to poke out further between the over-strained halves of his checkered shirt.

"And blood of live humans is in short supply in your sanitized, demographically accurate modern societies. There's only so many trips one can take to Third World countries. As for the Pucks, they do not need blood, but they appreciate the turmoil that comes from wars, revolutions. Feeding on human feeling, as they do, they like the raw emotions better than the bland ones.

"So provide us with wars and revolutions, with sieges and devastation enough on a regular basis, so we can feed, and we'll leave your little wealth-creating empire alone. Otherwise, you've seen we have the power to crush you. We'll bring the anti-monopoly laws down on your computer megaliths and the Vlads will sabotage you from the inside, ensuring that your released products are full of bugs. The computer industry will come crashing down about your ears. So, tell me, Drake, which will it be?"

All right, so I reacted without thinking—or without thinking it through. My panic at the realization that I'd been trapped, my paranoid fear that my own family had known just what would happen and had sent me in, as a sacrificial lamb, to give them the time to think through and negotiate a better deal. . . . All those emotions knotted up inside of me.

A little war, a little revolution. . . .

But my family needs stable times for the computer era to continue flourishing. We need our wealth as much as the other races need their odd fodder.

My wings, growing to their full seven-foot span, tore through my shirt, brushing the chandelier on the ceiling. My forked tail poked through the pants at the back. The rest of my suit and my expensive white silk shirt, well, my guess is that they tore as my body expanded to ten times its normal size.

Since the mass remains the same—only more spread out—this made it possible for me to fly to the ceiling of the room and flame, left and right.

The Puck was the first one to go—an expression of extreme wounded surprise in his blue-grey eyes—engulfed in flames and burned away. I took out the Vlad, too, though I had to flame her longer to ensure she was truly dead.

The werewolf made it out of the room, though.

I was right. There was something wrong about the valets. Most of them were Pucks, I think, with a few carefully shaved Lupus thrown in.

However, my people had taken over the maids. The battle was nasty, though I don't know—and you probably can't remember—how nasty.

I have no idea how I escaped unharmed. I bit and clawed, and flamed. Oh, boy, did I flame. Not even the fire sprinklers could prevent my burning half the treacherous bastards who would wrest power from my family and send all races of humans into primordial violence to satisfy their animal hungers. . . .

I woke up with you putting handcuffs on me, while I sat, dazed, on the floor of a hallway that had been charred, flooded, and bloodied beyond recognition.

Do you mind if I smoke another cigarette?

Thank you.

You see, I'm not exactly afraid of your justice, detective. Your ape peace-enforcement doesn't scare me.

I've rested long enough. When I'm done with this cigarette, I shall change form, rush out of the station and fly through the clear blue air to my family home.

Conspicuous? Nah. No one, not even yourself, will actually believe what he sees.

Faced with what it has been taught is only mythological, *Homo sapiens* edits it out. It's a defense mechanism, like possums playing dead. Doesn't always work, but it's comforting enough.

No, I don't fear your justice.

What I fear is that my father, savvy creature of the world that he is, will have cut a deal. . . . A deal involving a few disasters, a few revolutions, a few wars.

He won't realize this is just the slippery slope into a new dark age that will allow the werewolves to rage amid the humans once more and raise their bloodied muzzles to the sky in triumph.

Which is why I decided to speak frankly to you detective. All the supernaturals are allied against the Drakes but, as I said, we're the ones who don't feed on human flesh or human suffering—we could forget that our ancestors created you from the native life forms. We might be willing to treat you as humans, as allies, if you put aside your ape-fears and stand beside us and help us.

We could start with you, and your closest friends.

Quietly spread the word of what is really going on. Drag the Vlads out of the offices into the full noon-day sun. Surround your local politician with cold metal . . . no need for knives, just wrap them in iron chain. As for the werewolves, lock your doors at night, secure them, do not allow hairy strangers in. . . .

The apes and the Drakes, allied, we can do great things. The apes and the serpents. . . .

So, take a sip of your coffee, detective, and tell me . . . what are you going to do?

The Fae

Elves have survived to see internal combustion engines, fast-food, and reality TV. Elemental spirits have adjusted to the near-ubiquitous presence of man. Some have attempted to hide away, while others are making do, eking out an existence in this brave new world of yuppies and druggies.

Kindled Morphogenesis
Alexa Grave

Two visions scorched Fiona's mind: the horror before her eyes and the flames smoldering in her psyche. She dropped her house keys, and they clattered on the linoleum.

Fiona cried out, falling to her knees. Dailon had told her to leave for the afternoon, so she had gone on a hike in the woods near their house. Now, she came back to this. Her elven lover's eyes stared up at the ceiling.

She dug her hands into her hair and yanked. A few strawberry-blonde strands came away with her fingers, and she stared at them. They flamed with the flashes in her mind. She disregarded the image and crawled across the kitchen floor.

"Dailon, wake up." Fiona shook him, but he didn't move, didn't react to her touch. Instead, residual magic clung to Fiona's skin. It inched up her arms and threatened to strangle her with its potency.

She jumped back. Dailon had taught her to sense magic, but she had never felt anything so wicked before. Fiona caressed his cheek, smooth and cold, allowing the residual magic to weave around her. She read into the power that killed Dailon, and it assaulted her senses.

Two other elves did this.

The image in her mind overlaid that of Dailon's body; flames engulfed her, but they didn't burn. Fiona failed to comprehend where the fire sprang from, and why it ignited now. If it was part of the memories she had searched for so long, she wanted nothing to do with it. Dailon mattered now, not this conflagration in her brain.

She stroked Dailon's pointed ear. His lifeless body and the flames melded into one otherworldly picture. He lay on a pyre, his body surrounded by flickering orange, refusing to be consumed.

Fiona shouldn't have listened to Dailon, or she should have at least questioned why he wanted her out of the house. The peaceful walk she had had in the woods felt tainted. While she had relaxed and embraced the world around her, Dailon died.

She flung herself over him. Dailon had stood at her side for five years. He had found her and given her memories to replace those she had lost.

There had to be a reason for this, and she intended to find it. The magical residue tugged at Fiona. She memorized the intricacy of both strands and knew she could track whoever did this. Dailon had taught her well.

She would hunt down the elves who killed her lover and kindled the fire.

A sharp pain tugged at Fiona's brow, and she woke, tangled in sweat-soaked sheets. With consciousness came the emptiness. It had been one month since Dailon's death, yet the anguish over his absence hadn't dulled.

Fiona kept her eyes closed, not wanting to face the world. The dream she woke from lingered. Each flame licked over her skin. She breathed the fire in as if it were oxygen, every hot tendril necessary for her existence. Pleasure radiated from the warmth.

Something pulled at Fiona's hair again, forcing her to open her eyes.

"Your skin is scalding again. You need to go to a doctor," the fairy said.

Mitay worried too much. The fevers weren't really fevers. They started after Dailon's death, growing in frequency, always paired with her visions of fire. She felt fine when they struck, more comfortable than when she was without them. Fiona didn't think it had anything to do with sickness.

The flames.

She didn't want to be tested, poked, or prodded until they finally said they didn't know what was wrong with her. It would all resolve itself once she found Dailon's murderers. His death had triggered the convoluted memories. Once she faced his killers and gained the answers she needed, that would cure her. This knowledge burned in her.

"No," Fiona said. "And get out of my hair."

"Tish. How many times do I have to tell you, it's the best nest." Mitay snuggled deeper into Fiona's locks.

"What did I ever do to be cursed with such a fae for a friend?"

"You know you love me. Where would you be without me?"

Indeed.

Tires screeched and car horns blared outside. Mitay said, "I know where I'd be, though, if I didn't worry about you. Somewhere in the country, not in this foul-smelling city."

"You know why we're here."

"How long are we going to hunt them, Fiona? We can't even be sure they're in this city."

"I know they're here. I can feel it." It had taken her a while to pick up their trail, but their magic thrummed through her entire body, vibrating her bones. It was only a matter of days before she pinpointed them.

"Your magic sense is awfully strong for a human."

"Do you doubt me?"

"No. And you know I'm with you until the end. Whatever that might be."

"I know." Fiona rolled out of bed.

Mitay clung to her hair. "Hey, warn me why don't you." She untangled herself and flew to the bedpost.

"Sorry."

Fiona could sense the magic of the murderers, but she couldn't use magic, and depending on how things played out, it might be needed. Mitay was her only friend once Dailon had died. Her magic would have to do.

All this for Dailon, who gave her a name and his love.

And to douse the blaze.

Fiona stepped into the shower, the water quenching the heat of her feverish skin and scattered memories.

Fiona stared at the candle, match in hand. She wanted to try something, and since Mitay was out getting food, this was the best time. Her hand shook as she struck the match. The scent of smoke stung her nose as she lit the candle.

The flame danced before her eyes and in her head, its light beckoning to her. She stuck her finger into the fire. It flickered, enveloping her flesh. She waited for the pain, even longed for it, but it didn't come. A calm washed over her, starting from her fingertip and spreading throughout her entire body.

The blaze in her mind rose up, reaching new heights, as if it had been doused with gasoline.

Fiona pulled her hand back from the candle, and the fire in her mind died down. Her finger was whole, no burn or blister marred her skin.

It only took Fiona two days after the candle incident to discover their hiding place.

She paused in front of an abandoned warehouse. Sweat rolled down her face, even with the cool night breeze.

The magical vibrations emanating from the building matched those that killed Dailon.

Mitay perched on her shoulder. "You're hotter than ever," she said. "We should go."

"Hush. I feel fine." Fiona felt well enough, except for a slight desire to plunge her hands into the flames that shot out from a metal drum in the alley. "I think you're turning into a chicken."

"Far from it. I just want to make sure we're prepared. And that we're doing this for a good reason."

"Do you want to find out why Dailon was killed?"

"Of course," the fairy said. "Not knowing why he died is a horrible way to end a fifty-year friendship. But if we go in there, we might not come back out."

Fiona swallowed. "I know." She dug in her purse and pulled out a small handgun. The clerk had said it was perfect for a woman wanting to protect herself, but Fiona had already forgotten what he called it.

Mitay squeaked and fluttered off Fiona's shoulder. "I was wondering why you brought that bag."

"This is if your magic doesn't work against them," Fiona said, and tossed the empty purse into the alley.

"Do you know how to use that thing?"

"If you don't want to go in with me, you don't have to, but I'm not stopping here." Fiona walked toward the warehouse.

"Dailon made sure you weren't at home when it happened. He wanted to protect you," Mitay said.

Fiona stumbled in mid-step. Dailon had wanted her to live. "I have to know why." She also needed to throw off the inflamed memories.

"And you're seeking vengeance."

"Maybe."

"When has that ever been a good reason?"

Fiona turned back to Mitay. "Vengeance is a perk. You're worried about my fevers. Well, this is the way to end them. They started when Dailon died. And the memory flashes paired with the fevers are consuming me."

"Memories? You never said anything about that. And what makes you think killing them will stop it?"

"I just know. They triggered it, their deaths will stop it." *Hopefully.*

Mitay hovered in the air, silent. Then she finally flew over to Fiona. "You know I can't let you do this alone."

The rusted lock on the warehouse door was already broken off. It was dark inside, except for a light further in. This place had been abandoned for a long time. A thick layer of dirt was on the floor, and the few boxes that were left were scattered, trampled, and battered.

"Should I scout ahead?" Mitay asked.

"No. Let's stay together."

A smooth voice echoed from the back of the warehouse. "Don't be shy, Fiona. Come in. We've been expecting you."

Fiona followed the voice and the light, cursing under her breath. She hadn't been careful enough, and they knew she was coming.

Two male elves greeted her in the fluorescent-lit back room. Mitay stayed behind in the shadows. There was a chance they didn't know Fiona had come here with a friend.

"Welcome, welcome," one of the elves said. Both smiled at her. They wore white lab coats, pocket protectors and all. The only things missing were thick-rimmed glasses.

These are Dailon's killers? The two magic strains she had sensed on Dailon's body undoubtedly belonged to them. Fiona's stomach turned from the tainted feel of their power. She raised the gun, and her hand shook. "Why did you kill Dailon?"

"He wouldn't give you to us, of course," the other elf said.

Fiona faltered, the sweat streaming down the back of her neck. There was nothing she had that they could want, but if they were telling the truth, Dailon had died for her. "What game are you two playing at?"

"No game."

She aimed the gun at one, then the other.

"You look a bit perplexed, Fiona. If you want things clearer, I guess I can oblige," one of the elves said, and stepped toward her. "When Dailon refused to hand you over, we felt it was best to kill him, otherwise he would have stopped us from taking you. So we waited for you to arrive, and were we surprised at your reaction."

"You were watching me?" Fiona struggled with the details of that day. She had been distracted with Dailon's death and the emergence of her memories, and she hadn't started tracking the elves until after the funeral.

"Yes. And we thought we'd let you be for a while. To observe you naturally. Some of our colleagues took it upon themselves to keep tabs on you, since we couldn't get close to you until we wanted to be found."

"It's all been intriguing, to say the least," the other elf said. "It looks as though the heat is getting to you, Fiona."

This made things anything but clear. "I have nothing you need," she said.

One elf looked at the other. "Her lover wasn't lying. She has no clue."

"Amusing," the other elf said. "How are those memories of yours, Fiona? Coming more frequently?"

The muscles in her arm twinged, and she lowered the gun. "How do you know?" She hated to think how closely they might have watched her.

"We've been searching for you for a long time. Dailon had you quite secluded out in the middle of nowhere. We know about your past. It's a pity we didn't know you before you lost your memories, then it wouldn't have taken this long to find you."

Fiona raised the gun again. "Did you trigger them on purpose?"

"No. That was your own doing."

The fire sprang up behind her eyes. *Her own doing.* Something inside herself brought the flame and heat.

Dailon had known things about her that she didn't, and he wanted to save her from these elves, these scientists. He had protected her and whatever was inside her. This was no way to repay him, by running from the memories and hunting these murderers. The blaze grew inside her, and she embraced it.

Fiona released the gun. It clattered to the ground, echoing the fall of her keys when she had found her lover dead.

The elves frowned at her. "You disappoint us. We were looking forward to see what you'd do," one said. They approached her.

Mitay darted from the shadows, throwing up a magical barrier between Fiona and the elves. "Leave her be."

Fiona smiled at the fairy's courage. "No, Mitay. Shield yourself, not them. Protect me when I'm weak." Mitay turned to her, brows drawn together and unasked questions hanging from her slightly open mouth. Fiona wasn't even sure what she meant, but she would soon.

Flame licked down Fiona's arms. She studied her burning hand, shocked yet comforted by the intense heat. The inferno was beyond her control, consuming her when it deemed fit.

Mitay yelped. The barrier flickered out, and a blue orb appeared around the fairy. Both elves retreated, flattening themselves against the back wall.

The fire wrapped itself around Fiona, until her entire body was engulfed in yellows and oranges. Her clothes burned to ash, leaving her naked to the world. And her memory came alive.

She had a name before her life with Dailon, but what it was didn't matter because now she was Fiona, changed in every aspect from who she used to be. Fiona had done the unthinkable. She had been young and arrogant. How the flames had enticed her.

In this life, she had hunted for these scientists, and in her former life, she had hunted the phoenix. Fiona had wanted to see the immortal phoenix consume itself and give birth to a new being. She hadn't just desired to see it, she longed to be a part of it.

The heat grew, and Fiona touched the minds of those around her. How these elves reminded her of her former self. They sought the key to unsurpassable power, to immortality. Their greed drove them. Fiona was the first and only one to ever accomplish the feat that gave her a new life.

Immortality had drawn her to the phoenix, and she let the fire take her away. She had entered its flames without a second thought. The phoenix had engulfed her body, feeding off of her flesh. Now she remembered Dailon. He had been hidden behind a boulder, watching the whole thing. She had noticed him as the phoenix embraced her. He must have been hunting the legendary bird, too.

The blaze had devoured everything, both bird and human turned to ash. Fiona had been reborn from those ashes, but she was no longer human, and her past had been erased.

Now, the fire surrounding her intensified. Blue flame tore at her flesh. Fiona knew if she wanted to, she could reach out with the flame, touch the elves, and incinerate them. But she wouldn't.

Her skin flaked off. Fiona touched Mitay's thoughts and read her panic. Her friend worried too much. "Mitay. No fears."

Fiona lost her vision. This time she hoped to keep her memories, so she'd always have Dailon's face to return to whenever she felt empty. Her body dismantled itself. The fire remained warm and reassuring until her mind fluttered to ash.

Salvation in a Plastic Bag
P. Kirby

If he had to do the killing, drive the bolt through their big thick heads, he would never eat beef. At home he rarely ate meat; at home he was expected to hunt. But here, meat came in neat packages, a once-living critter sliced, diced, and wrapped in plastic and Styrofoam.

Or in this case, folded inside a warm corn tortilla. Talis angled the taco sideways and bit down through tortilla, lettuce, cheese, and spicy shredded beef. He chewed, watching the restaurant's doorway and the dark street beyond. He was midway through his second plate, beef burritos, when Breas finally showed up.

"Talis," the vampire said. Even as he sat down, his gray eyes continued to roam the restaurant. A consummate practitioner of the art of survival, Breas Montrose took his immortality seriously.

"Hey, Montrose," Talis said.

"Hey, yourself." Breas's gaze fell on the empty plate. "You got some kind of Fey tapeworm?"

Talis shrugged and swooped up a forkful of rice. Better than any fad diet, his habit worked like Teflon, keeping any weight from sticking to his tall frame. A friend had once described him as a chocolate-covered skeleton.

The waiter returned and filled his water glass. "*Gracias*," Talis said. The waiter nodded and moved on, seeing only a thin, dark-complexioned human.

With his rich brown skin, sky-blue canted eyes, soot-black hair and pointed ears, Talis was anything but human. A cloaking glamour kept his true features hidden from human eyes.

Breas glanced at his watch. "You done? We're supposed to be across town in twenty minutes."

"Yeah, I—" Talis stopped, his mouth open. Across the room, in a short hallway that opened to the kitchen, the waiter stood talking to a busboy. As Talis watched, the waiter's olive complexion faded and bruises bled across his face, dark irregular islands on a sea of dead gray skin. Behind the man, the restaurant dissolved and was replaced by—

Pain.

Talis had fumbled blindly, found a fork, and driven the tines into his thumb, banishing the portentous vision. Haloed by yellow light that poured from the kitchen, the waiter laughed, hearty and hale.

"I, uh, gotta run to the restroom," Talis said, ignoring the look of disgust on the vampire's face.

A few minutes later he emerged from the restaurant, finding Breas waiting in the parking lot.

"You're still using, aren't you?" Breas asked.

"Why do you ask, if you already know the answer?" Talis said.

"Stupid kid," the vampire muttered. "That crap won't cure whatever ails you." Without a glance at Talis, he turned and walked toward a parking lot next to the building.

Talis shivered, the drug trickling though his nervous system. "I know," he said.

The Elf Dust did nothing to mask the vision. It hit Talis just as they passed Asarco, the copper refinery on the far west edge of El Paso. His sight tunneled to a pinprick of light. The spot of light then expanded, the scene shifted and he stood in the middle of a wide lawn. Someone—Breas?—spoke, his voice muffled, distorted. A duct-taped cardboard box sat on the ground about six feet away. Talis shivered. Little rivulets of blood dribbled through various tears in the cardboard, leaving vertical red stripes down the brown surface. Pain shot up Talis's arm.

"Hey!" Breas said. The vampire's fist had pummeled Talis's upper arm. The vision evaporated, replaced by the lights of Westside El Paso, a carpet of bright pinpoints huddled beneath the dark mass of the Franklin Mountains. "What the hell did you take?"

Talis's head slumped forward and he stared at the buttery soft leather car seats. "Nothing," he said, rubbing his arm. His lank black hair fell over his face and he risked a glance at Breas. "I'm fine," he added, in an effort to sound reassuring. He pushed his hair off his face and looked out the window. Catching a glimpse of a thin, dark face blinking pale eyes, he turned away and stared at the dashboard.

Breas didn't indulge in trite vampiric flamboyance. He wore blue jeans, a sweatshirt with a sports team logo and hiking boots. His blond hair was short and he never wore black. But Breas loved sleek overpriced European cars. Talis's gaze wandered over the rich walnut dashboard, pausing on the radio. He scanned through frequencies, stopping on a country station.

Breas punched a preset button. The station changed and something heavy on strings and low on twang sang out of the speakers.

"Hey! That was Reba!"

"My car. No hillbilly shit," Breas said.

"You're a snob."

"I put up with *you*, don't I?" Breas's jaw clenched. "Can you even do magic?"

"Of course—"

"I mean, hopped up on—" Breas paused and sniffed, "at least four hits' worth of Elf Dust."

Talis lifted his hand, elongated fingers moving with the ease of a fluent speaker of sign language. Magical energy vibrated and pushed through his skin. The radio crackled. Reba McEntire replaced Vivaldi. "Not many Fey can do that, surrounded by iron," Talis said.

Breas nearly smiled.

Hiding the pain the effort had cost him, Talis faced his reflection.

Thirty-thousand years ago, spurred on by precognitive visions of seers that foretold vast riches beneath the fishing waters of another race of Fey, the Elves set about exterminating their only obstacle to prophesized wealth—the Mar'Gwynt, Talis's people. The Elves were nearly successful. The few surviving Mar'Gwynt were driven far inland. Though they would rebuild much of their civilization, Talis's people still longed for the sea and cursed the Elves.

Talis watched bright signs, motels, gas stations, and warehouse stores whiz by, grateful for the glare that washed away his reflection. El Paso was a long way from any ocean.

Born on Fey Plane nearly 150 years before, Talis had spent the majority of his life on Earth. When life on iron-rich Earth Plane didn't quell his precognitive visions, he had resorted to chemical controls. *Using* led to *dealing*. If he needed extra money, he ran errands and provided backup for Breas, who called himself a "procurer of hard-to-obtain artifacts." Talis called him a smuggler, but never to his face.

Salvation in a Plastic Bag

Talis's visions started when he turned forty. His father, scandalized by his son's gift—precog ability was an Elf power—promptly disowned him. Not all visions were bad. Some—lottery numbers and winning slot machines—paid the rent. The foreknowledge of his sister's death initiated the darker phase of his visions.

Talis could not save his sister or any unfortunate soul he "saw" thereafter, no matter what he tried. The fate revealed by the visions had the consistency of glue, never relinquishing those it caught.

"Done brooding?" Breas said. "We're almost there."

Talis ignored the vampire and tried to picture his sister's face, finding, as usual, that her features eluded him. The swift current of Elf Dust carried away most emotion and eroded memories.

The car skimmed up Country Club Road, passing older homes on large lots. Tall trees, anomalous in the desert, flanked the road. The turn signal tick-tick-ticked and Breas turned left on a narrow street. A flickering streetlight winked out as they passed. Breas shot a questioning glance at Talis.

"Wasn't me." Despite his bravado, Talis's demonstration a few minutes before had stripped him of his innate power. It took a lot to cast through a drug-addled brain.

They drove up a curved driveway, stopping before a two-story brick house that sat back on a grassy lot, hunched like a dog over a bone. Breas pulled down the window long enough to test the air before shutting down the car and getting out. Talis followed. Two bulky shadows separated from the dark of the porch and moved toward them. Talis sniffed, detecting the earthy scent of Sharet demon.

The four stood in two pairs, five feet apart. Both demons were tall with comical proportions—massive shoulders set on torsos that tapered to narrow waists. In the dim light, their green skin took on a grayish cast. The taller of the two inclined his head. "Breas Montrose?" he said with a grating metallic voice, yellow eyes settling on the vampire.

Breas nodded. "Yes. And my associate, BelTalis'aresh ap Darafinet."

The demon nodded at Talis. "I am called Fred. And this is my brother Mel."

Breas's mouth twitched. "I have the requested item. You have payment?"

"Yes." Fred gestured at his brother.

Mel stood motionless, his stare fixed on some point on the ground.

"Mel!"

Mel jerked awake and stumbled toward Breas. His shaking green hands gave the vampire a cloth bag. While Breas counted the money, Talis studied Mel. Little rivulets of nerve tremors slithered up and down the demon's neck. *Mel's strung out*, Talis thought.

"Sixty-two thousand in Elf currency, as specified by the contract," Fred said.

Breas smiled, the expression bypassing his eyes. "It's all there." He turned his hand in the air, as if to unscrew a light bulb. A tiny flash, the smell of ozone and a lacquered box appeared in the vampire's hand. Fred nudged his brother and then nudged him a second time. Mel retrieved the box and gave it to his brother, who inspected it.

Talis, Elf Dust humming in his system, studied the ground.

Grass. Winter-brown grass.

In his vision, it had been day, the grass green. But things often shifted in his visions, filled with symbolism his untrained mind could not interpret. Talis lifted his head and scrutinized the place.

The box sat about twenty feet away. No blood. No duct-tape.

Talis was just a step away from the box before he realized his feet had moved.

"Talis, what the hell?" Breas said.

"Kittens," Talis said, crouching by the box. Six small cats raised their heads and meowed. He smiled. "White, ginger, calico, even a black one." He turned to Fred. "You giving them away?"

The demon looked shocked. "Of course not. They are for the Tithe games."

Tithe games? Talis thought, stumbling over a gap in his memory.

"The main event at the Sharet Tithe festivities. Their warriors fight blood-crazed Fhomor bears," Breas said. "This time of year, the bears are just coming out of hibernation. They're lazy and hard to provoke."

The loose connections in Talis's brain snapped in place. "Y-you throw the kittens to the Fhomor bears?" Talis's heart pounded, a deep bass to the kittens' high-pitched snare drums.

"Yes," Fred said, a happy glint in his eye. "They are easy prey. The bears tear them apart—"

"That's horrible," Talis blurted, glancing at Breas.

Breas shrugged. "Blood-sucking creature of the night, remember?"

Talis stood up, his attention squarely on the box, listening to the thumps and mews of the playing animals. The black kitten sat apart from its compatriots, tawny stare fixed on Talis.

He took two quick steps back. Every year the humans sent thousands of these creatures to "shelters" where most were killed. The little cats were doomed; it made no difference whether they died on a demon world or here on Earth. His guilt wasn't a problem. The Elf Dust may have started to lose its efficacy against the visions, but it still reined in pesky attacks of conscience.

"Yeah, let's go," he said to Breas.

"You doing an impression of a statue?" Breas said when Talis didn't move. "Less movement and you'll have pigeons crapping on your head."

Talis turned to face the demons. "Perhaps we could work out something—"

"Talis," Breas said.

"Got any Surreal?" asked Mel, his eyes picking up an eager orange tint.

A spark of hope flickered in Talis's chest. *It can't be this easy, can it?* "Yeah. Yeah, I do." He fumbled in his jacket pockets. He never took the stuff anymore; it had stopped working years ago. Now he just sold it. He pulled out the bag and held it before the demon addict's eyes. "You can have it all. For the kittens."

Mel nodded, but Fred interrupted. "One kitten," he said, scowling.

"No," Talis said, desperation squeaking in his voice. He tried for his power, thwarted by the Elf Dust that rode his blood.

"Yes. In Sharet homeland, these creatures are worth four bags of HallowBone," Fred said, referring to a premium hallucinogen.

"Let it go, Talis," Breas said.

Talis, hands shaking, pulled out the last of the Elf Dust.

Fred sneered. "No Dust. My people don't—"

"But you can sell it," Talis said.

"No," Fred said, but Mel eyed the package of Surreal like a starving dog near a steak.

Breas groaned. "Come on, kid. Give him the junk and grab a cat. Or—"

"Okay, okay." Talis lowered his hand and jammed the drug back in his pocket.

He shut his eyes and reached into the box. His hands closed around fuzzy heat and pulled the creature from its siblings. He carefully tucked it in his jacket pocket and walked to the car. Breas unlocked the vehicle and both men got in.

The ignition clicked, the engine purring to life. "You got the black one," Breas said.

Talis's thin shoulders rose with a sigh and he eased the kitten out.

Breas reached over and scratched the kitten behind its ears. "I'd wager this is the first time Surreal *saved* a life."

Talis bowed his head and met the cat's yellow eyes. *This is the first time I've saved a life, changed fate.* He pushed thin fingers through ebony fur, feeling warm possibilities in the cat's vitality. The spark of hope he had felt earlier ignited dry despair.

"So what's its name?" asked Breas.

"Her," Talis corrected gently. The cat sat on his lap, quiet and proud, fierce gaze demanding an answer.

"Eithne," Talis said. "Little fire."

Joy, Unbottled
RON HORSLEY

A chorus recital. Tammy standing in her starched white blouse buttoned up to the neck and her severe blue skirt, singing "There's a Little Wheel Turning in My Heart" and "When Johnny Comes Marching Home Again." She'd spent four weeks, three hours after school, practicing with the rest of the second-grade recital group. Dad complained about having to go pick her up so late after work, but the night of the recital he'd been dressed in his best, not complaining.

My father, in a suit and tie he never wore to work. Standing in my bedroom doorway.

Gray tweed. The black tie an upside-down exclamation point. Above this, his head the oversized pink period. His hair was thinning. He smelled of cologne I can't find in department stores anymore.

My last memory of my mother is a silhouette in my bedroom doorway. Her hand like cold wax on my forehead, feeling how hot my fever was.

� ☽ ♀ ☿ ♋

They didn't survive hitting the embankment on the way home from the school. Something went wrong: bad alignment, a tire blown, a panicked grab at the wheel.

My mother had been driving. My father probably tried to do something in the last seconds: grab the wheel, put his arm out to protect her; who knows?

Tammy survived ten minutes after paramedics arrived. Long enough to declare her comatose from the trauma before her life completely ebbed out of her.

☽ ♀ ☿ ♋

Lives can be summed up in the total number of boxes it takes to make them disappear. Every bit of silverware, every piece of clothing. Every starched white blouse and exclamation-point tie. Every songbook and carefully-kept Little Tyke reading primer.

I didn't cry. Even when I saw the yellow-and-red plastic wheel of Tammy's play shopping cart sticking out of the cardboard Maytag box on the back of Uncle Carl's truck.

She'd often badgered me into playing the clerk while she and her friend Sheri from across the street spent the summer afternoons out of school, playing shopping mall. Counting up imaginary items. Picking up a teddy bear that was pretended into a baby, or picking up empty cereal boxes and checking their price tags. All in the imaginary aisles of our backyard.

All that gone; packed and boxed in the back of Uncle Carl's truck.

☽ ♀ ☿ ♋

A week after the funeral, I came to my Uncle Carl's house to live.

Carl was bigger than my father; heavy-bellied and shaped like a bullet-headed, close-cropped gnome. Rough hands; the skin always had splotches of oil or marks of grease on them no matter how scrubbed they were at dinner-time. I liked Carl.

Carl was the kind of man who never held a steady job or had the exact parts for anything. When a side panel came off a van's driver-side seat, the owner came to Carl. Carl fixed it by re-screwing the bolts that held the panel back in. But he didn't have the right size screw, so instead he'd hammered in a couple of plastic screw anchors, the kind used for hanging pictures firmly into weak plaster. Then he'd screwed in smaller screws that fit the anchors, and that'd worked.

Carl poured the beer into the Mason jar glass like any classic barkeep in the Old West.

"Here." The foam slathered onto the table as he shoved it to me. I picked it up and drank a heavy sip. Ever since I was nine, my dad had let me have beer during football games when Ohio State was trying desperately to beat Michigan, or the Browns were making another losing season's bid for the Super Bowl. It was the only thing Carl could think of to ingratiate himself to me.

We sat in the dining room of his dilapidated, mongrel house. It had been in the family for the last few generations. When he'd settled on a place of his own, Carl had kept the family grounds to live on.

He was a perpetual bachelor. Not picky about women, not gay . . . not anything but simply lazy and not caring enough about companionship to seek it. The house was 'bachelor's neat' as my mother once called it: scattered pop cans and magazines. Clothes left on the floor until every other laundry day; the unused rooms left closed, piled with junk and assorted furniture. Not dirty. Just undusted, disused, and comfortable.

Someone had grafted a mobile home to the house's ass end to give extra space carpeted and dressed up as a dining room. The chairs didn't match and it was always hot, even in the last dregs of evening with the fan overhead turned on.

I drank the beer, then clunked the foam-rimed jar back on the table. The liquid sat in my stomach like an acid bath.

"It happens." Carl stared at the bottle in his hands. "It happens."

My only other relatives were my grandparents, who lived in a 'senior community' and couldn't care for me, and a married aunt on the other end of the country with five children of her own. Aunt Sammy could've taken me if she'd *had* to, but Carl and my father had only been separated by four years.

"Your dad tell you he saved my life once, Marty?"

"No."

Carl nodded to himself. "Yup. Sure did."

"How?"

He looked out at the lawn through the huge bay window of the prefabricated back wall.

"We were taking our bikes up this hill path. Had no business doing it, actually. I can't remember what it was . . . I think we had some stupid idea there was a silver mine up in the hill . . . those Shawnee silver mines they always say Tecumseh's people had hidden somewhere in the hills." Carl chuckled. "I slipped off the path. Wasn't more than a gravel cut in the side of the hill, no real path to speak of. I went sliding." Carl's hands rolled the bottle between their palms. He looked from the lawn, to me, to the bottle, then the lawn again. Shadows were drawing shapes across the easel panel of the emerald grass. "Somehow, he got off his bike and caught me before I slid down the slope. There was a barbed wire fence that ran along the base of the hill. My bike slid right under the bottom run of wire. Razorwire. Just an inch or so off the ground. If I'd followed my bike, I'd've gotten my head cut clean off, tangling up in that mess."

I nodded, apropos of nothing. A beer burp shoved hard against my tongue, whispered between my lips.

"You want to order a pizza?"

"Yeah."

That was my first evening in Uncle Carl's house.

The summer had come into full swing when I moved in with Carl, and he wasn't worried about enrolling me into school just yet.

The house was part of a loose neighborhood where the nearest neighbor was over a mile down the county road. Places where streets had route designations instead of names. It was probably what would be called "the sticks."

We were ten minutes' ride from town, and you could find plenty to amuse you if you were willing to dig around burnt-out barns and Mail-Pouch Tobacco signs. Southern Ohio is a geography of abandoned farmsteads and gray-board barns left to ruin.

Usually I helped Carl in his garage, handing him a wrench or a socket adapter while he lay his bearish bulk against the rollback and crab-crawled under some transmission or axle joint. He did moderate-to-easy engine repair for folks around town. People would bring their Caddies and Buicks, or someone might need their John Deere fixed so it didn't rattle. If they wanted a guarantee with paperwork and warranties they went to the Faslube or Meineke in Cheotha Village, twenty minutes' drive away. If they wanted something reliable and a lot cheaper than the professionals, they came to Carl's Backwoods Garage and Auto Repair. No ad in the Yellow Pages, just a nod and a grunted mention from a mechanic to some frustrated Joe Average who couldn't afford new parts.

Three weeks after arriving, I asked Uncle Carl to let me mow the backyard. Carl was lying on the rollback, head craned up to look at a bearing he was greasing. That gunoil smell of grease and WD-40 covered everything; the metallic tang of old oil-spills on the floor.

Carl gave me a strange look, part curiosity and part suspicion. "What for?"

"Nothing special." I was sitting on top of an old slat barrel that was used for holding spark plugs. The lid was splintery; every so often I shifted my weight or my back would go numb on its lumpy surface. "Just bored. Figured you wouldn't mind. You don't mow it much, either."

"That I don't," Carl mused casually. "I don't get visitors, and it doesn't matter to me if there's grass or not. Sure . . . I guess I could even slip you a fiver for it, if you'd like."

"Yeah." I grinned, shifting on the lid.

"Just be careful of the washtub, okay?"

I knew about the dirty-pearlescent shape in the backyard, but hadn't really thought to ask about it before. "What about it?"

"Some junk from great-grandpa's time, I guess." Carl blew through the hole of the metal doughnut shape he was greasing, blowing a small spat of green-brown grease from it. "I don't know what-all it's about. I figure since this was a horse barn, it was probably what he used to water his ponies. Who knows? Maybe it was what he used to cool off hot shoes that he'd just had made before he shod the horses." Carl lay back and shoved himself under the Toyota he was repairing. "Figure you could mow the lawn for me while you're here this summer. Just watch mowing around that thing."

"Why?"

"Because there's some bricks that were used to lay the thing to the ground, only now you can't see them, and I've lost a bitch of a good lawnmower blade or two chipping those damned things when I can't see them in the high grass. If you mow the lawn, don't get within more'n a few feet around the thing, so I don't have to come take you to the emergency room when a chunk of Snapper lawnblade cracks off and comes flyin'out at your ankles."

Carl's house was quiet, and despite the piles of books and magazines I didn't want to sit and read. It seemed like too much time was spent sitting or walking around, looking at nothing, left with nothing but my own head to consume itself.

The next afternoon, Carl toted out the huge green lawnmower from the back depths of the garage and put gas in it. Its carriage bag smelled of molded grass, and the bright green exterior, almost day-glo, was marked with gouges in the plastic. Streaks of soot-dark oil and grease warpainted it like everything else in Carl's world.

He checked the mower's single spark plug, put fresh two-cycle oil in it, then showed how to rev it with the clutch bar and the jerk-snap of the pull cord.

The mower fought reviving—it coughed, hacked, and chugged, then went cold again. Carl cursed, took beefy hold of the pull cord's black plastic knob handle, and gave the thing another snap-pull like a fisherman giving one last heave to land a Marlin. The mower spat out a blossom of blue-gray smoke that smelled of gasoline and grass blades. Carl held the clutch bar down flat against the handle. He showed me, through hand-motion over the roaring, how to throttle the mower to keep the engine going, or let the clutch bar pop up to kill the engine quickly. He gave me a rough idea of the L-shaped path he wanted me to follow, then let me lead the chuddering thing around the gate into the backyard.

The bag needed emptying after a few laps of the mower. It got so I emptied the carriage bag at five-minute intervals, carrying it to the large compost heap—the flecked-red, slat-board box that came up to my chest. I had to heave the bags up onto my shoulder to dump it. By the time I got near finishing the yard, all acre-and-a-half of it, I was coated in grass dust and dry bits of lawn debris.

Past the lawn's edge were thick trees and scrub brush. Witch hazel and poison ivy mixed with sunflowers that somehow dotted the property line like retired soldiers from a gardening war. The treeline was shadows; dusk had lobbed the sun past the trees.

I mowed the last lap, but the compost box was full. Uncle Carl poked his head out of the garage as I was finishing up. "Just dump the bag near the parts pile."

Lifting the bag by the plastic mouth that latched into the lawnmower, I dragged it across the face of the newly-cut lawn. I had overfilled the bag the first several passes; there were dune-drifts of blades around my feet as I reached the parts pile, beyond the washtub. Carl dumped odd or broken auto parts to form a disjointed Modern Art monstrosity of gears and axles, alternators and cracked gaskets.

I unzipped the bag, grabbed the handle of the plastic mouth, and let fly. Lifting the bag, swinging its heft, the mass of grass cuttings flew out with a soft *whump* sound down onto the car parts. I shook the bag harder to dislodge the clumps of wet grass trapped in its folds, and there was a tea-kettle hiss as they slid out easily. A drift of blades and seeds wafted against me. I gagged on a seedling, coughed, sneezed, and recovered the bag in both hands again, zipping it shut.

I smelled like motor oil and summer sun. Bronze and grease, grass and gears. I was tired and numb. The bag emptied, I turned back.

The sunlight was at my back, and I could see it illuminating the worn siding of the house like an orange peel, soft and spotted. I paused to look at the sky over the house.

I heard a whisper behind me. Like the sloughing sigh of leaves bothered by a wind enough to brush against each other. I turned around.

Just the washtub.

Past that, behind the corner of the garage, the car parts pile joined with a small, hairy hump of grass clippings and crabgrass seed. The red wall of the garage ran the side of the yard. Distantly, I could hear Carl banging his socket wrench at something while Lynyrd Skynyrd's "Freebird" played on his beaten ghetto-blaster that always sat on the garage workbench.

The washtub was an immense, chipped, bone-white affair. The weight of it had buried it to the hilt of its lion-claw feet. It held a good fifty or sixty gallons of water, and had been set with its head against the wall of the garage where it would have sat underneath the mouth of a faucet in a bathroom.

It looked bad; the water dark and dirty. Frog territory, maybe even a snake or two. I could hear a thin, reedy noise of crickets ratcheting up a squall in the trees.

Just another part of the motif known as Americana Backwoods Refuse, alongside such famous pieces as *Rusted Kid's Tricycle in the Yard* and *Corvette Up on Blocks*.

A few thin ropes of weed twined up the sides, clinging to the unsanded edges with a horticultural tenacity that outlasted many hot summers, but other than that the tub was untouched. In the cool of the late dusk I smelled the fibrous scent of cut grass and honeysuckle.

The washtub was light blue in the twilight. The water was black with a thin scum of freshly-flung grassblades spotting it like a strangely unraveled sweater's weaving; a flat mat that slowly revolved in the dark.

A sigh . . . a brush of lips. . . .

". . . *boy?*"

A kissing sound in the air, the slight hiss that made the word. The smell of honeysuckle blossoms became cloying, like trying to breathe deep in the perfume section of a busy department store. . . .

I held my breath . . . and a breath was taken for me.

A dead rabbit—its fur matted and soaking—lay just a few feet away from the sunken claw feet of the tub. One eyeless socket regarded me with horrific placidity, as if it were calmly waiting for me to leave so it could continue on its hopping way. There were no flies that I could see, which should have been swarming given the warmth and shade afforded to the corpse near the base of the tub. Yet it was clearly picked-over—dirt smeared parts of its body that had been exposed, ripped, and laid bare like the work of a butcher's bad apprentice.

". . . *come, boy . . . come and dip your toes . . .*"

The voice was coming from the washtub.

If I had thought I was crazy, if I thought it was a trick of my mind that I'd heard anything, it was stopped when I saw the grass blades on the surface of the water twitching in time to the sounds of that voice.

A treebranch sawed against another. The breeze was dank and faint like the pleasant smell of a cellar come up through a thrust-open kitchen door . . . dark yet inviting . . . it blew through the yard, making me shiver.

Yes. A warm place, wet and refreshing . . . springs in the mountain and valleys with cascading falls. . . .

I blinked.

I could see those places.

I could see those mountains, with hidden grottoes lined with soft beds of moss.

Ron Horsley

I could feel the spongy give of putting my palms to that moss as I rested my weight, then shoved off to float aimlessly, easily, across clean springs of pulsing water . . . the feeling of each molecule of water like hands: brushing me, buoying me up to float. To lean, to list and roll in the current . . .

 . . . the grass blades twitched, revolving faster . . .

 . . . *hands linked, water . . . the wave of motion that coursed through their bones . . . goodbye and love . . . goodbye and let's* try *again.* . . .

An immense sadness hit me, turning depths of depression into a physical weapon and simultaneously striking me in the chest, head, and stomach with it. Something panged in time with my heartbeat, a rhythmic stabbing.

My fingers relaxed, letting go of the carriage bag. It puddled at my feet, a whipped dog, deflated and forgotten.

I saw . . . I *felt-saw-heard* a crying, a weeping . . . a weeping that cycled on itself, water mingling into flesh back into tears . . .

 . . . *salt flowing into clean waves that beat on a forever shore of pain to be re-salinated—*

—a sense of the cycle being suddenly *cleaved.*

Hands, smiles, jeers, colliding into the meat of that lovely circle, sending its components scattering.

"What are you?" I whispered. My feet twitched; my hands clenched. My knees were tight as padlocks left to rust.

". . ."

I felt the pause hang like a raincloud, wanting to answer.

I got a fading impression of the pain. The cycle, the flood into the recession back into a deluge, feeding itself in a beautiful matrix of water and love . . . it tried imparting this again, as if this were something I could then put into letters, words, a concept.

I was losing the connection. The empathy flowed away—

(like a wave like a current like a stream drying up)

—and *it* knew that the connection was not what it had been. It had struck out at me, made its best play to get hold, but I could sense a rueful regret in its pulling back. It had no more choice in the fading than it had had in trying to begin with me.

". . . *child* . . ."

Was it addressing me, or trying to answer?

". . . *child* . . ."

The grass blades were sinking, the water darkening in the way that it does when it reflects a cloud passing over the sun. The rabbit's corpse seemed to dim as if it was decaying faster, its corruption exponential as the light faded to mute glimmers.

It was part lust . . . the touch on all my body . . . the fast intimacy impressed on a child that was only beginning to understand what defined a man from a woman. The rabbit's eyeless stare was back in my face, and somehow the idea came to me that this was my own death, seducing me. This was death coming back to finish the temptation that had claimed the rest of my family. The thing in the tub was as much responsible for its loveliness as for the brutal death of the twisted animal at its base.

I was crying. Hot, spontaneous, sobless. My chest shook, my shoulders shivered in their sockets. I coughed, choked, and the feeling was pulling back *harder,* like a hand from a hot stove.

I tore free and ran for the house, not looking back.

I didn't say anything to Carl at first. We had macaroni and cheese. I washed the grass stains off my hands in the kitchen sink.

Later that night we watched television. Like most folks living past the normal reception of city stations, Carl had a sizable satellite dish installed in his front yard. We watched old reruns of *The Outer Limits*.

"Carl, do you believe in ghosts?"

"I'll believe in anything if it pays well enough."

"Seriously, Carl. Do you believe in them?"

He pressed the mute button on the remote. Leonard Nimoy, who was playing the reporter in an episode about a robot on trial for murder, suddenly went silent.

"Marty, is this something you want to talk about, about your mom and dad?"

I felt uncomfortable, sitting alone on the big couch, his eyes on me as he leaned forward from his recliner. "No. Not really. Just . . . I heard something tonight, out back by the washtub."

"What did you hear?"

"Something. It sounded like a person talking to me."

"What did it say?"

"It just said my name, I thought. Maybe it was the radio in the garage, but it sounded like it was in the washtub."

Carl reflected a moment. "Probably was the radio, Marty. Anything else?"

"No. Nothing else."

Carl sighed. He sat back in the chair, a creaking sounded in its stuffed depths.

"It happens." He spoke as if I wasn't there. "That thing out there, that washtub, it's a weird thing, I admit. I think grandpa or great-granpa brought it over with a bunch of the family's junk on the Turkey side of our little clan. But it's still just a washtub."

I didn't look, but I knew that his eyes were looking at me, curious and resigned.

"It happens, Marty."

We went back to watching television.

Two days later Carl took the truck to go for groceries. I told him I wasn't feeling good and stayed home. After he left I went out to the washtub.

". . . *child?*"

"Yes?"

". . . *close* . . ."

I walked to the tub's edge, not caring about snakes or mosquitoes. The grass parted easily, and I stood within inches of the lip of the tub. The rabbit, if it was still there on the other side of the tub from me, was hidden.

". . ."

Another answer in sensations. A wash of forms. Lithe, dancing things that ran hands over each other, melting into each other . . . there were cries . . . sounds of joy that quickly degenerated into what I could only dimly understand were the sounds of love at climax.

The smell of berries and pure, scentless water . . . earth and rain, ozone like a blanket bathing me . . . cradles . . . shores of sand, earth, clay . . . feet dangling . . . the feel of everything flowing. Everything in a cycle of regeneration, recreation, revivification . . . renewal ever-after. . . .

I tried to breathe . . . my blood roared, brought up and out. My body was a lily stem, and something was tickling out the substance of me like the bloom, my soul the pistil that was rising . . . coming up to meet its kiss of liquid warmth—

"MARTY!"

Carl was screaming, slapping my wet face. I was lying on the ground, looking up into my uncle's panic-ruddy face.

Carl kept saying how lucky it was he'd forgotten his parts list and returned in time to find my head and upper body submerged in the brackish water of the tub, for all intents and purposes blissfully drowning myself. Uncle Carl was one of those people who get angry at the focus of their fear, once panic drained off their adrenaline-shivered shoulders.

"What the hell were you doing?"

We sat in the living room, a terrycloth towel draped around my shoulders. My shirt was bonded to me like a second skin with filthy water. I only shook my head, teeth chattering.

I was awake again, I was *here*, and I was cold. No matter how hard I rubbed the towel against myself I couldn't get warm.

He shrugged, patted my shoulder, and ordered a pizza.

I remembered the feeling that had happened the moment I'd heard Carl saying my name. The moment before his hand slapped me, breaking me free.

I heard a breaking, shattering *scream* in my head, faded to a whisper before I'd even registered it.

Those dancing forms, falling through endless air, glassy shards of unreality ripping at them as they faded out.

"Marty, it doesn't make any sense."

I'd tried explaining, chattering and hiccuping, about the voice from the washtub. Every time I put it into words the same thoughts kept coming out wrong: voices, hands, pain, screams, laughter, water. Nothing would come out the way it had flowed in. He made the honest assumption: it was me, it was my grief showing its head.

"You imagined it. I understand."

"N-no!" I slammed a fist into the dinner table. Dishes, still sitting there even in the late afternoon, rattled like sabers. A spoon clanged to the floor.

"Marty, this is something we're going to have to deal with. And I think the best way . . ." He sucked in a breath. "Is to deal with first things first."

Numb, I followed him out to the yard.

"Now just wait here a second. This thing's bound to be settled-in, and it's going to be a bitch to move. You just watch me and I'll call if I need you. Otherwise, you'll just be in the way and I don't need you in the wrong place at the wrong time to get squashed if I lose grip on this thing."

I couldn't have moved closer if he'd commanded me to.

There was something *wrong*.

Something in the way that the light shifted blue like it was evening, but it was only three-thirty in the afternoon. The way that I could smell everything so clearly: Carl's sweat and shaving cream residue, the grass, the dirt; like it had just rained.

"I'm just trying to take care of you, you understand." He had on work gloves, and his bib overalls that he wore when we worked in the garage. "We'll work on this together, get rid of this crazy deal, and I promise we'll talk more about this, okay, man?"

I nodded, my eyes alternating between Carl and the washtub.

"But for now, we'll deal with the easiest things first. I've been meaning to clear this thing out forever, guess this shows me it's about time I got off my ass." He took a deep breath, looked down at the tub for one measuring moment, then bent over. His hands sought each edge for a handhold. As he came down, I heard a *plip*, a bubble-pop in the water.

The water in the tub detonated upwards, rising to meet Carl's downward bend. It *flowered*. Not a haphazard spray like the aftershock of a kid cannonballing into a public pool, but like a crystal forming. Liquid and flowing, it rose in a smooth, sidelong arc . . . a multicolored deluge, slamming in one motion into Carl's face.

Carl gagged. I heard the sound of a garbage disposal gnarled on something just hard enough to resist its spinning rotor teeth. Cracking, gulping noises.

I ran forward, sweat down my face, cries of *help* and *stop* stuck two degrees below audible in my throat. It was like watching a stop-motion film of a morning glory closing in the sunlight.

The water was a shape. A shape that rose up, gelatinous and shivering constantly as it rose, waves of itself rising, falling . . . a fountain that was hardened but not into ice . . . into cohesion . . . a shape. . . .

The shape was a woman.

Long, gaunt, but with a clear curve to the edges, at the middle, where the torso became the hourglass hips. I could see the shape of the belly as it flattened, smoothed and came down like a gentle hillside, becoming the dim pubis. The arms wrapped like thick cables around Carl's neck, pulling at him. The face and head were still poorly formed, smashing into Carl's face; a weirdly kaleidoscopic mold around his features, like thick glass poured taffy-soft from a heated oven. I could see his lips distending, his eyes bulging, through the very substance of his attacker.

. . . the shape was water, but also flesh . . . it looked like smooth, creamy pencil shavings, rose petals slowing and twining around the water . . . so much that she was a woman and she was a figment in the same blink. Dark lines, small staccato shapes that were bits of grass and molded plantflesh. . . .

The water was the sound of rushing through a creek, the babble and crack of it muffling the bubbled scream my uncle was gargling. But as his lips parted and his teeth came away from each other, I saw a draining vortex form, and knew it was shoving itself down past his tongue, into his throat, down into his belly . . . filling him, crushing and expanding to break him and protect itself.

As I came within arm's reach the same closeness exploded in my skull. I felt everything fade away, the real world of touch and sight useless as all of me became enveloped by the feel and soul of it.

The washtub became the white-porcelain pool of every Greek god's palace, and I saw every speck of muck, every twist of vine-roping grass that was crawling up its side and over its rim, jewels in the obscure afternoon. I could hear something like a guitar being plucked in a lovely rhythm, in perfect time to my swelling heartbeat. . . .

Numerous forms, curved and angular, roiling in a never-ending swirl . . . a maelstrom feeding itself with flowers and blossom waves, froth and foam that sizzled away to become smooth, glassy water. . . .

childhood, painted in ochres and tinctures of aquamarine . . .

Meratae . . . the name is Meratae . . . oh yes, Meratae sweet water breath like the swimming air of a Raphael afternoon . . . Meratae that means sea-love, water-daughter . . . keepers. . . .

(No . . .)

The spirits of water, the Sisters of the Fluid, the throb in your heart, in your groin, in your spine and up the nerve caverns, up the sensation rivers to your luxuriating, bath-swimming brain in its red brine solvents . . .

(Oh god . . . *love*)

As she held me, my mouth filled with dirty, filth-slimed water. I tasted something like excrement and sour milk . . . the earth that was dissolved had poisoned her . . . turned the water to vile wine.

. . . the Spirits of the Wash, we cradled Achilles in the Styx, we carried Moses to his Pharaoh, we swept up the earth in tide and flood . . . the Sisters of the Cistern . . . we bear your sailors to beds in the deep where we make love forever until the day when the world tips its oceans into the black basin of Night evermore. . . .

(But I love you)

. . . how were we repaid? With disdain, with being cast aside, with the very breath we gave you, amniotic sons and daughters, you said we no longer were . . .

(I didn't know)

. . . no . . . nor did we . . .

I was choking, my head was struck by my heart like a symphony of gongs, clanging with dull, cotton-wrapped roars. . . .

(I can't)

no, you can't . . . nor can we. . . .

(breathe)

I blinked.

I woke up on a soaked-wet back, grass sucking at me as I sat up, immediately assailed by the smell of rotten water; swamp smells.

It was later in the day. Brighter. So bright I had to keep blinking until my eyes adjusted. The sun was lower . . . was it five or six?

The washtub loomed. Sitting on the ground as I was, it looked like a white monument. Porcelain shaped into a stony wall, curled at its end; a bulwark for eternity. Carl was slumped over its edge, his rear end towards me so that I only saw his limp legs. His upper half was in the water, out of sight.

My shoes were gone. One of my socks remained. I sniffed, sneezed water from my nostrils. My head ached.

I hadn't dried. I remained soaked and wet where I lay.

Carl had drowned in the washtub, the coroner's report determined. From my statement, it was assumed that He had tried to move the washtub for some reason and suffered a heart attack. How the water had so violently propelled into his throat that veins in his neck had burst from the pressure was something that couldn't be adequately explained, so was left out of any attempt at explanation.

Aunt Sammy agreed with the courts that things were best left to keeping me in an environment I was used to, seeing as how I'd gone through too much with most of the family I knew dying in less than a year. I was sent to live with the Darrens—Noel and Shanna—as my foster parents.

When I turned eighteen, just before graduation, the state notified me that I was heir to Carl's property, which had been held in probate for the last few years.

The Darrens celebrated my birthday and graduation with a small party. Shanna cried and presented Flounder, a mixed-terrier puppy who barked about as often as he breathed. It was while giving Flounder his first bowl of puppy food that I announced I was moving out to go live on Carl's property. They frowned for a moment before smiling and wishing me luck.

She's still there.

When I mowed the lawn, I would only cut a line as close as ten or so feet. After a couple of months, I found myself slowing down when I started to near that corner with the mower. Slowing down to a stop.

Staring at the thing.

Wanting to know what it would be like to breathe her mist, to know those mountain spaces again, those bubbling, secret pools . . . the crush that was part lover, part revenge.

It got so bad, I finally quit cutting the lawn at all.

A year after moving in, I found Flounder, a few feet from the washtub amongst the highest blades of grass. Sodden to the skin, fur matted down and his twisted body bitten so deeply in some places that the jagged bone showed through. It looked as if he'd been taken by some mad shark.

His head was gone. I buried him in the backyard with the rusted parts pile as his gravestone.

Naiad.

I looked it up in a mythology text the night after burying Flounder, tears blurring my reading to a crawl.

"*Ancient Greek. A water sprite/spirit, mostly noted for living in or around rivers, creeks, springs, and ocean shores. Naiads represent the purity and spirit of the water or body of water in which they reside.*"

Every summer night, when it's been hot and dry, and the grass is thigh-high, faded and gray-beige, I can *hear* it. I hear the *lap-lap* lolling sound of the water inside the tub.

I can hear a thin, papery *creeeeeeeee* from crickets and cicadas making their low concert noises.

I remember the taste of dirt-salted water in the back of my throat. I taste weeds and water . . .

. . . *it's the finest, most intoxicating vintage I've ever had in my life, all over again.*

It's her licking, stroking embrace that holds, cool and wet, so refreshing, like a kiss from a lover returning from a long trip. . . .

Dry summer becomes chill dusk.

I know that there is something out there waiting for the day when no beer will suit me. No lemonade will taste sweet enough, no soda will satisfy me.

I will feel a hard, iron ache in the middle of me that will draw me out like an old song; an old movie where the lovers have to separate at the end before the credits roll. . . .

She's waiting for when I finally have a thirst . . . a thirst for the only kind of drink that Death and Love can offer from a shared chalice. . . .

It will taste like joy, unbottled.

Souls of Living Wood
Eugie Foster

Morning was not Aria's preferred time to do business; the din of workaday bustle overwhelmed the lazy, more dulcet voices she preferred.

She checked her watch. Twenty minutes now. The Bellingers were late. Were they lost? They had seemed so interested in this property, stressing again and again how much they liked the pictures they'd seen on the Internet.

The view *was* striking. The predawn sky was a lovely cobalt blue, brushed with dusky clouds in somber purples and gray. Tingeing the horizon, a breath of smoky silver promised a sweeping blanket of gold and white just an exhalation behind. It silhouetted the luxurious two-story house before her, framing it in a nimbus of light.

It really was a wonderful structure. Four bedrooms, each spacious and brimming with personality. The master bedroom had blue glass transoms that fragmented sunlight into prisms of azure. The house deserved a good family, one who would care for it and love it, maybe with children or a friendly dog. She stopped herself from checking her watch again. The Bellingers had her cell phone number. They would arrive or call her, or they wouldn't.

Aria inhaled the soft air. How long had it been since she'd greeted the rising sun? She remembered eras long past when her skin was burnt earth-brown from afternoons sprawled in golden light, and her red-wheat hair was a gossamer tangle that brushed the backs of her knees. Once, the wind had burnished her cheeks ruddy, and she had communed with the wind and rain. But those days were gone. Now she was pale from long hours spent in her office; her hair was neatly cropped to her shoulders—though it still retained a shimmer of red in its depths—and she no longer exulted a song to the heavens. But she could still hear the old melodies.

She smiled at the house, listening.

It was an older home. Its foundation was rooted deep in soil that had passed through economic skips and lags, thunderstorms, hurricanes, and lightning, all with the calm, unperturbed certainty that tomorrow would arrive as today had, inevitably and with serenity. A cloak of branches and underbrush crowded the yard—sturdy oak, lithe willow, bold holly—creating warm shadows and a kiss of mystery. A gifted gardener could sculpt such chaos into a cornucopia of welcoming colors and scents.

One had, the house sighed. But she was gone, and without her nurturing hand, the flora had become overgrown.

The house apologized for its scruffy appearance, its tone meek and self-effacing. Aria soothed it, sending reassurance and tender humor to hearten it.

Houses like this one had to be coaxed to step out, pushed protesting into the spotlight like the shy girl at a dance or the stuttering poet. But patience and encouragement were rewarded with delicate grace and halting eloquence. Houses like this—unlike younger houses that bragged of state-of-the-art appliances and new paint—told stories of time, the ache of loneliness, and the joy of completeness. While Aria indulged the youngsters, matching them with owners who babbled just as happily about the automated features and shiny newness, she loved these gently aging homes. And she felt keenly for this gracious dwelling, lonesome and forlorn for so long.

She drummed her fingers. Where *were* the Bellingers?

More than halfway inclined to give up on them, Aria saw the searching flash of headlights enter the lane. The lights resolved into the squat bulk of a dull-blue minivan. It careened down the street, breaking the early-morning peace with the rumble of its engine and the muffled squeal of voices within.

It pulled into the driveway—the Bellingers it would seem.

The minivan's driver, Mr. Bellinger, popped his door open. "Sorry we're late," he called. "Traffic was a nightmare, and the gym gave us the runaround. They didn't want to open up the exercise room. What sort of place still has their treadmills locked up at 5:30, I ask you?"

Aria hadn't finished formulating a reply (she had never touched a treadmill in her life, and she hoped to be ashes and dust before she ever did) when Mrs. Bellinger chimed in.

"And then on the way here the kids started fighting over their Game Boys. We had to stop for a time out. You know how kids can be." Mrs. Bellinger emerged from the other side of the vehicle. Her hair was a plastic blonde and she wore a lime-green pantsuit with embroidered daisies on the lapels. It reminded Aria of wallpaper she'd seen in '70s era pre-fab houses.

Two youngsters—a sullen-looking boy with headphones trailing from his ears and a bored girl chatting on a pink cell phone—emerged from the back of the minivan.

"The ad said there's a pool?" the girl said, snapping closed her phone.

"Mom, do I have to go?" the boy said.

"Jeffrey—" Mrs. Bellinger began.

"I could wait in the car." His voice pitched up in a whine.

Aria blinked. She needed to take control before this showing turned into a fiasco. She extended her hand. "Hello, Mr. and Mrs. Bellinger. I'm Aria Kearn. After all our phone chats and emails, it's a pleasure to finally meet you."

Mr. Bellinger's grip was tight and overly vigorous. Shaking hands with him was like having her hand worried by a blunt-toothed dog. Mrs. Bellinger's hand was limp and clammy, like a cooling lasagna noodle. The children seemed disinclined to partake in social niceties.

This wasn't going to work. She knew it the same way she knew when termites had destroyed a house's skeleton or a wall was unsound. The lie was almost on her tongue: the house was no longer for sale, had been pulled from the market. She'd even begun mentally riffling through the houses on the north end where all the subdivisions were so new the trees still needed braces to support their supple stems. Cookie-cutter in design and layout, she knew they would be more suitable for this family.

But the house was so hopeful. It keened a welcome to the Bellingers, and the eagerness in its tone put to rest the words, the lies, on Aria's tongue. Maybe she could find a way to make this work after all.

Mrs. Bellinger sniffed at the yard. "That tree must shed terribly in fall. All that raking. And the acorns!" She gave a delicate shudder.

"We can hire a service," Mr. Bellinger said.

"Or we can chop it down. That would let some light in. It's so dark under all those branches."

The oak tree was centuries old. Aria's heart ached at the idea of the needless death of that ancient soul. But if she mourned every venerable death, she would wail away her remaining days in desolation.

"The pool?" the girl said.

"It's in the back," Aria replied.

Her hand lingered over the dark wood of the front door before she opened it with a flourish. Made of a heavy, solid mahogany, a delicate stained-glass window—translucent bellflowers and jewel-scintillating attendant hummingbirds—was inset within it.

"We'd have to remove that window," Mrs. Bellinger said, as though she were a malevolent eavesdropper on Aria's thoughts. "A burglar could smash it and undo the locks from the outside." She frowned, standing in the threshold. "This isn't a deadbolt!"

"No," Aria said. "This house predates deadbolts, and the previous owner never had one installed."

"Isn't that against the law?"

"A locksmith can be called in before closing."

"I should hope so."

"Ugh, are all the walls white?" the girl asked, pushing past her mother.

"I believe they're cream." Aria surveyed the soaring ceilings and the walls bordered with hand-carved molding. She preferred neutral shades like these that brightened the space and soothed the eye.

"That's totally behind the times. White, yuck."

"Kelly's right," Mrs. Bellinger said. "Can we get a painter in before closing?" She pointed at the foyer. "This would be nice in garnet or paprika."

It would look like the walls were bleeding, Aria knew, but she just nodded.

"And the kitchen would look so cheery in a bright peach, or maybe even an orange," Mrs. Bellinger continued. "They say orange stimulates the appetite center of the brain. Wouldn't that be smart?"

Mr. Bellinger wandered into the living room. "The walls probably aren't wired for sound," he said. "I'd need to get an electrician in to get my planar speakers installed. Probably have to cut through that wall."

Aria realized she was grinding her teeth behind her smile and forced the muscles in her jaw to relax. No. This was *not* going to work out. These people would leech out every bit of soul and beauty from this stately, old house, leaving behind a traumatized, fragmented psyche. Already, she heard the gentle bewilderment in the house's voice. They didn't like it the way it was? They were going to splash garish color on it and tear down walls to string electrical arteries through it? Why?

Not to worry, Aria reassured the house. *These people will be leaving soon. I'll find you a family that won't try to change you, to destroy what you are.*

"I believe you wanted to see the pool?" she said. She ushered the Bellingers through the family room and the kitchen, and pulled open the French doors that led to the back. This area was of a newer era than the rest of the house; the pool added in a time of whimsy and good fortune. Even so, the previous owners had taken care to blend the edges of the pool in with the existing backdrop, creating a miniature tiered waterfall in the far corner as a segue from the rowan trees that clustered in a tiny forest at the back of the lot.

The sun hung like a molten coin in the sky, spreading rays of white gold, topaz, and tawny fire over the still water.

"It's gorgeous!" Mrs. Bellinger said.

"Why don't I let you all wander around back here, folks?" Aria suggested. "I've got to check in with my office. I'll be right with you."

The Bellingers ignored her as she retreated into the house.

I'm so lonesome, the house murmured. *Maybe I won't mind the changes. Maybe it's better this way.*

"No." Aria spoke firmly. "You deserve someone who appreciates you for who you are, who doesn't want to change you because of some fad. You deserve someone who will take care of you, not ruin you, someone who sees how beautiful you have been, are, and always will be. You deserve people that love *you*."

I had a family like that, once, the house whispered. *They're gone now.*

Aria ached for its grief. But down that path lay ruin. As she well knew, a despairing house was a dead house—nothing but rubble and dilapidation.

"I'll find you another family. I promise. But first I have to get rid of the Bellingers."

She knew from her brief association with them, and by instinct honed from years of matching hopeful people with earnest homes, that the Bellingers would make an offer. They were the kind to buy quickly, once they'd put their mind to it, and bluster until they got what they wanted. She would have to make sure they didn't get that far.

In her purse, next to her sunglasses case and her bulging keychain, was a velveteen pouch, tied with a braided, tri-color string. At her touch, the intricate knot released. For any other hand, the knots would prove insuperable and the string resilient to even a razor's edge. Aria rummaged in the bag until she found what she needed: a tiny vial of camphor oil, a crumble of ochre, and a pinch of sage. Taking her Swiss Army knife out, she sheared off a lock of her fire-touched hair.

"Camphor for discord, ochre to ward, sage for magic," she chanted. "And with my body, I bind it."

She anointed the tiny brush with the oil, dusted it with the ochre, and crumbled the sage over it. The knife served her again, pricking the tip of her finger. One drop of her blood sealed the spell.

"In the name of the forests I have guarded," she intoned. "And the trees whose boughs were my home, I call upon the old magics to protect that which is mine by birthright and ancient decree."

Crooning words in a language ancient as time, she made a circuit of the house, upstairs and down, daubing each archway, doorframe, and lintel with a speck of the mixture from her makeshift brush.

When she was done, she tucked the bundle of fragrant hair into the velveteen pouch and re-knotted the cord.

The Bellingers returned from the backyard, their faces alight with pleasure. But as soon as they crossed through the French doors, they began squabbling.

"You always get the big bedroom," Jeffrey shouted at his sister. "Just because you're older. It's not fair!"

"Maybe if you didn't live in your room you wouldn't care so much, you freak!" Kelly shrieked back.

Mrs. Bellinger ignored their bickering, preoccupied with her own clash with Mr. Bellinger. "We have to sell your convertible. If we're going to live so far away from the city, you'll need to do your share of driving the kids around, and I don't want them riding in that speed demon."

Mr. Bellinger's face took on a brick-red flush. "We are not getting rid of my car! It was your idea to live in a quieter area, remember? I'll have a longer commute living way out here in the boonies. I figured it was worth it if it was good for you and the kids, and now you want to sell the only thing that would make my drive tolerable?"

Aria let the fracas mushroom out, the voices growing louder and more strident with each passing moment. When it seemed the Bellingers were on the verge of blows, she cleared her throat.

Like guilty thieves, they fell silent, reminded that a stranger stood witness to their discord.

"If I'm correctly interpreting your feedback," Aria said, "what you'd like is a modern house in a well-to-do neighborhood that's a little closer to the city but still away from downtown? A roomy four-bedroom just went on the market in the Pepper Ridge subdivision on the north end. Perhaps you'd like to look at that?"

"Does it have a pool?" Mrs. Bellinger asked.

"No, I'm afraid it doesn't."

The children's faces turned sour.

"But there *is* a private clubhouse with a heated pool, sauna, and Jacuzzi tub. It can be rented by individual families for private parties."

"Price range?" Mr. Bellinger snapped.

"It will be a little more than this house. It's a brand new construction, you see. You'd be the first owners. Why don't we all drive back to my office and we'll set up a showing?"

The Bellingers nodded warily.

Back in the sanctuary of her office, Aria took the velveteen pouch from her purse. Plucking forth the little brush, she regarded it.

The Bellingers had loved the new construction in Pepper Ridge. A little blueberry powder and essence of sandalwood in their eyes had guaranteed their delight. Even though she'd *influenced* them into it, something she disliked doing out of professional pride, she knew they would be well pleased with their glossy, new house. The house itself had prattled its silly head off in welcome.

But now to fulfill her promise to the wonderful old house with the mahogany and stained glass door. She twirled the brush of hair between her fingers.

"Gods that oversee the souls of living wood," she whispered, "hear the plea of your daughter once more. Help me keep my promise."

She knew the gods were there, listening, for she understood the great secret, the one she and her sisters had not learned until almost too late. Mortal man, when he hewed down the forests and slaughtered the trees, was not always wantonly destructive. The gentle consciousnesses—maple, elm, pine, birch—were transformed, reborn at the hands of artisans and builders. When they realized this, the guardians moved from their dwindling forest homes and assumed new mantles of nurturance and protection. It was a different life, but a good one nonetheless.

She breathed on the tiny brush and set it into the ashtray on her desk. It began to smolder, and a green, fragrant flame engulfed it.

The couple arrived, skirting the edge of a spring rainstorm. His white shirt was paint-flecked, dotted and swirled with sea green, ginger, sultry raisin, and marigold in glossy acrylic. She hummed a merry tune while twirling their ragged umbrella.

"We need a place with a lot of natural light," he said. "I'm a painter."

"A house with high ceilings and plenty of character," she said. "Someplace with music in it. I give piano lessons."

"But we don't have a lot of money. We've been saving. Enough for a down payment, we hope."

"I'm tired of living in apartments," she said. "I want a dog, someone to keep me company while I garden."

Aria smiled. "I think I have the perfect place for you."

Peter I Am Lost
Kelly Hale

Once upon a time, I clung to him like a shadow, clutching his coattails, the tangle of his hair. Still, I fell. I am the Wendy-bird, doomed to fall."

Boy. Spotted earlier outside Peet's Coffee. Trickling a packet of sugar into the foam of his latte. Oh, the darling pointy shape of his ears. Ropes of hair smoothed back beneath a sheen of candy-apple red. I almost stop to ask him where oh where did he get his hair, but am swept past his table on my way to an altogether different destiny. A movie or something. Then, later, coming back, waiting for the crossing light, I hear, "Wendy is that you?" Not my name, but I pretend for a moment so I can say, oh hi, how've you been? He looks hard at my face. I say, no, ha ha, I'm not her; I just wanted to meet you. His eyes go up and down all over me. But not in the way guys usually do. Weird. Different. "It *is* you," he says with delicious, mad certainty. "Sit. I'll buy you a coffee." I sit. He buys. We talk.

Up close his hair looks like Medusa's serpents tamed by styling mousse, errant heads and tails snipped into a blunt line at the nape of his neck. And something even stranger than the hair keeps distracting me from the flirty precursors of our inevitable boinking, something the reptile nubbin in my brain stem notes instantly, though my eyes sidle away from the impossibility as we converse. The afternoon crowds flow around our table. I'm caught. I'm held. I am at the absolute center of his attention, so damned charming he thinks, so like this someone he once knew. I feel compelled to *be* her just to make him laugh. As he laughs, his teeth seem too small for his mouth—too perfect, pearly, and a little too sharp.

"So, *Wendy*..." he says, and the name is a game we're playing together now. I wet my lips. Do the sultry thing with my hair. He leans across the table, close as a whisper, distant as the sun shining hot on my face. "Do you still have it? Because I really *need* it."

Mmmm. Mad, yes. Exotic. Strange. There will be dangerous games of trust and betrayal I think. Led blindfolded by this strange boy through a maze that winds upward.

His room. Not what I expected. No manacles, whips, or instruments of play torture. I had been sure of something. Now I'm not.

It is a round space, like a tree turned inside out. There are no windows, just a rough, door-shaped hole with a flap of green over it. The green moves slightly, but not from the wind. Our own movements cause the flutter, I think. And the glimpse beyond is nothing I want to see. I'm afraid it is literally *nothing*. So, I look around a room that needs sweeping and a woman's touch.

No woman has been in this room. Not for a long time. Or ever. There is no after-image of *woman* imprinted upon the ether. The space is in casual shambles, and its treasures make no sense. Balls of dirty string and strings of pearls. A cowboy hat. A rolled up Persian carpet.

Empty bottles and empty plates, jewel colors dimmed by the crusty remains of macaroni, or drowned gnats in the dregs. A bow and quiver of suction cup arrows. Big, fat sultan pillows loll about amid the carcasses of shiny black beetles on a floor that is part buckled linoleum and part hard-packed earth.

But the bed is huge, incongruous; like an afterthought plunked smack in the middle of an intention he's only just thought of. A mess of patchwork quilt and puffy duvet like an ocean wave frozen mid-crest over the footboard.

He wades through the pillows, kicking gold tassels and silk fringe, pulling me along behind him, an intrepid explorer grimly determined to reach the pinnacle, the peak. He *will* plant his flag in virgin territory, damn it. But then he just stands at the side of the bed staring at it. Doesn't look at me. So, I look more closely at the bed. I start to laugh. The sheets printed with big, gaudy sprigs of lilac. My favorite flower as I've only just told him.

"I don't remember those sheets," he mutters. He cocks an eye at the walls, the ceiling, as if sensing a conspiracy between me, and this—his fortress of solitude, bat cave, or what-have-you.

I can hear him swallow. It's *that* loud. He's terrified. He's about to change his mind. Any moment he'll spin around and hustle me out, saying, this is a mistake, a terrible, dreadful mistake.

But I don't want to go. His fear excites the mother in me, the power to comfort and manipulate.

I wrap myself around him from behind. My hands slide beneath his shirt, massaging his belly. The full frontal me commences a body rub assault upon his spine. Unbalanced, he falls face first across the bed with me sprawled over him. My hands are pinned, and we wriggle and grunt until finally, we roll apart, laughing. Lie on our backs, laughing.

I like his laugh. I like the way he'll throw his head back when he laughs, the way his eyes crinkle up. He looks wicked, instead of crazy and sad.

I stare up at the dome of rough wood, waiting.

His move.

He lays his hand flat upon my left breast. Just keeps it there. I wait.

Nothing.

Getting irritated now. I look at him again. His eyes are closed. Is he asleep? I open my mouth to say hey and he says "Ssshhh." Then I feel it. Pain boring through the breast and leaving a hollow in my heart like a core sample from the tundra.

What're you . . . ? What are you doing?

"Ssshhh . . ."

Heat moves from his open palm back to my heart. His hand tells my heart to beat a strange, sultry rhythm, and it does. It melts, pools and bubbles between my legs like butter in a microwave. The feeling's a little like ecstasy, the drug I mean, but smoother. I just say aahh. . . .

We haven't even kissed, so in a way it's like that time I took X with that guy whose name I can't remember but do recall being convinced we were having the best sex of our lives only it turned out the next day we didn't have sex at all though we had decided to get married. Didn't, thank God.

But here I'm wide, wide open, and we still have all our clothes on. Not for long. Susurrations, the sighs of linen and cotton, the flap of leather—that's him, his belt. Me, I'm moving through water, and he has to help me out of my T-shirt, free my ankles from the tangled bondage of my panties.

He's posed above me, ready to do a thousand push-ups. I try to focus on the way he looks naked but my eyes go blurry, as if there's a band of excited pixels over the area where his naughty bits should be. And we haven't even *kissed*. I need the kiss. The kiss is the knock on the door.

Kiss me, I demand. He leans in. His eyes are the color of the sky, every mood of the sky. I can't look at his eyes because they remind me of time-lapsed photography, of watching something sprout, grow, and decay in a matter of seconds. I look instead at the vaguely pointed tips of his ears. I see two ridges in his brow, the hint of horns that haven't sprouted. We smash our mouths together. Our tongues do a little waltz. It's all terribly courteous. Too polite. I suppose I want to see the horns. Cloven hooves. The impossibly huge cock of God.

I slip my hand between our bodies, and there it is—not impossibly huge, but thick and weighing heavy in my palm. My fingers curl around it, feeling the velvety soft skin, the tiny beads of moisture at the tip.

Normal. Perfectly normal. I experience a moment of disappointment before his mouth moves to a nipple, and his hand seeks out mine, and we frantically rub our parts together to make fire, if fire can be made entirely of slick and gooey interstices.

Comes the wiggle, and the push, and the oh, ah, oh, as if this first connection is the very *first ever*. We would spend every moment having this moment if we could, wouldn't we? This oh, ah, oh yes, ah, how could I forget *this* moment moment. He's bang—up against my cervix, then back out, and bang—stunning me breathless. A twinge of panic. A thrill of anticipation. His whole body shudders and—

It's over. He rolls off and lies with one arm flung across his eyes. Snuffling. Oh shit. He's crying. Breath catching stutters of snot and sighs.

"Five thousand years old," he moans, "and I can't even make it last two seconds."

We can do it again, I offer lamely. My mind is busy trying to ignore the implication of counting one's years in the thousands, of me having been led blindfolded to this place, possibly by a madman, or worse, a pathetic loser of a god.

He wants to talk. Bleah. Total death. No hope of recapturing the mood. But I'm being nice. Nice, nice, nice. I consider masturbating while he talks. I put one hand on his sticky prick, the other on my clit. His voice drones on and on about old days and old gods shrunk down to the size of little boys. Monsters and Mermaids. Pirates and Indians. The shadows of conquest in the neverlands. Things lost forever. I'm half asleep and halfway to orgasm when his voice startles me out of both.

"I forgot all about you once. You fell."

I concentrate hard on the diddle and jerk. Mediocre sex is a kind of falling. I can lose myself even in that.

"We were flying. Do you remember?"

I don't remember flying or falling. If this is some sort of allegory about love I swear to God, I'll scream.

"Anyway, I just wanted to say, I'm sorry."

I don't care. I don't want to talk, I tell him. Fuck me now or let me out of here. And he's hard again. This time he goes on forever and ever and ever. There is no happy medium with the creature. Too much or too little. Perhaps he is a god.

Afterwards we lie tangled, sweaty and numb. He runs a finger up and down my arm. "So . . . do you still have it?" he asks.

What? I'm prickly with the urge to leave now, like always after sex, when they touch and talk and want something else.

They always want something else. A song, a soothing salve. A bit of mending done.

"I'm stuck between worlds, 'twixt ancient and ever-young. I need delineation. A sense of diurnal." So he claims. "Do you have it? Do you have my shadow, Wendy?"

What? That little bit of grayish-ness wadded up in the pocket of my jeans on the floor, along

Kelly Hale

with the condoms we're not using, and a plastic baggy full of Demerol?

It could be my parachute, my sail, my veil, my shroud. I could toss it to the Nothing outside and see if it floats. Flies. Whatever.

It doesn't belong to him. Or to the monsters, or the mermaids, or the everlasting twilight.

It's mine. Mine now.

"No," I say. "I don't."

Magic Users

Some who use magic wield it to gain money, power, status, and celebrity. Others us it quietly from their living rooms or office cubicles. Some fight for the lives of those around them, while others spend the lives of mortals cheaply. What would you do if you could reshape reality?

Zaubererkrieg

Stephen D. Rogers

I barely escaped him at Kiev. The troops missed me by less than a day and Hitler made no effort to hide his displeasure. He massacred a hundred thousand Jews and gypsies at Babi Yar despite the fact that not one of them had any idea of my whereabouts.

Hitler then countermanded his directive of 19 July and resumed the attack on Moscow, probably hoping to follow the original lead. Whatever he might have told his inner circle, his generals, or his people, the real reason he invaded the Soviet Union was me. I was the wizard who could deliver him England.

By breaking off from his original plan, however, Hitler had handed me the weapon of my choice. Winter arrived.

I have never created snow so deep, cold so severe. I stopped tanks from functioning, dropped horses by the herd. The men I put through hardships that rivaled those of a frozen hell.

Needless to say, Hitler never did reach Moscow. Even if he had, I was a hundred kilometers away, spinning my spells of bitter snowfalls, piling up the misery that would later mire him in spring thaw, mud the likes of which he had never seen.

No, I was not working with the Soviet leadership. The Communists were no more fond of rumors regarding me than they were of churches or religious icons. I was merely protecting my source of power.

That is true. And that is why I am talking to you now about this war you're planning to fight.

I'm sorry that word slipped out. I mean, this offer of UN-sanctioned military assistance.

The American people are tired of seeing their children return in bodybags. I can end this situation with minimal casualties providing you delay your assistance until the winter solstice. I will also require the establishment of a forbidden zone measuring sixty-three point three square kilometers, the location to be disclosed once we come to an agreement.

That's not a problem. After all, if you renege on your promise, I shall simply cover the United States with a sheet of ice six miles deep.

I'm glad you understand.

The wizard war will begin as scheduled.

Good day.

The Apprentice
Joy Marchand

The old witch hoisted herself out of the Buick and stood blinking in the blizzard of flashbulbs until the tourists got bored of the shot and lowered their cameras, keeping them at the ready like sports photographers waiting for a touchdown. She hefted her bag of tricks closer under her arm and nudged the car door shut with a thump, marshaling her long black robes, her grizzled gray hair—wouldn't do to step on a hemline now and ruin the dramatic effect. Not tonight, on All Hallows Eve, at the Old Burying Ground, edgy young witches already assembled on the green, smelling of patchouli and chewing gum.

"Madame Call, is tonight the night you choose your apprentice?"

The old witch turned, looked past the gawking tourists. There they were, all the young reporters who'd drawn the short straw in the editorial pool for the right to huddle in the cold, waiting to snap a single photograph that might end up on the back page of the Lifestyle section of the newspaper. "Every Sabbat and Esbat, the same lineup."

"Yes, ma'am." Julie, or Jenny-somebody raised a little digital camera. "When you pick your apprentice, can we have a shot for the paper?" Behind her, a few others shifted, hefting flashguns and reflectors. A familiar-looking blond kid, Tim-something, looking world-weary and embarrassed, concentrated on manipulating his lenses.

Madame Call grunted as she moved off down the green, toward the circle of girls waiting for her, their hands over their mouths, eyes shining in the moonlight. "Mayhap you'll get me to pose, as a reward for your persistence, aye?" Then she climbed the rise, waded into the assembly, set her bag of tricks down on the earth, the pressed powder of bones, hair and teeth, the coffin dust of centuries.

She forgot about the tourists, blocked out the sounds of cars passing the Burying Ground. Out of her bag of tricks, she pulled a black cloth, smoothed it over a nicely flat patch of ground for an altar. On it she arranged her bowl of salt, silver pentacle, plate of tiny cakes, a wand of crystal (just in case some grouchy spirit showed up and needed to be sent on its way) and a bronze chalice, into which she poured a measure of Evian from a plastic bottle. Then the candle in the lantern, lit with a match. And the athame—double-edged, its black handle etched with the symbols of her faith—flashed: down, up, across, down, and up again, the pentacle, cut in the air. And the circle, inscribed over the earth to the accompaniment of much grunting and shuffling. She was getting too old for this part, this kneeling in the dew, this blessing of the sacred space.

Let her apprentice take over that part. Her apprentice.

The girls arranged themselves along the edge of the circle and held hands, gazing at one another from the hoods of their cloaks. It would be one of them, chosen by the old witch

Joy Marchand

to continue the old traditions, to dip the athame in the salt, the purified water, then draw it through the candle flame, catch the smoke in curls on the tip. They watched the old woman stand, with her arms to the heavens, asking the spirits of the north, south, east and west to protect them as she drew down the power of the moon to infuse their circle and lend majesty to the proceedings. As they watched, they shuffled their feet. Looked at the tourists, yawned.

Madame Call saw everything that happened in the circle. Saw it with a heavy heart. But her favorites—splotchy Celia, nose-pierced April, scarecrow Jen—were all wide-eyed and silent as the old witch assumed the aspect of the goddess. To faithful witches, this was the best part of the ritual, watching the aspect settle across Madame Call's shoulders like a cloak of night. The faithful would see her grow pale of skin, dark of expression, as beautiful as deadly nightshade, as tall as oaks, shining with the power of the moon and stars. No more a bent old woman, worrying about hemlines and tourists, but a creature of dark energies, a temporary goddess, with the crackling fire of creation dancing in her fingertips, boiling in the palms of her hands.

The girls passed around the little cakes while the old witch did the work of the evening. Blessings and wellwishes for sisters too old or sick to attend. Healing energies sent to them on the winds, gratitude sent into the earth, into the sky. Requests for happy times in childbirth, requests for fortune to fall on those whose hands labored hard and long. Requests for good harvests, warm houses, strong families. In one case, smiling, Madame Call send healing energies toward an ailing poodle, Trixie the Dust Jacket Dog, a fixture in a local bookshop, who'd gotten kennel cough from a visitor's black Labrador.

Then, exhausted, the old witch bid farewell to the aspect, cast it back into the sky from whence it came. Bent and poured the salt back into its plastic baggie, sprinkled the water on the earth, blew the cake crumbs into the wind. The girls huddled together, red-faced from the cold, and it seemed very much like they were excited about the selection, for they were huddled around the favorites, listening to them whisper, watching them toss their heads and preen. The old witch gave a smile, caressed the athame before putting it back into the bag of tricks and stood, ready to throw her arms around her new apprentice, to bring her favorite back to the house for her first lesson.

After we're done, anybody wanna get a Jamba Juice? God, I'm parched. I could really use a Jamba Juice. Anybody wanna come? God, I'm cold. This is taking forever. Why does this always have to take forever? The favorites went on and on, chattering like demented magpies. They didn't notice when the other girls winced and moved away from her, their heads lowered, eyes on the buckles of their fashionably gothic shoes.

Madame Call stood on the green with the aftereffects of channeling the goddess still tingling on her skin. She gazed upon her favorite girls, the girls she'd nurtured and petted, groomed and instructed, the girls who held the future of the craft in their hands. She saw, as if for the first time, the flowing cloaks of crushed black velvet, the black lip liner, the silver and crystal jewelry, the pentacles dangling from wrists, necks and ears. Trappings, glinting with the motion of their oblivious chatter. And then the old witch tucked the bag of tricks under her tired old arm and turned away from the gaggle of girls, limping sadly down the green, through the shifting ocean of tourists and the blizzard of flashbulbs, to the Buick.

Of the reporters, only one had remained. The embarrassed one, fiddling with his digital camera, flipping through his shots with tears in his eyes.

Poor thing, too skinny—needed feeding.

"And here's Tim Reavy," said the old witch. "Reavy, aye? Disappointed not to get his shot of Madame Witch and her Apprentice. Think they'll fire you now?"

He lifted his eyes from his camera, looked at her through his dirty-blonde hair and said, "You were wearing the moon. All over you like a mist. You were nine feet tall and there were stars in your hair. But the stupid camera—"

The old witch's hands began to tremble, and she nearly dropped her bag of tricks.

But young Tim was there, in a flash, to steady her. "Need a hand, Madame?"

"Yes," she said, blinking. "Oh, yes."

Office Magic
Jon Sprunk

Michael Crawley finished the last entry on the page and sat back with satisfaction, twirling his pencil. He glanced at the clock on the wall. It was only ten thirty-five. He had time to tabulate another page of receipts before lunch.

An associate bookkeeper for Brisby & Lowman, an accounting firm of high reputation, Michael took pleasure in the orderliness of the accounting universe. He found meaning in a column of figures arranged perfectly straight on a clean white sheet, each line contained within its own tiny domain, never intruding on its neighbors. His father had never approved of his career choice, said Michael could have been Someone Important with the world at his fingertips. All Michael had ever wanted was a quiet place where he could tally his numbers in peace.

The shelves of his cubicle held a score of leather-bound tomes like Bank Accounting Practice, *Bookkeeping By the Numbers* by Al Hazred and the voluminous *Federal Guidelines for Receipts Payable Computation*. On his desk were only a ledger book, an old-fashioned hand-turned pencil sharpener, and a can of new pencils. He did not use a calculator—his computations were never wrong—and he disdained personal computers. In his estimation, accounting software was an aberration. They were sterile, distant programs designed to alienate the user from the numbers. Also, Michael liked the smell of pencil erasers.

The walls of his cubicle quaked as a large blond head leaned over the partition.

"Heard the latest, Mikey?"

Michael hated being called Mikey, but he tolerated it from Les, if for no other reason than Les looked like he should be playing linebacker for the Giants rather than crunching numbers for a living. He was tall and ruggedly good-looking, and he had shoulders as wide as a city block. Besides that, Les was an honest-to-goodness, salt-of-the-earth, great kind of guy.

"I've been tied up all morning with the AAMP account. What's up?"

"The PaperTrail Project just got tanked. Vince is cleaning out his desk as we speak."

Michael sat up in his chair. The PaperTrail Project? That was Vince Goldman's baby, an innovative way to track accounts all across the country by computer networking, or something like that. Michael didn't really understand how it worked, but he knew Vince had pioneered the idea, pitched it to the Board, and gotten approval despite the hefty price tag.

"You mean they fired him? Just like that?"

Les shrugged, his thick neck straining the collar of his shirt. "Just like that."

Michael didn't realize he was twirling his pencil until he looked down. "There's got to be something we can do."

"Like what?"

Michael lowered his voice. "We could go to the Old Man and fight for Vince's job."

Jon Sprunk

Les's tanned face turned a shade lighter. "Whoa, Mikey. Who's going to do that? You?"

"Someone's got to do it. We could go together."

Les rubbed his close-cropped head. "I don't know. It sounds risky. I got Amy to think about, ya know? She'd never understand if I lost this job."

"Maybe we need to do something risky here, to shake things up."

Before Les could reply, something down the hall caught his attention. "Hey, there's Nancy. I got to tell her the news."

As Les clomped down the hall, Michael leaned back in his chair, the figures in front of him forgotten. He and Vince had started at Brisby & Lowman at the same time, both of them fresh-faced youngsters with big ideas full of numbers and revolutionary calculation methods. Michael had been proud when Vince came up with the PaperTrail Project, just as proud as if he had thought of it himself.

In that moment he made up his mind. He stood up and left his cubicle.

Even on his feet, Michael wasn't a large man, being of average height and build. Countless hours living under fluorescent lighting had washed out his complexion and ushered the first strands of gray into his hair. However, he was well-groomed, always smooth-shaven, and professionally attired in Dockers, a shirt and a tie.

Michael knocked as he opened the door to Bob Nelson's office. Nelson was Michael's supervisor and a decent guy, for middle management.

Nelson was on the phone, so Michael walked in and sat down.

"Yeah, Frank," Nelson said into the phone. "We'll have those numbers for you by the end of the day."

Michael sighed, twirling his pencil. He tossed it into the air and caught it neatly with his thumb and index finger. In the past nine years, Nelson had gotten progressively fatter and, if Michael's eyes weren't deceiving him, shorter. You hardly ever saw Nelson out of his desk and every time Michael stopped by his office, Nelson had sunk a little lower behind a growing mound of ledgers, legal pads, and memos.

"You betcha." Nelson hung up the phone and glanced over his paper-strewn desk at Michael. "What do you want? You got that AAMP account done yet? Those guys are crawling up my ass."

"I've got a problem."

Nelson picked up a blue binder and started paging through it. "Yeah? I got all kinds of problems. My wife isn't happy, I never see my kids, and my doctor says I've got three ulcers. Three! So what's eating you?"

"It's Vince. Isn't there anything we can do about him? The guy's a real asset to the firm."

"Hey, I got nothing against Vince," Nelson said. "But the word came down from On High. What can I do?"

"You could go to bat for him."

"Are you out of your mind? I'm not setting myself up for one of the Old Man's tirades. The last person who went up there looking for a favor was Charlie Cavanaugh. You remember Charlie?"

Michael remembered. Charlie Cavanaugh had been one of the firm's top guns in marketing. One day Charlie came to work bearing terrible news. His house had been struck by lightning the night before. He lost everything. His family barely escaped with their lives. Still, he came to work the next day wearing a borrowed suit. He went up to the Old Man's office to ask for a couple days off. Michael had seen Charlie on the way out looking like he had gotten into a fight with a meat grinder. And lost. He didn't talk to anyone, just left the office and never returned.

"This is different," Michael said.

Nelson checked his watch. "You want my advice? Forget Vince and watch out for your own butt. It's no secret that this quarter's forecast has put a bug up the Old Man's ass. If things don't get any better, Vince isn't the only one who'll be looking for another place to work."

The phone rang and Nelson straightened his tie. "I've got to take this call. Go finish that account, Mike. I need it today, by four at the latest."

Michael got up and left. It took every ounce of self-restraint not to slam the door on his way out. He returned to his cubicle and slumped into the chair. It wasn't goddamned fair! A man works for years in a company, displays loyalty and an earnest desire to succeed, and as soon as some cryptic margin drops a couple points the suits upstairs toss him out. The more Michael thought about it, the madder he got.

Riding the wave of his fury, he snatched up the phone and punched in four digits. The tones rang in his ear like the jangling, discordant notes of an infernal chorus. It took six rings for the other end to pick up.

"Mr. Brisby's office," a nasal voice said.

Michael affected a professional demeanor. "Yes, I'd like to speak with Mr. Brisby."

"Who's calling, please?"

"Ah, this is Michael Crawley . . . from Accounting."

The voice paused, and then said in a more officious tone, "He's in a meeting. I'll tell him you called."

Michael knew the voice was lying. His anger returned. "When will he be available? This is important."

"He'll be in meetings all day, Mr. Crawley. I'll tell him you called."

The receiver clicked in Michael's ear. He flung it back into its cradle. "Damnit!"

His pencil was twirling furiously in his hand.

Les peered over the wall. "What's the problem?"

"That does it!" Michael snarled. "I'm going up there."

"Up where?"

Michael thrust himself to his feet. "Brisby's office."

"What? Are you crazy?"

Les came around the partition, but Michael lifted a hand and the big man backed away.

"Think about what you're doing, Mikey."

The words followed Michael as he charged down the hall with long, measured strides. Out of the office pool, he made a left and turned into a broad, well-lit atrium. Only one elevator went all the way to the top. Its doors were flanked by a pair of security guards in navy blue uniforms. They eyed Michael's approach. He twirled his pencil and they blinked. He walked right past them, hit the button, and stepped through when the doors opened. The guards didn't move.

Michael hummed an old television super-hero theme song as he pressed the button for the top floor. The elevator began to rise.

He was doing it. He was on his way to see the Old Man. When he got there, he would march right in and demand Vince's reinstatement. It was a bold move, so unlike his normal self. The impetus was a heady drug.

The elevator car ground to a halt between the sixth and seventh floors. The overhead light sputtered and went out, plunging Michael into darkness. He waited for a moment. And then another. And then the realization sunk in. They were trying to stop him. He had gotten past the outer defenses and now they were upping the ante. Michael had no doubt that more security guards were on their way with crowbars and handcuffs. They would be ready for any tricks.

Michael twirled his pencil in the dark. A thought came to him. He found the control panel. His questing fingers located a small hole beneath the rows of raised buttons. The emergency keyhole. He stuck the tip of his pencil inside.

The lights flickered back to life. The car resumed its journey upward through the innards of the office building. He was back on track.

The elevator doors opened on the thirteenth floor and Michael stepped out into an intimidating hallway. Varnished oak doors were staggered down the hall. Executive suites. The air smelled different. It was more pleasant, sweeter in some ineffable way. Yet, Michael detected a menacing undercurrent in the atmosphere. Yes, life was better up here, but one wrong step could mean a long fall.

As soon as Michael started down the corridor, people appeared. Dressed in tailored suits and dress-suits of varying shades of gray, they emerged from the doors. With piercing eyes they skewered him, ready to block his advance.

Michael twirled his pencil, but the executives blocked his thaumaturgy with a horrendous litany.

"Stock options," they chanted. "Company BMWs with leather interior!"

"401k," he shouted back. "And responsible asset managing."

"First-class accommodations at the Four Seasons!"

Michael shivered under the onslaught. He felt his resolve crumbling. In desperation, he unleashed his most potent weapon. "Smith, Keynes, and Greenspan! By these Names of Power I banish you!"

The executives fell back, their voices hushed.

Michael pushed forward. "Begone, parasites of the workingman, back to the Hell that bred you!"

The suits fled before him. Expensive Italian shoes clacked on the marble tiles and doors slammed shut.

Michael continued his march. The silence was unnerving. A massive door stood at the end of the corridor.

"Can I help you?"

A familiar nasal voice pulled Michael away from the door. Mr. Brisby's receptionist was a short, squat woman. Her bright red sweater made his eyes hurt. It was difficult to tell her exact age through the thick layers of makeup caked on her face, but Michael guessed somewhere in the mid- to late-forties.

"I'm here to see Mr. Brisby," he said.

The receptionist regarded him with large, bulbous eyes that—despite several layers of mascara and a liberal coat of 'Seductive Sapphire' eye shadow—made Michael think of a giant frog.

"Your name?"

"Michael Crawley, from Accounting."

If possible, those eyes bulged even further. Michael took an involuntary step backward.

"I told you," she snapped. "Mr. Brisby is in a meeting."

Michael made his move when she reached for the phone to call security. He dashed for the door, turning the brass knob and throwing it open before he could be stopped. As he caught the door's edge, he heard jackboots echoing down the corridor at double-time. He slammed the door and locked it. Then he turned around.

Mr. Brisby's office occupied the entire east wing of the thirteenth floor from corner to corner. It was floored in perfect one-foot squares of black marble, polished to a high gloss. Yet, the vast majority of the space was empty save for a tiny, 1950s-style gray-metal desk, the top of which was obscured by stacks of paper, some of them over a foot tall.

A small man wearing silver-rimmed bifocals peered over the document towers. His head was bald except for a sparse white halo of hair.

The company letterhead said 'Brisby & Lowman,' but Arthur Lowman had retired five years ago. The last Michael had heard, Lowman was living in the Bahamas, enjoying his vast fortune. Since then, Mr. Brisby had run every aspect of the company.

"What is the meaning of this?"

Michael cleared his throat. "Pardon the interruption, Mr. Brisby. I've come because of Vince, Vince Goldman, sir. I don't think it's fair what the firm is doing to him."

Michael knew he was babbling, but all of his strong words had evaporated from his mind and he was grasping at shreds.

"Who are you and what is all this about . . . what was that name?"

"Michael Crawley, sir. I mean Vince Goldman. I'm Michael. Mike Crawley, sir. Vince is the one you're firing."

The eyes behind the glasses squinted. "Ah, yes. I remember signing the order yesterday. The Papermill Project or something."

"PaperTrail Project, sir."

"Yes. I ended the project. A frivolous waste of money! What of it?"

"Well, sir, Vince is a good friend of mine and I thought—"

Mr. Brisby stood up from his desk. "You thought you could just barge into my office and demand that I reconsider? Is that it?"

"Sir, I mean, I know it sounds bad, but I had the best intentions."

"Good intentions do not pay the bills, Mr. Crawley."

Michael's anger returned, but this time it wasn't hot and scattered. It was more focused. Righteous indignation. That was it. He was indignant. How dare this old geezer treat his employees this way?

"Sir, I really think—"

"Is this what I pay you for? To interrupt my work during business hours?"

Fists pounded on the door. Shouts echoed from the hallway. It was only a matter of time before the security goons battered their way inside. Michael knew he had to do something quick.

"Tell me, Mr. Crawley. Why shouldn't I fire you along with your incompetent friend?"

"Sir, I . . ."

Michael's pencil was twirling like a bandleader's baton. Around and around his fingers it spun, trailing tiny slivers of starlight. Brisby's form wavered. Michael stared in amazement as his boss transformed before his eyes. The little man's hunched form straightened and grew until he towered over Michael. His withered flesh fell away to reveal a coat of slimy, black scales. Titanic wings unfolded from his back, filling the office chamber.

"Yes, Mr. Crawley?" Brisby's voice resounded from protruding jaws laced with rows of curving fangs. "You have something to say?"

In the face of this horror, Michael retreated to his bastion of logic. "I . . . I believe a detailed cost analysis reveals that the PaperTrail Project conforms to the most stringent parameters, and furthermore places Brisby & Lowman at a highly advantageous market position."

Mr. Brisby's roar shook the building. "You dare quote elementary economics to me? What of the normative portfolio? What of the falling margins, Mr. Crawley?"

Michael stumbled and fell to the hard tiles. The pencil shook in his fist. He had one bullet left in his arsenal. He conjured the terms of Final Termination. "In the event of a contract prematurely dissolved, the guilty party shall Surrender Damages *In Toto!*"

Mr. Brisby howled and the windows of his office shattered. His monstrous body shrunk, returning to its original shape. He collapsed in his chair as a great wind blew through the chamber and swept his papers away.

Voices from outside shouted over the tumult.

"Mr. Brisby, are you all right? Mr. Brisby!"

The employees of Brisby & Lowman talked about the incident for days and weeks, of how one of their own, a mild-mannered associate bookkeeper, told off the Old Man and survived to tell of it. Brisby retired soon afterward. To the aghast of his executive staff, he appointed Accounting Manager Bob Nelson in his place. That year, for the first time in Brisby & Lowman history, Christmas bonuses appeared in the paychecks of every worker, great and small. In the years following, the company's bloated management was trimmed back and its profit margin surged.

Michael Crawley declined all attempts to reward or promote him. Instead, he returned to his cubicle where he worked happily ever after.

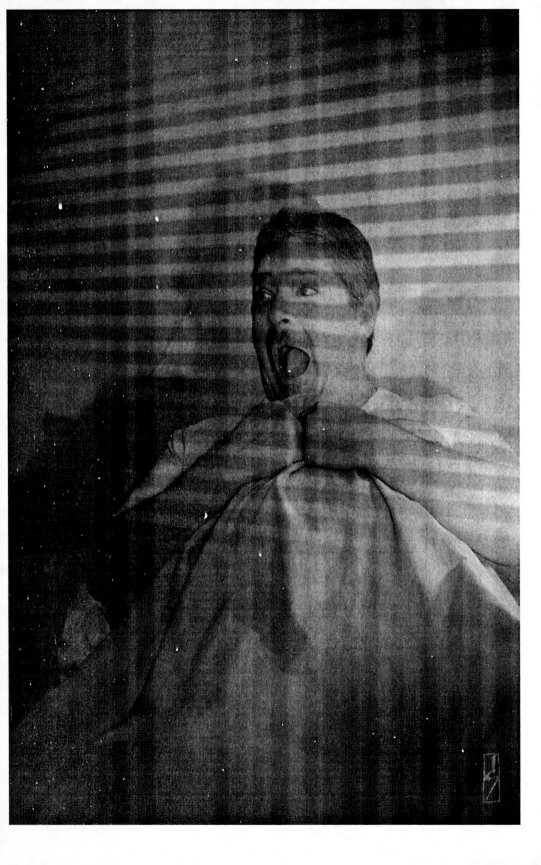

Raven

Elaine Cunningham

People move to the suburbs to get away, am I right? I mean, what other reason could they have? Yeah, I know: safe neighborhoods, good schools, back yard barbeques, little league, mowing grass on weekends, yadda yadda yadda. But if you got no kids—and as far as I know, I don't have any—then what's the freaking *point*?

Like I said, it's all about getting away.

So I bought a house in the suburbs last month, and lemme tell you, it's about as far away from my old life as I'm likely to get without crossing an ocean or two. The house is this little blue box with wood shingles on the walls instead of the roof—something people around here call "a Cape." And it's in this little New England town that looks like something out of a freaking coffee table book. Seacoasts around every other corner, white steeples on the churches, houses with historical plaques on the front porches. Lots of smug little blonds driving around big SUVs, looking for ways to spend all that money their gastroenterologist hubbies bring home.

To cut to the bottom line, this town is about the last place anyone who's into Our Thing would go to look for me. Sure, Rhode Island used to have a pretty decent organization with solid ties to New York, but that went to shit after Ray Patriarca's day. Business is still being done around here, don't get me wrong, but nobody's got reason to be looking for a low-level, burned-out soldier from New Jersey.

And I fit in pretty good, if I do say so myself. Probably half the names in the phone book end with a vowel, and even my accent is close enough to the blue-collar Rhode Island natives that it doesn't raise eyebrows. People just figure I'm from Cranston, which is to Providence what Jersey City is to New York. Yeah, I know—not *too* freaking lame.

So anyway, here I am. At first, it was mostly okay. The neighborhood is quiet. Lots of kids around, but they're usually being driven to tennis lessons and soccer games. The two kids across the street sure as hell don't have much to say. They're a couple of pasty little blond girls with these big freaky deer-in-the-headlights eyes. They go to the Baptist school in town, which probably explains why they look at me like they're mentally reciting the Commandments, and expecting me to break one of the top ten any minute.

At first, that worried me a little. Old habits—if you're interested in staying alive, paranoia's a pretty important part of the package. But then I saw the way the Children of the Corn looked at the lady next door to them. For no reason I could see, they were really freaked out by *that* broad.

From a distance, she seemed pretty much like any other middle-aged suburban mom. A week or two went by before I actually met her. I was in no hurry. It wasn't like there was anything in it for me. Besides, I had this little situation to think about.

Thing is, there was something wrong with the house. The first night I slept there, no problem. But the next night shit started hitting the fan. For starters, I had nightmares for the first time since I was a kid. Scary stuff, and so real it took my eyes a while to adjust after I woke up. I'd be sitting bolt upright in bed, sweating like a pig, and *still* seeing this transparent, half-rotted corpse sitting in the bedroom chair, swinging slowly around to face me and taking its own sweet time to fade away into moonlight and shadows. I guess when dreams are vivid enough, it's like looking at the sun: after you look away, it takes a while for the spots to disappear.

Anyway, the dreams were so freaking real that for a while I shrugged off everything else that was happening. Weird thumps and creaks? Hey, it's an old house. Murmured conversations I couldn't quite hear? The TV was on—if not mine, then probably a neighbor's. Lying in bed and hearing people that I *knew* were long past talking whispering together in the corners? I must be asleep and dreaming. Waking up gasping for air, feeling a black cloud pressing down on me like it was trying to smother me in my sleep? Just another bad dream, most likely due to all the Portuguese food I'd been eating recently—spicy sausages like chourico and linguica, high-voltage seafood chowders, snail salad. I mean, *snail salad*? That *had* to be worth a nightmare or two, am I right?

Things went on like this for awhile, and frankly, I was starting to get a little ragged around the edges. Then one night I turned out the lights and was beating the pillow into a more comfortable shape when I heard this crash downstairs. Not a crash like a coffee mug falling off the counter—this sounded like someone had picked up a pool table and thrown it down an escalator.

There was no way I could write this off as a dream, so I pulled out the gun I keep under the mattress (old habits again) and got ready to take care of things. I don't scare easy, but lemme tell you, my heart was pounding, and the back of my neck felt cold and prickly. When I ran a hand over it, every hair was standing up like I was some freaked-out watch dog. But I pulled my shit together and went downstairs for a look around.

Nada. Zip. Zilch. Everything was perfectly in place. The doors were all locked, none of the windows had been opened or broken, and the alarm system (top of the line, and about half the price of the damn house) hadn't been triggered.

By this time I was seriously spooked. So after I checked everything three or four times, I went upstairs and threw some clothes in a suitcase, and grabbed a bottle of scotch on the way out. There was no freaking way I was going to get any sleep in this place—not tonight, anyway.

As I pulled out of the driveway, I noticed the lights were on in the suburban mom's house. Kind of strange, seeing that it was past two in the morning. But as I drove past, I noticed that the lights were not actually *in* the house, but sort of *around* it. And the closer I got, the brighter *they* seemed to get.

But by that point, I was already way past my weirdness threshold and didn't have much brainpower to spare on this. So I drove about fifteen minutes to a town that had less charm and more strip malls, and checked into a motel behind the Bugaboo Steakhouse. I figured if there were any ghosts around there, they'd mostly be beef cattle, and since I hadn't personally killed any of them, they had no call to be pissed off at me.

Yeah, that's right: *ghosts*. Because at that point, there wasn't much sense in denying what was going on. I'd bought a haunted house. The question was, what the hell was I going to do about it? Complain to the real estate agent? Get myself a lawyer and sue the old owners? Check the Yellow Pages to see how Rhode Island was fixed for ghost busters? I mulled it over for a while, then, thanks to the scotch, I managed to get a couple hours of sleep.

The next morning was Monday, and it was one of those bright, crisp New England mornings I found so freaking annoying when I was hung over. As I drove up to the little blue Cape, the setup seemed so freaking *normal* that I felt like a complete moron for thinking... what I'd thought the night before. I was a reasonable man, and there had to be a reasonable explanation for all this.

The suburban mom who scared the crap out of the Children of the Corn was in her front yard, digging in one of the flower beds. Her house was basically a plain, off-white box—the real estate guy had called it a "Federal-front colonial"—but the little gardens all over the yard were something else. She looked up when I got out of the car and waved. For no reason I could think of, I started to walk over.

My neighbor wasn't any more impressive at close range. She was on the shady side of forty, close to my height—just short of six feet—and probably a good twenty pounds heavier than me. She was wearing black jeans and a black T-shirt, probably because someone had told her black was slimming. Her hair was short and not quite red. No makeup. Glasses. A few silver rings. Pretty average stuff, except that she was barefoot, and her T-shirt read, "If I wanted your opinion, I'd read your entrails."

Hmm. I was starting to see where the kids next door were coming from. But she was walking toward me now, and I figured what the hell. She introduced herself as Frances Connolly and told me to call her Frankie, and I gave her the name I was using these days and told her to call me Bobby.

"Connolly—isn't that an Irish name?" I said. Hey, small talk had never been my strong point.

She smiled a little. "That's my husband's name. I was born Franceska Kwitowska, which should explain a few things."

Actually, it did. I knew some Polacks back in Jersey, and she would have fit right in with the kielbasa crowd.

"How are you settling in?" she asked. "I've been meaning to do the welcome thing, but the two or three weeks have been fairly hideous."

"You got that right," I agreed with feeling.

Apparently I put a little *too* much feeling into it, because her gaze sharpened. "Anything I could help you with? Starting out in a new place can be tough, and this town has more red tape and strange bylaws than most."

I was about to say thanks but no thanks, when I noticed one of the rings on her left hand. It was that star in a circle thing you see in movies about werewolves and devil worshipers.

"A pentagram," I said out loud—again, before I could think. Geez, a couple of weeks without much sleep had taken more of a toll than I'd thought!

Frankie got this schoolteacher look on her face. "Strictly speaking, it's a *pentacle*. The suffix 'gram' indicates writing, as in 'telegram.'"

Like I give a shit. I was a lot more concerned about what this meant for me. I was having a hard enough time sleeping, without knowing that someone in the neighborhood was chanting over chicken bones every full moon.

"A pentacle, huh? So you're... what?"

"Careful."

That wasn't what I'd expected to hear, and my confusion must have showed on my face. Again she did that little smile, then she pulled a silver chain out from under the T-shirt. On it was a little twisted horn made from red coral. It was a charm against the *mallochio*—the evil eye. A lot of people I used to know wore it, but they're all Italian. And more importantly, they weren't serious about it. It was a tradition, that's all. An ethnic thing. Something told me this broad had a different view, and since she was still wearing the schoolteacher look, I figured she was about to tell me about it.

But like I said before, I'd already had all the supernatural shit I could handle. So I said, "Yeah. Well . . . nice to meetcha and so on, but I've gotta get to work."

She nodded and went back to her flowers, and I headed into Hell's Little Outhouse to get ready for the ten-to-six shift at Lombardi's Volvo. Take a shower, put on the shirt and tie, take out the trash for Monday pickup—that routine.

Work was the usual civilian bullshit, and afterward I stopped by the Italian deli to pick up dinner. I got home to find trash scattered all over the front yard. My first thought was that maybe my ghosts had started working days. But of course, there was no lid on the trash can. I'd thrown the plastic bags in and hadn't given it another thought. There were a lot of trees in this town, so there were probably animals and shit around.

Frankie wandered over with a plate of something. "A belated welcome to the neighborhood."

I looked down at a dozen or so chocolate cookies, big suckers that had little peanut butter cups stuck in the middle, and melted chocolate drizzled over the top. They looked pretty damn good, assuming there was nothing funky mixed in. Eye of newt, human blood—whatever.

"You shouldn't have gone to the trouble."

She shrugged. "It's nothing out of the ordinary. I have kids. They have friends. Baking is part of the package." Her gaze shifted to the litter scattered over the grass. "Yikes. You know what will stop that?"

"A lid for the garbage can?"

"Well, that too. But if you have to put out extra garbage bags some weeks, take a couple pieces of bread, tear them into small pieces, and scatter them near the trash. In fact, do this every trash day. The ravens will eat the bread and leave the trash alone."

"Ravens."

I must have looked skeptical, because she gave this little shrug to let me know she realized how that sounded.

"They're extremely intelligent birds, and if you pay attention, you'll notice some pretty interesting behaviors. For example, if you pay 'protection bread,' they'll leave your trash alone. I've even seen them chase other birds away from it."

It sounded to me like someone had been watching too many *Sopranos* reruns. "Protection bread, huh?"

"It's a figure of speech. But yeah—I guess you could call ravens the feathered members of the suburban mafia."

"How about that."

She didn't seem offended by my lack of enthusiasm for this scenario. "They have close-knit family groups, and if anyone messes with one of them, the others can hold a serious grudge. I read a story about a woman who found a baby raven who'd fallen from the nest. Its leg had been mangled in the fall. The bird couldn't survive in the wild, so she took it to a wildlife shelter. A small flock of ravens dive-bombed her, squawking in protest. They followed her car for a couple of miles before she lost them. And for years after that, they'd be watching for her and would mob her whenever she came out of the house. They never bothered anyone else in her family."

This was really out there, but to my surprise, I was starting to get interested. "No freaking way! No bird is that smart."

"Sure they are." She turned and pointed to a big tree, the one the real estate agent had told me was a maple. Like that should mean something. "Every Monday morning, there's a raven perched in that tree waiting for me. When I come out of the house, he lets out this loud series of caws. The call is repeated from a tree not too far away, then another a little farther, and so on. On a quiet morning, you can hear the relay go for quite a ways. Ravens gather in those two trees and wait until a certain number arrive—usually no fewer than six."

"You're telling me they communicate?"

"Sure, and not just with other birds. In the wild, ravens sometimes form partnerships with wolf packs. Ravens are the eye in the sky, and the wolves are the muscle. If ravens fly over carrion or a wounded animal, they'll find the wolves and lead them to the food. In return, the wolves let the ravens eat alongside them when they make a kill."

It was enough like the system I grew up with to make sense. "As long as nobody eats alone, everybody eats."

"That's one way of putting it. My ravens have this down to a routine. They take turns, some eating, some standing sentry. Same thing, every week."

"So how do they know it's Monday?"

She lifted one eyebrow. "That's the day people in this neighborhood put out trash cans."

"Oh. That makes sense, I guess."

Frankie chuckled and gestured with the cookie plate. "Do you want me to take this in for you? Here—let me take that bag so you can open the door."

Since she was determined to be helpful, I gave her one of the deli bags and dug my keys out of my pocket. I unlocked the door and held it open for her. There's a little table in the hall. She took two steps toward it and stopped dead, like she'd run into a wall I couldn't see.

The cookie plate clattered to the floor and she probably would have followed, if she hadn't caught herself against the table. I've never seen the color drain out of someone's face like that—not when they were alive, anyway.

She turned around and pushed past me. Once outside, she sank down onto the stairs, breathing slow and hard. There was a wheeze to her breathing that I recognized from way back. My brother always had to use an inhaler when he was a kid. The sound was comforting, in an odd way. Familiar. I sat down beside her and waited for the worst of it to pass.

"Asthma?"

She nodded. We sat there like that until she got her breath back, and then for a while longer. It was like both of us knew there was more to say, but neither wanted to be the one to start.

"Maybe you're allergic to something in the house," I ventured.

"Possibly," she agreed. Her voice was still a little scratchy, but she was pulling it together. "I'm still pretty new to this—I developed asthma a couple of years ago. One of the joys of getting older. All things considered, though, it beats the hell out of the alternative."

"I guess."

"But there's definitely something in that house," she added softly, and the expression on her face made it plain that she wasn't talking about dust, pollen, or cat dander. "Not that I'm surprised."

"Why's that?"

She grabbed the railing and pulled herself to her feet. "Let's talk somewhere else. My house is pretty well protected."

That was a strange choice of words, but I was interested enough in what she had to say to follow her across the street and through the attached garage. There was a small bundle of dried herbs on either side of the door leading into the house. She took one of them off the hook and waved it over her head, then she crossed herself with it like a good Catholic—only she used five points rather than four—and brushed at her shoulders like she was flicking off dandruff. She did the same to me, which gave me the feeling that I was going through some kind of decontamination process.

Elaine Cunningham

We went inside, and Frankie nodded toward the kitchen table. I took a seat and looked around while she got out mugs and put the kettle on. A pair of Siamese cats slinked in. One of them jumped up on the table and gave me a long, flat stare—the kind of look I used to give people to let them know I had orders to shoot if they pissed anyone off. There's a reason why I don't much like cats.

The place seemed pretty normal, except for a dark painting on one wall—a portrait of a dark-haired, barefoot woman drawing a circle around a small fire. Smoke rose from the flames in hazy curls that seemed to be shaping up into something pretty fucking significant. Several ravens gathered outside of the circle, maybe waiting for the smoke to get its scary shit together.

"That's a Waterhouse print," she told me as she gently shoved the cat off the table and set a steaming mug in its place. "But you didn't come here to talk about art. Let's focus on your problem."

"You said you weren't surprised there was 'something in my house.' Why not?"

She gave a vague wave of her hand to indicate the area in general. "This part of Rhode Island has been settled for over four thousand years. There are all kinds of oddities around, if you know where to look. Some of the things are recent and fairly mundane—for example, there's a black bear buried behind the house two doors down from you. I get a sense of it from time to time."

"You get vibes from a dead bear? So you're like, a medium?"

That amused her. "Thanks for the thought, but I've got another twenty pounds to go before I'm down to a *large*."

"No, what I meant was—"

"I know what you meant," she said, still smiling. "Ever heard of self-deprecating humor?"

"Oh."

"But to answer your question, no, I'm not a medium and I don't want to be. For one thing, I'm still working out what I believe about all that. I don't know if it's possible to talk with the dead, but I'm pretty damn sure I don't *want* to. With my luck, I'd be hearing from dead telemarketers at all hours."

By now I was starting to get a feel for Frankie's sense of humor: pitch black, delivered with a straight face and a bone-dry tone.

"I had the same problem when I moved into this house," she went on. "Nothing quite so . . . specific as you have, but a lot of negative energy. It took me a while to get the place cleansed and warded. Protected, in other words."

I thought about the dim light that had lingered around the house the night before, and how it seemed to get brighter as I got closer. That raised some interesting questions, but for the moment I was more interested in getting rid of my ghosts than figuring out why I was setting off magical alarms.

"So, how do you set up this protection?"

"It depends on what the problem is. Give me your hand."

After a short hesitation, I held out my left hand, palm up. She dropped a small, smooth, very shiny black stone into it.

"That's polished hematite. I found it when I was breaking sod for the garden out back. Hold it tightly, and tell me what you feel."

I clenched my fist around the stone. It gave off a slightly fizzling energy. It was sort of like holding a damp Alka Seltzer tablet, only it was hard and dry. Slightly freaked, I put the stone on the table. Frankie picked it up and dropped it into a little silk bag. She added a couple shakes from one of the salt shakers on the table, pulled the bag's drawstring shut tight, and tossed it onto the kitchen counter.

"Hematite absorbs negative energy. And let me tell you, it *works*. I learned that a few years back, when I was visiting my parents in Florida. I love my father dearly, but he's one of the most negative and critical people I've ever met. A couple of days into the visit, my sister-in-law took me to a New Age shop. I tried on this little black ring, not knowing what it was. Suddenly I felt this *whoosh*, like something had pulled a plug and all this tension and bad energy drained right out. Needless to say, I bought the ring." She paused long enough to send me another of those half smiles. "The ring shattered on my finger when I was on the way to the airport. Apparently Dad had exceeded its capacity. It was a little messy, but I'd do it again."

I didn't believe a word of it, but it was a pretty good story. "So you're saying someone buried a hunk of hematite in the back yard to keep away negative energy?"

"Actually, it's not a bad precaution. There's a lot of strange energy around here. My guess is that there's enough psychic energy in this area to magnify whatever people bring with them."

I wasn't sure I liked the sound of that. "For example . . . "

"I started work on a book about Stregheria—that's hereditary Italian witchcraft—shortly after we moved in. There were a few strange occurrences, but mostly just a lot of unexplained tension in the air. I planted rue and fennel by the doorways and set up a *Lare* shrine inside, and things calmed down." She gave me a small, one-sided smile. "There's still a lot more dust generated by this house than any rational explanation can justify, but things could be worse."

For a while I sipped at the coffee and tried to make sense of this. The woman was a fruitcake, no mistake about that, but I knew enough crazy people to realize that being nuts didn't mean you couldn't also be *right*. Maybe she was some kind of psychic.

On the other hand, how good could she be, if she'd let a guy like me into her house?

"You have a very strong affinity for death," she announced casually.

Her timing was too good to be accidental. Surprise made me jump, and coffee sloshed over my hands and onto the table. Frankie handed me a paper napkin and waited while I pulled myself together.

"That's an interesting theory," I said cautiously. It also raised an interesting question: if she *was* some kind of psychic, how much did she know about me? And how much of a problem was that likely to be?

Frankie took a sip from her mug. "Green tea," she said sadly. "I'm decaffeinating. There ought to be a clinic for it, or at least a goddamn patch. But that's my problem. Yours is more interesting."

"Oh yeah—it's freaking fascinating."

Apparently she found sarcasm amusing, because that rated a brief smile. She took another swig of the tea, then pushed the mug aside and got down to business.

"There's a pretty dark presence in your house—most likely more than one presence. But you already know that."

There wasn't much sense in denying it, but I shrugged and gave her a look that suggested we should move on.

"I never got a strong read from that house before, but it's possible that the entities were already there, and the kind of energy you brought into the house gave them the strength to act out. Sometimes houses are quiet until someone with an affinity for death moves in. I've seen it happen."

"So you're saying I bought a haunted house?"

"Possibly," she said, drawing the word out to add emphasis. "But it's more likely that whatever I sensed in there followed you here. The energy in this area gave it, or them, enough of a boost for you to see what has always been there. Frankly, I don't particularly care how they got here. The question is, how do we persuade them to move on?"

"We? You make this sound like it's your problem."

"It's absolutely my problem!" she snapped. "I lived next to a seriously haunted house right after I was married, and I'm here to tell you that sometimes these things wander. I don't want my kids dealing with that. Besides, what else are neighbors for?"

As God is my witness, I had no idea how to answer that question. The whole suburban neighborhood thing was new to me, but I was pretty sure an offer of cookies and witchcraft wasn't the usual welcome package.

I drained my coffee mug to buy some time, then asked, "So what should I do about the house? Call a priest?"

Frankie smiled and shrugged. "If you feel more comfortable going that route, sure—give it a try."

"Or..."

She sipped her tea and considered. "It's odd that ravens came into the conversation earlier. A lot of the old religions considered them to be psychopomps—that's a sort of messenger that can move between this world and the spirit world. Some people thought ravens carried souls to the next world. Their presence on the battlefield was considered a blessing, as well as a practicality."

My patience was starting to wear thin. "This is freaking fascinating, but it doesn't solve anything."

"You know," she mused, "it just might."

The "protection bread" I could almost see, but this? I pushed back my chair and stood. "Thanks for the coffee."

Frankie rose with me. "Meet me in my front yard next Monday morning, just before dawn," she said softly. "This time of year, that's around five o'clock. Not many people are awake at that hour—"

"No shit!"

"—so we should be able to wrap things up without raising too many questions."

Since I had more than a few questions myself, I seriously doubted that.

"Leave all your doors and windows wide open," she told me, "and come into my yard. The wards on it are pretty good. The ravens will do the rest."

"Sure," I said, which struck me as a pretty good way to go. Fairly polite, but it didn't make any commitments. Fact was, I had no intention of carrying out some half-assed exorcism.

Still, I played and replayed that bizarre conversation over the next few days. When Monday rolled around, I woke up before dawn pretty much the way I'd been waking up every morning, not to mention several times a night: drenched in sweat and fighting my way free of tangled sheets.

After I'd beaten back the nightmare, I noticed the faint, gray light rimming the window shades. Morning was just about here. I glanced at the clock. It wasn't much past five, so I just lay there for a while, waiting for the now-familiar panic to recede, and my pounding heart to crank down the volume.

As the thumping in my ears faded to manageable levels, I became aware of the noise outside—a chorus of rough caws, growing louder by the moment.

I swung out of bed and stumbled over to the window. Frankie was standing in the middle of her yard, wearing some sort of long, black dress. There was a silver chain around her neck, and hanging from it was a fairly large cloth bag. She was barefoot—big surprise—and looking up into the maple tree.

I followed her gaze, and my jaw dropped. The branches were black with birds—big, sleek, glossy birds that scooted down along the limbs as they made room for the newcomers winging their way in from God-only-knows where.

Just then Frankie looked over to my window, and even from this distance I could feel her eyes on mine. There was something in them that made me begin to understand why the ravens came to her call.

A long moment of indecision passed. Obviously there was something to what she said; otherwise, how'd she manage to recruit all these birds? On the other hand, it looked like a scene from a Hitchcock movie out there, and if my memory was holding up, that movie didn't end real well.

Then something changed in the air around me. There was this electricity in it, like the supercharged, super-still feel the air has just before lightning strikes. The bedroom was still fairly dark, and things not yet visible began to rustle and whisper in the shadows.

Suddenly one middle-aged Polish-American witch and a couple hundred ravens seemed like a much better bargain than whatever was stirring *in*side the house.

I moved away from the window long enough to pull on a pair of pants. Open the windows, she'd said, so I threw that window wide open and moved on to the next one. When all the bedroom windows were open, I went to the next room, working my way downstairs. The feeling of a gathering storm grew stronger with every step, pressing in on me from all sides like a smothering cloud. The dark energy in the house was stronger than it had ever been, and it was starting to feel so familiar that I could give it a name: unfinished business. Whatever was in my house had a score to settle with me.

Once the house was wide open, I ran across the street and realized too late that I was barefoot. I sort of hopped my way across the rough pavement and loose stones and hurried onto the Connollys' yard. Frankie gave me a distracted nod, then she swung one arm like a sidearm pitcher firing off a high fast ball. She finished off with a sharp snap that left her pointing at my house.

What happened next was pretty much like the scene after the starting gun goes off at the New York Marathon. Hundreds of birds leaped out of the trees and headed straight for the little blue Cape. That was pretty bizarre, but I wasn't prepared for what happened next:

The windows started to slam shut.

Ravens pulled up short as best they could, but some of them whapped into the glass and slid down the side of the house. There were enough birds still on the wing to circle the house like a dark tornado, and it occurred to me that their shrill, harsh cries were getting loud enough to wake half the town. Oddly enough, no one else seemed to notice. The neighborhood houses stayed dark, and a passing dog casually lifted his leg on some bushes and trotted on. Apparently Frankie and I were the only ones seeing this particular show.

She didn't much like what she saw. Her face creased in a frown, and she let out a string of words I was trying to get out of the habit of saying. She took off for her garage at a run, calling for me to follow.

I closed my mouth, which had been hanging open like I was some small-town tourist who'd just gotten a sales pitch from a Times Square hooker, and I followed her into the garage. She was taking a solid-looking shovel off a wall rack of tools and giving it an experimental swing.

"Whatever is in that house is stronger than I thought, and they don't want to leave," she told me. "Windows and doors are portals, in more ways than one. If the ravens can't get through, we're screwed. We've got to open the windows or break them. Grab something."

I looked around and noticed a black leather sports bag someone had dropped in the middle of the garage. The zipper was half open, and a bat handle stuck out. I pulled it out and hefted

it. It was a one of those fancy new metal bats, dolled up with metallic blue paint.

Frankie snatched it out of my hands in mid swing, looking more shocked by my choice of weapon than by anything that had happened so far. "Are you *kidding*? These things cost a small fortune."

She threw the shovel into my hands, grabbed another, and ran across the street, ducking this way and that as she made her way through the feathered wind tunnel that was still circling my house.

I've had some strange moments in my life, but nothing like the feel of all those black wings sweeping past. The weird thing is, none of them actually *touched* me. It was like the ravens were already halfway into whatever world they were heading to.

I made it through without completely freaking out and tried the front door. It wouldn't budge. No luck with the windows, either—the place was locked down tight. So I swung the shovel at the dining room window, bracing myself for a shower of broken glass.

That turned out to be a mistake. Something was behind the window—or maybe *in* the window—turning it into something that was more like hard rubber than glass. The surface gave a little, but it didn't shatter or even crack, and the shovel rebounded so hard it flew out of my hands. I lost my balance, overcompensated, and fell face-first into the unbreakable glass.

Holy *shit*, that window was cold!

I stumbled back, surprised that my skin didn't stick to it, like my brother's tongue had stuck to the stop sign that one winter he was young and stupid enough to take a dare.

I looked around for Frankie. She wasn't doing much better. Her first attack on the house sent her reeling back hard enough to land her on her backside. She pushed up from the ground, grimacing in pain, and reached into the cloth bag she wore like a necklace. She took a handful of whatever was in there and flung it at the window.

A small dust cloud hit the window, and the glass promptly blew inward. Ravens flew in right behind, streaming past Frankie as she hurried to the next window and did the same thing there. She started around to the back of the house, then spun on her heel and yelled at me to get over into her yard.

Too late.

The first wave of birds burst out of the house, dragging behind them an invisible cloud of cold and darkness and sorrow and rage. As it swept over me, I remembered why I'd decided to get out of the family business—every fucking moment and every bloody detail that had led me to that decision. Let's just say it was a bad few moments, and leave it at that.

Fortunately, it was over pretty quick. Just like that, the ravens were gone, including the ones who'd pancaked themselves against the house. The neighborhood was as quiet as a church, and I noticed that the grass was cool and damp. I didn't remember falling to my knees, but there I was.

Frankie stumbled over and sank down onto the grass beside me. A long moment of silence passed, broken only by the yap of someone's dog a couple of blocks away, and the faint echo of the raven chorus.

"Well, that should do it," she said.

I had to grin. I mean, she sounded like some mechanic telling me my muffler ought to hold until I got the car over to the nearest Midas!

My smile faded abruptly. Come to think of it, that's *exactly* what it sounded like—an admission that the measure was successful, but temporary.

"So . . . what next?"

Suddenly I noticed that Frankie looked very tired, not to mention several years older. She took off her glasses and began to massage her temples with both hands. I figured I hadn't been the only one to sense the departing ghosts. She'd probably been hit pretty hard by the psychic shit left behind by all those bad men I'd turned into dead men.

Several moments passed before she spoke. "The stuff I threw at the window had salt in it, so you'll want to dig out the soil around the windows and have it taken to a landfill. Not much will grow in salted ground. Once you replace the soil, I'll tell you what things to plant. If they grow, it'll help." She shrugged and sighed, then admitted, "Not much, but some."

"So what'll help *a lot*? What'll keep . . . stuff like that out of the house?"

"You're not going to like this," she murmured.

"Like I'm crazy about *any* of this!"

Frankie lowered her hands and met my gaze. "You could move."

That wasn't what I was expected to hear, and something closed down inside me. I hadn't realized until this minute that I was actually starting to like the ditzy broad. I couldn't blame her for giving up on me, but her answer came as more of a surprise than it should have.

"You could move," she repeated, "which would probably solve the problems in that particular house. And maybe the next place you go would be better for you. Maybe the energy levels will be low enough to keep something like this from happening again. But if you want to make sure, go back to wherever you came from. Face whatever there is to face, make whatever restitution you can. *Then* it'll be over."

That was a true statement, if I ever heard one! If I went back to Jersey, I'd be dead, which is about as "over" as it gets.

Or so I'd always thought, up until, say, last month.

I flopped back to lie on the grass, one arm flung out wide and one thrown over my eyes. All of a sudden I felt more tired and hopeless than I'd ever been.

The soft rustle of skirts and a creak of protest from middle-aged knees informed me that Frankie was leaving. I wanted to stop her, but there wasn't much more to say.

Fact was, I was pretty sure I understood the problem. I didn't need a witch to tell me my karma was fucked beyond recognition.

Maybe she sensed what I was feeling, because I heard her hesitate. After a moment, something cold dropped into my palm. I felt the faint fizzling energy, and I closed my fist around the hematite stone.

The tingling increased, until it took all my strength to hold my hand closed over the vibrating stone. It felt good—scary, but somehow cleansing. After a while I stood up and clenched my other hand around that fist, determined to let the stone suck out as much negative energy as it could.

By then Frankie was long gone. The sun was up. Her family would be awake soon, and she'd have the usual mom stuff to do. That was okay—what I was doing now, I could do alone.

So I held onto that stone until senses I didn't know I *had* screamed at me to drop the thing. I threw it at the salted ground under the nearest window. Not quick enough. The stone shattered, and slim black shards burrowed deep into my hand. Blood welled up from several small wounds in my fingers and palm, like scattershot stigmata.

Suddenly I understood why Frankie had given me the stone. As she'd mentioned earlier, there was only so much negativity a chunk of hematite could hold.

I walked over to the window and let a drop of my blood spill into the tainted earth. It seemed like the thing to do. Blood calls out for blood. I might not know shit about magic, but some things I know.

So I walked around the house, making small offerings to appease the dead. Fortunately, the place was small. I managed to squeeze a drop or two by each window and door before the bleeding stopped.

I was sitting on the step, picking out the last of the stone shards with a pocket knife, when a sharp, grating call came from the maple tree. I glanced up. One of Frankie's ravens was back, and damned if he wasn't looking right at me. There was a very familiar expression in his black eyes, and I could almost hear the feathered motherfucker saying, "Not bad, kid, but you might want to take out a little extra insurance, if you get my meaning."

Yeah, I got it. So I went into the house for the rest of the garlic bread I'd had last night. It was trash day, and apparently the ravens and I had this little arrangement.

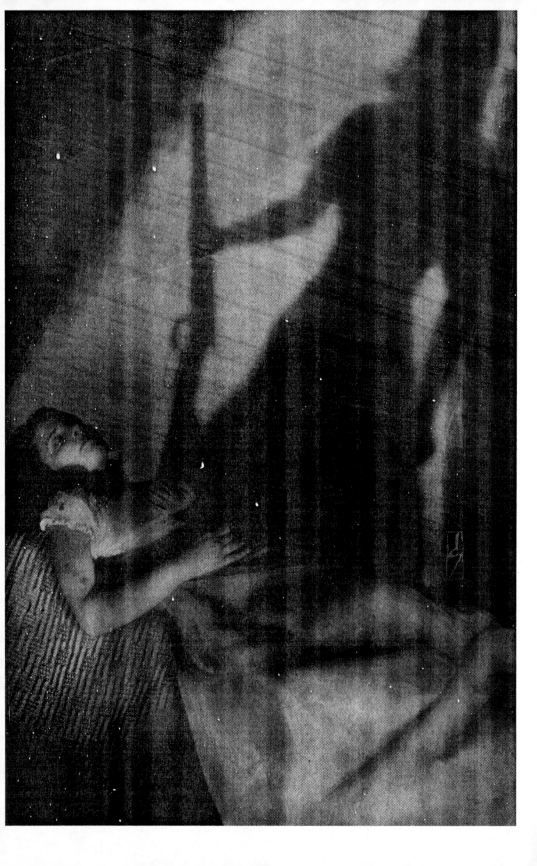

Beauty, Sleeping
Melissa Frederick

Rose lay motionless on the guest bed, just as Trudi had arranged her: hands folded, blankets snug under the elbows, head propped and tilted 45 degrees to the left, in case she vomited. Every candle Trudi could get her hands on stood watch around the room—a flickering chorus of heights, widths and perfumes. It was the closest she could come to a room of prayer. She had no vials of holy water and didn't keep incense around the house since the smoke bothered her eyes. Candlelight had dissolved Rose's acne and chicken pox scars so that her face looked more than ever like a porcelain egg nestled in red curls. Too perfect for this world. The only detail that disrupted the scene was the shadow cast by Trudi's rifle, a dark gash across one eyebrow and part of the forehead. Trudi reached over to where the gun leaned, shifted the barrel, and continued to admire.

"Hello, princess."

This shouldn't have been necessary. Trudi sighed and twirled the syringe between two fingers. If any one of five people had listened, but then, no one ever listens to the witch. Her kind were a marginalized group back in the days when the Brothers Grimm had Cinderella's stepsisters lopping off chunks of their feet to fit into the glass slipper. It occurred to Trudi that she should consider destroying the syringe somehow—by flushing it down the toilet, maybe—since it was evidence against her, and fairly damaging at that. But she didn't seem to have the energy. On the opposite wall, the needle distended into a cigarette holder, sleek and black, the kind they used to smoke in a good rich man's tragedy, a Fitzgerald novel. The willowy heroine, eyes bright as her sequined flapper dress, slips the stem between her teeth and manages to inhale before one wide hand encloses her neck and snaps it. Earrings shift, her head dangles like an apple. It didn't take Trudi long to figure out that this debutante was a mirror image of Rose.

Trudi shuddered, releasing herself from her vision. Blood buzzed through her cheeks, a sure sign she needed to get to her tea leaves. First, though, Rose deserved an explanation. "Don't be afraid, now, sweetheart. You're with me, and I always told you I'd keep you safe and sound." She shifted on the comforter and watched Rose's lids for any sign of recognition. "You're still in the Cristiana, in case you were wondering, and you're going to stay here for as long as I can fend off the world. It could only be for a few hours, but that might be as long as I need to set your future straight. And him. I told you darling, I told you that boy would be the death of you."

She caught herself in time. No need to tell Rose everything in the leaves. Gingerly, she laid her fingers on four purple bruises, forming a line down Rose's delicate upper arm like a flute. Trudi boiled. "I want you to know, if I'm not around to explain when you wake up, I never meant to hurt you. No matter what your mother or father or . . . Todd"—she expelled the word from her teeth—"or the news men or anyone else may try to tell you later."

A ripple along one eyelash. No, Rose wasn't conscious. Trudi was digging too far. "I injected you with insulin, princess. Just enough to keep you resting while I do what I have to do. Now, I know what you're gonna say, and you're right. We're practically family, we don't keep secrets from each other. But I can't let you see how this turns out. It's gonna get messy, trust me."

It's starting all over again, Trudi thought, biting her lip against tears and the pressure in her veins. There was still a chance that Rose wouldn't listen, wouldn't learn. Todd could escape. The two of them could fly off to Europe as planned. Then this whole overblown, Third-World-coup-style maneuver would wind up nothing more than a front-page thrill for some ski instructor over morning coffee. Couldn't let that happen. She'd have to resort to the fire water. With shaky, swollen fingers, she began buttoning her black cardigan as she scanned Rose's face, serene and smooth as a Michelangelo. The Mother of God had nothing on Rose.

Seventeen years ago, Trudi Hobart found her deepest calling when, on a whim, she bought the Cristiana Guesthouse in Crested Butte, Colorado. For months, she'd been looking to settle on some remote mountainside, in a log cabin, preferably with a smoky wood stove and a few acres of forest where she could collect ingredients for her extracts. She knew, even with a trust fund, the world didn't have much use for a Croatian-American, Pagan-Catholic, diabetic pastry chef. Too many labels for a job application—though she'd never really needed one—and way too many ambiguities. Hyphens made people nervous, even "sophisticated" natives of the east coast urban sprawl, upstanding Christians who turned up their noses at astrology columns as they sat at their kitchen tables in towns with names like Bala Cynwyd. That always made Trudi snort her Oolong. So you think you're above all that mystical, new-age, tree-hugging nonsense, hmm? Well, then, show me in the Bible where Jesus came up with that big red dragon on the flag you wave when you want to celebrate your Welsh heritage. And those Easter bunnies humping in fields sure don't have anything to do with our dead and risen Lord, unless you know something I don't. She'd decided, finally, that the problem was a simple flaw in human nature: the average citizen couldn't tolerate history or gray areas. When both openly flourished in the same person, watch out.

So after a divorce and one too many slaughtered rabbits showing up on her doorstep—gifts from the neighborhood Villanova students—the prospect of a move west loomed bright as the sunset in a bad cowboy movie. One Tuesday, almost without thinking, she packed the car and stuffed Bryn Mawr and the rest of Pennsylvania into the back of her glove compartment to be cheerfully forgotten. It was a straight shot to the Rockies, and once she got there she traveled on instinct, stopping at any mountain town that gave her an opening for clear vision. At that time, Crested Butte was still what real estate agents back east would call "underdeveloped"—a minuscule ski resort, lots of bars, a haven for aging hippies. But when Trudi drove through, she felt the future slam into her brain unannounced. Even without tea, she realized something was going to impact her here, but she couldn't tell what. She found a room at a Swiss-style hostel, the Cristiana. When the British couple who ran it wanted to quit the business, she took it off their hands, since, she figured, if Crested Butte wasn't what her future had in mind, she could always dump the place on some other wealthy vagrant.

For two months, Trudi woke up at 4 a.m. to bake five different kinds of Swiss pastries for her visitors, usually skiers who liked to hit the slopes by seven. She spent midday hiking the trails and familiarizing herself with the new flora. Glacier Lilies. Mule's Ear Sunflowers. Indian

Paintbrush and Colorado Columbine. All these would fast become new extracts more potent than anything she'd squeezed out of tired eastern land. Rumors flew from town to town that Crested Butte had attracted a witch. Trudi didn't mind the reputation, since it attracted curious tourists, and Crested Butte didn't mind, either, since the curious usually had extra cash. Still, she wasn't sure. She paced the upper hallways when the guests were asleep and couldn't shake the feeling that she was passing through.

Then, at the business association's annual Christmas party, she met Max and Dorothy. They were an older couple, German-Americans, both schoolteachers. There was nothing remarkable about them separately: he was on the short side of average, balding, had round eyes with low-hanging lids, dressed in gray suits; she was straight and slender as a birch, but with a slight bend at the pelvis—possibly from scoliosis—and her face was flat and plain. But when they stood side by side, they gave off an aura of clear blue light, like a gas jet, and smelled like an inland sea. Trudi knew this potential existed but had never seen it before, especially joined in two people when nothing emerged from one. It took Trudi a whole evening of small talk to figure out what was staring her in the face.

Max and Dorothy had a problem: they couldn't have children. Trudi informed them: before a year goes by, you'll be blessed with a daughter, and she'll be the most beautiful child on earth.

"I'll be back in a minute, dear." Trudi scooped up the rifle like a pool cue and rushed into the hallway. Her hot pot was wafting streamers of fog over the balcony, meshed shut with Trudi's barbed-wire perimeter. A dense cloud had already begun to obscure tree and tinsel at the bottom of the stairwell. The whole set-up was eye-catching, at least. Thank God her new extra-potent sandman dust had settled the guests for the evening. She hadn't used that precise combination of poppy seed and sweet everlasting before, but she knew she didn't want to use sleeping pills (way too unreliable) and she needed something that wouldn't be affected when baked into a pastry. Trudi had gone around to each room with a tray of samples—her latest recipe!—and made sure at least one buttery square went down, even if she had to pop one in someone's mouth while he was still talking to her. The guests thought she was playful. She also made sure to have a few, less powerful tidbits ready for the handful of children: "No, dear, you wouldn't like this one, it's for grown-ups. Here, try a bit of chocolate croissant, what little French children have for breakfast. Open wide." She knew how to work her charms. The whole house would be out until this mess was done.

Quickly, she nudged aside the pillowcase full of her extract bottles, which she'd had the presence of mind to collect before constructing the barricade, and poured a splash of water into her stone mortar. Planting a Virgin of Guadeloupe figurine so the long, wistful face stared squarely at the cup's white throat, she crossed her legs and peered into the staggered bits of brown, swirling like dust in a sunbeam. There was nothing special about the leaves, of course. They were just from a mixture she'd picked up from the organic grocery on Main street. But when steeped just so, they worked as a butterfly net to pluck the future out of a possible flow of events. With practice, Trudi had learned to interpret and use the information she was given, like any scientific instrument. She'd even developed a flavor system to give her the best results: Orange Pekoe for the weather, Jasmine for worldly affairs, Chamomile for relationships, good and bad.

Since she didn't quite know how to categorize this situation, Trudi had chosen Earl Grey—dangerous circumstances. Even with the house drained of noise, though, the brew stayed cloudy. As she jostled the base of the mortar, she began to see an image grow from the thumbnail edge of liquid. She focused her mind more to clear up the image and finally made out . . . herself on the guesthouse pay phone.

Five seconds later the phone rang. Trudi sighed. Not surprising the damn leaves would go haywire when she was under pressure. Quickly, she stood and plodded across the empty balcony.

"Hi, Trudi, I tried to call your private line but you weren't answering." There was a defensive twang in Dorothy's voice, not much different than her usual chat. "I figured you were entertaining guests. Listen, have you heard from Rosie at all today? She hasn't been home yet, and she really needs to get packing if she and Todd are going to make that flight out of Denver."

Trudi's chest tightened. "You're home already?" This was not a good turn of events. When she'd hashed out her plan, Trudi had assumed Dorothy would be busy with her usual chaperoning at the junior high Fun Friday Dance. The monthly festivities always kept her at school till 9:00 or later.

"Oh, yes, I came home ages ago. Got someone covering for me at school. I figured Rosie'd need all the help she could get in the trip prep department. You know as well as I do how much it takes just to get that girl on the bus in the mornings." Dorothy started laughing. "God, you should see the state her room's in right now! Not so much as a folded sweatshirt in sight. Piles everywhere. At this rate, she might be walking to Paris."

Trudi tried to force a giggle, which came out like a snort. Suddenly, all her carefully considered plans, her grand rescue mission, seemed as flimsy and transparent as a jailbreak on *Hogan's Heroes*. She might actually lose Rose before she could begin to defend her. Trudi's eyes began to well up.

"Anyway, I can't get her on her cell phone, and the weather's going to be iffy tonight, on top of everything else, so I don't want Rosie staying out too late. Could I possibly bother you to drive down to Gunnison with me? I'm guessing she's at the Wal-Mart with Crystal, and since Max is coaching right now, I'd really feel more comfortable with—"

"No, wait . . . you don't have to . . . I mean, Rosie's here, actually." Fingering each metal ridge on the pay phone cord, Trudi prayed ferociously to St. Jude to help her control the wavering panic in her voice.

"Rosie's with you?" The disbelief registered immediately. "What time did she get there? Why hasn't she come home by now?"

"She came . . . she's . . . waiting for Todd to pick her up." Trudi took a deep breath, in and out. The plan could still work. Todd would be coming soon—Trudi had seen to that. The only urgent matter now was throwing Dorothy off the trail. "Plus, I could hardly send poor Rosie off to another continent without some provisions. I've got a corn lily powder that works wonders on jetlag, but I have to refine it a bit more before it's ready. Then there's a tincture of belladonna I'm whipping up, just in case Rosie gets plane sick, and I'm trying to dig up my medallion of St. Christopher, for safe traveling, you know—"

Trudi's litany seemed to go right over Dorothy's head. "Why on earth would Todd want to pick her up at the Cristiana? He told me he'd come straight here after he punched out at the ski lodge."

"Oh, well . . . slight change of plans. I think he might have said something about a . . . lesson being cancelled. In fact—oh, wait, I think I see him pulling in the parking lot now." She held the phone away from her ear. Waited two beats. "Yes, it's definitely him. I'll send the two of them over as soon as everything's brewed and bagged. Won't take long. Call me tomorrow, dear."

"Wait a minute, could you put my daughter on the ph—"

Trudi held onto the receiver long after she'd cut the connection. The dead line felt smooth in her ears. Calm. The pressure was back, burning in her throat, but at least whatever happened would happen her way. Todd would come on his own, and she would dispatch him without stirring up any more trouble. But if Todd escaped, if the police got involved and thought this was a hostage situation . . . no, she was thinking like TV. If the police came, they'd just set up a few automatic weapons and try to mow her down as soon as she passed a window. The fire water would be necessary then. She hoped it would never come to that.

Hello again, princess. That was your mother on the phone. I bought us some time with a little white lie. It almost didn't go over, though. She was all set to send out the National Guard to look for you. She's your mother, you know. Oh, but you don't take after her. You hate it, I know, the way the school secretary mistakes your voice on the phone, how the other teachers gasped and pointed when they saw you clopping down the hall in a sundress and your hair in a French twist. I admit, I used to play hairdresser for your mom while you were still brewing in utero, but honestly, it was your head of hair my heart ached for. My lovely tiger. I set aside my silver combs and clips for the minute when my fingers could dip into your salt-smelling mane and tease out every snarl. Some rituals are so sacred they're worth cashing in your whole life for. You'll understand one of these days.

Darling, your life is special, never forget. It's my reason for going to war. Why do you think they put the god in mother? I've watched you grow from when you were a pearl wrapped in a blanket, a mouth wrapped around a teddy bear's leg. The blue light's grown, too, darling. I look at you now and it outshines the sun, the moon, every light bulb in Colorado. I heard your spirit call from your parents' genes. You wanted to be born more than anyone I'd ever heard of, then or now. So I assembled the ingredients: three violets, cornflower, a white rose, and something from every wild bloom that grows along the trail up Mount Crested Butte. Those were for endurance. I knew when you grew up, you'd have a fondness for them.

You have to realize what this means, princess. Your life can't be frittered away. The other kids in school may have one hand on a beer can and another rummaging in someone else's crotch. But that's their road, not yours. Your duty is to keep moving. To walk the slope, always ahead and rising, with your eyes glued to the ground.

It was wrong of you to hide those bruises from your mother. Just like it was wrong of her to let Todd's family take you to Europe. Her eyes aren't strong like yours and mine. She can't see past Todd's Ray-Bans and the Jeep Cherokee his parents bought him for Valentine's Day or Halloween or St. Stephen's, whatever holiday that lets them celebrate the purchase of a status symbol. Plus that palace those people live in has utterly blinded your father. Read up on your European history, precious. You'll soon find out it's only in fairy tales that castles redeem sin.

The view through the window had become a blue tunnel. After the last trace of sunlight disappeared, it didn't take long before a pair of headlights pierced the lining between dark and snow. Trudi held her breath. The car rumbled to a stop, the lights snapped off. Then, eventually, a slouching shadow reared up through the driver's-side door. Hallelujah, Trudi thought. Todd was right on time. No fretting Dorothy, no Max, no sheriff. She'd even gotten a good reading from the leaves: Todd slumped on concrete, shattered in the middle as if someone had stepped on him like a wine glass.

Letting the blinds drop, Trudi fumbled in the candlelight for her gun and box of bullets. She hated having to take such primitive, technological measures against Todd, but she couldn't see any other way to get the job done. She refused to tap into demonic forces. That ruled out poisons and grave dirt and the like. The judicious use of ball lightning had always scared off drunk Villanovans tramping through her herb garden back in Pennsylvania. But any sort of electric spell would be too unwieldy, no to mention dangerous, in such a tight space. That only left the gun. Hopefully, with this method, she'd get the pleasure of seeing Todd's cocky smirk dissolve into terror and trembling right before she blew a hole in his head.

Since the sun had set, the lack of power in the Cristiana had gone from nuisance to obstacle. Her fingers, she could tell, were turning purple, one stage before blue, but there was no time to locate any winter gear. She didn't need the protection, anyhow. Rose still felt warm to the touch, had a pulse. Trudi put a quick palm on the forehead to make sure before she left. While she'd been keeping watch, Rose's right arm had lifted from the blanket and now lay parallel to her head, fingers curled like a Russian icon's. Shivering, Trudi wondered what it meant. There was also a noticeable current of smoke blowing across Rose's face and making her blue aura flicker. The clock was officially ticking.

Creeping along the wire border, Trudi positioned herself so that the Christmas tree angel would temporarily block her from Todd's line of sight, at least long enough for her to aim. For weeks she'd been practicing on old hubcaps she'd collected along the highway to Gunnison. She knew she only needed one shot. Cautiously, she slid her rifle between two coils and waited.

The first-story windows let in enough light from streetlamps to help Trudi monitor the double doors, even though her night vision wasn't half what it was twenty years ago. She could tell when the rectangle's watery outline shifted its shape then dropped back into place. A brown form swam toward the check-in counter. A barrage of clicks sounded, like Morse code. Without warning, the darkness was on the move again, accompanied by a slow tap—new Nikes, probably—headed toward the lobby, the Christmas tree, the open center of carpet and hardwood. Trudi inhaled. She lifted the barrel. Her head was starting to hum, a blood sugar fluctuation. She made sure to brace her elbows against her knees. The trigger felt dull against her numb finger, which she twiddled until the joint ached.

Suddenly, a face cut into the fluorescent light. A pale wedge, black hair falling across an eyebrow ring. The eyes, unnaturally sunken, carried three lifetimes of black venom. Trudi's elbow slipped. The barrel scraped an inch of wire, which gave him two seconds extra to look up and bolt before the angel burst, a spray of twinkling plastic splinters.

Head ringing, Trudi scrambled to her feet.

"You don't scare me, Mrs. Hobart."

Trudi struggled to pinpoint the voice. "I don't want you scared, just dead." Wrapping her fingers tightly around the stock, Trudi peered into the well. "Or too far away to do any more harm."

Pause. "You don't seriously think *this* is going to stop me from seeing Rosie."

It was coming from the left, the check-in counter. She began to pace. "It may come as a shock, but if you had even a scrap of soul in that bottomless sewer you call a personality, you'd be wetting your pants right now."

She swung the rifle and fired. The barrel exploded in white sparks.

"I really wish you'd tell me what the problem is." The voice traveled up, loud and clear, from the fireplace beneath her. "I'm sure I could show you there's no need for all this fuss."

"Don't patronize me, you little yuppie bastard." Her hands shook as she stormed across the balcony, rifle and bullets rattling under one arm. "You know exactly what the problem is, and I know the solution. She has bruises . . ." Trudi's throat caught. No tears, absolutely none. "You filthy pervert, there are bruises all over her body!"

"I think you're exaggerating, Mrs. Hobart." Now the words, sarcastic and snarling, drifted up from near the windows, opposite the counter. Trudi realized he must have been crouching behind the curtains all along. "I only ever hit her once," Todd went on. "We were . . . experimenting. She told me to hit her and I did. I just smacked her a little too hard, that's all. We already had a big blowup about it, I apologized. It's over. Anyway, I don't think it's any of your business."

Heat rippled in Trudi's cheeks. "She is fifteen years old!"

"Okay, and I'm seventeen. Do you want to charge me with statutory rape? I doubt if it would hold up in court. The whole thing was consensual, I promise you that."

The third and fourth shots sliced through a cardboard santa hanging from the balcony but didn't sound as if they had lodged in anything living. Sure enough, words that seemed to swell from the tree trunk: "So is this some weird reverse female oedipal complex or an extreme version of empty nest syndrome? Every little girl has to grow up sometime. Rosie's more mature than most."

Trudi hadn't planned on this much difficulty. One more round and she'd have to stop to reload, giving Todd a chance to disappear. Frantically, she circled the wire railing in a last-ditch effort to figure out which direction would give her the best shot. "I am trying to save her from your kind. Carpetbaggers like you who steal little girls' futures. But I wouldn't expect the spawn of evil and materialism to understand spiritual destiny."

"Hah! What sophistry! Pure new age drivel." Suddenly Todd appeared, framed in branches and glass bulbs. "You should know you can't win this one. I'd commit myself now, if I were you."

For an instant, the sight of his triumphant sneer froze Trudi. Then she ran hard and pulled the trigger. But again, he anticipated, his wire-thin frame bent and sprang toward the far wall. Smoke stung Trudi's nostrils as she heard the latch bang shut.

Princess, I'm sorry I let you down. This would have been so much easier if things had worked out according to. . . . But I suppose even the best laid plans. . . . Anyway, the damage is done. You shouldn't have hidden those bruises from you mother, darling. She could have. . . . Wouldn't have made a single mistake, no, she's way too meticulous. She's your mother, you know. No, darling, I know. The silver combs, the clips, and my extracts are yours. You'll find them in a pillowcase in the hallway, the other things are locked in my hope chest, key behind the oatmeal box in the. . . . Pantry. . . . For the guesthouse. Remember I loved you with all my heart. Always know that, if this doesn't work, I tried to save you. The blue light's burning low, it breaks my. . . . I still have one more card to play, but if it doesn't. . . .

The police had set up a barricade with bright yellow tape and swirling lights. Red and blue, but not the true kind. A man's voice on a loudspeaker bounced off the window every few minutes, but it sounded like static in Trudi's ears. She'd read the tea leaves. An older Rose had looked back at her, a cold face, scowling picturesquely with bitter eyes and a wisp of black running from her forehead to her cherry-red lips. The Virgin had wept brown tears.

As she watched Rose in bed, the blue glow continued to weaken. A smoky breeze had turned into a stiff gale, and the light couldn't compete. It was now or never. After Trudi had blown out the last candle, she checked Rose's pulse one more time, then headed for the balcony. The bottle she wanted was, naturally, lying at the bottom of the pillowcase. It was an old perfume vial with a cork in the neck and the label scraped off. Inside, a thick iridescent oil clung to the glass like a tongue. With a deep breath, Trudi drank every last drop of the fluid, burning a wide furrow in her esophagus as it went down. Patiently, she waited.

Beauty, Sleeping

There were drawbacks to turning into a true monster. A strange existence, opening like a door on the face of a new sun. Never returning. Worst of all, no one would ever understand. Innocent comments would be misinterpreted, sacrifices laid waste by the spectacle. But Trudi had to admit, the end result did have its attraction.

Fever came first, then stretching, as if her skin would tear along some invisible seam. She felt her face elongate, teeth crushing against each other as they extended and sharpened, a growing jaw rushing to accommodate. Hands and feet became three-toed claws that bent her spine permanently when all limbs touched the ground. She could also sense the torso growing longer, a thin appendage swiping the ground, two papery folds where shoulder blades had been. Finally, her skin grew hard and shiny—not quite an exoskeleton, she couldn't put her finger on it—and a coal began rising from her stomach. It burst over fangs as a red and gold plume.

Once she felt comfortable in her own skin, she took off and, after a few false starts, was circling the iron chandelier. The room had brightened, so she could take stock of the damage below: glass shards, a broken window, a chunk bitten out of the sooty check-in counter. She hadn't realized she'd done so much damage, but then, her new identity entitled her to wreak a lot more mayhem. Diving past a window, she caught a glimpse of her body, red and fluid, and understood how beautiful it was.

But now she was wasting time. Quickly, she climbed and blew a long stream of flame at the ceiling. Instantly, the roof exploded into a field of wavering day lilies, which she easily pushed her way through as if emerging from a shell. No burns, only a tickling warmth. It had been a long time since Trudi had felt no pain.

A spitting mist met her face, which she gradually recognized as snow. She could get used to this immunity to temperature. Retiring to a remote mountain peak might not be out of her ball park now. She'd always loved Independence Pass, 12,095 feet above sea level, its silent crests that had stood for centuries, collecting wind and ice, without concern for human observers. But first she had a job to do. Aiming for the tiny band of lights in the Cristiana's parking lot, she lunged into a steep plummet, wings pounding like cannons, claws outstretched and a roar that echoed off the face of Mount Crested Butte and all the other peaks that enclosed the drowsy valley. Figures began to shout and scatter, except one, straightening proudly from his slouch. He held a carving knife in his hand as he waited, patiently. Trudi inhaled, bracing her limbs to strike.

Unsung Hero
Michael A. Pignatella

Ian Walker lay still in the darkness, listening to the sounds of the city trickle into the cheap motel room. He folded and unfolded his long legs, his feet hanging from the edge of the mattress like icicles, his knees cracking from years of abuse. *Soon*, he thought. *Soon it will be time for battle.* The steam radiator hissed, straining against the midwinter cold, and Ian smiled. The warmth helped him summon his powers of foresight, the "seeing" as it was called. This power, along with Ian's other talents, would be needed to avoid catastrophe.

He had read the newspaper headlines in his visions—"Congressman Stephenson Assassinated—Rioting in Detroit and Chicago." So he knew that Carl Stephenson, Michigan congressman, a charismatic African-American with a bright future, would soon be killed. He knew this would spark full-scale rioting, starting here in the Midwest and then spreading to both coasts, and he knew the black magicians of the Coven would incite it. It was his mission to stop it, and he waited for the knowledge that would allow him to do so. It would come, but the waiting was frustrating.

He thought of his family back in Connecticut. It helped him relax, even though such thoughts were bittersweet. He hadn't seen Carrie or the children in over a year, and wasn't sure when he might see them again. It gnawed at him.

It was not a problem that any of the other white wizards of the Peaceful faced. But he was not like any of the others. Orphaned at birth and adopted by a "normal" family, he had spent his first twenty-one years unaware of his heritage. By the time the Peaceful had located him and revealed his powers he had fallen in love with Carrie, had already conceived Ben. It had been a concern. Yet despite the fears of the Peaceful that his love for his family would compromise him, he had served for ten long years, battling the Coven while protecting his family from discovery by the dark magicians.

Lately, he found himself wanting more and more to leave the service of the Goddess, to live a normal human life. What he really wanted was to be with Carrie and Ben, with Samantha, his daughter and Tommy, his youngest son. Thinking of Tommy made his heart ache. Yesterday had been his fifth birthday. Ian used to think protecting humanity from the Coven was his most important role. He was no longer certain.

Scratching his short, somewhat unkempt goatee, he closed his eyes. A tingly, pleasant sensation trickled over him, starting with his face and then blanketing his body. He heard the tiny scuffle of a cockroach picking along his backpack and inhaled the dankness of the room, the must and mildew and body odor of a thousand prior occupants. Then his ears flooded, not with noise from the room but with the sounds of some not-so-distant future, and his closed eyes filled with color. He was seeing.

Michael A. Pignatella

He was in a hall or auditorium—a drab room lined with dented folding chairs and festooned with red, white, and blue banners. A placard reading "Re-elect Congressman Stephenson" was attached to a wooden podium that stood on a raised, well-worn stage area. The hall was filling with an interracial mix that was Congressman Stephenson's calling card. Ian could see the congressman off to the far right of the stage, pacing back and forth like an expectant father. Stephenson, the son of a janitor, was a true success story, rising from the rubble of an urban Michigan town to college football stardom, with a 3.9 grade point average to match. He had shocked sports fans, when, after finishing second in the Heisman Trophy balloting, he had forsaken professional football to take a position as a staffer for Michigan Senator Harold Ketchings. Fifteen years later he was the darling of the national political media, as much for his rags-to-riches story as for his always-quotable demeanor.

The Coven wanted him dead.

Ian scanned the crowd in hopes of identifying how they might strike the congressman. He saw nothing. People milled around, talking in small groups, waiting. The institutional clock on the wall ticked off the final seconds until five o'clock, and then a small, intense black man, his forehead exposed by his receding hairline, approached the podium.

"Ladies and gentlemen, welcome," boomed the man's rich, stentorian voice, belying his small stature. "Today we have a special honor. We have with us here, today, a man who needs no introduction, a man who has thrown off the shackles of his disadvantaged youth, who has succeeded because, and in spite of, the system. Ladies and gentlemen, let's get it on for Congressman Carl Stephenson!" The crowd exploded in applause and whistling and deep booming cheers of "Carl, Carl, Carl." The gathering was electric, almost religious. No wonder fringe elements of American society felt threatened. No wonder the Coven had chosen Congressman Stephenson as the crucible in which to foment their chaos.

The congressman began to speak, but Ian was not listening. Instead, he searched for clues as to what would happen, and when. A flyer lay on the ground, trampled by the attendees. Touting Congressman Stephenson as a politician "for *all* the people, by *all* the people," it advertised his appearance at the Amity Zion church hall at 5:00 p.m. on February 5th. Tomorrow. *Now I know when,* Ian thought. But he still did not know how. He continued to search but couldn't locate anyone suspicious, didn't see any obvious threat. If he didn't locate the danger he couldn't stop it. He had to—

Ian's vision went black. His stomach lurched, and for a moment he felt weightless. Air rushed against his face, as if he was moving at a rapid speed, and he felt pressure, as if being squeezed by some unseen force. For an instant he thought he was under attack, that the Coven had located him and penetrated his mental defenses, but his protection spells should shield him from any such attack. *You're safe,* his intuition said, and he listened. His intuition was rarely wrong. His perception cleared, and he was no longer in the assembly hall.

He was in a vehicle, an old van by the looks of it. The floor and sides were lined with thick, inky-blue shag rug, dirty with bits of unknown substances, the floor strewn with a couple of screwdrivers, an old hack-saw, and a large hammer with a broken handle. He seemed to be looking through the eyes of the van's occupant, whose soiled hands coiled a long loop of rope with thick, skilled fingers. The man placed the rope on the van floor and reached into the pocket of his stained overcoat, pulling out a switchblade. Pressing the release button over and over, he folded and unfolded the knife in rhythm. Then he retrieved a manila folder from a worn black gym bag, and Ian felt a wave of revulsion.

Inside the folder were dozens of pictures, some cut from magazines, some grainy photographs taken with a cheap camera. The pictures were of young boys, all under age ten, and as the man shuffled through them he glanced into one of the van's tinted windows. Ian saw the look of pleasure in the man's unkempt, scruffy face, saw the dead look in his ferret-like eyes, and knew what the man was about. Loathing washed over him, and if he could have controlled the man's body he would have thrust the switchblade into the man's eye and pierced his brain. As Ian began to search for clues to the man's location he felt himself slipping, and then the vision faded. Hearing the hissing of the radiator, he knew the seeing was over.

Ian opened his eyes. He was soaked in sweat, his heart pounding. *By the Goddess*, he thought, *what happened?* He had never glimpsed two futures, seen two possible realities during one seeing. And to what point? While he had sensed the evil in the van's occupant and knew his fetid desires, he had no idea who or where he was. Did the Goddess wish him to quell this man's foul urgings? He would do so with pleasure, but he would need more information. And what about Congressman Stephenson? That vision had been interrupted, and although he now knew when the Coven would make its move, he did not know the means. Without that knowledge, preventing the assassination would be like trying to catch a ninety-mile-an-hour fastball with his eyes closed—possible, but unlikely.

Ian flipped the pillow over, welcoming the coolness of the fresh side. He looked at the alarm clock. *2 a.m.* Ian sighed. No sense going into battle fatigued. Exhausted and confused, he closed his eyes and welcomed the embrace of sleep.

The Miss Roosevelt diner was three blocks away, the desk clerk had said, and served the "best darn chili in Michigan." Ian didn't think he wanted chili at eleven in the morning, but had thanked the man anyway. Now, sloshing through the gray, soulless slush, the remnants of a winter storm that had paralyzed the city two days ago, he thought chili might be a good choice. He could use something warm to ward off the foreboding that had iced his every move since the seeing last night. Congressman Stephenson was going to be assassinated tonight and Ian didn't know how it would occur. This was disturbing—he had never been sent on a mission without enough knowledge to complete the task, and the added repugnancy of the child predator befuddled him. And time was running out.

The Miss Roosevelt diner appeared as old as the city itself, tucked into the corner of a decrepit brick building in the heart of what must have once been a thriving downtown. A pink neon sign proclaimed that it offered "good grub at a good price." Entering, Ian inhaled the smell of fried food and strong coffee. "Seat yourself," ordered a handwritten sign propped on the front counter, its stools occupied by a mix of diners, from street people to government workers to businessmen. Spying a booth in the corner, Ian sat and picked up the menu, a laminated booklet spotted with the grease and stains from prior diners.

Now that he was here, his hunger was not so urgent. Instead, he felt the low creep of fear and anticipation that was always a precursor to a clash with the Coven. Nevertheless, he needed to eat, as Carrie would say. He ordered a mug of chicken soup, a cup of black coffee, and a glass of water from the waitress, a bottle-blonde, middle-aged woman. He closed his eyes and let his mind wander home.

Despite the danger, he was unable to let go of his family. Truth be told, Carrie did not want to be let go. She found his tale of dark and white magic ridiculous at first, but he had persuaded her, first with words and later with an exhibition of his newfound abilities. He spent the first two years of their marriage training in England, learning the skills necessary to battle the Coven, while Carrie raised Ben, a single parent. The Peaceful supported them financially, one of the benefits of the secret society. But over the past ten years he had spent no more than a week at a time with them, always wary that the Coven would discover and destroy them. It was a never-ending cycle—even if he wanted to quit, he was not sure he could. The Coven would relish destroying a white wizard and his family, even a retired one. So he continued to serve the Goddess and continued to miss his family.

"Here you go, sweetie, nice and hot." Ian's reverie was interrupted by the waitress's shrill voice. She placed an overlarge bowl of soup in front of him, followed by his coffee and water. "Anything else?"

"No, thank you." The waitress left in a burst of perfume and hairspray and Ian set to his meal with gusto, his appetite awakened by the meaty aroma of the soup and the strong tang of the steaming coffee. Finishing, he wiped his soup bowl clean with a napkin. He poured water into the bowl with one hand while he rummaged through his backpack with the other, pulling out a small pouch. He looked around. No one was watching. He opened the pouch and removed a pinch of fine powder that flickered and shimmered in his hand in a kaleidoscope of color. Mumbling, invoking the words of power, he scattered the powder over the water bowl.

The water shimmered as the powder dusted the surface, and then it began to bubble and steam. Ian glanced from side to side, but still no one was looking. The powder burned off and Ian gazed into the water's surface, now glazed with a silvery, metallic coating. He relaxed and conjured memories of the small Cape Cod that was home, the paint flaking from the windowsills, the perennial garden that Carrie tended as if the flowers were her fourth child. He focused on her face, her dark, almost black hair, on Tommy's small button nose, on Samantha's crystal blue eyes. The silver coating filled with white and then cleared to reveal the front yard of his home, where Carrie and the kids were making a snowman. Tears formed in Ian's eyes.

His family was the picture of health, their faces rosy and robust as they patted and smoothed the snowman, a huge specimen that towered over even Carrie. The snowman wore one of Ian's old ski hats, left over from his skiing days, before the Peaceful had found him. He felt tired and drained. As Carrie screwed a huge carrot into the center of the snowman's face, Ian let the vision fade. His family was safe and happy. Using his magic to view them carried the risk, however small, that the Coven would sense it, would follow his spell and discover their existence. He couldn't resist a peek sometimes, but that was all. No sense further endangering them.

He sloshed the water back into its glass, retrieved the waitress and paid his bill. His mood tinged with a mixture of sadness and contentment, he headed back to his room.

He spent the afternoon lying on his bed in a state of self-hypnosis, waiting for the seeing to enlighten him, but no visions came. He refused to panic, instead putting his trust in the Goddess. At four o'clock Ian's eyes opened and he sat up in bed. He rummaged through his backpack, checking and double-checking the hodgepodge of powders and potions and trinkets that made up his arsenal, secreting them in the pockets that lined his old army coat. Prepared, he slung his backpack over his shoulder and went to meet his fate.

The Amity Zion Church was located in the heart of what Ian knew people would call the "bad" part of town. It was 4:40 p.m. and the sun was low on the horizon, a dark dusting of winter clouds painting the sky gray. There was a small crowd waiting, who streamed in when the door opened, sweeping Ian in with them.

As was the norm, everything was as the seeing had shown him—the worn podium on the stage at the front of the hall, the battered folding chairs, the institutional clock on the wall. Noting his surroundings, Ian stood in the back of the room and leaned against the wall, so he could scan the crowd for threats. Wherever they might come from.

Nervous, Ian let the sounds and smells of the hall envelop him, opening himself up to them, hoping to induce the seeing. He was running out of time. The low murmur of the crowd continued to build, the attendees discussing the congressman, weighing his potential Senate run, his charisma. The sweet, greasy smell of doughnuts and the tang of humanity filled his nose, excitement charging the air with nervous energy. Ian began to fear that he would receive no more visions of the future. He would need to improvise, cause some emergency to cancel the congressman's appearance. As he began to think through this possibility, the seeing began.

He was in the hall again, and a glance at the clock told him it was 5:07. Fifteen minutes from now. Congressman Stephenson was speaking, a deft mixture of old-time tent revival and political stump speech, and Ian appreciated why his assassination would cause such turmoil. Stephenson moved people with his words; he transcended racial, class, and political party lines with ease. Ian was not here to admire him, however. He noted the bodyguards, two thick, bull-necked men posted behind the congressman, their eyes scanning back and forth in a measured rhythm. Ian followed suit, studying the crowd. No assassin here that Ian could see.

Then Ian felt evil, hot and fierce, emanate from the podium, and the vision flashed to a small explosive device concealed within the structure of the podium itself. Time slowed as the podium exploded in a fury of flame and splintered wood, the microphone burying itself in the congressman's chest. Shrapnel littered the front two rows, raining spectators with bullet-like shards of wood and the hot breath of the explosion. One of the bodyguards, his face burned and melted in a disquieting mask of agony, crawled toward the congressman's body before shuddering in one last gasp of duty. Ian's perspective widened and he watched the crowd stampede toward the exit, an avalanche of panic. That panic would transform into a thirst for vengeance that would set America on fire.

Once again a sudden change in perception made him queasy. He was back in the van, peering from the eyes of its foul owner, who was donning a pair of stained leather gloves. Ian noted the time on the man's watch—5:09 p.m.—and his heart sank. Almost exactly the same time as the assassination attempt.

The man opened the van door, and a hard knot of fear lodged in Ian's throat. He was outside his family's home, the familiar Cape Cod that was the center of Ian's spiritual universe, where Tommy was putting the finishing touches on the snowman Ian had watched his family building hours earlier. Dusk had settled and, combined with the heavily falling snow, it rendered the two shapes mere silhouettes—one slight and carefree, the other ponderous with the weight of his malevolent intentions. The man approached Tommy and began to talk, weaving a web that had undoubtedly snared other children.

"Would you like to see my puppy?" he said, and Tommy looked, intrigue obvious in his eyes. Despite all the parental warnings, Tommy nodded and smiled as the man drew closer, hunched over as if he was holding something between his arms.

"Take a look," the man said.

Tommy leaned in, rising on his tippy-toes, and the man reached out and pulled Tommy's wool cap over his face. With surprising quickness he tossed the boy over his shoulder and made his way to the van, its back doors open like the gateway to Hell. The man dropped Tommy into the back and trussed him like a calf, his moves practiced and sure. As he closed the doors and shuffled to the front of the vehicle, Ian screamed to himself, calling his son's name. The van sidled down the street, becoming a speck in the white blanket of snow that continued to fall.

Michael A. Pignatella

The seeing stopped, jolting Ian to reality. He heard the booming, confident voice of Congressman Stephenson and realized that the game was on, that he had precious little time to save the congressman (*and my son*). He glanced at the clock—5:05 p.m.—barely two minutes until the podium would explode (*and my son is abducted*). He pulled his cell phone from his coat pocket to call Carrie. No signal, as he suspected. There was a confluence of evil here poised to overwhelm him. For one moment his mind grew fuzzy and his heart beat fast in his chest. There was no way for him to get back to Connecticut in time to save Tommy; his magic was not that strong. Then a glimmer of an idea struck him and he smiled. He wondered if the smile looked as sadly ironic as he felt.

He reached into his backpack and pulled out a small vial of clear liquid, thick and viscous like honey. Calling forth the powers of the Goddess, he cast a spell of binding on himself, on his soul. Next to him, an elderly black man, his face gnarled in annoyance, shushed him, but Ian ignored him as the magic coalesced. He unstoppered the vial and swallowed the thick liquid, feeling the magic harden inside of him. Hopeful that the spell had succeeded, Ian turned his attention to the congressman.

5:06. Time slowed. The beefy bodyguards focused on him as he approached the stage, his pace brisk. Congressman Stephenson continued to speak, glancing briefly at Ian. Ian saw all of this in the blink of an eye, and processed it subconsciously. Then, his overcoat flapping behind him like a cape, he leapt to the stage.

The two men were on him in an instant. As the first attempted to wrap him in a bear hug, Ian, wiry and strong, grabbed his forearm and flipped him over his back and off the stage. The man landed on the unforgiving cement floor with a thud and the cracking of bone. Ian grunted as the other bodyguard, bald and thick, buried his head between Ian's shoulder blades, driving him forward. They crashed into the podium, destroying it. Splinters and shards of the podium scattered around them and Ian saw the bomb skitter across the stage. He could feel it tensed to explode. He needed to reach it.

The bodyguard had Ian on his hands and knees, straddling him, squeezing Ian's head in a headlock. Ian's forehead pulsed with the pressure of the man's exertion, a tight, sharp pain flashed across his brow, and tiny red pinpricks of light danced before his eyes. *Time to end this*, Ian thought, and thrust an elbow into the man's stomach, twisting out of his grasp like a six foot-five eel. He stood up, prepared to deliver a final blow, but the man rolled out of the way, quicker than Ian had imagined. Rising, the man pulled a gun from his coat.

At the sight of the gun, the crowd screamed and began running toward the exits. Ian reached into one of the myriad inner pockets of his overcoat and pulled out a handful of red powder, hot and pulsating in his grip. He tossed the powder onto the gun as the man raised it to fire. The weapon began to melt, its barrel dripping liquefied metal, and then the bullets exploded like a package of M-80s. The man bellowed, his hand caught in the heat of the powder, shrapnel peppering his face and neck, his hair singed and burnt. Ian stepped forward and wrapped his hand around the man's forehead.

"Norcolanthus... sleep," Ian said. The man's eyes closed and he crumpled to the ground. Ian turned to Congressman Stephenson. "Please, Congressman," he shouted over the panicking crowd, "I'm here to help." Ian's heart raced as he noticed the object in the politician's hand.

Congressman Stephenson was holding the bomb, drawn to the evil of the Coven like a coyote to a carcass.

"Please give me that," Ian said as the clock clicked to 5:07. *The witching hour.* "Now!" Ian leapt as the congressman backpedaled, stumbling. Ian landed and snatched the makeshift bomb with his left hand even as he pushed the man down, face first on the ground. "Stay there and lie low," Ian said. Not waiting to see if his command was heeded, Ian ran off the side of the stage to a small room and closed the wooden door behind him, clutching the bomb to his chest. The room was empty, except for a worn wooden desk and chair in the corner. Ian scrambled underneath the desk, mouthing a quiet prayer for the congressman and the others in the hall, and then another prayer for his family and his final plan.

As you wish, Goddess, Ian thought, seconds before the bomb exploded with tremendous force, blasting the small wooden door clear across the stage. The explosion tore through Ian's body, scattering chunks of flesh and spattering blood in a macabre collage.

Ian's senses returned a moment later. He was hovering, observing the room where his body lay broken and battered. He floated out over the stage. Dust and debris scattered the floor, covering Congressman Stephenson and his supporters with bits and pieces of wood and glass. One man lay motionless in the corner, a large sliver of wood impaling him through the eye, and another writhed on the floor, bleeding profusely from a jagged tear across his neck. But Congressman Stephenson rose to his feet, brushing his coat jacket, looking dazed but intact. Alive.

Ian looked at the clock. 5:08. He had precious little time to save Tommy. The binding spell had been successful, anchoring his soul to the earth after his death, barring it from the afterlife. But the magic was temporary. He needed to get to Tommy now, and as a spirit he could do what he could not accomplish alive. Concentrating, he felt a great shift, as if moving on a giant treadmill, and then he was hovering over the front yard of his family's home.

The man was approaching Tommy just as in Ian's vision, and Ian found he was not quite sure what to do. He was not corporeal and could not act upon the man physically. But he could possess corporeal objects, including people. He entered the man's body but found a never-ending well of darkness that tangled and caressed him, trying to seduce and capture him. He extricated himself, realizing he could not overcome the corruption of the man's soul. Trying again, he entered Tommy and exerted a concerted but gentle attempt to gain control. "I'm here, son," he soothed, and he felt Tommy's psyche relax, but then Tommy's woolen cap was pulled over his face and he was hoisted over the man's shoulder. The boy retreated into his mental prison, shutting Ian out.

Leaving Tommy's body, Ian searched for an alternative, but didn't see one. *Dear Goddess, I can't save him,* he thought, and it tore at him like a rabid dog, threatening to drive him insane. *Stay in control.* He entered his family's home to alert his wife or one of the kids, but the kids weren't home and he found Carrie asleep in an overstuffed chair with the lights out and a cold compress on her head. *Migraine,* he thought, realizing again that there was more evil at play here than he had recognized—not the organized evil of the Coven but rather random evil that struck without warning. He touched his wife's mind, but a sharp, hot flare of pain drove him out. He'd never rouse her in time. Leaving the house, he had one last, desperate idea.

The man had almost reached the van. Ian focused on his target—the huge snowman standing in the front yard, almost as tall as Ian himself, and plunged in. He felt instantly cold: not the coldness of evil, but pure elemental cold. As if to reassure him, he felt the call of the Goddess to his soul, a gentle caress that promised rest, promised peace. *I can't have peace if I don't save Tommy,* he thought. Determined, he animated the snowman.

It was more difficult to move an inanimate object than it would have been a person, but the house was built on a sloping hill, and by possessing the snowman, Ian was able to jerk it forward, once, twice, three times, until gravity was overcome and the weight of the snowman, the slickness of the snow, and Ian's continued efforts started it sliding down the incline toward the street.

Michael A. Pignatella

The man did not notice the snowman approaching him, even as he pulled the coil of rope from his pocket. He looked up just as the snowman crashed into him, driving him backward, his head striking a glancing blow against the van. He fell to the road and the snowman plunged upon him, driven by Ian's need and rage. The man reached up and grabbed the snowman's head with both hands, his eyes widened in apparent disbelief. With the man's defenses lowered, Ian drove the snowman's head down onto his face, guiding the crisp carrot nose into his eye socket, piercing his eye with a pop like roasting corn, and then into his brain.

Ian watched as the man's soul, black and paper-thin, left his body and sank into the road. His final task complete, Ian felt a tremendous urge to rise. His spell was fading.

He left the snowman and entered his son, who lay in the van shivering and crying, the hat still over his face. "Tommy," he whispered, "it's all right. Run to the house, find your mother." Tommy pulled the hat up.

"Dad?" the boy said. *He can't see me*, Ian thought. Tommy looked down and Ian followed his gaze, spying the dead man, the blood dribbling from his eye socket, melting the snow around his head. Tommy scurried out of the van and ran toward the house.

"Mommy, mommy, come quick," he yelled, and Ian felt relief as a light turned on inside the Cape Cod. His urge to leave the world became overwhelming, but he touched Tommy's brain for one final moment.

"I love you son," he whispered, and then the darkness surrounded him like an immense tunnel, at the end of which was a bright light. The light approached and tears trickled down his ephemeral face. Releasing his mortality, he went to meet the Goddess.

Infernal Encounters

There are deep, hidden powers that mortals should think twice about tapping. There are creatures in existence whose sole purpose is to tempt and torment mankind. Sometimes you can make a deal with these beings and come out on top. More often, your only reward is pain.

Swan Dive
CHRISTA M. CALLABRO

I love to dance. Don't believe it when they say all I do is sit on my throne and laugh at the poor souls clawing at my feet with charred hands and broken, blackened nails. Nor do I stand behind stupid mortals all day and whisper temptations in their ears. Don't get me wrong; it is quite enjoyable. But ninety-five percent of the inhabitants of my quaint little kingdom end up there on their own. And the other five percent aren't usually worth my time anyway.

So what's a devil to do, when these delectable past-times sour in my mouth? I thrive on constant amusement. And dancing never bores me.

It reminds me of flying.

I enjoy ballet the most. Surprised? Don't be. I could watch those doomed, graceful creatures all day, in their satin and tulle, leaping and twirling like leaves in a brisk autumn breeze. Most of them never realize how close they come to belonging to me. Dancers, especially ballerinas, sell their souls to their companies and their art. They pay a heavy price for a hard dream, just to perform for the throng that lusts for their delicate beauty and eats up their sweat-soaked glory. I can't think of a better Saturday night than dressing to the nines and catching the newest production of this or that. It gives me a chance to show off.

Occasionally, a young girl catches my eye, a fragile flower with too much ambition and fate against her the whole way. I can instantly see it in the trembling line of the arm, the spark of anger deep in the pupil. Those are the girls I love best. I don't own very many; you'd be amazed how many actually turn me down. The few I do possess delight me so much more than the other souls I've personally collected. How do you think the flames in Hell dance with such allure?

I am about to add another to my collection. She doesn't see me back here, cloaked in the shadows from the curtain wings. Andra Ferrone, prima ballerina, with more genius than the ballet world has seen since Margot Fontaine. My genius, of course. She's dancing the role that started her career, that of Odette/Odile in *Swan Lake*. I always preferred Odile the black swan, but white so easily captures every little stain of sin.

Swan Lake is my favorite.

When I first saw Andra, about ten mortals' years ago, her flame had burned so bright I knew a moment of nostalgia. White-hot, searing to the eye, but temporary all the same. All it would take was one more rejection, and little Andra would be joining me through the path of the suicides. Those souls are so devoid of color, or spark, or anything at all. I knew I had to save her life, and make it last, and make it mine. I met her on a night much like this, though her swan costume was much plainer. Other swans swarmed about her, but she was an isolated island, too intent on warming up her feet to pay attention to the other girls in the *corps de ballet*.

It was too easy to get her alone. A frayed ribbon instantly sent her worrying into the dressing room, which surprisingly had just emptied out of dancers.

I can remember her so clearly, directing all her anger at me, because she had nowhere else to throw it. "What the hell are you doing in here?" she had yelled, holding up her shoe like a dagger, the wooden toe ready to nail me between the eyes.

I held up my hand in peace. "Stay, Andra. You don't want to get all upset before your big debut."

She didn't lower her shoe of course. All that fire, my little ballerina wouldn't give up that easily. "What do you mean? And how did you know my name?"

"Why, you are the one meant to dance Odette tonight, that's how I know."

"Jenelle is dancing Odette. I'm just the understudy." I could see her curiosity was piqued, even if she still didn't trust me. I could also see the flush on her cheeks as she gazed at me. I have that effect on women. Must be the blonde hair.

I decided to go out on a limb for her. She could still refuse, in the end. But I knew inside that she wouldn't be able to resist me. Or my offer. "Could you dance Odette tonight, if you had to?" Of course I knew she could. I'd watched her in the studio, hours before and hours after classes and rehearsals, going over the steps, dark hair whipping about her reddened cheeks, a look of rapture on her face.

Andra nodded slowly, the shoe lowered to around her hip. I smiled and bowed my head. "Then dance it you shall. I promise you. And if you enjoy your triumphant debut, I hope you care to join me after, for a celebratory drink." With that carrot dangled in front of her, I turned to the new set of shoes that waited for her on the make-up table. I ran my fingertips across the tops, and made sure they glowed with just a touch of red, enough for her eyes to pick up. Then I placed my business card on top of them, with the name of this particularly nice hotel that I know of, that always has my favorite suite empty. I tried not to smile as I left her dressing room. Andra could still say no, but call it instinct or just past experience, I knew that she was even now strapping on the shoes I'd blessed.

As I walked down the hall the director hurried past me, shouting for Andra. On his heels was a gurney pushed by two paramedics, Jenelle stretched out on it. Her lower leg was swathed in bandages and a splint. Blood seeped through the dressing. Must have been a nasty fall.

As predicted, Andra went on as Odette and wowed the audience with her easy grace and bright light. I know; I was one of them. I think I might have outdone myself with her. And later when I opened the door to my suite, there she stood, still glowing from her triumph and smelling of make-up, sweat, and rosin. I love that smell; I have to admit it's a bit of a turn-on. I breathed it deep as I kissed her trembling lips. Her skin held traces of sparkle left over from sweating in her costume. I traced those lines of luminescence with my tongue and fingers, enjoying the soft little moans from the throat of my swan. I don't have to possess the body to possess the soul; in reality, I don't have any flesh to do it. But Andra didn't know that. She gave herself to me body and soul that night, and demonstrated why men always fall for dancers. I must say it is a beautiful and rare thing to have something so powerful as a ballerina's legs wrapped around your waist.

In the end she agreed to all my terms. Ten years, a lifetime in the dance world. Ten years of fame, of genius, of diva status. Andra would live her dreams, have any man she wanted, and be the darling of the ballet. But she wouldn't be dancing for herself, or her company, or for her audience. She would be dancing for me.

Andra dances for herself now.

I don't like that.

I can hear her inner voice as she chants the same mantra she has for years, right before her first entrance. *The stage is my kingdom, the audience my slaves.* Three times for good luck. My sweet ballerina, luck has nothing to do with it. That lady forsook you the moment our tongues touched. Still, Andra takes a breath and glides onto the stage, a floating dream in feathers and tulle. Immediately my gift captures the audience. My gift, not hers. She only channels it through her sinews and bones, the flesh that I personally molded and plied. Every person has to stare at her, and think of nothing else save her grace. Once, I enjoyed their open-mouthed appreciation of Andra, and drank their longing for her like a fine wine. No more, my dear. You've expired. And I think I've already spotted your replacement, gazing at you from the wings with these huge, liquid doe eyes. She doesn't look like she would forget her place, unlike you.

Sometimes I do grow bored. Especially of insolence.

I think perhaps I should play with her a bit, before we have our talk. As Odette, the lovely Andra dances with her prince, shy and tentative swan maid that she is, but soon she warms up to his charms. The boy that dances in the prince's role has the same cow-eyed look as the audience. I know she's seduced him already; I can tell from the press of his hands against her sides as he lifts her, intimate knowledge radiating through the lines of his body. It doesn't matter, her conquests of the flesh. I'd promised her that. She didn't know at the time, though, that my gift taints the world through every press of the lips, every stroke of skin. And that, no matter how many men she takes to her bed, she will never be able to forget our passion.

The prince's role has never belonged to me, no matter how many call me by that title. I always preferred the villain, the evil wizard, the despot. Go figure. In this ballet, he bears the name Rothbart. I easily slide into the role, and the *danseur* playing the part. He'll remember this all as an unpleasant dream, and take many showers in the upcoming days. I see the world through the eyeholes of a hawk-faced mask, a cloak that mimics bat wings billowing from my shoulders. I push my borrowed body to its limits; it's been a long time since I've actually danced. My performance should be remembered too.

I can see that Andra is intrigued, even as she tries to run away from me. She cannot though, not yet. It's still too early in the show. I pull her close and lift her, a reminder to the prince that this swan maid belongs to me. The audience sighs. Andra's toes hit the ground and she stares into the eyes of my mask, her face full of heat and surprised expectation. She thinks it this body that warms her blood. I smile behind the wizard's features, and let her see the glint of red deep in my pupils. Instantly, her skin turns cold, even as she whirls away from me, back to the prince. It is enough. She knows I am here. I leave Rothbart and wait for the right time to speak to my ballerina.

The climax requires perfect timing.

The last act of *Swan Lake* is the best.

Such drama and heartache, and sometimes triumph, if the choreographer meddles with the original story. Andra stands on a high platform in the wings. Wires are attached to her back, to make her float down to the stage and her prince. She shifts from one foot to the other and fans her red cheeks. I watched her fight with her company director, and witnessed her make a stagehand cry. 'Diva' and 'bitch' and 'stuck-up' are the words whispered behind her back, even though every single person envies her talent. It would all be fine with me, if she didn't let the praise go to her head. A slightly humble attitude would be best. Andra carries the title of Diva as a badge of honor and as a right of her talent, when she should be offering it up to me as tribute. Selfish little one. She'll learn soon enough to pay me my due.

I whisper her name, but she refuses to turn around. Instead, she wraps her arms around herself and shivers. Head high, she murmurs, "I thought you weren't real."

I try not to let my laughter leak through my words. It's hard to do. After all the things I made her cry out that one night, and she still convinces herself that I'm not real. "Do you think your success just make-believe?"

Andra turns then, and I feel the breath catch in her throat as she sees me as she did that first time, stylish by mortal standards in a black suit, blonde hair longish and floating around my face like the feathers of her tiara. I look exactly the same as I did that night ten years ago. She frowns at me, a cute pout that makes her look much younger than she is. "My success is mine. You're just trying to trick me into joining you. It won't work."

A chuckle breaks through my serious guise, which upsets her. She turns away again. I rest my hands on her bare shoulders and let my heat sink into her skin. I can feel a fine tremble shake her flesh, one that has nothing to do with revulsion or the cold. Her head bows, a single strand of dark hair curling against the nape of her neck. I tease it with my breath. "You joined me many years ago, my dear. Your body remembers at least, even if your mind does not."

She shrugs my hands off. "Excuse me, but I have a show to finish. One that has a happy ending, which is something you can never offer."

I sigh as if her words really hurt me. "Don't you remember how the original story of *Swan Lake* goes? The swan maid always stays with Rothbart at the end." This is too savory sweet. I knew I liked this one more than the others.

Andra whirls toward me and takes a threatening step forward. Chin high, she spits out, "That story was written hundreds of years ago. This is a new age. My age. I will write my own ending." With that, my pretty swan turns and steps off the platform.

I smiled after her. "That you will, my love. That you will."

Look at her now, little ballerina girl, as she glides on air down to her adoring fans. Her smile never falters, even when the wires suddenly catch and tug. She beams like an angel as she lands on toe and begins to twirl. Lovely swan maid, she does her *fouettés* and her *piqué* turns with every ounce of her soul, to prove that she never needed me. What a shame. She's concentrating so hard the gasps and screams of her beloved audience never penetrate past the swell of the music. Not until the soft rain falls and spatters that pristine tutu red does she look up. And finally misses a step.

Now I can't help but laugh. She's confused now! The real Odette was never confused, only resigned to her fate. My little Andra, she should have been more reverent. I could have let her go for years on end. But she forgot that she danced for me. For my pleasure only; not her audience's, and not her own. Now she watches her own body dance on the wind, garroted by the wires that made her fly.

The expression on her face is priceless. Still a trick, she must think. Andra desperately looks off into the wings, like a five-year-old in her first recital, needing assurance from the teacher hidden behind the curtain. Only I am there, waiting in the dark for her. I know she can feel me there, but she can't see me. Just my eyes, winking red in the black.

Little swan, the story always ends the same.

Just the way I want it.

Feast of Clowns
Robert Guffey

Eliphas grabbed Marisa about the throat, began to squeeze. His black-painted thumbnails dug deep into the softest, most delicate spot in the middle of her throat. Marisa gagged, reached out for Eliphas's face. Her fingernails clawed at his pudgy cheeks, scraping off the black and white face paint of his profession.

The smell of sawdust filled her nostrils as life escaped her.

"I want to make people laugh," said Eliphas Kane to the old fakir. The two men sat in a battered trailer filled with nothing more than stacks of ancient tomes with evocative titles like *The Book of Coming Forth By Night*, *Mani Padme Hum*, *Ceremony of the Stifling Air*, and *The Angry Book of Dragonflies*.

The fakir's modest home smelled like a mixture of old leather, incense, and cat piss. This latter scent may have been due to the thirteen cats that appeared to spend their days scrounging for a new book they hadn't urinated on yet.

Whenever the fakir wished to support an enlightening point about the interplay of magick and the performing arts, he would withdraw a particularly thick book from a teetering pile and begin to read out loud. The flickering shadows cast by the black candles scattered around the trailer added to the profound nature of the millennia-old texts. Unfortunately, the smell of cat piss somehow dampened the overall dramatic effect.

The fakir spent his days performing telepathic tricks for local yokels in a dirty, sagging tent. At night, he hid in his trailer, drank his chamomile tea, and tried as much as possible to dissuade Eliphas from pursuing the career of a clown.

"Why do you want to make people laugh?" said the fakir. "Why not learn sword swallowing from Linko the Magnificent, or fire-breathing from Captain Bullion? These tricks are easy to learn, and you'll be able to make a good living from them for the rest of your life."

"You've got to understand," Eliphas said, "my father, and his father, and *his* father before him were all clowns. I've never had any other career in mind. But I'm not satisfied with just being a normal clown. Sure, I know all the standard routines like the baby in the burning house and piling into that stupid little car and juggling banana cream pies, but that bullshit can get old real quick, you know what I mean? I want to do something different. Something that'll set those damn tents on fire." He paused, staring at a mangy black cat that had begun to use a pile of hardcover books as a scratching post. He felt uncomfortable asking the next question. "Why did you ever give up being a clown?"

The skinny, frail man just shrugged. "Because I grew bored with the old routines, as you just said, and I didn't have what it took to push my talents beyond the known. I thought it'd be easier to read the minds of assholes. And I was right."

"Learning magick is easier than making people laugh?"

"Sure. All you have to do is read a few books." He gestured nonchalantly at the towering piles as if there were only a few dozen books in the room. "Making people laugh takes something else altogether."

"Like what?" Eliphas leaned forward expectantly.

The fakir sighed. He opened a coverless black book and read from it aloud. "'The Path of the Fool is the secret extension of the Path of the Tower.' Those are the words of a man named Kenneth Grant, former member of Ordo Templi Orientis and founder of the Nu-Isis Lodge."

"What did he mean?"

The fakir held up his index finger. He pulled out a different book and read aloud once more. "'The clown is so close to death that only a knife-edge separates him from it, and sometimes he goes over the border, but always he returns again.'" The fakir nodded, shut the book, then remained silent for an interminable amount of time.

"Who said that, another one of your magicians?"

"Sort of. It was Charlie Chaplin."

Eliphas waved his hands impatiently. "Yeah? So what does it *mean*?"

An orange tabby leaped on the fakir's lap, and proceeded to make a bed on his silver robe. The fakir stroked the cat's fur as he said, "It means . . . you'll have to get over your fear of death."

Eliphas sat on the back of his father's trailer, staring up at the stars. Father had died only two nights before. The manager had told him he could take a few days off, but made it perfectly clear that if Ogo the Clown was going to remain with this circus he'd have to be back in the ring sooner rather than later, mourning be damned.

Angry, Eliphas smashed his fist into the sharp stones lying in the dirt beneath the sawdust. It had rained earlier this morning, transforming the sawdust into a caked, wet mass. Unfortunately, some idiot had forgotten to paraffin the nearby cook joint in order to make it waterproof. Dinner had been a damp, chilly affair. He'd left after eating only two biscuits. He couldn't take the endless barrage of condolences. What good were they?

Idly, Eliphas scooped up some of the sawdust and rolled it into tiny balls between his thumb and forefinger. He tossed them into the night sky, as if aiming for the stars. Just as he thought about the utter uselessness of apologies, he heard a soft voice behind him say, "Sorry about your father."

Eliphas turned and saw a dark-haired, petite girl standing beside his trailer. She wore an oversized trench coat to protect her from the biting wind. She was about sixteen years old, two years younger than Eliphas. He recognized her as Marisa Chassin, the youngest member of the high wire team. They'd spoken to each other only occasionally.

"Why, did *you* kill him?" Eliphas snapped.

Marisa seemed taken aback by his rudeness. "I-I'm sorry. If you want to be left alone . . ." She began to walk away.

Eliphas immediately felt stupid. "Wait a second, I'm sorry. It's just that everyone in the world has told me that and, I don't know . . . it's just becoming a bit annoying."

Marisa nodded. "I understand. My mother died a few years ago. I should've known not to say that. I always try to be different from everyone else, but then I just end up being exactly the same." She shrugged.

Eliphas frowned and returned his attention to the sky. "You shouldn't have to *try* to be different from other people. You should be the way you are."

"That's easy for you to say. You've got that face paint to hide behind. You can be anyone you want under there. The rest of us are stuck out here in the cold, always frightened of looking foolish."

"'You have to be clever to make a fool of yourself.' Nikolai Poliakoff said that."

"Who?"

"Coco the Clown."

"Is he one of the clowns you work with?"

"No no, Coco the Clown was born in 1900. He died in 1970."

"That's too bad."

Eliphas grinned as he turned toward her once again. "Why, did *you* kill him?"

Marisa hesitated before saying, "Yes, I ran over him with one of those midget cars."

They both laughed. Eliphas grew excited as he felt an idea sprouting somewhere in his mind. He said, "Hey, that'd be a funny scene in the ring: a clown being run over by a car."

"Being driven by a monkey."

"A *bunch* of monkeys."

"Even better. And when the clown gets up he can have a flattened torso with a tire mark running over it."

"Maybe." Eliphas pulled on his lip thoughtfully. "Or when the car runs over him, blood will shoot out of his stomach and shower the audience."

Marisa wrinkled her nose. "Isn't that a little *too* disgusting?"

Eliphas grinned. "Yes."

"You may offend a lot of people. They'll demand their money back."

"That's fine. There'll be a hundred more to replace the few blue noses who leave. I think we have to do something to broaden our audience. No one goes to the circus anymore, not when there's TV and movies to go to. We have to offer them something more, something they can't get anywhere else."

"And what's that?"

"Magick."

"They've got Doc Templar and his illusions for that."

"No, that's not the kind of magick I mean." He studied the ball of sawdust in his hands. "Have you ever heard of a book called *Mani Padme Hum*?"

"I don't think so."

"It's very rare. It's about the interplay between chaos and magick. It's about manipulating the central nervous system from afar. In a way, it's a psychology text."

"And what would a clown need with a psychology text?"

The smile on Eliphas's face grew quite wide. "What are you doing tonight?"

She glanced from side to side, as if he might be referring to someone else. But she was the only person around. "Nothing, I guess. Why?"

"Would you like to come inside?" He gestured toward the trailer. "I've got some hot blackberry tea for your refreshment, a psychology text for your entertainment."

"Sounds wild."

"No need to be sarcastic. It *is* wild. Trust me."

She accepted the offer. Later that night she learned that "Mani Padme Hum" meant "The Jewel in the Lotus." She lost her virginity that evening as well.

Marisa lay in the cramped trailer giving birth to her first child. Eliphas held her hand and whispered encouraging remarks in her ear. The doctor kneeled before her widespread legs, waiting for the baby to appear.

They'd been at this a long time now, Eliphas thought. Too long. If only they had access to a hospital. If only this damn circus wasn't so isolated.

"You'll be all right, Marisa," Eliphas whispered. "You'll be walking the high wire again in no time. All eyes will be on you again. There'll be so much applause your first night, you won't believe it. It'll be better than it ever was before. You'll see. You'll see."

Marisa smiled, shook her head. He wished she could squeeze his hand in return. But she was so weak, oh so weak.

"He's coming out the wrong way," the doctor said, panic rising in his voice. "We may have to cut her open."

"No!"

"I'm sorry, Eliphas, it's not up to you."

Eliphas grew enraged when he saw the surgical knife. He tried to take it from the doctor. Linko the Magnificent dragged Eliphas into the rain outside. Threw him into the mud. Told him to calm down for his own sake. For Marisa's sake.

Eliphas had never been able to stand the sight of blood. He remained in the downpour while his son was born . . . while his lover died. . . .

Eliphas laid young Joseph on a wooden bench in his trailer. The boy was only three months old. Eliphas had named him after Joseph Grimaldi, the most famous clown of all. The Ur-clown.

Grimaldi, like Grock after him, had been famous for a grotesque bow-legged stride.

Eliphas stroked his son's bald head, then removed the special hammer from its silver casing. It had been passed down from generation to generation. He didn't want to do this, not really. He himself had undergone such treatment from his own father. This was a family tradition, the most important one of all.

Every clown must have a funny walk; it came with the profession.

He raised the hammer above the boy. He stared into Joseph's clear, blue eyes. He hesitated. He heard the voice of his dead father telling him, ordering him, to go through with the deed. It was expected of him. He couldn't let the family down.

He closed his eyes and imagined Marisa's sweet face. How lovely she had been. How caring. Until Joseph.

You're a murderer, he said silently to his son. He said it over and over again until he nearly believed it. Believed it enough to obscure the sharp wrenching in his throat.

Tears moistened his cheeks as he brought the hammer down on the boy's left knee. He heard a sharp swift crack, like the breaking of a walnut shell. Joseph wailed in pain. Eliphas winced and averted his eyes. He saw a placard hanging above his bed on the far side of the room. Inscribed in the plank of wood was an epigraph he'd found in one of the fakir's many books:

"I never saw anything funny that wasn't terrible.
If it causes pain, it's funny: if it doesn't, it isn't."
—W.C. Fields

Eliphas turned his attention to the boy's right knee. Better to get this over with as soon as possible, he told himself uncertainly.

The hammer came down once again.

Eliphas was surprised when the fakir appeared on his doorstep early one evening to tell him that he was leaving.

"I've grown tired of this circus," he said. "Time to move on."

"To where?"

"Another circus, of course. Where else? Maybe I'll try being a boss canvas man. I always wondered what it would be like being responsible for putting up and taking down the tents in every town."

"C'mon, that stuff's beneath you."

The fakir laughed. "Believe me, once you've swallowed and regurgitated rats for a living nothing is beneath you. I just came by to tell you, you could have my entire library. You can probably get more use out of the damn things than me."

Eliphas felt his jaw dropping. "The *whole* library? I don't know if I have room for it all."

"You'll make room. All I ask is that you let little Joseph read the books as well. Just looking into his eyes, I believe he has a touch of the Am-Smen inside him."

"What's Am-Smen?"

"The Place of Chaos." The fakir turned to stare at the surrounding attractions. "Ah, how could you ever get tired of the circus? Listen to that." In the distance, Eliphas could hear the roaring of the Whirling Octopus, the dissonance of three separate bands playing at once, the clever patter of the talented talkers (only a naïve First-of-May would call them "barkers"). The fakir looked up at the night sky. "Look at that, the lights of the circus are so bright they actually blot out the stars. That says a lot, doesn't it? It'll be fascinating to see them from a different perspective, at another circus." The old man breathed in the cool night air, then began to hobble away. "You can pick up the books any time before tomorrow afternoon. Otherwise I'll just leave them lying in the horse shit."

"Wait a second," Eliphas said. The fakir paused and glanced over his bony shoulder. "You know, you never told me your real name."

The old man smiled. "Sid Moskowitz."

"Huh? How did you get from Sid Moskowitz to Mahatma Baba Ram Shree?"

The fakir spread out his hands; his smile widened. "Magic," he said.

As Joseph grew, so too did Eliphas's sadness. Marisa's absence haunted his life like a ghost. He missed her warm body beside him at night. He missed the smell of her damp hair after she'd taken a shower. He missed her funny little comments, non sequiturs that would somehow inspire an entire comedy sketch in the ring.

His performance wasn't affected by his sadness, at least not for the worse. In fact, he gradually gained a reputation as one of the most innovative clowns in the circus world. But even this level of acceptance failed to ease his pain. He searched for answers elsewhere, outside the ring, like a bloodhound on the trail of an unknown scent.

He continued to search through the fakir's books. Though Mahatma Baba Ram Shree was the first to admit he was an utter fraud, the books in his library were not . . . particularly the books dealing with Chaos Magick.

The book Eliphas studied the most was *Mani Padme Hum*. He read it forty times over the course of the next five years. One day, five-year-old Joseph climbed up onto his father's lap and asked to see the cover of the book. After staring at the title for a few minutes, Joseph said, "*The Jewel in the Lotus*."

"How did you know that?" Eliphas whispered.

Joseph merely shrugged. The boy read the entire first chapter that afternoon.

For Eliphas, the next eight years passed very slowly indeed, as if time itself had been fed into one of the vendors' numerous taffy machines. Most of his life was spent in rings: either under the big top before a laughing crowd, or alone inside a pentagram surrounded by black candles. Occasionally, when he had the time, he would prepare immense pentagrams within the three rings themselves. That way he could occupy both worlds at once. The purpose of both environments was the same: to lead him toward the Answer, the cure for the vast void in his heart.

The Path he had chosen was not an easy one. Constant practice was essential. The books warned against so many possible dangers that might occur from enacting such rites: possession by the dead and even worse entities, permanent insanity, the irrevocable distortion of time and space. The books even warned against the inadvertent creation of *tulpas*, physical beings brought to life by the raw energy of the human imagination. Such beings could be quite troublesome, enacting the subconscious wishes of their creator without the creator's conscious knowledge. But Eliphas had convinced himself he was protected against such a contingency. After all, he had trained for so many years. He was almost a Master. His imagination was a mere tool to be manipulated by his mind, not the other way around....

And it was his mind, honed to perfection through years of meditation, that led him to attempt the most ambitious rite of all.

On the twenty-third of April, Eliphas knelt within yet another pentagram drawn into a thick carpet of sawdust. He used his own blood to draw esoteric, Kabalistic symbols into his traditional clown face paint. He didn't look so funny anymore, but at least he'd gotten over his aversion to blood.

Tonight would be a total lunar eclipse. It was now 6:00 PM. The sun would set in seven minutes.

Eliphas chanted words forgotten by most humans, words to summon etheric entities ... from the other side? From the electromagnetic spectrum? From his own mind? No matter their source, Eliphas knew the beings to be real.

At 6:30 the lower edge of the moon began to darken. The chant continued.

At 6:58 the moon entered the umbra, the darkest section of the Earth's shadow. Slowly, a figure began to form within the pentagram. A human figure—adult-sized, crouched in a foetal position. As the lower edge of the moon grew darker and darker, the entity grew more distinct. Wisps of long, dark hair sharpened into focus.

By 7:48 only a sliver of the moon remained visible. To the northwest, a bluish comet slipped out from behind a thick cloud cover. Directly above the moon a blood-red dot called Mars stared down upon Eliphas's ritual with an impassive glare.

At 8:23, amidst the utter blackness, the entity took its final form: a nude woman in her late teens.

For the first time in a long time, Eliphas smiled. He beckoned the woman toward him. She approached.

Oh God, she's so beautiful.

Marisa....

On his thirteenth birthday, Joseph lay in bed, trying very hard to fall asleep. It was going to be a big day tomorrow. He would be performing in the first sketch he'd developed without the help of his father. In the ring, his father was known as !!Ogo!the!Clown!! He was one of the most gifted clowns in the United States, perhaps in all of history. Everyone at the circus told Joseph he would be as famous as his father one day if he kept working hard, and listened to everything his father told him. Even the other clowns had begun to call him by his stage name: Dementia the Clown.

The audience loved Dementia's funny walk. It felt strange when they laughed. It was nice, of course, but it wasn't like he had to work very hard at it.

He wondered about his father's whereabouts. He wasn't in the trailer, this much was for certain. Their trailer wasn't very large. It would've been impossible for his father to hide from him in here—unless, of course, his father had discovered how to become invisible.

A single beam of moonlight peeked through the thin curtains that covered the tiny window above his mattress. The beam shone upon the placard hanging above his father's bed, illuminating only the bottom line:

"If it causes pain, it's funny: if it doesn't, it isn't."

Joseph massaged his imperfect legs, and wondered for the first time what the epigraph actually *meant*.

Shadows separated from the wall. They coalesced into a dark-haired woman with a childish grin. She was about four years older than Joseph. Nude. Oh so beautiful.

"Who . . . who are you?" Joseph whispered.

The woman kneeled down beside his bed. She lifted her index finger to her lips. "I've been told my name is Marisa. You don't need to know anything more than that."

How strange. One time, many years ago, Joseph had pleaded with Captain Bullion to tell him the name of his mother. Father refused to discuss her at all. Reluctantly, Bullion leaned down and whispered a name in his ear . . . seconds before Father entered the tent and demanded to know what was so secretive. Bullion backed away, never to repeat the name again, no matter how much Joseph pleaded. In that brief moment, he thought he had heard the name *Marisa*, but could never be sure. And that was so long ago. . . .

Now this lovely woman, this stranger named Marisa, slipped into bed with Joseph . . . caressed his hair, slid her hand beneath the sheets, stroked his penis. He quickly became erect. Joseph wondered if this was another of Father's "initiations," another one of his "harmless" practical jokes.

"Did Father send you?"

She shook her head and kissed him on the lips. Tentatively, he placed his hands on her warm shoulders, then allowed them to wander down to the small of her back. He felt the smooth surface of her legs as she straddled his thighs. For the first time in his life he forgot about his father.

I hope this isn't a practical joke, he thought, 'cause it sure doesn't feel funny.

Nor was it painful, not in any way.

Ogo the Clown was killing the audience once again.

Ogo's world lay within the center ring, beneath the candy-striped big top. In Ogo's world, anything could happen. Pigs could fly and be shot out of the sky, children could turn into chickens that were then beheaded by Ogo himself, policemen could be impaled on stop signs, old women could be raped by kitchen utensils, bears could be mauled by kittens. Ogo's comedy usually involved blood. A great quantity of blood. Ogo, however, was never hurt. Not permanently, at least. Not even the laws of life and death could bind him for long.

At the moment, he was performing one of his most famous sketches. Ogo was dressed as the Grim Reaper. The Reaper needed to meet his weekly quota of dead people or else God would get angry and whap him upside the head. Thus, the Reaper waited outside a retirement home with a plank of wood and clubbed old women over the head as they left the building. He

accosted men on crutches, women in wheelchairs, babies in strollers. No matter how much his victims cried in pain, the Clown always remained silent. This was one of Ogo's expert theories. The Clown must never utter a sound. He should only smile.

After the Reaper glided out of the ring on spiked roller skates, the brass band began to play the jaunty entrance music of his son. Dementia rode in on a twisted unicycle. He sat down at a piano and fell through the chair. He kicked the chair across the sawdust floor. He tried another, but the back legs collapsed. He kicked the remnants across the floor, cursing silently. Snapping his fingers, he gestured for yet another chair to be carried into the ring. Smiley the Clown, one of Ogo's new understudies, gave him a real one this time. Dementia sat down. It held. He cracked his knuckles, loosened his neck. Placed his fingers on the keys. . . .

Nothing happened. No sound. He cupped his hand over his ear, leaned forward. Tapped the keys some more. No sound. He grew angry. Tapped another key, which sprang into the air. It wasn't even connected to the piano! He pulled off two more keys and threw them on the ground. *None* of them were connected! Dementia stomped out of the ring, grabbed Smiley and pulled him in front of the piano, swept his gloved hand across the keys, knocking them to the floor. Smiley shrugged helplessly. Dementia slapped him upside the head. Smiley swung back. He and Dementia proceeded to beat the crap out of each other—Dementia trying to kick Smiley in the butt, just barely missing, Smiley trying to sock Dementia in the head, just barely missing. They tackled each other, fell to the ground, still beating one another furiously. At last they separated. Smiley remained on the ground, groaning. Dementia staggered backwards, whipped out a gun and shot Smiley five or six times, blood spraying everywhere.

The deed done, Dementia stomped out of the ring once again. Then returned with an axe and proceeded to hack away at the useless keyboard. The audience could now hear the distinct, raucous sound of piano strings being severed by the axe. Despite the fact that it had no keys, it now made wonderful noise. Happy for once, Dementia sat down again and played a beautiful rendition of Beethoven's Fifth Symphony on the now non-existent keys. As abruptly as it began, the music ceased. Dementia leaned forward, cupped his ear again. Tapped the unseen keys. Nothing! He grabbed the axe and devastated the keyboard once and for all. Having released his frustrations, he opened the piano and out jumped a dozen midgets playing flutes and harps. Dementia joined them in a jig. They all danced over the corpse of Smiley the Clown. The spotlight shrank to nothing, darkness fell upon the dance.

The audience applauded for a very long time.

While the audience was still showing its appreciation, Ogo and son (with the help of a few more clowns) carried Smiley's dead body out of the ring.

"Where do you plan on dumping this one?" said Melanoma the Clown. "We're not pawning him off on one of the hot dog vendors again, are we?"

"No, no," Ogo said. "What's the purpose of performing Chaos Magick if you're just going to repeat yourself? That's somewhat of an oxymoron, don't you think?"

"Where're we gonna get another Smiley?" whined Petit Mal, one of Ogo's most loyal clowns.

"Where are we *going* to get another Smiley?" Ogo said. "Watch your grammar."

"Okay, where're we *going* to get another Smiley?"

"Another will show up, they always do. Remember what P.T. Barnum said."

That last word transformed into a groan as the bloody corpse almost slipped out of his hands. Ogo yelled at Dementia to pick up the slack.

Joseph did so, waiting to be complimented on his fine performance in the ring. He'd never heard a single compliment from his father. Probably never would. Nonetheless, he always hoped . . . maybe, someday. . . .

Behind them, the rubber cows (or elephants, as the natives called them) lumbered into the ring with a dozen dwarves standing on their backs; the dwarves juggled torches and snakes and tire irons. Both the rubber cows and the jugglers had been painted in bright day-glo colors. One of the dwarves was playing Wagner on a day-glo violin. You could barely hear him over the monkeys in the brass band.

They carried Smiley to a nearby graveyard and plopped him atop a coffin in someone else's grave. Ogo was still dressed as the Grim Reaper. After the last pile of dirt had been shoveled back into place, Ogo dismissed the other clowns and took Dementia on a little walk. He placed his hand on his shoulder, led him from grave to grave. They played a favorite game of Ogo's: making up clever stories about how each person might have died. The goal was to see who could come up with the most obscure diseases in existence. When they ran out of these diseases, the trick was to make up new ones, the most horrible you could imagine. Ogo almost always won. Dementia would rather not have played, but hid his reluctance behind the painted smile.

Later that night, lying in a darkened trailer, Joseph hoped Marisa would visit him again. Odd how she had simply vanished into the shadows. Had it all been a dream?

In the trailer that formerly belonged to Smiley the Clown, Eliphas sat amidst his sawdust circle and received fellatio from his long-dead wife. Marisa asked her lover to close his eyes and wait for her to return from the *Meon*, the other side. Eliphas did as he was told. *I'll be back soon*, she whispered in his ear. He wished he could go with her.

While on the verge of sleep, his tense hope having been replaced by disappointment, Joseph suddenly felt a hand stroking his cheek. He smiled. Opened his eyes. *No*, Marisa said from the foot of the bed. *Close your eyes, child. Feel the Meon. Feel what it's like on the other side.* She dug her long nails into his thighs and lowered her head into his lap.

Joseph closed his eyes. . . .

The Tower of Silence stands twenty-two stories high amidst a continually shifting landscape. First a desert, then a forest, a sprawling city, a swamp, a beach, sometimes all of these at once. Sometimes none of these. Sometimes only starry space. A vulture the size of the big top is perched atop the tower's crown. Strange symbols are carved upon the outer walls. The most prominent symbol resembles a stylized bee with its antennae twisted into a spiral. The scarred surface of a full, golden moon hangs above the vulture's outspread wings. The carrion eater rears its head into the twilight sky, opens its razor-sharp beak. A fountain of blood spurts out of its mouth and appears to stain the moon itself.

When Joseph opened his eyes, he found himself alone once more.

"I almost thought you'd left me," Eliphas said.

No, she said, *I could never do that.*

She wrapped her lips around his penis, flicked her tongue rapidly across his foreskin.

He closed his eyes. Moaned in pleasure.

He thrust himself inside her violently as if she were nothing but a warm hole.

Behind his eyelids, he saw nothing he hadn't seen a million times before: utter darkness, as black as the moon during a lunar eclipse.

Feast of Clowns

They found another Smiley, some young kid just out of college with a BA. All of a sudden he wanted to be taught the secrets of sword swallowing. Naturally, Linko the sword swallower told him to beat it. The kid ended up in Clown Alley, the area just outside the big top where the joeys waited for their cues. There was always room for another clown.

Joseph forgot the new Smiley's real name in less than a day. What was the use of remembering it when he'd be replaced by another Smiley within a few weeks? This Smiley was rather odd in some ways. Outside the ring he was shy and self-effacing, while inside he was as enthusiastic and bubbly as Petit Mal himself. He had a penchant for hanging around the children rather too much. Joseph had seen this pattern before. It was common among circuses, which often served as a refuge for outsiders of all kinds, even criminal ones. *Especially* criminal ones.

One day after the show, Eliphas took Smiley aside and told him quite emphatically that the last thing they needed was the law breathing down their necks. "You get caught pulling this shit and we'll have a clem on our hands in no time. A fight with the towners always turns out ugly on both sides. It'll turn out *real* ugly for you." Eliphas slapped him around a bit and ordered him to shape up. That was usually all it took with such people. But not this time.

Inevitably, a clem erupted in a small coastal town outside San Francisco. Just before the first act, the taming of an emaciated white panther, Smiley lured a small boy behind the calliope with the promise of cotton candy. What he got was something quite different, something quite different indeed.

The mother found the child curled in a foetal position, his pants pulled down around his knees, blood streaming out of his anus. The child couldn't speak. He stared straight ahead, his mouth wide open, no sound emerging.

The police arrived soon after. All the clowns were pulled out of Clown Alley, prevented from taking their part in the final act. Smiley was the only clown not present. Eliphas knew where he might be, but said nothing. He would never leave a fellow clown to the mercy of mere towners.

As the police scoured the grounds, Eliphas slipped into the horse stables, found Smiley curled up beneath the straw near the Amazing Unicorn Stallion. The second he saw the look on Eliphas's face, the clown immediately began crying, as if on cue.

"God damn you," Eliphas said.

"I'm sorry," Smiley whimpered, covering his face with his hands.

"You're going to be a hell of a lot more sorry pretty soon."

"You're not gonna give me over to the police, are you?"

"No, of course not. I'd never rat on a fellow joey. We have to put you someplace where the cops won't ever think to look."

For the first time, Smiley looked up at him with hopeful eyes. "Where?"

"Oh, I've got one or two ideas," Eliphas said, withdrawing a long, serrated knife from his jolly bag of tricks.

The cops wouldn't let them leave town. This was bad, very bad. The manager called his 24-Hour-Man and warned him they might be held back a day. Meanwhile, the entire circus was in danger of losing money. All because of one damn joey. The responsibility lay on Eliphas's shoulders, for it was his job to keep the other clowns in line. He'd failed miserably, miserably.

"Either arrest every damn one of us or let us leave town," Eliphas shouted at a police detective. "We haven't got the rest of our lives to dick around with you people."

"Listen, Bozo, don't tell me how to do my job," the detective said. He gestured at a vendor behind a hot dog stand; the angry vendor pointed at a sign marked CLOSED. The detective turned the sign around: OPEN. "Mustard only," he said and snapped his fingers. "Hop to it." He turned back to Eliphas. "I'm afraid you people are going to blow a date. I'm not leaving here until I get my hands on that pervert." The vendor gave him the hot dog, mustard only; he held his hand out for his coins, but the detective ignored him.

Eliphas smiled. He disliked repeating acts of chaos, but emergencies were emergencies, after all. "You might just get your wish," he said and walked away, trailing generations of ghosts behind him in the form of a funny limp.

Joseph couldn't stand the chaos on the circus grounds: police with flashlights, panting dogs, roving searchlights. It was all too much. He took refuge in the soothing darkness of his trailer.

"Marisa? Are you there, Marisa?"

Yes, said a voice inside his head. Soft hands wrapped around his thighs from the shadows behind him.

He sees a dark tower and a vulture perched atop its crown. With each encounter, the tower seems to be drawing nearer and nearer. He peers through a window in the structure, a narrow slit carved out of the ebony walls eleven stories above the ground. Inside the tower he sees a chamber devoid of any distinguishing features except for an E-shaped sigil painted on a gold-speckled, emerald floor. The sigil glows pale yellow and casts a reflection of itself against the stone ceiling. Between the two upper bars of the E-shaped figure are rigid black marks that resemble teeth, as if the sigil is baring its fangs. Marisa's voice echoes between the ebony walls of the chamber: *Would you like to stay with me here forever, Joseph? For the entirety of this life and the next? We can enfold ourselves within each other and never emerge. . .*

. . . never separate . . . endless pleasure . . . never pain, never pain. . . .

Yes . . . oh God, yes, you don't even have to ask.

Then please help free me.

Free you from what?

The tower dissolved around him. He found himself lying naked in his bed, Marisa straddling his thighs once again. She leaned forward and whispered in his ear, "Your father."

"What?" Anger welled up in his throat. "You told me you had nothing to do with him."

"I said he didn't send me to you. And that's true. I came because I had to."

"Why?"

"You're the jewel in the lotus. You're touched by the *Meon*. Your father is touched by nothing, except old hates and old loves. They're both the same to him. Nevertheless, his imagination is powerful. Powerful enough to summon me from the other side. I can't free myself from his control. Only you can do that, Joseph."

"How?"

Marisa peered into Joseph's eyes. She didn't respond, at least not out loud.

Eliphas, exhausted from the day's strangeness, lumbered towards his familiar old trailer. He paused outside the door, placed his hand on the knob. He was just about to turn it when he peered through the tiny window in the door. His gaze alighted upon a ray of moonlight bathing the long dark hair of a woman he knew all too well . . . in sickness and in health . . . inside and out . . . alive and dead. A woman who was now lying naked with his own son, straddling his thighs, moving slowly up and down as Joseph melted inside her. The Fool's first instinct was to tear into the room, kill both of them at once. But no. No. The reason of the Magician held him back.

He lifted his hand from the knob, silently stepped back from the trailer.

The sound of barking dogs ripped through the usual quiet of the sleeping circus.

Eliphas sprinkled sawdust on the floor of Smiley's trailer. With a gloved finger he traced a pentagram into the thick layer of dust.

Flashlight beams slashed through the closed curtains, briefly illuminating the inside of the trailer. Hounds sniffed at the door, then moved on in their futile quest. Eliphas frowned and thought of the lines composed by the Kabalist Isaac Luria:

The insolent dogs must remain outside and cannot come in,
I summon the Ancient of Days at evening until they are dispersed,
Until his will destroys the shells.
He hurls them back into their abysses, they must hide deep in their caverns.

How like those hounds are the rest of the human race, forever darting about within the great gulf dividing the phenomenal world of Malkuth and the noumenal world of Kether, forever hunting a prey they will never find. For too many years I allowed myself to be fooled by the shadows of Maya, by the worlds of the physical. I thought I'd risen above such transitory concerns, but I now know that I simply allowed Maya to trick me all over again. For years, I studied ancient tomes in order to become one with Kether, sacrificed soul after soul to develop more and more power. But for what purpose? To bring back Marisa. To surrender myself to Malkuth all over again. Marisa betrayed me thirteen years ago by leaving me trapped here in this shell.

My biggest mistake was in believing that the dead could be any more trustworthy than the living.

"I don't know if I can do it."

Joseph lay on his back as Marisa idly ran her fingers across his bare chest, tracing imaginary symbols in his flesh.

"You can," she said. "You *have* to, unless you want me to be imprisoned in this world for the rest of my life. You don't know what it's like where I come from. The *Meon* is the opposite of Death. It's non-being, eternal bliss that makes this place seem like a perpetual Hell."

"Even when you're with me?"

Marisa remained silent for a moment before she finally responded, "Of course not," then kissed his neck. He closed his eyes, ready to make love to her once again, but suddenly Marisa screamed. She was wrenched off the bed as if by an invisible force.

Joseph shot up to a sitting position. Marisa lay sprawled on the floor.

"Oh my God," she whispered. "He's calling for me. You've got to do it *now*, Joseph. Do it before he destroys me forever. He's that powerful. You have to believe m—"

Marisa's words were abruptly cut off. She clutched at her stomach and groaned in pain as her body seemed to melt, collapsed in upon itself, compressed into a single bright point in the middle of the air that shined a blinding pale yellow for one second before it flickered and was gone. . . .

For one second there was a blinding white flash and then Marisa was kneeling in the middle of a sawdust pentagram. She raised her head slowly and found Eliphas standing over her. She was not at all surprised.

"I trusted you," he said through a blood-red frown. The twenty-two sigils of the Kabalah had been woven into Ogo's face paint in a stunningly artistic design that she might have found beautiful under different circumstances.

Marisa didn't utter a sound. She stared back at Eliphas with no expression at all.

"I loved you," he said.

No response.

"I gave up thirteen years for you."

Again, a long silence. Finally Marisa shook her head. "You're playing with energies you don't even understand. You stand there reading your esoteric tomes, beating your chest with pride and declaring yourself superior to everyone else because you've lost your ego. You're so blind you don't even see the contradiction.

"None of this should ever have happened. I'm not your wife, I never was. I'm a product of your diseased imagination. Everything I've done, I've done because you wanted me to. Everything you've lost, you've lost because you wanted to lose it. You believe Joseph stole your wife away from you; therefore, he must steal her again. Because it was ordained. Not by cosmic forces, not by gods or demons, but by *you*.

"Your pain is self-inflicted. You're the only one who can stop it . . . stop it before this whole sick comedy becomes even uglier. Just back away. Let go. Let me go.

"That's your problem, Eliphas. You've forgotten that everything is essentially *funny*. What happened to the man Marisa fell in love with, the man who said you have to be clever to make a fool of yourself?"

Eliphas clenched and unclenched his fist. He thought about stepping out of the circle. Stepping back, just like he'd done outside the trailer. Stepping back from his ego. Stepping back from Malkuth. Stepping back from . . .

. . . *a ray of moonlight bathing the long dark hair of a woman he knew all too well . . . in sickness and in health . . . inside and out . . . alive and dead. A woman who was now lying naked with his own son, straddling his thighs, moving slowly up and down as Joseph. . . .*

Eliphas grabbed Marisa about the throat, began to squeeze. His black-painted thumbnails dug deep into the softest, most delicate spot in the middle of her throat. Marisa gagged, reached out for Eliphas's face. Her fingernails clawed at his pudgy cheeks, scraping off the black and white face paint of his profession.

The smell of sawdust filled her nostrils as life escaped her.

Joseph leaped out of bed, pulled on a faded pair of Levi's and dashed out the trailer, not even bothering to close the door behind him. Where could his father be? In the stables? The Fun House? With Petit Mal in his trailer?

He paused near the cook joint, glancing right and left, not knowing where to turn. Perhaps he was with Smiley himself, trying to help him escape . . . or at least getting rid of the remains. . . .

The remains. Of course. Smiley's trailer.

Joseph weaved in and out of the grimy, battered trailers, cursing his limp for slowing him down. Except for the occasional Coleman lantern dangling from a post, the only light to guide him was the full moon, casting its pale glow through the spokes of the distant Ferris wheel. Winding trails of dog prints were scattered about the sawdust beneath his feet. At night the smell of the sawdust was always the most intense. It overwhelmed even the sweet, lingering scent of cotton candy. From a few yards away came the distinct scuffling sounds of canine paws scraping against metal. Somehow he knew they were outside Smiley's trailer. When Joseph finally arrived, the dogs had already moved on. They were nowhere to be seen, though he could hear their nearby whines over the shouts of the ubiquitous policemen.

Joseph swung open the trailer door to find his father bent over Marisa's body. Her head was hanging limply to one side as if her neck had been twisted like that of a child's plastic doll. Marisa's eyes lay wide open, staring up at nothing.

Joseph released a single whimper that trailed off into a long, drawn-out scream as he launched himself on his father's back. Eliphas spun around, wrenching out of his son's grasp. Joseph saw the three trails dug into his father's face paint by Marisa's fingernails. The magickal sigils were smeared, running together like wax crayons left to melt in the sun. One of the sigils resembled the letter "E" with teeth between the upper bars, a symbol very much like the one Joseph had seen in the tower not long ago. This made him even angrier. He punched his father in the gut.

Eliphas crumpled to his knees, falling over Marisa's corpse. He scooted backwards and grabbed his bag of tricks, the same one he'd brought with him while visiting the stables. His hand blindly reached inside the bag and withdrew a long serrated knife. Smiley's blood still stained the blade. Joseph kicked it out of his hand. The knife skittered across the floor. Joseph fell on his father, landed blow after blow against his face. Eliphas raised his knee into Joseph's stomach, knocking the wind out of him momentarily. He pushed his son aside and crawled toward the fallen blade. Joseph forced himself to rise from the sawdust floor. He jumped on Eliphas, grabbed his arm with one hand while reaching for the knife with the other. Eliphas jabbed his elbow into Joseph's chest, but to no avail. Joseph refused to feel the pain, not now. His fingertips drew the knife closer, then at last closed around the hilt of the blade. Eliphas shouted something as Joseph shoved the blade into the back of his father's neck. Blood splattered on Joseph's bare chest. He thought he heard the sound of a spinal cord snapping. Nevertheless he continued to thrust the blade into his father's back over and over again.

Once the thirst for death drained out of Joseph, he staggered away from his father's body and collapsed to his knees. He sat there staring at the bleeding mass of flesh a long time before at last throwing the knife away and crawling toward Marisa's body. He couldn't help but slide his arms around his lover's shoulders, expecting her to respond with passionate whispers, but this didn't happen. She simply hung in his arms, as lifeless as his father.

Joseph began to cry, until he saw the smattering of blood he'd left on her bare back. His father's blood. Ogo the Clown had to foul her body even in death. Anger consumed Joseph's mind once again. He gently lowered Marisa to the floor, then approached his father's body. He kneeled down in front of Eliphas, flipped him onto his back so he could stare into his empty, painted eyes. He wanted to see a trace of regret somewhere inside them. Instead . . . nothing. His gaze wandered downward. He stared at his father's stomach and saw the vulture and the tower so clearly in his mind. The vulture and the tower told him what to do. The sound of hunting dogs drew nearer. He pulled open Ogo's brightly colored shirt. Dug his hands into his chest, ripping his fingers right through the skin. No blood appeared. He slowly peeled off the flesh in long strips; it gave way as if it were the merest tissue paper. Layers of his father's skin piled up around Joseph until there was nothing left of the stomach except a bottomless black hole. Inside the hole: a stone stairway leading down into darkness.

Behind him, dogs scratched at the trailer door once again. The sound of brusque voices surrounded the trailer, heavy boots tromped through dirt and gravel. Joseph didn't have time to think about it. With one final glance at Marisa's beautiful face, Joseph descended the stairway inside his father's body. Darkness swallowed him. His bare feet padded softly against the stone steps. He stretched his arms out to either side of him but could feel no walls whatsoever, just endless space and a cool wind blowing against his cheeks from some indefinite source far below him. Behind him could be seen the same utter darkness. At some point he almost tripped over a body sprawled across the stairway: a haggard man, his face marred by scars, slumbering with a thick book hugged tightly to his chest. Joseph couldn't make out the whole title; all he saw were two ones and a zero followed by six or seven words that might have been English, but the blackness obscured them so he couldn't be sure. For a moment he considered waking the sleeping man, then thought better of it when he saw the pistol tucked into his belt. This man's destination, Joseph knew, was not the same as his. Joseph continued his journey. After what seemed like many days of descending and descending and descending, punctuated by brief intervals spent curled up on the uncomfortably small steps (trying to lose himself to sleep, just like the scarred man he had left far behind) he at last grew impatient with the seemingly endless stairway and leaped into the wind. . . .

The Tower of Silence stands twenty-two stories high amidst a continually shifting landscape. First a desert, then a forest, a sprawling city, a swamp, a beach, sometimes all of these. Sometimes none of these. Sometimes only starry space. A vulture the size of the big top is perched atop the tower's crown. Strange symbols are carved upon the outer walls. The most prominent symbol resembles a stylized bee with its antennae twisted into a spiral. The scarred surface of a full, golden moon hangs above the vulture's outspread wings. The carrion eater rears its head into the twilight sky, opens its razor-sharp beak. A fountain of blood spurts out of its mouth and appears to stain the moon itself.

Joseph peers through a window in the structure, a narrow slit carved out of the ebony walls eleven stories above the ground. Inside the tower he sees a chamber devoid of any distinguishing features except for an E-shaped sigil painted on a gold-speckled, emerald floor. The sigil glows pale yellow and casts a reflection of itself against the stone ceiling. Shadows separate from the walls and coalesce into a beautiful dark-haired woman with a childish grin . . . endless pleasure, she had said . . . never pain, never pain . . . and for a brief moment, her words are true . . . then comes a final kiss on the forehead, and a whispered command to return home . . . his life, she says with a distinct trace of sadness, is not yet over. . . .

The police broke down the door of the trailer and found three dead bodies sprawled out amidst soft, fresh sawdust. The woman's neck was broken, the clown had been stabbed in the back dozens of times, and the boy was simply staring up at the ceiling with a rictal grin frozen on his face. Blood trickled out of his mouth in bright streams.

The police detective strolled onto the crime scene and rubbed his hands together with glee, knowing a mad man must be loose on the circus grounds. The man was capable of child rape and triple homicide. Innocent lives had to be protected from his insanity.

"Don't worry," he said to his men, "we'll capture this nut sooner or later. He couldn't have gotten too far."

Within minutes, officers with flashlights swarmed the circus grounds once again.

The hounds resumed their search even more furiously than before.

He limped slowly toward the silent freight cars in the switching yard on the outskirts of the city. He planned to head south if he could, the opposite direction of the circus . . . and Marisa. And Eliphas. And all they represented.

He would never again call himself Dementia. He no longer saw himself as a disease, but as a flower growing from the manure once known as Eliphas Kane. He thought: What better way to disgrace a man's memory than for the murderer to steal his victim's most cherished possession?

Humorously, ironically, he would hereafter be known only as Ogo the Clown, while his old self lay moldering beside his father in an unmarked grave with the rest of the nameless, faceless clowns.

Subversion Clause
RICHARD PARKS

It was Ahazat's first day on the job as a procurement specialist. A little confusion could, perhaps, be understood. He looked at the white-robed young lady standing just outside the perfectly calligraphed mystic pentagram and frowned.

"I didn't quite catch that."

She smiled at him. "I said: I want you to subvert my present expectations."

Ahazat stared at her. "That's what I thought you said."

So much for orientation. It was simple, they said—Mortals want things. Silly things, usually, but they want them and they're willing to trade their precious immortal souls. Usually for some very minor magical service. Eternal youth was popular, as was beauty, but there was always a catch that allowed the buyer—Hell—to collect. They knew all the tricks, they said, all the various dodges that mortals had tried over the years. Just call if you get into trouble. Ahazat decided to do just that.

"Just a sec . . . what's your name, anyway?"

"Martha."

"Thanks. Just a moment, Martha. I need to check with the home office." Ahazat pulled out his hellphone.

"That looks like a cellphone," Martha said.

"Show me a cellphone that can reach the Infernal Regions," Ahazat said. "Most of them can't call out of the Holland Tunnel. Can you give me a little space here?"

Ahazat, being conjured, couldn't leave the middle of the pentagram. Martha politely stepped back out of immediate earshot and Ahazat pressed *H. In a few moments he got a response.

"Hell Helpdesk."

Ahazat recognized the voice. Matkalak. Just his luck.

"Listen, I've got an odd one here . . ." Ahazat explained the mortal's question. Matkalak just hmmmed in a way that wasn't very helpful at all. Ahazat heard the click of a keyboard, then a very long and empty pause.

"There's nothing in the database," Matkalak said.

Ahazat blinked. "I thought that wasn't possible."

"So did I. I'll make a note. You will report your result, won't you? We need to keep the records up to date."

"To Bliss with that! I need to know what to do!"

"You're the field operative," Matkalak replied, totally unmoved. "It's your discretion. . . . And your ass, by the way. So logged. Bye."

Ahazat heard the click of the connection dropping, followed by the buzz of eternity. He switched the phone off. The mortal was still waiting. She was smiling as she approached the pentagram again.

"Think you're clever, don't you?" Ahazat said. "You're not the first mortal to think so, you know."

"I know," she said, and that was all.

Ahazat found himself taking a closer look at Martha. Time as such didn't mean much to him now, but he knew she was young. Pretty, too, in a way. Her hair was the color of cornsilk and her skin was flawless, though she seemed a little thin. Ethereal, almost. That had aroused his suspicions at first, yet Ahazat checked his wrist monitor and a human soul was definitely present; she wasn't a sprite or some soulless earth-bound fairie playing a joke. The only question remaining was, what the hell was he going to do?

"So let me be sure I understand you," he said, partly for clarity, partly to stall for time to think. "You want me to subvert your expectations in exchange for your mortal soul?"

She smiled wider. "Nice try. This is a challenge proposal. You know the sort—I wish for something and, if you can't fulfill that wish to the letter, you don't get my soul. My wish is that you subvert my current expectations, for as long as I live. That is, what I expect of you right at this moment. If you can do that, you have my soul upon my—natural, unaided—death. If you ever stop, you don't. Simple."

Ahazat just stared at her again. It made no sense. Why would a mortal give her soul for no gain? There was no gold, unsurpassed beauty, eternal youth, or anything else in it for her that he could tell.

"This is foolishness, Mortal. Do you expect me to know what your expectations are?"

The smile never wavered. "Don't you?"

"I—-" Ahazat stopped. He realized to his horror that he *did* know what her expectations were, to the letter. They were what every mortal with even half a brain expected: that he would do whatever he could to renege on his promise, or make it turn into something terrible that the mortal didn't expect, and *still* use the legalities to collect her soul. That was the way this scheme worked, the way it had always worked.

The way it was not going to work this time.

It's your discretion . . . and your ass.

Ahazat didn't need Matkalak's reminder. Still, if he took a pass on his very first assignment. . . . Ahazat tried one more time. "Why would you give your soul for nothing?"

"Are you so sure that's what I'm doing? Suffice it to say I have my reasons, and free will says I'm allowed. That's all you need to know."

Cheeky thing. Ahazat decided he *would* have her soul, and wipe that cheerful smile off her face in the bargain . . . so to speak. He was a demon. That's what demons did.

"Done," he said, and it was. There was still the formality of the formal contract, but the Verbal Contract had a life of its own and morphed their spoken words into blood and parchment. The Document appeared floating in the air in front of the girl, along with a quill pen dripping blood.

"Read it, but I think you'll find it's in order. My signature will already be present," he said.

"To the letter," Martha said, after reading it carefully. "Done." She signed the paper, ending her name with a flourish. The contract disappeared.

"It's gone to Legal. Once approved, it's on to Accounting. Another formality."

"Did Hell actually invent legalisms, or did your lot just see the advantages sooner?"

"Only Himself knows for sure," Ahazat said. "I'm just a level three procurer."

Subversion Clause

"Yet my soul is actually yours, technically," she said. "Not Himself's, if you won't say his name."

"Yes, but in practice they're all signed over once the contract is forfeited—and it is always forfeited," he said.

She shook her head slightly. "Not always."

Ahazat shrugged. "Well . . . so seldom that the difference is hardly worth mentioning. Unless, I suppose, you're one of the two or three who've managed."

"Precedent doesn't require multitudes," she said.

Blast the girl, she was still smiling. In fact, if anything, she looked happier now than when he'd first seen her. It was getting a little annoying.

The contract reappeared briefly, rolled into a scroll, tied with a red ribbon bearing the official seal of Legal: a scale of justice with a big red thumb on one pan. It was a reminder: cheating was perfectly acceptable—more, encouraged—so long as it didn't violate the actual letter of the contract. The spirit of the contract was problematic at best.

Ahazat wanted to cheat. Which was, of course, exactly what she expected. Which meant he couldn't do it. The force of the contract was as binding on him as it was on her. That was one legalism that Himself had never quite mastered.

This is going to be tougher than I thought.

"Everything's set."

"Fine," she said. "Now I can let you out of the pentagram. You're staying with me for a while."

Ahazat blinked. "I am?"

"You have a lien on my soul but not my body, and this body still has some time left on it. How can you subvert my expectations if you're not around?"

"Now wait—" Ahazat stopped. It was useless. He weighed his protests against the Force of the Contract and found his quibbles wanting. She was right. While he had no doubt of the eventual outcome, he had to admit that, as of this moment, this silly blonde girl had him under her little pink thumb.

"Ok, fine. Do you really want me to accompany you in the mortal realm looking like *this*?"

Martha looked him up and down, not that Ahazat really needed such careful inspection. His horns and tail were standard issue, as was his scaly, ugly body. The barest glance to even the most obtuse observer would tell the whole story: demon.

"Do I really need to explain this? Of course I wouldn't! Yet my expectations of you assumed nothing less. Therefore?"

Ahazat knew what followed. He managed to smile, but it wasn't easy. "I will considerately change forms to convenience you, rather than creating shock and disturbance wherever we go."

"Very good."

Ahazat tried, but it wasn't as easy as it sounded. Transformation itself was a basic skill; appearing handsome or beautiful in order to deceive was Demon 101 stuff. Yet he wasn't trying to deceive now, or rather he would have if he could figure out *how*. He was still a little at a loss in that regard, but there was plenty of time. For now he just needed a suitable form, and he didn't have one. He said as much.

"Were you always a demon?"

"No, I was once mortal. Most demons are recruited from the ranks of the Damned, these days. The original lot are spread much too thin for the workload."

"So what did you look like then?"

Ahazat tried to remember. As a freshly-minted demon his old appearance had been taken from him at orientation, and the new form imposed. Ahazat hadn't thought about his original form in some time, and most of his mortal memories had been suppressed. There was a buzzing sound in his mind whenever he tried to recall them, and yet, to his own surprise, Ahazat could remember his old mortal face with no difficulty. He wondered if that was due to the terms of the contract, since he needed a mortal form now to satisfy the client. He didn't know, but decided it didn't matter. He had the memory, and he used it. In another moment the transformation was complete. He summoned a mirror and studied the effect.

The face that looked back at him was softer and pinker than the one he was used to. The hair was very dark, cut short. He had a dark stubble of beard and no scales at all that he could tell. He wore jeans and a black shirt, and short black boots. Ahazat waved the mirror away, and it was only then that he noticed Martha staring at him, an odd look on her face. He could almost swear there were tears in her eyes.

"Ummm . . . is something wrong?"

She shook her head and looked away. "No, no, it's fine. You look . . . fine. Contrary to what I expected."

Something about her tone made him question that. Ahazat summoned the mirror again and gave himself an even closer inspection. He was a little out of practice at looking like a mortal but he was fairly familiar with the range of body types and appearances and, so far as he could tell, this one was fairly ordinary. He shrugged, and banished the mirror for good.

"Well, then. What now?"

Martha reached down and, using her hand to erase a small section of the outer circle, broke the pentagram. "Now you do as the contract directs."

Ahazat stared at the dirty water in the sink and the pile of clean dishes that had left the water in that state. He looked at his hands, still not scaly but now definitely far more wrinkled than they had been before.

"What did I just do?" he asked the universe at large.

Perhaps the universe wasn't listening, but Martha was. She glanced at him from the dining room window where she'd just finished adding the tie-backs for her new curtains. "You were helpful. Again, contrary to my expectations."

"I'm a Demon of the Ninth Circle. I shouldn't have to wash dishes!"

"Of course not. Which is precisely the point. Good job, by the way." Then she smiled again.

"What's so funny?"

"That bit about not having to do dishes. There are some men who would use the same logic, you know. 'I'm a man, I shouldn't have to, et cetera.' I'll bet when you were a mortal you did the same."

"You assume too much. You can't know."

She shrugged. "Just an observation. It wasn't important."

Ahazat wanted to agree, but then he knew sarcasm was definitely a violation of the contract. He sighed. *When will this be over??* Purely rhetorical; he knew it would be over when he had completely subverted Martha's expectations, that is, all those she held at the time of the contract. Yet he didn't have a list; that would have been too simple and sensible. No, all he had was a situational understanding of a particular expectation at a particular time, and so far all that understanding had bought him was a soft pink mortal body and a set of dishpan hands.

Matkalak must be laughing his ass off.

Martha came away from the window. "All done?"

"Yes," Ahazat said, keeping his tone as neutral as possible.

Subversion Clause

"It's better isn't it?"

Ahazat wasn't sure he understood what she meant at first, then he sighed and looked around the apartment. After a moment he had to admit that the tidying and straightening that Martha had insisted on were somewhat of an improvement. Ahazat realized that he preferred a certain order in his surroundings; even in Hell, his personal space, such that it was, tended to be spare and simple. Not that a few rocks next to a sulphur pit lent itself to much in the way of design.

"You like things tidy."

"Is that an expectation?"

She demurred. "Speculation, that's all. Are you still looking for the 'gotcha' that gets you off the hook and loses me my soul immediately? Think carefully before you answer."

"It would affirm expectations," Ahazat said. ". . . wouldn't it?"

"What do you think?"

It wasn't a question of thinking. He knew. The very act of trying to obtain the maximum benefit with the legal minimum of effort was exactly according to expectations. So he couldn't do it. Even explicitly looking for the angle was a violation of the agreement.

I knew I made a mistake, Ahazat thought, *but I didn't realize just how big a one.*

He was starting to understand, and what he understood was that pretty little demure Martha had him by the short hairs, and not in a good sense. Yet there was a way. There was always a way.

Wasn't there?

"I'll be good," Ahazat said.

She reached up and patted him on the head. "It's not as hard as you think. You'll see." She yawned. "Time for bed."

Ahazat blinked. "Bed?"

"You're wearing a mortal body now, and mortal bodies get tired. You'll need sleep."

"Fine. Where are we sleeping?"

"We? What do you think?"

There it was again. "A seduction would be corrupting, potentially, and therefore . . . expected. I'll be sleeping on the couch?"

"See? You're getting better already."

"There's no reference *anywhere*? Matkalak, are you sure you looked?" Ahazat kept his voice to a low whisper; Martha was sleeping in the next room and the last thing he needed was a test that would prove that even talking to the home office was a no-no in contract terms. After all, at this point he hadn't actually *tried* to use any knowledge gained to his advantage.

Mostly because there wasn't any.

Matkalak's voice bubbled up through the speaker, sounding more like an expression of lava, if lava had an expression. "It's like I told you from the start, if you'll recall—no precedent. No 'a priori' data. It hasn't happened before. How many ways do you want me to say it?"

"That's impossible."

"That's what I thought. This is something new, old sod, and to think I was present. What luck."

"Maybe for you," Ahazat said dryly. "What am I supposed to do?"

"Whatever she doesn't expect. That's for you to figure out."

"Fine, but what is she really after? This deal makes no sense as it stands."

"No? She's got what amounts to a personal servant, from what you've told me."

The connection went dead. Ahazat thought of calling back, if for no other reason than to vent a little invective, but it was pointless. Matkalak would only smirk a bit, and enjoy Ahazat's predicament that much more. No scales off Matkalak's ass, as he said from the start. Ahazat put the hellphone away.

A servant?

Well . . . it sort of made sense. There were mortals who would do anything for the sake of appearance, and status, but he measured Martha against that particular metric and the numbers made no sense. Martha wasn't like that. Trouble was, absent that rationale, *none* of it made any sense. Martha had to have an angle, and he had to find it. More, he had to finish meeting—in reverse—her expectations as said expectations stood at the beginning of the contract, and all without cheating . . . at least, not directly. That was the main reason he'd contacted Matkalak at the help desk; since Matkalak wasn't in the contract, his efforts were outside its bounds. If, of course, he had made any efforts other than what his duties required. That would have required initiative on Matkalak's part, so naturally that's where Ahazat's plan fell splat.

It's up to me.

Once the thought was there, Ahazat felt a sense of relief. He realized that he didn't like depending on others. Demon, human, it didn't make any difference. They disappointed you. They did not go the extra step. They didn't care. Like Matkalak. Like. . . .

Again there was that buzzing in his brain, like white noise, but now it was much worse. He had been allowed to remember his former appearance, probably to please his client, but now. . . . What had he been trying to remember? He finally shrugged. It was forbidden. More, it didn't really matter. His old life, whatever it had been, was long over. There was only here, and now, and his present problem.

Which, he also realized, was fairly straightforward. There was nothing really complicated about fulfilling the contract; it was *not* fulfilling it in a creative, nasty, and typical way that was the problem, only because there didn't seem to be a way.

Maybe . . . too straightforward?

Perhaps what was required was a little legal ambiguity. Ahazat looked around the apartment, and saw the computer sitting on the desk in the corner by the western window. For the first time in two days he smiled, and meant it.

"You look terrible. Have trouble sleeping?"

Martha stood in the doorway, holding a steaming cup of coffee.

Ahazat yawned. "No, no trouble."

It was true enough; he'd had no trouble sleeping because he hadn't tried to sleep. He'd spent all night on the computer. Yet there was nothing in his contract, so far as he could see, that compelled him to say so.

"Here, you need this more than I do." Martha gave him the cup.

"I don't like coffee."

"Yes you do."

Ahazat frowned. Was that in the contract? He hesitated and Martha sighed. "Just try it."

Ahazat tried it. Much to his surprise, Ahazat did indeed like coffee. He drank the whole cup and accepted another when Martha brought the pot from the kitchen.

"Feeling more awake now?"

He eyed her suspiciously. "Yes . . ." He was certain there was more to this than coffee. He was right.

"You know, my car is really dirty."

Ahazat almost groaned. "So a considerate person would wash it for you, yes?"

"Are you offering?" Martha asked.

He nodded, resigned. "I think I am."

There was a hose near the front of the building for the tenant's use. Martha pulled the car off the curb and into the driveway. Ahazat got to work with a bucket and cloth while Martha sat on the front steps, watching him. It was a beautiful day; sunny and warm. There were people about on the sidewalk, many heading toward the nearby park. Ahazat thought he remembered a park, somewhere. He thought about visiting this one.

I'm a demon. I don't care about that.

Even so, he still thought about it as he washed Martha's Toyota. After he'd finished the first rinse, he noted that Martha was smiling. It wasn't an unpleasant smile at all; she wasn't smiling at his predicament, or the idea of having a demon washing her car. So what *was* she smiling about? Ahazat decided to ask.

"I was just thinking. You know, in many ways you're the perfect man."

"Because I do cars and dishes? Only because the contract forces me to be nice. Besides, I'm not a man, Martha. I'm a demon."

The smile didn't waver. "I know that, silly. Yet you used to be a human; you said so. They take all that from you, don't they? Who you were, what you were?"

He nodded. "That's standard procedure."

"Why?"

Ahazat blinked. "What do you mean?"

She shrugged. "It was a simple question. Why? Why does it matter to the Infernal Powers that you don't remember being human?"

Ahazat thought about it as he washed the wheel rims. "I think it has to do with hope. Humans have it, even when they're not supposed to. Demons have no use for it."

"As in Dante's *Inferno*, 'Abandon All Hope, Ye Who Enter?'"

Ahazat wondered how much he should be telling her, but then he didn't see any reason why she shouldn't know. "Don't joke about that, Martha. It's true, as you will eventually discover. Or are you forgetting our contract?"

She shook her head. "No, but a contract has obligations on both sides. I'm not in Hell yet."

"Sooner or later," Ahazat said. "Not a threat, understand. A fact."

She smiled again. "We'll see."

Ahazat dropped the towel in the bucket. "Done. Anything else, m'lady?"

She nodded. "I want to go to the park."

"So I should offer to escort you?"

"Why thank you, kind sir. Let's go."

Martha had him flying a kite before the day was over. Part of him thought he should feel insulted, but he didn't. He was, however, so worn out by the evening that he was only able to spend a little time on his computer project before his eyes began to cross from the strain. He yawned. There were limits to this human body; perhaps a little more memory would have been a good thing then. He would know better what to expect. He encrypted the file and then placed it in its hidden folder, then logged out just as his hellphone chimed.

"Ahazat here."

"Hey, Haz. It's Matkalak. Time to report in, guy. How's it going?"

"Not too badly." Ahazat described his current project.

"A database search? I told you there was nothing in the database."

Ahazat couldn't keep from grinning. "No there isn't. *Yet.* I'm compiling new data every time I subvert one of Martha's expectations."

"So? How does that help? You still can't use it to correlate; that's attempting to circumvent the contract, which is against the contract."

Matkalak didn't get it. Ahazat was enjoying himself now. "Is it? How can I best fulfill Martha's wish if I don't know what her expectations are? Am I circumventing the contract or fulfilling it?"

"That's nonsense."

Ahazat shook his head, and grinned wider. "No, it's *ambiguous*. It has more than one legitimate interpretation. Practically . . . and legally."

Ahazat could almost hear dawn breaking in Hell. There was admiration in Matkalak's voice. "You sick, sneaky bastard. That's a compliment, by the way."

"Taken as such. Later."

He hung up and put the hellphone away. It only took him a second to stop smiling.

She's the one who made a contract with Hell. What did she expect?

Nothing less, he supposed, and that was rather the point. Yet violating the spirit of the contract without actually violating the contract technically was rule one in this scenario and always had been. Ahazat had a job to do and he was going to see that it was done. No choice, really. No point in even considering another option. There were none.

Were there?

The buzzing was back, so intense it made Ahazat's head hurt. Why? He wasn't trying to remember anything. At least, he didn't think so. Well, not precisely true—Ahazat remembered aspirin. He went to get some.

Martha was standing in the kitchen, sipping a cup of tea. She was wearing a plain flannel robe which, for some inexplicable reason, Ahazat found quite charming. "Oh. I didn't know you were up." He wondered briefly if she'd heard any of his conversation with Matkalak but he didn't see a trace of guile on her face anywhere.

"Obviously. Looking for something?" she asked.

"Ummm . . . oh, right. Aspirin?"

"Third drawer from the left."

He'd taken a step in that direction before her words even registered. Ahazat stopped, confused.

"You don't look well," Martha said. She put her cup down, then stepped forward to feel his brow. Her touch was cool and light and suddenly Ahazat felt the room spinning. It was only the fact that Martha now had a firm grip on his arm that kept him from falling over.

"Come along. Past time you went to bed."

She led him through the living room, past the couch, toward the bedroom door. "Um, where are we going?"

"For a demon you need a lot explained," Martha said.

"What . . . what do you expect?"

She smiled. "You'll find out."

Lace curtains. For some reason, Ahazat had not expected lace curtains. It was a woman's bedroom, and Ahazat didn't remember being mortal and therefore certainly did not remember the rules—if indeed there were such—for a woman's bedroom. Still, the curtains were a revelation. Airy, lacy, fluttering slightly in the breeze from the open window, they filtered the morning light into very interesting patterns. Ahazat put his hand on top of the covers and watched the flow of light and shadow across his skin.

This is what being mortal is like.

His head wasn't hurting because this wasn't a memory, exactly. It was now. Ahazat looked over to the other side of the bed where Martha had been. There was still a slight depression on the sheets where she had slept; her scent lingered. Ahazat sighed deeply.

You're being awfully mawkish, old sod. Especially considering that nothing happened.

At least, he was pretty sure nothing happened. Martha had talked a bit, about nothing in particular, as if having a demon in her bed was the most natural thing in the world. He'd tried to stay awake, aware of the potential havoc that Martha was courting here and looking for the best way to take advantage, yet his weariness had caught up with him. He'd gone to sleep with Martha stroking his arm. So much for 'the perfect man.' Ahazat sighed. This was getting more complicated than he'd thought possible.

There was a buzzing noise. At first Ahazat thought it was another unbidden memory being squelched, but his head didn't hurt and the noise didn't stop. He finally realized that it was his hellphone ringing. Where? Of course. In his trousers. Which were just now hanging over a chair near his—what a concept—side of the bed. He sighed and dragged himself out to answer it.

"Ahazat here."

It was Matkalak. Who else? "What the blazes is happening up there??"

Ahazat rubbed his eyes. "It's too early in the day for riddles. What are you talking about?"

Matkalak, clearly upset, still hesitated. "Where's your pigeon? Have you noticed anything unusual?"

"Her name is Martha and she's a contract technical consultant of some kind, so naturally she's at work. And define 'unusual.'" Silence. Ahazat sighed. "Look, Matkalak, I've got work to do myself. If you're just going to be cryptic, go away."

"You disappeared," Matkalak said.

It was Ahazat's turn to go silent. Then, "Um . . . excuse me?"

"Your signal disappeared. Vanished. Poof."

Ahazat shook his head. "My signal? What are you talking about? Hey, you don't have some kind of spy camera in Martha's bedroom do you?"

"Well . . . sort of. Look, I didn't want to say anything, but this is getting critical. Standard protocol puts this on a 'need to know' basis, but right now you need to know: as a demon you have a personal 'aura,' a diabolic energy field that is unique for each demon. Our tracking device doesn't show pictures; it's more like your aura serves as a transponder. Helps us keep tabs on your whereabouts since there are so many field operatives. You vanished from our scopes."

"I didn't *go* anywhere," Ahazat said. "Your radar or whatever must be broken."

"It's magic, you dolt! It doesn't break. And I didn't say you personally went anywhere; it's just that for several days your diabolic signal has been weak. It's weak now. For the last seven hours it disappeared completely! We don't know where. Frankly, Command and Control is getting a bit . . . concerned. There's been talk of alerting Infernal Relevance."

"Damn. IR?" He shuddered. "What should I do?"

"I don't know, but I suspect that Martha woman is a threat to your diabolic field integrity somehow."

"Martha? Don't be silly."

"I don't do 'silly.' Listen, Boyo, there's something weird happening. Whatever the cause, I think you better get to the bottom of it yourself, unless you want Infernal Relevance to do it for you. Or do you want a Debriefing?"

Ahazat did *not* want a Debriefing, to put it mildly. Demons of the Inner Circle didn't want a debriefing, and Ahazat was nowhere near that class of demon. Like as not he'd simply be flayed over hot coals just as an example, no matter what answers he gave, and the sad fact was that he didn't have any answers in the first place.

Better find those answers, and soon.

"I'll call you back, Matkalak."

Ahazat hung up and put his pants on. *So much for mooning over curtains.*

Since Ahazat was already in the bedroom, he decided to start there. After all, it was the first time he'd managed to see Martha's room and, if there was any clue as to what Martha's angle was, it had to be here in her most private of spaces. Ahazat knew he was on dangerous ground in terms of the contract and expectations, but he wasn't even sure that should be his priority now. Besides, he still had the rationale that "Knowing her better helps to better subvert her expectations." It was a thin line of reasoning, but it allowed him to continue.

He found the Grimoire right off.

Well, of course. He knew there had to be one; demon summoning wasn't something you did without a guide. Preferably a good one; a bad one would get you killed or worse. Martha had a good one indeed: Johann Correlli's *Ars Demonica*. Easily several thousand dollars for the 1922 Melshic reprint edition, assuming you could find one. Martha had clearly gone to some trouble and expense, but why?

There was a mystic circle in the center of the room, but Ahazat had been too tired and pre-occupied to notice it the night before. He instinctively recoiled from it, but then realized that it wasn't complete. There was about a three-inch gap in its circumference where it passed about three feet from the door of Martha's walk-in closet. It was rather like the one she'd summoned him with in the first place, in her den. As long as the circle was incomplete, it was powerless, but Ahazat had to admit that this was a particularly fine one, easily capable of holding him or fiends fifty levels higher if finished. But why was it there? To trap him? Yet if she'd wanted to do that, Martha could have done it last night when he'd stepped right into it. More strangeness. Still, he wasn't sure when Martha would return and he didn't take long to either admire the circle or puzzle over it. Ahazat kept looking.

It took a while, as he was being careful not to be too obvious in his search and leave underwear drawers in disarray or clothes on the floor, but he finally found her notes tucked away in a bag on the floor of the closet. He settled himself on the floor next to the bag and started reading.

This is strange.

Not the notes themselves; they were the sort of carefully recorded procedures that any halfway competent witch or sorcerer would distill from a grimoire as they designed a specific ritual in accordance with the basic concepts in the book. There were various sketches for different pentagrams and mystic circle variations. All pretty standard.

Except that the name of the demon was missing.

Ahazat studied the notes from first to last, and found nothing at all to indicate the name of the demon that Martha had intended to summon. That is to say, *his* name. This wasn't so unusual itself; there was a generic procedure for summoning *a* demon, any demon, if the magicker didn't know or care which one he or she was getting. This wasn't it. It was a very specific and carefully designed ritual for summoning a particular demon. Just the name was missing. Why? In such carefully prepared notes, why omit this key piece of information? It didn't make sense.

Unless she didn't know.

That didn't make sense either. If Martha wanted a specific demon, then there were several more famous and much more powerful field operatives to choose from. Ahazat had no illusions about his own place in the Infernal Order of Precedence: Demon of the Ninth Circle roughly translated to 'bare beginner.' There were pit-imps that ranked higher than he did. If Ahazat was right, then Martha had gone to some trouble to find a specific demon, and that demon was him.

"Maybe she *wanted* a beginner, and took the first one she located," he said aloud. "It didn't have to be me . . . did it?"

Ahazat started to put the notes back in the bag and realized the notebook hadn't been the only thing in there. There was a piece of red chalk, apparently the same one she'd used to draw the circle. Then there was a photo album. The chalk made sense; the album did not. Ahazat pulled it out, frowning. He flipped it open.

Odd place to keep holiday photos . . . oh.

There were holiday photos, among others. Martha at the beach looking rather winsome in a yellow bikini, Martha in hiking gear standing against a backdrop of autumn leaves. . . .

Ahazat, somber, holding up a fish.

Ahazat, frowning, paddling a canoe.

Ahazat, at the beach with his arm around Martha. It was the only picture in which he was smiling. Not that this made a difference. He and Martha had never done those things. At least, Ahazat had not.

The buzzing was deafening, but only for a moment. His head hurt for about the same amount of time. The memory suppression mechanism never had a chance.

"Oh. My. God."

The hellphone rang. And rang. Ahazat finally picked it up.

"Yeah?"

"Ahazat, what did you just do?" Matkalak's voice sounded strange. Even for Matkalak.

"I don't know," Ahazat said, though he was pretty sure he did know.

"Well, whatever you did, you've done it. They're coming."

"Who's coming?"

"Guess."

"Oh," Ahazat said, and that was all. He hung up.

Martha stood in the closet doorway, looking down at him. Not angry, not happy, just looking.

"Hi, Michael," she said. "I'm home."

"Martha, are you nuts?"

Martha shrugged. "Possibly. The wave function hasn't collapsed yet."

Ahazat—he was still having trouble thinking of himself as Michael—frowned. "Wave function?"

"I stole the term from Quantum Mechanics. All possible outcomes of an experiment are equally valid until the observer notes *one* outcome. Then all the others go away. In mathematical terms, the wave function has collapsed."

"This is not an experiment; you've put yourself in incredible danger, and you don't seem to realize it! You just don't sign a pact with Hell out of nostalgia!"

Her mouth set in a hard line. "Don't pretend to know my reasons, Michael Dunn. And I didn't sign a pact with Hell, remember? I signed it with *you*."

"A technicality. Look, we don't have much time. There are some very nasty beings on their

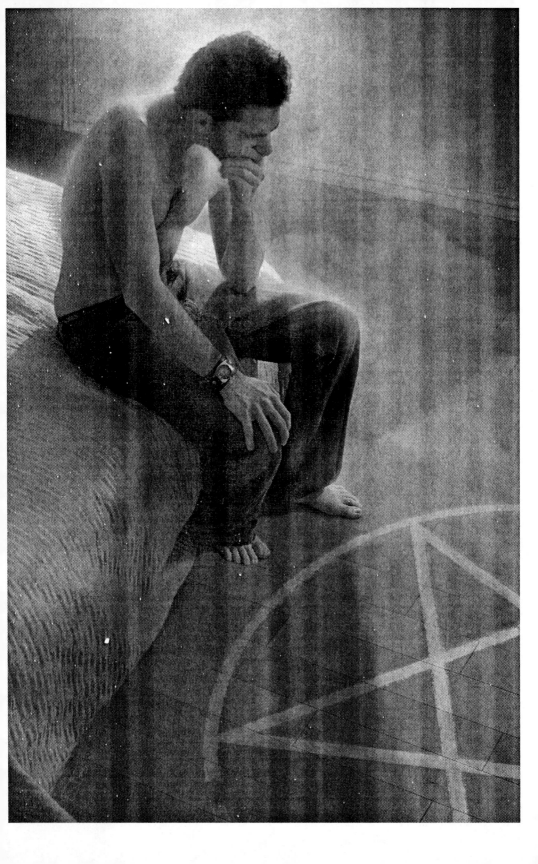

way here and I'm not sure what's going to happen. I do know that it won't be pleasant for either of us. So, if you don't mind, I have a couple of questions."

"Fine."

"How did you know . . . where I was?"

"We had a fight. You were drunk and confused and you said a lot of things that you meant at the time. Then you walked in front of a truck. It didn't take a genius to know you wouldn't be hobnobbing with the Almighty anytime soon."

"I killed myself?"

"Not consciously, deliberately, but deep down at that moment I think you wanted to die. You never quite learned how to be happy, Michael. I hoped I could teach you, but we ran out of time."

Ahazat reached out and put his hands on her shoulders. She brushed his left hand with her cheek. "Is that what this is about?" he asked.

"Among other things. So. Aren't you the least bit curious as to how I found you?"

"Now that you mention it."

Martha led him over to the computer. She punched in a code and a long column of text came up on the screen.

"Your demon name is just a random collection of letters; did you know that?"

He frowned. "I thought it was Aramaic."

"It just sounds like it; it doesn't mean anything. Doubtless the sheer number of you dictated this sort of naming convention; it took a while to track down the right combination."

"So you used a database? Just like—" he stopped.

"Like yours, you mean?" Martha tapped out another command, and her column was replaced by one more familiar. Martha's subverted expectations, tabulated and cross-referenced by table.

"You knew?"

"I'm an IT consultant, silly. Of course I knew. Or rather, I assumed you'd do something of the sort. Drawing inferences from raw data was a specialty of yours. You were always the intuitive one. Of course, my methodical nature came in handy when I was tracking you down." She brought up the column of names again. 'Ahazat' showed up about fifteen down on the column. "First, I had to learn the spells to summon just the names, and then correlate those with creation date. I had to be precise, there."

Ahazat shook his head. "There wasn't enough data. You couldn't be sure!"

"And I wasn't. Not until I saw your signature on the contract."

"My handwriting . . ."

"Bingo. If I hadn't recognized it, I wouldn't have signed the contract. And I'd have gone on to the next demon on the list. Simple."

"But . . . this is all pointless!"

"Not to me, Michael."

He shook his head. "Ahazat. I'm a demon now, remember? Nothing's changed. I thought I was being so clever, but apparently I did exactly what you expected me to do. I've violated the contract, so it's no longer binding."

"Not exactly."

The whiff of sulfur came too late for warning. The looming shapes appeared one after the other and when the materialization was done, two large and ugly creatures stood in the center of Martha's bedroom. No human forms for them; they weren't trying to pass as anything other than what they were—demons, and rather nasty ones at that. The one who had appeared first looked at Martha and licked his thick, rubbery lips, like a gourmet anticipating his next meal.

"Um . . . Infernal Relevance? I'll go quietly," Ahazat said.

"Only at first," said the demon. He was distinct from his companion only in that he was just a skosh bigger and uglier. "Later, I imagine you'll both be making quite a bit of noise."

Martha stood up. "So you came for me, too?"

"Of course," said the second. "Not our primary target, which is this misfit. You're dessert. So to speak."

Ahazat shook his head. "No."

They both stared at him as if they couldn't quite believe what they had heard. "No? Pipsqueak, for that alone I should blast you."

"You're going to do that anyway. Listen, I'm not thrilled about it, but I breached the contract, and so it's null and void. You have no claim on Martha! The contract is paramount. Even Infernal Relevance doesn't muck with Legal!"

"Fool," said the first. "Do you actually think we'd come here without clearing it with Legal? What do you think took us so long?!"

"But . . . I don't understand," Ahazat said.

"There's a shock," said the second.

"I think I do," Martha said, and the Infernal Relevance agents turned their full attention on her.

Ahazat felt his heart sinking in despair. "Martha, don't make it worse—"

She pulled away from him and went to stand before the two demons, right at the circle's edge. "It's Addendum C, Paragraph 2, isn't it? The Bad Faith Clause."

Number two nodded. "You should have seen their faces when Legal finally spotted it. I don't know why you'd pull such a stunt, lady, but it's going to cost you. A lot."

"What are you talking about?!" Ahazat asked.

"They mean that the deal was impossible from the start," Martha said. "I had two sets of expectations: one for Ahazat the Demon. One for Michael. Many—not all—were contradictory. It was impossible to subvert them all."

Ahazat finally understood. Entering into a contract in bad faith was as good as breeching it. In Infernal Law, the penalty was clear: contract conditions were immediately binding and permanent. "Martha's soul belonged to me from the moment she signed the contract."

She turned toward him and smiled wistfully. "It always did, Michael. Even before that."

"And *you* belong to us," said number one. "So let's get down to business . . . oh, get up! Groveling won't help."

Ahazat crawled across the floor on his hands and knees and bowed at the edge of the circle.

"As my friend said, that won't help at all," said number two. "In fact, it rather reinforces your image as a victim, which is not really one you'd want to emphasize."

Ahazat did not rise. He did not look at them.

"Perhaps you didn't hear me," said number one, flexing his long black claws. "I said stop groveling!" He lashed out at Ahazat only to snatch his hand away, yowling in pain.

Ahazat sat back on his heels. "Who's groveling?"

The red chalk was in his hand, and the three-inch gap in the open circle had disappeared. The circle was complete, and the two demons were standing right in the middle of it.

"Gotcha."

Number two swore an oath that made Ahazat's ears sting, then unleashed a torrent of hellfire directly at him. It struck the barrier and rebounded. The two demons lost all interest in both Ahazat and Martha as they danced and yowled and slapped at the sparks and glowing cinders that the backblast had forced under their scales.

"Tacete!" Ahazat commanded and they both fell silent, though they continued to worry at the embers. Ahazat stood up and took Martha's hand. "That'll hold them, but we've got to get out of here. Maybe in time we can think of a way—"

Martha didn't move. "It's ok, Michael. We don't need to go. They do."

Ahazat shook his head. "It doesn't *matter* that these two are in the circle. Nothing's changed; there's a lot more of them in Hell and you're still forfeit!"

She nodded, smiling. "Yes. To you."

"Same thing. I belong to them!"

"No," she said. "You don't. If you don't believe me, ask them yourself." Martha looked at the confined demons. "Isn't that right?"

The demons just glared at her, and she smiled.

"Oh, right. Michael?"

It took Ahazat a moment to remember the Latin. "Um . . . Dicete."

They were still silently glaring. Martha sighed. "No point being tricksy, now. You're in the circle. You have to tell him the truth."

"Well, truth is a matter of opinion . . ." began number one.

"Facts, then," Martha said. "Fact: Michael's bond with Hell was growing tenuous. That's the real reason you came, isn't it? It wasn't about me at all, was it?"

"Yes to the first, and no to the second. We were sent to investigate," said number two, reluctantly.

"Matkalak warned me about that," Ahazat said. "Do you know what it means?" He directed the last at the two demons, but they kept silent. "Answer me!"

"They don't know," Martha said. "But I do."

Now they were all looking at her. She sighed. "It's simple: Michael may have been a morose sort, but there was one thing that made him happy: working on a problem with no apparent solution. I provided just such a problem. Fess up, Michael—searching, pondering, gathering information, trying to break the contract without breaking the contract . . . wasn't it fun?"

"Yes," Ahazat said. He was beginning to get used to Martha using his old name, even if he didn't quite feel as if he really owned it now. "But how does that . . . ?"

Martha sighed. "Michael, since when can a truly happy person be in Hell?"

"Damn."

Someone swore. Maybe it was Ahazat. Maybe all three demons present.

Ahazat shook his head. "I'll grant you that one, yet Matkalak said my signal strength was just weak. There was one point when it went away."

"When was that?" Martha asked.

"When I spent the night sleeping in your bed," Ahazat said. He actually blushed.

"Well," Martha said, smiling, "maybe there are two things that can make you happy."

"I think I'm going to be sick," number one said, and number two agreed.

"Not on my floor," Martha said firmly.

Ahazat shook his head. "But I *died*, Martha. I went to hell. They made me a demon. How can I be free of it?"

"You almost weren't. There was still one thing missing besides the problem, and I couldn't provide that. You did, Michael." Martha turned to the captured agents of Infernal Relevance. "Will you tell him or shall I?"

"I don't care what they say, Martha. You tell me," Ahazat said. "Please?"

Subversion Clause

"Free will. No demon has free will; that's why it's safe for Hell to sign the pacts that gives the victim's soul to the demon in the first place. A demon, having no choice, will hand the soul over once it's forfeit. Yet you completed the circle, Michael. You tried to protect me. That was sweet, but why you did it doesn't matter; what does matter is that you made a free choice. No demon does that. No demon can."

Ahazat didn't need to ask the demons in the circle. He knew she was telling the truth. "What now?"

Martha shrugged. "You completed the circle, not me. That's really up to you."

Ahazat turned back to the circle.

"Look, Ahazat," said number one. "You're in enough trouble. If you'll just come quietly—"

Ahazat smiled. "I'm not the one in trouble. I imagine you'll find that out when you get back."

It was a little hard to tell because skin color didn't show well through scales, but Ahazat was pretty sure numbers one and two had both just turned a little pale. Ahazat thought of all the possibilities, even the one that might return him to Hell in triumph. He wondered if that fit in with Martha's expectation, but only for a moment. He didn't bother with Latin this time. As a beginner demon, his language skills weren't very good, and he wanted to make certain there were no misunderstandings at all. He faced the circle.

"My name is Michael Dunn. By the Power vested in me by this mystic circle, I declare you two officially and legally screwed. Go to Hell," he said, "and stay there."

And, because as demons they really had no choice, they obeyed.

Michael finally found his voice again. He'd been too busy hugging and kissing Martha to use it for a very long time. "I asked it before, I'll ask it again: are you nuts?"

She propped up on one elbow. "Why?"

"Don't you realize what might have happened to you?"

"Still might," she said. "My life's not over yet. Lots of potential for mistakes there."

"You know what I mean!"

She sighed. "Would it surprise you to know that I kept a piece of red chalk in my pocket the whole time? I'm not crazy, Michael. Reckless, maybe."

"Going up against Hell itself? It was *damned* reckless, and almost literally. Listen, my love: you may be smart, and brave, but lots of smart and brave people have come to ruin over the years doing what you did! How—"

Martha put her finger across Michael's lips, silencing him for the moment. "It's not about being smart, or brave, or sneaky, or anything of the sort. It is about giving a damn."

He blushed then. "Even so . . ."

"I knew the risks, Michael. I accepted them. Not unlike the day we got married."

He sighed. "I remember something about 'till death do us part.'"

Martha grinned. "Another technicality."

Michael lay back on the bed, wallowing in the bliss. After a while he said, "I hate to ask, but what do we do now? I'm out of Hell, but I'm not quite human either. I did die, you know. Or is that another technicality?"

Martha shrugged. "You can't stay here forever," she admitted. "We have to get you the rest of the way, if you know what I mean. Getting you out of Hell was only Phase One."

"What's Phase Two?"

"I think it's called 'Life.'" She kissed him. "We'll work on it."

Love's Consequence
Rhonda Mason

The streets of Boston were relatively quiet at 2 a.m. Not surprising, considering it was January and the wind howled along ice-slicked sidewalks. Raine kept to the shadows as she strode down Boylston Street. The dead of night, and she was restless.

As usual.

A dark shape swooped from the roof of the Palace Theater and glided toward her. The garish light of the theater signs reflected off red scales. Any normal person would have run. Raine kept walking.

The creature landed with an indelicate thud beside her—she didn't stop, but a scream rose in her throat.

Keep walking, just keep walking.

"Raine." Its thunder voice uncoiled and wrapped around her. Against her will she slowed.

"Leave me alone." She put one foot in front of the other, striving for forward momentum, but she felt the irresistible pull. Fight though she did, her path angled toward the buildings until she came to an alleyway. He forced her into it without laying a hand on her.

The frozen air stuck in her lungs. For a minute, the hammering of her heart drowned out even her labored breathing. Then she forced her panic down and turned to face the mouth of the alley.

He was a silhouette with the street light behind him, nothing visible but the glowing embers of his eyes. Even so, she could still picture him—every gruesome detail. Though she'd seen him but twice in her life, once as a child and once a month before, she knew she'd never forget the demon, Goran. Her fingers curled in on themselves.

"I have refused you twice, I will do so again," she said as best she could through chattering teeth.

"Oh, I don't think so."

She heard the smile in his voice. He walked past her, deeper into the alley, studying the snow-covered refuse and buildings like a prospective home buyer.

Raine eyed the open end of the alley.

So close.

But paradoxically far.

She didn't have any illusions about escaping. Goran would leave when he was through with her, and not a moment before. Until then, he'd trapped her as effectively as if he'd bound her in chains.

Goran left off pretending to study the alley and speared her with a glance. She met his gaze, but immediately flinched away from the delighted malice she saw there.

Foul creature.

Molest me and be done with it.

She shook with the memory of the last time he'd visited her. In her bedroom. At this same hour. The shiver intensified.

"My little Raine is chilled?" Goran's lips stretched in smile, red flesh pulled taut across gleaming fangs. "Here, a fire to heat you up."

He waved one scaly hand and a pillar of flame, the height of a man, rose up from the ground to his right. The heat of it scorched her face but she refused to look.

It couldn't be.

Please.

"She makes a lovely addition to my collection, don't you think?" Goran gestured toward the flame.

His movement forced her to glance in that direction. Somewhere deep within her mind she'd known what she'd see—her twin sister Sunne, writhing in silent agony amid the demon's flames.

Her gaze went back to the demon, a slightly less torturous sight than her sister's pain. She'd stare at him forever if it would erase what she'd just seen.

Trapped.

He had her now—and he knew it.

Fucking hellspawn.

She took a breath of the crystalline air, then another. Her blood burned like the demon's fire, even while guilt fell upon her like a blow from heaven. She forced another icy breath into her lungs. Somewhere on the street a taxi rolled by, tires crunching on crusted slush. The driver might glance down the alley, but she knew he'd see nothing. The demon was invisible unless he desired otherwise. She'd learned that the hard way.

Surrender set in, deadening her.

"Whatever you want, I'll do it."

"That I don't doubt. But perhaps I want to keep her." His low, rough-velvet voice rose the hair on her arms through her jacket. "She's almost as delectable as her sister."

Raine refused to be baited. "I know you have a bargain for me, Goran; you wouldn't have come here otherwise."

"Perhaps I brought her here simply to gloat." The demon released a steamy breath that even the frigid air couldn't cool.

That breath on her face, the stench of blood—it was seared into her memory.

Goran lifted a hand and stroked Sunne's cheek through the flames. She screamed, a silent scream that nonetheless pierced Raine's heart.

"Are you so small a being that you need a mere mortal's validation for your coup?"

The demon's smile disappeared. His black leathery wings rustled, arching slightly before folding back into position.

"I thought not." It was her turn to smile, though her stomach roiled. Bile rose to the back of her throat as Sunne turned pleading eyes on her.

Help me, Raine. I would do the same for you.

The demon growled, an earthquake of sound. He continued to stroke her sister's cheek and Raine kept herself from charging across the space between them and ripping his scaly arm away by the sheerest strength of will.

She didn't ask why he had done this. Why did a demon do anything? Because he could. But why hadn't he simply trapped Sunne and moved on? Why involve her? If what he'd told her long ago was true, the energy he could drain from Sunne's captured soul would feed him for months. What more did he want?

He turned his burning gaze on Raine once more. The terror she'd felt the first time he'd come with an offer of power returned. She couldn't forget for one instant what Goran was.

A demon. Dedicated wholly to serving his Dark Mistress and Her twisted whims.

How did Raine, who had refused Goran's offer of power more than once, fit into Her schemes?

"You're right of course, I care not one whit for your precious Sunne." Goran advanced on Raine with the intentness of a predator. "Except that she provides such delicious . . . leverage."

"Tell me what you want and be done with it."

He *tsked*.

Raine's temper snapped. "Cut the shit. You know I'll agree to whatever twisted bargain you've concocted."

"I know." Goran's ember eyes flared. "That's the beauty of it. At last, Raine the Righteous is forced to bargain with a demon." His laugh was a scrape of nails across slate. "This is too precious."

Raine the Righteous. What the hell did that mean?

She hadn't refused him out of righteousness, only self-preservation. She'd read enough accounts to know that the Devil, or Her demon, in this case, extracted a disproportionate payment for any power offered. Such as your soul.

But now the creature had her well and truly trapped. She would do anything to save her sister, and he knew it.

"Tell me what you want, Goran."

"It's quite simple, actually. I want Aryntir. Dead."

She raised a brow. "Aryntir?"

"A fellow demon of mine."

"What does that have to do with me?" Suspicion uncurled in her gut.

"I want you to kill him, and bring me his heart."

Her hands clenched tighter. "Demonic humor—funny. If you want me to switch places with my sister, I'll do it, but don't make me go on some futile mission before you steal my soul. Just take it now."

He seemed to consider it a moment. She didn't know what she wished for less: that he'd refuse her offer . . . or accept it.

"My dear Raine, you have so much to learn." His polished horns gleamed in the firelight. His scales flashed as he moved closer and she resisted the urge to step back. Barely.

"Why do you think I've been trying to persuade you to accept an offer of mine all these years? Because you're a powerless mortal I amuse myself with?" He scoffed, a sound like bones grinding together. "You have something the rest do not. An . . . ability, of sorts, that makes you more than human."

Lies.

She was human, no more, no less.

"Much more," he purred, as if he could hear her thoughts. "Though, still human. Sadly." His talons scratched the frozen pavement as he took another step toward her, and his fetid breath fanned across her face. He reeked of death. Of suffering. "You have the strength within you to kill Aryntir. With help. My help."

"Why not kill him yourself? Surely you are a better match for him."

"True. But my mistress has certain . . . rules against killing fellow demons." His lip curled in distaste. "Else I would not hesitate to end his pathetic existence."

She didn't doubt it. A feral light gleamed in his eyes. Her gaze flicked toward her sister.

Sunne screamed and clawed at her prison of flames while her skin burned endlessly. Raine asked the only question that truly mattered.

"How?"

She refused to consider what she was doing. It was the only way. Sunne would do the same, were their positions reversed. Still. The look of satisfaction on his face chilled her more than the New England weather.

He waved a clawed hand in the air and a dagger appeared from nowhere, hovering in front of her.

"Aryntir's own dagger. The only weapon capable of killing him."

She didn't bother to ask how he'd come by it. She didn't care. She felt tired, impossibly heavy, and so terribly alone. She knew without a doubt this mission would be the death of her, one way or the other. But it didn't matter. What was her death compared to the torture her sister now endured?

She reached out and gripped the golden handle of the dagger. The warm metal fit her hand perfectly. She glanced at the snakes etched on the blade before shoving the thing into her belt.

"Two questions. How will I know him, and how will I get close enough to use the dagger?"

"Smart girl. I knew you'd accept."

"How could I not?" *Damn him.*

She nearly laughed at her choice of words. Clearly, she was the one who'd been damned.

"I shall point him out to you. As for how you'll get close to him . . ." Goran frowned. "That should be easy. The fool has developed a fascination with you. One might even say he's fallen in love with you."

The breath left Raine's body in a rush. "What?"

He nodded. "It's true. Our Aryntir spends entirely too much time among the mortals. And with one in particular. You. He's been following you like a shadow for years. You couldn't feel it?"

She shook her head. Horror crowded in, threatened to smother her. She'd attracted the lust of a demon?

"So. Do we have a deal? Aryntir's life for Sunne's soul?" Goran extended his hand, crimson palm upward.

Raine took a frantic look at Sunne. This was happening too fast. For the briefest of moments, she hesitated.

It was Raine's fault her sister was there.

My fault.

She laid her palm atop his, wincing as his flesh seared hers.

"I accept."

The familiar hum of voices did nothing to soothe her nerves as Raine sat near a window at Café Olin. Somehow, eating at her favorite restaurant with hellspawn for company just didn't seem right.

"You said he would be here," she muttered as she studied the bundled-up passersby. No doubt the people at the next table thought her insane, talking to herself.

"Patience." Goran sat across the table from her, invisible to all but her. Still, he had adopted a human appearance. But even if she didn't know he was a demon, she would have known he wasn't human. For one thing, he didn't sweat, and they had cranked up the heat in the restaurant.

It had felt good when she first entered from the frigid evening air. Now it smothered her. For the first time since winter began, she was glad that obscenely short skirts were in style this season. She shuddered to think of the ankle-length wool skirt she had almost worn. Sweat trickled between her breasts.

"Nice display," Goran murmured, staring at her expanse of bare leg.

His gaze felt like the hand of a corpse caressing her leg. So much for being hot.

"Ah. There's our quarry now."

Raine stiffened.

It begins.

She turned in the direction Goran indicated, scanned the sidewalk on the other side of the street. The usual black Audis and yellow H2s crawled past as she studied the people gathered there. She saw bankers, college students, families, and homeless mingling in front of the Barnes and Noble despite the frigid air, but no demons. She glanced quizzically back at Goran, who nodded at the intersecting street.

There.

A single man rounded the corner, the collar on his black floor-length duster pulled up to his ears. Even from across the way she could tell he was tall, powerful; solitary. He wore his sleek black hair in a topknot and the light from the streetlamps sparkled off his golden skin.

No.

She couldn't see from this distance, but she knew his ears would be pointed, knew his irises would be black. Knew his scarred hands would feel like satin on her bare skin, and his kiss would taste of power and blood.

She knew this man. *Demon*, her mind corrected.

"No." She shook her head. "It can't be."

Goran gave her an odd look. "Is there something I should know?"

She ignored him, eyes riveted on her lover's face. The one who came to her only in dreams, the one she thought she'd imagined. The one who'd stolen her heart years ago.

The one she had to kill.

"No." Raine shook herself. "No, there's nothing you should know." She tore her gaze from her lover with effort.

Goran's ember eyes burned in his unnatural peach face as he studied her. Apparently satisfied, he stood and flexed the wings he hadn't bothered to hide.

"You have one week."

Then he was gone.

She turned back to see her lover studying her from across the street, the sole stationary object in a shifting sea of people. She finally had a name to go with her beloved's face.

Aryntir.

Raine signaled the waiter, a young man with an over-eager smile, and paid him for her drink. "But you haven't ordered yet."

She ignored him as she rose on unsteady legs. Her world reeled, but a creeping numbness settled inside her. She strode from the café and hailed a cab.

He beat her home.

He stood in the living room of the modest apartment on Commonwealth Ave that she shared with Sunne.

Waiting.

For her.

She pretended she still couldn't see him. How many times had he been here with her, during her waking hours, and she hadn't known?

She felt his eyes on her as she flipped through the mail, felt his hungry gaze slide down the length of her bare legs. A shiver coursed through her and she clamped her teeth against it. Affecting nonchalance, she tossed her keys on the counter and opened the freezer. With her hand balanced on a lower shelf, she kept her legs straight and bent slowly at the waist. Inch by inch she bared her thighs to him as she leaned over the shelf, ostensibly fishing for a chilled glass.

The trick worked as well in real life as it did in her dreams.

One second he was across the room, the next he was directly behind her, radiating heat. Armed with the knowledge that he was truly real, she could feel his essence in the kitchen with her for the first time. Felt his skin against hers as he slid his palm up the back of her bare thigh. Heard his short, tight breaths. Smelled the arousal racing through him.

This close, he overwhelmed her senses.

Before the rising tide of desire could drown her, she straightened and slammed the freezer door shut. She spun and caught his gaze lingering on her breasts before he raised it to her face. In silence she met his eyes, held them a minute before breathing his name.

"Aryntir."

He froze. Every inch of his golden skin tensed and his ebony gaze bored into her. He held himself motionless, as if by not moving he might avoid detection.

Raine didn't look away, didn't blink. She held his stare and said his name again, with more conviction. What she wouldn't give to keep a picture of the stunned look on her lover's face in that instant. Desire quickly replaced amusement. This close, he was sexy. Exquisite. Unnaturally so, and now she knew why.

She reached a tentative hand toward his face, not surprised to find her fingers shaking. Lightly, as though one touch would ruin the illusion, she skimmed her fingertips down his cheek. He flinched, golden lids dropping closed.

"You're real." The words rose unbidden to her lips. Bittersweet tears stung her eyes. She wasn't crazy. The man she loved—had loved for years—*did* exist.

And he was a demon. A tormentor of man.

Her heart squeezed and she couldn't draw breath. He was a demon. Her brain refused to acknowledge it, no matter how many times she said it. Or perhaps it was her heart that resisted.

His eyes drifted open, searched hers.

She brushed her fingertips across his skin again, this time lingering on his full lips. His eyes began to glow and his tongue flicked out to tease the pad of her finger.

Then he was crushing her to the refrigerator, his mouth locked on hers, his hands everywhere. She felt cool air on her backside as he hiked her skirt to her waist, only to be burned a moment later by the heat of his palms on her bare flesh.

The breath sighed out of her when he finally broke the kiss.

"Aryntir."

His eyes were fierce, possessive.

"I've waited so long to hear you say that."

Then he pulled her to the floor, and the time for words passed.

The nights slid by too quickly after that.

Their passion was fierce, and Raine woke each morning with a satiated smile and a cold hollow in her heart. Though she did her best to ignore it, reality slammed into her at dawn when Aryntir took his reluctant leave and she felt under the mattress for the gold-handled dagger hidden there.

A week.

She had two days left. Two days in which to save her sister by murdering her lover, or to doom her sister to eternal torment.

Raine peeled herself out of bed. She smiled at the sight of her torn garter belt and corset on the floor. She'd thought Aryntir would like them—and he had. Which meant they were unwearable now. Just as quick as the smile came the tears, and the bittersweet lump that rose in her throat. Raine slumped to the floor as the room blurred.

Why?

Why did it happen like this?

It was too much coincidence to stomach.

She lowered her head to her knees and sobbed. Cried for all the 'what-ifs' that could never be, cried for her sister's torment. Her sobs turned to screams of rage as she pictured Goran sitting across the table from her at Olin's. He knew. He had to. He set the whole thing up. She screamed her throat raw while tears burned her eyes. As if anger alone could stop the relentless flow of time, the inevitability of events.

There had to be a way. *Had* to.

At last she quieted.

Even memories of Aryntir's whispered words of love were no comfort now. He loved her. And she would betray him. She knew that with certainty.

It was her fault her sister had been captured by Goran in the first place. If Raine had accepted his last offer, none of this would have happened. Sunne never would have suffered. It would be Raine writhing in the flames, and she'd never have to feel the pain of betraying her only love.

She hugged her knees to her chest and wished for the past to change. For the present to change. For anything to change. She wished for death. Wished a god she'd never respected would strike her dead, so she wouldn't have to choose between Aryntir and her twin sister.

This was her punishment.

She knew that now.

Raine leaned back against the bed and conjured up the evening one month ago that set this whole nightmare in motion. Sunne had been gang raped by her boyfriend and his roommates. Brutally.

Raine remembered the helpless anger that had burned white hot within her when Sunne came home that night, glassy-eyed and silent. After a listless account of the incident, Sunne had allowed herself to be put to bed, but Raine knew she didn't sleep.

Raine couldn't sleep either.

As she lay in her bed in the dark, Goran appeared before her as he had all those years ago, and offered her the strength she needed to avenge her sister. Offered her his powers to extract vengeance from the cock-suckers who had hurt her sister.

Raine had refused.

She of all people knew the price for the deal he offered. Had seen their mother pay it. Raine wanted nothing more than to beat all three men to death with a baseball bat, then bring them back to life and tear them apart with her bare hands, but she'd said no. If she'd known Sunne was at the door, listening, she would have accepted the offer in a heartbeat; to keep her twin from it.

Instead, Goran found a willing soul in Sunne, who traded her life for the chance to make her attackers pay. And pay they did. Raine had seen the pictures. Blood splattered from ceiling to floor, and not a whole body part in sight.

His half of the bargain fulfilled, Goran collected the debt owed him.
Sunne.
Raine pounded a fist against her knee.
"Damnit, Sunne!"
There was nothing else to say. Her puffy eyes drifted closed and Raine sought the oblivion of a sleep that wouldn't come.

Raine lay awake in the dead of night, listening to Aryntir's gentle snores beside her.
So like a man's, and yet—
There was an otherworldly quality about even that mundane sound that marked him as more than human. As if his golden skin, black irises and mild fangs didn't do that already. She rolled onto her stomach and her arm draped over the edge of the bed.

Her body ached in all the right places. The tang of sweat and sex still hung in the air. And beneath her, tucked between the mattress and the frame, lay the golden-hilted dagger destined for her lover's heart. For a wild second she considered drawing the dagger and plunging it into her own heart. But that wouldn't save Sunne.

Would anything save Sunne now?

Even if Raine could bring herself to kill Aryntir, would Sunne ever be the same after the rape, the use of dark powers to rend men to shreds, and her time as Goran's prisoner? What kind of life awaited her sister now? Would Sunne even want to live?

Deep in her heart, Raine acknowledged that all she was really buying her sister was a death without torment. She didn't doubt that Sunne would end her life once Goran released her. All she could do was free her sister from the pain.

It was worth it.

Wasn't it?

She turned her head to gaze at Aryntir's sleeping form.

Wasn't it?

Her heart twisted within her breast. Doubt threatened to drown her in uncertainty. Her fingers grazed the pommel of the dagger and she yanked it from its hiding place. No more doubts. No more waiting. This ended. Now. For Sunne.

The warm metal hilt was alive in her hands, vibrating with each beat of her pounding heart. With the image of her sister writhing in the trap of Goran's flames fixed firmly in her mind, Raine rose up on her knees and drew the dagger overhead.

Would it hurt?

Would he bleed?

She swung the blade down without another thought.

Aryntir's eyes flashed open in that instant and the blade paused scant inches from his heart. How she'd stopped the furious downward arc she didn't know, but there she was, held motionless by the look in his eyes. She gripped the dagger and bit back tears. This had to be done. Had to. He'd understand.

He had to.

He reached out slowly. His gentle hand cradled the fingers wrapped around the hilt. Stroked them in a loving caress. He didn't say a word. Didn't have to. A single question shone in his eyes.

Why?

"Aryntir—" She choked on the name. Sobs tore through her. She loosed her grip on the weapon, releasing it to him. "I—" Words wouldn't come. In their place was the helpless wail she'd been fighting back all night. It clawed at her throat.

Then he was holding her. Pressing her to his bare chest as she cried burning tears. He murmured her name, stroked her hair, and she cried all the harder.

"Hush, love."

He held her until her tears were spent. Until she was spent. She was hollow, empty. A shell. She was already dead.

"Where did you get this?" His voice held no anger, no accusation, just a detached curiosity.

"Your dagger? I—"

"That's not mine."

She pulled away to look at him, at the frown on his face. He gestured with one hand and an ebony blade appeared from nowhere.

"This is mine. That looks like. . . ." He studied the snake markings on the other blade. "Goran." He spat the word out. His face took on a grim cast and for the first time since she'd met him, he inspired a frisson of fear within her. "That's Goran's blade. How did you get it?" He dropped both knives and gripped her shoulders.

"Raine. Where did you get it?"

She looked into his eyes, saw anger there. And fear. Fear for her.

"How did you get it?" He shook her lightly. "Tell me you didn't bargain with him. Please."

She dropped her head in a nod. Tired. So tired now.

"Oh sweetheart." His voice broke. "Why?"

How could this be? He woke up to find her trying to kill him, but he still worried about her? In that instant, Raine hated her sister for forcing the situation on her. *Damn you for being so selfish, Sunne.*

Guilt immediately followed. It wasn't Sunne's fault. If Raine had gone after those guys like any sister should have done. . . .

"Raine."

Her gaze snapped back to Aryntir's. "My sister. He has Sunne." The story spilled out of her in a monotone voice she didn't recognize as her own. She felt emptier than before.

"He wants your heart," she finished. "Because of me." She gazed into his bottomless eyes. "Because you love me."

Aryntir let fly a string of guttural words in a language she'd never heard him speak. A thought struck a spark of anger within her.

"The dagger's his?"

He nodded but didn't stop cursing Goran.

"Then it was all a joke. A sham. I never could have killed you anyway." A fire burned up the emptiness inside her. A week of torturing herself, of hoping for her sister's release even while morning the soon-to-come death of her lover. All for nothing. The tears, the heartache, the pain. For nothing. "He just wanted to watch me try."

Shameful relief flooded through her as she realized the choice had been taken away from her. She wouldn't have to choose between them.

Coward.

They sat together in silence.

The pink fingers of dawn had curled over the window sill before Aryntir finally spoke.

"You can still kill me with that blade."

Raine froze, unwilling to hear.

"Goran's blade will work as well on me as it would on him."

"But—how?"

An empty chuckle escaped him. "Goran is my brother. We share the same heritage. Either of our daggers would shed our blood, no matter who wields it." He took a deep breath. "Even a mortal."

Her head felt stuffed with wool, the wheels tangling and grinding in her head. "Brothers? But you look nothing alike."

"And you're a demon expert now?" He chuckled, again a dry, humorless sound. "Trust me. Though I might wish otherwise, Goran and I are of the same blood."

Grinding.

Whirring.

Wait—

"But that means. . . ." She could barely breathe for fear of breaking the tenuous strand of hope that spun outward from her heart. "He's given me the way to defeat him. I can kill him. With his own dagger."

Aryntir stared at her for a whole minute.

"No."

"But—"

"No." His lips tightened and he gave a sharp shake of his head. "It's too dangerous."

"It's worth it."

"No, Raine." He grabbed her hand as she reached for the dagger. He threaded slender fingers through hers and brought her hand to his lips. "You mustn't risk it." He brushed a kiss across her skin. "You can't."

"I could save Sunne, and we could still be together. That's worth everything." Though she tried to tamp it down, the hope spun out of control, building. It gripped her with a frenzy. "Everything."

He shook his head, sadness in his eyes. "You would leave Sunne trapped."

Raine didn't want to listen. "If she's tied to him, she should be free when he dies."

"You don't know Goran, not like I do. He's spiteful. He may have tied Sunne to the Mistress already. If that's the case, he's the only one who can free her. If you kill him . . ."

"Sunne stays trapped forever."

He squeezed her hand. "There's only once choice."

"No." She fought against the death of hope. "Maybe he hasn't given her to the Mistress, maybe he kept her. Maybe—"

He silenced her with a kiss that tasted of love and goodbye. She clung to him, refused the truth he offered.

"What if I—"

"Hush, love. You know what you have to do." He kissed her again, and Raine could feel him slipping from her with each passing moment. He finally broke the kiss, his breathing ragged. He pressed his forehead to hers. "Sunne is worth everything to you; you're worth everything to me."

He reached back and retrieved his dagger from the bed. He pressed the ebony hilt into her hand. She would have tossed it away if he had not wrapped his fingers around hers on the handle. He brought the tip to his chest.

"I never thought you would know I was real. Never dreamed I could hold you while you were awake and hear you say my name. That's more than I ever deserved." He forced her hand toward him and a trickle of blood ran down his chest. "Much more."

"How can you say that?" she whispered. "I love you."

"Raine—I'm a demon. If you knew half of the things I've done—no, a third—you would hate me more than you hate Goran."

"It's not possible."

He closed his eyes and his head sank forward an inch. "It's true, love. The things the Mistress has forced me to do, made me do against my will . . ." He sighed. "Believe me, death would be a blessing. I can never atone for what I've done." He opened his eyes and the bleakness she saw there spoke to her heart. "I am what I am. A demon. I can't change that."

He squeezed her hand.

"I can't escape it. I've tried to forget, tried to hide, tried to deny, but always the Mistress finds me. And always I am forced to—" He broke off and for that Raine was thankful. She couldn't bear to think of Aryntir as anything like Goran.

"Save me from it." He leaned into the blade.

"Wait!" Her hand trembled but she knew he was right. "We have one more day. He gave me a week." She silently begged him to listen. "Let me have one more day with you."

The blood flowed while she waited. She didn't breathe until he finally nodded and released his grip on her hand. She threw the dagger away from her and held out her arms for him.

He came to her with a rush of desire so hot it threatened to burn her alive.

When she awoke in the late afternoon he was gone. She'd expected as much. He'd left her alone for some hours everyday of this last week. She didn't want to know where he went, what he did. Didn't want to remember that Aryntir was a demon, Goran's brother. She only wanted him to return to her.

Raine sat in the wicker chair in her bedroom by the window, clad only in her silk robe. She stared sightlessly at the black blade where it had landed on the floor. Aryntir's blade. His death. Shadows crept across the carpet as afternoon settled to evening, and evening turned to night.

She expected anger. Pain. Desperation. A gnawing helplessness. Instead, she felt nothing. She was well and truly dead now.

It would all be over tonight.

She knew what she had to do and she would do it. She'd made that decision sometime during the long afternoon. A sense of inevitability, of peace almost, hung in the room.

The stars came out before he returned. He said nothing, just stood there, watching her. She returned his gaze, struggled to memorize every nuance about him. As if she could ever forget.

She didn't know how long they remained locked together like that. It didn't matter. She only knew that his voice was like the tolling of bells when he finally spoke.

"It's time." Aryntir picked up the blade and carried it to her. He knelt at her feet. "I would do it myself and spare you the pain, but then you won't have fulfilled your end of the bargain, and Goran would own you as well as Sunne."

He ran the back of his hand along her cheek. "My beloved." He smiled at her in a way no one ever had, and feeling returned in a rush.

Not this man, not her love.

She couldn't do it.

"You must."

Again he held her hand with the weapon in it, brought it to his chest, to the wound she'd made early that morning.

Tears leaked from the corners of her eyes and he reached up with his free hand to brush them away.

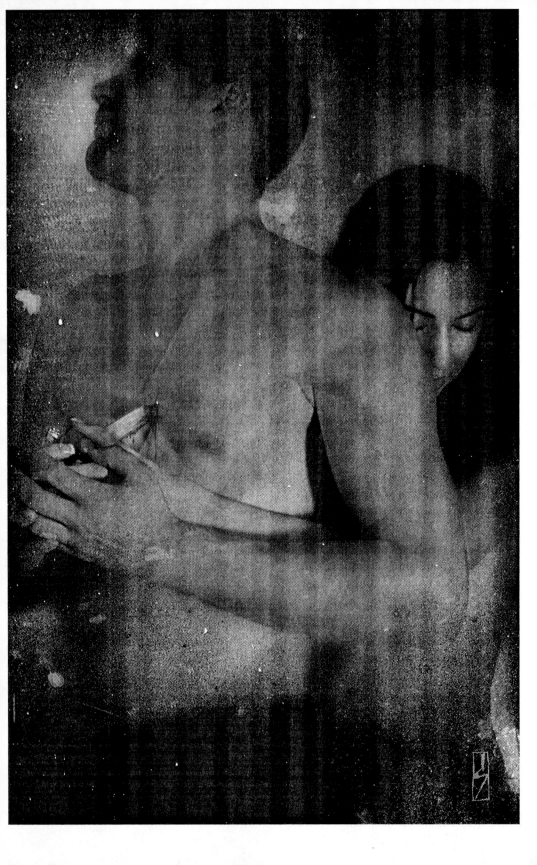

An acidic voice broke in on their private moment.

"Isn't this touching." Goran appeared in the corner of her bedroom. The pillar of flame that held her sister accompanied him and the firelight glinted off his red scales. He leered, revealing fangs. "How fitting, Brother, to find you kneeling at the feet of a mortal." He spat in Aryntir's general direction. "Weakling."

Aryntir said nothing. He hadn't even glanced away from Raine's face. "Do it."

"Yes, by all means," Goran said. "Don't let me interrupt." He fell back on Raine's bed and propped his head on her pillows.

The crimson demon's presence in her bed overlaid a blissful week's worth of memories. Tainted them.

"Get the hell off my bed."

Goran said nothing, he just smiled broader and sighed.

She couldn't take it. He was ruining the very last memories she would ever have with Aryntir.

"I said get off!" She shot to her feet and sent the wicker chair flying behind her. Aryntir's knife handle bit into her hand as she gripped it like a lifeline.

"My, what atrocious manners." He *tsked* and crossed his powerful legs at the ankles.

Something inside her snapped and she crossed the room in two strides, staring down at the demon defiling her bed. Raine felt disconnected, severed from her body. Events slipped out of her control.

Goran swung his legs to the floor, talons tearing the carpet, and rose to his full eight-foot height. Black wings flared behind him and his ember eyes danced as he beckoned his prison of flame closer. Raine turned to see her sister.

Sunne's mouth was open in a scream Raine felt but couldn't hear. Sunne clawed at the walls of her fiery prison even as she twisted and bent in pain. If Raine had tears left to cry, she would have spent them on the sight. Instead, she turned to look at Aryntir, still kneeling where she left him.

The intense sadness stamped on his face struck her like a blow. He understood. Understood her pain and offered his own death to free her from it.

"It's time to decide, Raine the Righteous. Time to choose." Goran's delighted voice boomed in her head. "Your sister, or your demon lover."

She had to choose.

Damn him.

Damn them all!

Raine closed her eyes and forced her emotions down. She gripped Aryntir's dagger, centering herself. Preparing herself. Forced herself to make the choice she'd known all along she'd make.

There was only one way.

Her eyes opened with a snap.

"I'm sorry, Sunne."

She lurched forward and plunged the ebony dagger into Goran's chest to the hilt. Twisted it with all the strength she'd ever possessed. His startled eyes met hers as black blood spurted from the wound.

She waited.

For a second, nothing happened.

Then she heard laughter. A biting, contemptuous, mocking laughter. It came from Aryntir. She turned, incredulous, as he rose to his feet, still laughing.

"I told you," he said, when he'd caught his breath. "They do it every time."

Raine's gaze flashed back to Goran in time to catch his frown as he yanked the dagger from his chest. The wound closed before her eyes.

Aryntir's voice was triumphant. "Every time. Every single time. Foolish humans." He shook his head and walked over to where Goran stood grumbling.

"I swear, I thought I had this one," the red demon said.

"You say that every time. What's my record, ten million to none?" Aryntir's laugh made her skin crawl. "I told you. The damn creatures can't resist the lure of 'true love.'" The scorn in his voice hit her like a kick to the gut.

No.

Not Aryntir.

Not her Aryntir.

He loved her.

She watched as he grew, changed. His golden skin darkened to red. Leathery wings sprouted from his back as horns broke through the skin of his forehead and his eyes lit to embers.

Demon.

Goran's brother.

"Oh god."

Both demons chuckled at that. "I don't think he can save you now, sweetheart."

"NO!"

Aryntir's grin revealed fangs longer than Goran's. "So, what do I get this time? I want both girls." He eyed the oblivious Sunne. "They'll make quite a meal."

Goran muttered something but Raine didn't hear. Her eyes were locked on her lover.

"You—all along—" She crumpled in on herself, gasping for air. "But, I loved you. I did it for you."

He stepped closer and scratched a black-tipped claw down her cheek, drawing a line of blood. "I know. That's what makes it so delicious. You betrayed your own sister for a demon." He winked. "As I knew you would."

"It was a game," she breathed, stunned. "A game."

They both nodded. The air around them shimmered and for a second they both looked human.

Sunne's boyfriend, and one of the roommates.

It was them, all along.

From the beginning.

"It was all a trap."

"See?" Goran said to Aryntir as they resumed their natural shapes. "And you said humans were devoid of any intelligence. She figured it out, in the end."

Aryntir shrugged. "Only after we spelled it out for her, let's not give the thing too much credit."

Raine sagged to the floor, boneless.

Heartless.

Hopeless.

"I loved you," she whispered.

He eyed her like she was an insect he considered crushing. Aryntir, who had adored her with his gaze on so many occasions, had nothing but contempt for her.

"They all did," he replied. "Every last one." He laughed and raised a hand. Fire sprang up from the floor in a circle around her. It closed, the heat searing her flesh. The flames rose high around her until she was locked within a pillar of flame.

She screamed without sound.

Monsters

What is a monster? Is it something bestial and terrifying? Is it something that hides deep within the human soul, awaiting the chance to strike? Do we fear and hate those who are different? Or do we hate those who are mirrors for our own twisted souls?

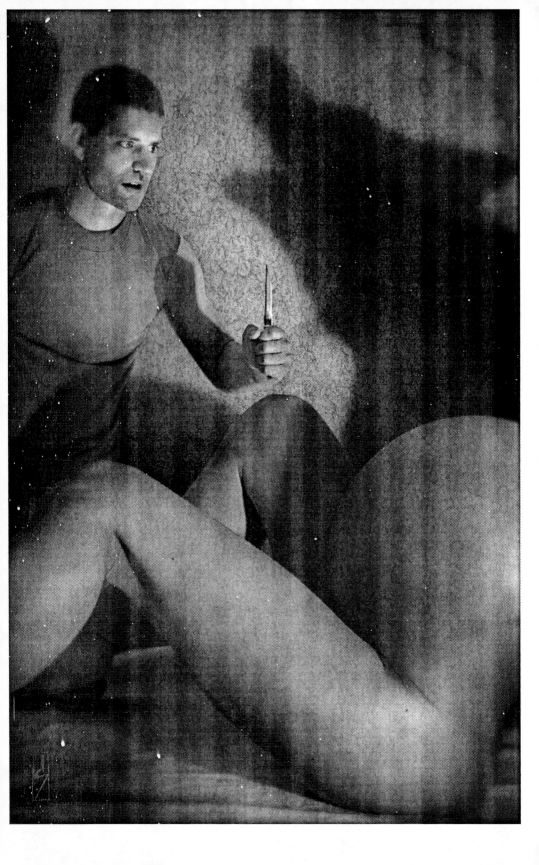

The Healer's Line
Jill Knowles

"Frankie?" Julia's voice was hesitant.

He opened one eye—the blue one—to peer at her, saw her expression, and abandoned his nonchalant slouch. She looked down at the floor, as if his mismatched gaze made her uncomfortable. "Let me guess," he said, taking pity on her, "their honored, uptight reverences have a problem with my clothes." A grin flitted across his lips. "Although how they could dislike this glorious ensemble," he gestured to himself, "is beyond me." Today he wore white tights, white Daisy Duke shorts with a belt made of heavy silver chain, and a sleeveless white half-shirt that showed off both his biceps and his abs. "It's the shoes, isn't it?" The black leather platform tennis shoes didn't quite go with the outfit, but they were the most comfortable for standing or walking, and he knew he would be standing for a long time tonight.

"They like the outfit just fine. They don't like the fact that you're wearing it." She shook her head and continued. "They want me to tell you that if you don't dress in 'a way that appropriately suits your duties and station,' they will be forced to take disciplinary action." Julia was a junior member of the Healer's Council, and functioned as an advocate for any healer facing reprimand from the Council.

He closed his blue eye, focusing the brown one on her. Blue and purple sparklies surrounded her. She was telling the truth and she was distressed by what she was saying.

"I'm sorry you got dragged into this, Julia. It's my wardrobe, and my fight. It really frosts my shorts that they're using you as a middleman." The bunch of uptight old bats just hated knowing that a young person—and a man at that—had healing abilities that rivaled the best of them. Especially since his specialty was working as a midwife. They would have tolerated him if he was gay, or even effeminate; but he was straight, masculine, and a cross dresser. Frankie opened both eyes, blinking to clear them of the aftereffects of his magic.

"You're a thirty-five-year-old man with an amazing knack for helping babies into this world, you're a size three, and you look better in a dress than most women. I'd hate you too if you weren't so darn nice," she said, wrinkling her nose in mock disgust.

"Nice?" Frankie winked at her. "Darlin', I'm much better than 'nice.'"

"So you keep telling me." She grinned at him. "Too bad I'll never find out." She and her girlfriend had been together for nine years.

"Alas, I must yearn from afar." A bell sounded, calling the next topic on the Council's agenda. Sobering, he said, "They want to kick me out of the Guild, don't they?"

"Yeah."

"Can they?" He bit his lip. He'd fought so hard for his place in the Guild. It had taken years before they would even condescend to admit him on trial basis. His probationary period had lasted nearly twice as long as that of the Guild's female members. Oddly enough, when he began his healer residency, his wardrobe hadn't been an issue. He had been granted full Healer status five months ago. His mentor, Joy Davidson, had been killed in a car accident soon afterward. It was then that he found out how much she'd shielded him from the pettiness of the Guild's most powerful members. The harassment about his clothing started three days after her funeral. *At least they gave me time to mourn,* he thought bitterly.

"The younger Guild members adore you—or at least respect you. But none of us are in power. You haven't done anything wrong, so the Council can't force you out."

"But?"

"They can assign you hazardous duties hoping you get scared enough to quit, or . . ."

"Or get killed." Defeat swamped him for a moment. "Goddess Bless, am I such a threat to them?"

"You've brought new ideas into the Guild. Change threatens the power structure."

Joy had been a licensed massage therapist and had been pushing for the Guild to "come out of the medicine cabinet" and admit its existence to the public. Frankie had apprenticed to her as a massage therapist as well as a magical healer. The Guild's rules about not offering mundanes his healing abilities frustrated him. "And if I stop dressing?"

"Then they win."

Before he could respond, the heavy oak doors opened and Councilor Honeymeade stepped out. In mundane life, she was an x-ray technician; someone who did her job well and was nearing retirement age. Frankie studied her as she stopped in front of him. Deep lines were etched into her plain face, her thin hair was more white than blonde, and she'd started thickening around the waist. Her dark blue Councilor's robes were her armor against fading away into old age. Pity welled up in his throat. Maybe he should put aside his dresses—at least for a while.

"You're wanted inside, Shirley Temple."

Screw pity. "Who?" He said, all innocence.

She glared at him. "You. Inside. Now."

Frankie strutted into the Council chamber, putting extra wiggle into his walk. Senior Councilor Bee Balm—or Bag Balm, as she was known to the younger Guild members—motioned for him to stand in front of her.

"Healer Casswell," she said, wincing as she said the name. Unlike most of his peers, he'd refused to take a pseudonym, preferring to use his own name. He felt that was the first step in removing the tradition of secrecy. "We have a most unusual assignment for you. We've received a petition from the Coyote Clan."

Frankie felt his mouth go dry. The Were Clans and the Healer's Guild were ancient enemies. They had, in fact, hated each other for so long that the cause of the original rift had been lost in time. No healer could go into a Were Clan household and expect to emerge alive.

A thin, dark-haired man stepped forward, toying with the heavy gold bracelet around his wrist. "I'm a Seer. All of my Clan claim that gift. My mate is heavy with child. Without a Guild Healer, she will die. I have seen it."

Frankie felt the caged power and impatience radiating from the other man. *You're in trouble Frankie, lad,* he thought, *there's no way you can back away from this and maintain your integrity.*

"And what assurances have we that our Healer will be returned unharmed?" Bee Balm asked.

The Coyote Alpha shrugged. "If no one kills him, he will be returned unharmed."

"Healer Casswell? Your decision?" The Senior Councilor's face was expressionless. Only her eyes betrayed malicious glee.

He was well and truly trapped. Pasting his most salacious grin on his face, he said, "Why Senior Councilor Bee Balm, you sweetheart, how'd you know I was just *aching* for a challenge?"

Shock and triumph warred on her face. Triumph won. She extended a hand to him, saying, "Good healing, Frankie." The "and good riddance" was unspoken.

Undaunted, he brushed his lips across her knuckles. "Why thank you, Senior Councilor. Your good wishes mean everything to me." He allowed himself to savor her discomfort for a moment before turning to the Coyote Alpha. "When will she go into labor?"

A distant look on his face, the other man said, "Two hours ago."

"We'd best be going, then," Frankie said before he could chicken out.

Julia caught him as they were leaving the Council chambers. "What are you doing? Are you crazy?"

He clasped her hand. "If I go, I might die. If I don't, she *will* die." He squeezed her hand and followed his client from the building.

"I'm called Frankie. May I know your name?" Some of the Were Clans were superstitions about telling their true names to anyone. Frankie didn't know whether or not the Coyote Clan held such beliefs, but he wanted to be able to call his client something besides Alpha.

"Woodward James Hunter Throckmorton III. Call me Woody."

Frankie bit the inside of his cheek to stifle a chuckle. "Nice to meet you, Woody." The car turned south on Mission. "I don't know anything about Coyote Clan birthing practices. Will you tell me of any taboos so I don't make things more stressful for your mate?"

"She'll be in human form, of course, as will the young when they arrive."

"Excuse my ignorance, but wouldn't it be better for your mate to give birth in her coyote aspect? I know Canids usually have easier births than humans."

"They do. The problem is with the young. They take whatever shape their mother wears. A cub who is born in coyote form will never be human. It leaves them—damaged." Woody's knuckles were white against the steering wheel.

"Damn. How are the mothers prevented from shifting in an attempt to get away from the pain?"

The car turned into a circular driveway and stopped. Woody turned to face him, sharp teeth exposed in a snarl. "Do you think I will give you Clan secrets so easily?"

Frankie took a deep breath, swallowing his fear. "I know nothing of Were physiology. I have to know as much as possible about my patient in order to keep both her and the child safe. When things start happening, I'll need information fast. I can be diplomatic or I can be effective."

"We use these." Woody held up his left arm, shaking his wrist so the gold bracelet clinked. "They're spelled to prevent transformations."

"Do all incipient fathers wear the bracelets to keep their mates company?"

"Is this relevant to the birthing process?"

Frankie grinned at him. "Nope. I'm just curious."

Woody grinned back. "Some do. Most don't." He pulled the car closer to the house, stopped the engine and stepped out. "Are you ready to meet the clan?"

Knees weak, Frankie grabbed the fluorescent green makeup case he used as his healing kit and exited the car. He threw his shoulders back and winked at his host. "Sugar, I was born ready."

The Coyote Alpha cocked his head, studying the healer. "You may actually get out of this alive." He led the way into the house.

They were met at the entryway by a young girl. She walked up to Frankie, stepping closer than he was comfortable with. "He doesn't smell right."

"Dorrie, it's impolite to make comments about a guest's scent, you know that."

"But Daddy," she squatted and took a long sniff of Frankie's crotch, "he dresses like a girl, but he smells like a boy."

Okay. Well, this is interesting. Willing himself not to blush, Frankie smiled at her. "I'm a boy who likes to wear girl clothes."

"Oh." Dorrie stood and offered her hand to him. "I'm Dorrie. I'm sorry I sniffed you."

"I'm Frankie. I don't mind being sniffed." They shook hands.

"This way," Woody said, nodding toward a door at one side of the short hallway.

Before Frankie could follow the other man, he was hit hard and knocked to the floor. He looked up at the person who attacked him, seeing an old woman caught halfway between human and beast. She snarled at him, her teeth very white against iron gray fur.

"Darlin', if you want to be on top, all you have to do is ask." His voice was breathy. She froze, staring down at him.

"Mother, please," Woody said, lifting her up and setting her down behind him. He extended a hand to Frankie, hauling him to his feet.

Dorrie was standing next to the now fully human woman. "Grandma," she said in a stage whisper, "you're not supposed to pounce people before you're introduced."

"You're right, dear." The old woman stepped around her son, offering a hand to Frankie. "I was dreadfully rude. My deepest apologies. I'm Agnes Throckmorton."

She didn't seem to be bothered by her nudity, so he paid no attention to it. "Pleased to meet you, Mrs. Throckmorton. I'm Frankie Casswell." He brushed his lips across her knuckles before releasing her hand.

She smiled at him. "You're going to get blood all over those pretty white clothes."

"It won't be the first time," he said, shrugging. "May I see my patient now?"

"Through here," Woody said.

"A moment." Agnes looked down at her stomach. A line of red welts marred the skin just below her belly button. "The belt's silver; it needs to come off."

He had been hoping it wouldn't be noticed. "Sorry, the outfit just doesn't work without it."

"Leave it alone, Mother. It's not right to take his only weapon from him," Woody said. He waited until she nodded, then went though the door.

Frankie followed him, stepping into a large bedroom. A petunia had puked all over the room. Everything was bright pink and aggressively ruffled and flower-bedecked.

"Trickster bless, Woody, you were supposed to bring a healer, not a fairy."

Frankie stepped up to the bed, smiling at the woman lying there. Intuition told him she was not the person who had created this room. He wondered if she was Woody's second wife, and what, if anything that answer said about the infant/mother mortality rates among the Were.

"*Love* what you've done with the décor." He reached out and gingerly touched the virulent, rose-festooned bedspread. Gaudy as it was, the room was uncluttered. He had clear space all the way around the bed, which would make his job much easier.

"I didn't decorate it," she said through clenched teeth.

"Really," he said, looking her over. She was a small woman, with sharp, feral features. Her dark hair was slicked against her scalp with sweat, and exhaustion had made her skin was so pale it was almost translucent. "And you seem like such a delicate little flower."

She glared up at him, sighed, and said, "Alright, you win. If you won't call me names, I won't call you names."

"Fair enough. I'm Frankie."

"Serena."

"I need to see your belly."

She flipped back the pastel comforter, baring her naked body for him. Her belly was grotesquely swollen against her small frame.

Gently, he skimmed his fingers across her taut skin. There was magic here, strong, unfamiliar, and barely tamed. He took a deep breath, centered, and pressed his palm against her abdomen. Bright green tendrils of his magic sank into her. Her magic fought against him for a moment, before receding. He could feel the spark of her life, and five smaller, weaker sparks.

"Quintuplets," he said, meeting her gaze.

She nodded.

"Are multiple births common among your people?"

She nodded again. Her belly jerked under his hand as a contraction hit her. Raw magic spilled into him, coloring his vision red. As Serena's body tried to push the babies out, the pain caused her magic to flare, trying to alter her shape. The bracelet she wore prevented her from shifting. The stress caused in the fight between instinct and necessity was very likely going to kill her.

Confirming his guess, Dorrie said, "Is she going to die like my Mommy?"

"Not if I have anything to say about it." Reaching into his kit, he pulled out a prosthetic testicle and handed it to Serena. "When the pain gets really bad, squeeze this."

She took it gingerly. "Is this what I think it is?"

He nodded. "I've found it helps most women focus."

"Oh yeah," she said, giving it a squeeze, "I can see why." Another contraction hit her.

"Picture the babies' father, and squeeze."

She smiled through the pain and followed his directions.

He sent soothing, strengthening energy to her. "Why can't we do a cesarean?"

Woody answered. "Steel doesn't harm us. You'd have to use silver to cut her, and that would cause her system to fight the bracelet and force her to shapeshift."

"Okay." He closed his blue eye, covering it with his hand. With just the brown eye open, he could see the aura surrounding Serena. Dull gray magic from the bracelet she wore swirled down around her, mixing with the red power that formed the basis of her shapeshifting abilities. The babies had their own distinct signatures, a red not as bright as that belonging to their mother. As he watched, one of the energy sources darkened. He opened both eyes and looked at Serena. "We're losing the babies."

She closed her eyes, defeat in every line of her body.

"I'm not through fighting yet. Are you?"

"No." She looked at him. "No, I'm not." Her face contorted with another contraction, and she concentrated on pushing while she squeezed the testicle.

"What to do, what to do," he muttered under his breath. Closing his eye, he studied the mixture of magic again. The power in the bracelet was the strongest, but it was passive magic, it wouldn't be of any use. The Were energy was active, but too dangerous to use. If he could just figure out a way to let Serena access her own magic without compromising the babies, he could save most of them. The glimmer of an idea hit him. "Agnes, let me see your stomach."

Wordlessly, she stepped forward, leaning back so he could see her skin. The welts from his belt were still visible, but they had faded considerably.

"How dangerous is it for you to have silver pressed against your skin?"

"For a short period of time, not very. Longer than a few minutes it will cause first-degree burns. Longer still, and it will draw blood."

"So I'd have to be fast." Only three energy sources were visible inside Serena's abdomen. "I have an idea."

"Do it," Serena said. Her eyes were glassy with the beginnings of shock.

Frankie opened his kit and pulled out the solid silver knife he used for ritual magic. The silver was too soft to keep its razor sharp edge for long, but hopefully, he would only need to make a single cut. Sending a prayer to the Goddess, he unsnapped the clasp holding his belt into place and pulled it free of his belt loops. "Woody, when I say the word, remove Serena's bracelet and try to keep her from killing me. Agnes, get ready to catch." The source of the Were's magic was located in the center of her chest. With luck, her power wouldn't be able to pass a barrier created by silver. He knelt on the bed between Serena's legs and laid the belt just above her swollen belly. She gasped when the chain touched her.

"Now."

Woody pulled the bracelet off Serena, and threw himself across her writhing upper torso.

Frankie visualized the skin, fat, and muscle he needed to cut. He had to be quick and accurate. If his cut was too shallow, he ran the risk of dulling the edge of the blade before he made the necessary incision. If he went too deep, he ran the risk of injuring one of the babies. Sinking his awareness into Serena, he positioned his knife and began.

Serena screamed, twisting madly beneath her mate. The silver belt acted as an anchor, holding her lower body still.

Blood and tissue sizzled as the silver blade cut Were-flesh. The acrid stench of singed meat and raw magic swirled around him. Narrowing his focus to the task at hand, he cut into Serena's womb, his movements sure and steady.

Screams turned to shrieking howls, as Frankie dropped the knife and used both hands to spread open Serena's belly and expose the babies. He ducked as a clawed hand swiped at his face.

"Hurry." The coyote Alpha growled, catching his mate's hand before it eviscerated the healer.

Frankie plunged his hands inside her and eased the first child loose, severing and cauterizing the umbilical cord with one burst of tightly focused energy. He handed it off to Agnes, and grabbed the next baby. It was dead. He let it fall to the floor beside him and reached for the next baby. This one was dead, too.

A loud wail cut through his despair, and he breathed a sigh of relief. At least one baby would live. Blood splashed onto the silver belt, bubbling and turning black. He had to hurry before the silver cut Serena in half. The fourth baby was alive, as was the fifth. As soon as the last child was delivered, he pulled the belt off Serena, tossing it to the side. He used both hands to press the edges of her wound together, flooding her body with healing energy. She went rigid beneath him, then relaxed as her abused flesh rejoined. The areas where the silver had been in contact with her skin resisted his healing efforts and he had to be stern with them in order for them to heal.

"You have some dangerous information about us."

The Coyote Alpha held his two sons while his new daughter suckled at Serena's breast.

"I guess I do." Frankie stretched, making the vertebrae in his back pop.

"You're never going to get the blood out of your clothes," Agnes said from somewhere behind him.

He tensed, expecting an attack. "Sure I will. It'll just take a lot of bleach." Something sparkled in front of him, and he jumped as his belt was dropped into his lap.

"Don't forget this." She said, moving into his line of sight.

"Thanks."

Serena said, "Agnes, it's time to put Francine down for a nap."

"Francine. A good name." Woody handed his two sons to his mother and stood up. He offered a hand to Frankie, hauling him to his feet. "I'll take you home."

"Thanks Woody." He pulled his business card out of his wallet. "Call me if anything weird happens."

"Will do." Woody pulled out a business card of his own. "The next time the Council sends you on a suicide mission, let me know and I'll play backup."

Frankie grinned at the Alpha. "Thanks. I guess I'll see you tomorrow night, then."

The Lamia
James S. Dorr

"They don't die like us," the panhandler said. "Instead, they shed their skins—that gives them new life."

"What?" Matthew said. He had seen the man before, outside his building, just like he was now. Bearded, dirty, of uncertain age. Dressed in a yellow-brown robe—a toga of some sort. Clutching a Bible.

"What?" he repeated, meeting the beggar's eyes for the first time, meaning to brush past just as he had the previous times the man had accosted him on the way back from lunch. This time, however, the beggar's gaze held him.

"Serpents," the man said, wild-eyed. "They don't die of old age. Not like you or I. Rather, they worm their way out of their skins when the time is upon them. That makes them young again. Try to kill one, chop it in half, and both halves become new snakes, filled with poison." He pointed to the book he carried, thumping it hard with his index finger.

"Mind they don't kill you."

Matthew laughed nervously, this time making good his attempt to push past. He stopped in the building's marble-walled lobby to talk to the security officer, asking if there was anything he could do to keep the sidewalk outside clear. The guard shook his head. "This is America, Mr. Ambrose. They got a right to free speech, same as anyone else. Now if he actually had prevented you from getting past him—you know, like grabbing your arm or something—then maybe you could swear out a warrant. Have him arrested for assault. But if he just looked at you . . ."

Matthew nodded. He thanked the officer, then took the elevator to his floor. When he arrived, the receptionist told him his project manager wanted to see him.

Three hours later he returned to his desk, shaken, having learned his partner had betrayed him, taking credit for work he had done. More importantly, she had foisted the blame for a setback on him alone—one that had cost the company thousands and had been her fault, although he, magnanimously, had agreed at the time to share the responsibility with her.

He saw her flitting past, down the hallway. Belinda Carmichael. Thirtyish, dark-haired, slim-figured—some people might even have thought her to be attractive—not meeting his eyes the way the panhandler had. And then he realized.

How long had she been here? Not just on his project—the one that she had just stolen from him—but hadn't it been at least several years since she had first been hired? Yet every morning, her hair fixed just so in a sensible bun, her makeup just right, always dressed in a gray pinstriped pants suit as if to pretend that she, too, was a man, to compete in a man's game . . . had she ever changed? Had she ever looked the slightest bit older?

Then, when five o'clock finally came, he looked for the beggar on the sidewalk, but found the man's usual place deserted.

That was Friday. In Sunday's newspaper he noticed an item, buried in the back, about a panhandler who had been found poisoned by methyl alcohol in a public park near his building. The beggar, the paper said, had had a yellowish-brown blanket wrapped around him.

On Monday he realized he was lucky to have not been fired, when he heard the rumors about him. He went to the boss and explained they were lies—he did not so much contradict the things Belinda had reportedly said, but rather just blunted them, showing how, in context, the impression that might have been left was untrue—and the boss looked at him in an odd sort of way, but ended by saying that he and Ms. Carmichael were still expected to be productive. That Matthew should make an effort to smooth out whatever differences might be between them.

So Matthew agreed. What else could he do? He remembered the beggar—the one-time beggar since no-one was outside the building this lunchtime—and wondered if he, too, might have once worked for a company like this. If he, too, had been betrayed by a co-worker.

He thought about serpents. How snakes were supposed to be known for their cunning as well as their venom. He thought of a proverb he had heard somewhere once, an admonition, to not take serpents to one's bosom—but then he thought, why not?

Could two not play this game?

And when, after lunch, Belinda came to his desk, full of tears and apologies, saying the rumors had not been her fault, that she had, in fact, put in a good word to the project manager—that she had never intended for what she had said to be misconstrued—he smiled and nodded.

He said, "I believe you."

Then several hours later, at 4:45, he knocked on her cubicle. "You know," he said, "I've been thinking about Friday afternoon. Some of the things Mr. Robertson mentioned about our project—it occurred to me we could improve them. I mean together, working as a team, just like old times. Whatever that misunderstanding was about, we were a good team . . ."

Belinda nodded. "I think we were too, Matthew. I really don't understand what happened either, but I'm so glad you agree we can put it behind us. I'd be delighted to hear your ideas."

Matthew smiled. "Possibly we could talk over dinner . . . ?"

Of course he did not think of her literally as a serpent. Not at first. But the metaphor seemed apt as they ate their dinner, she, tearing at the meat on her plate with small, pointed teeth, scarcely touching her salad, while he explained what he had in mind—a slight change in design, a different approach in the advertising—between bites of his own fish and stir-fried rice. Later, he learned that real snakes only ate meat too, never vegetables. But that was later.

For now he was interested just in observing, in finding out more about her. He paid for the taxi that took her home, not offering to drive her himself, but listened when she gave her address to the taxi driver.

The next day, he asked around the office about others who had shared projects with her before. Had they too been betrayed?

What he learned seemed mixed. Most, in fact, had left the company, several apparently having been fired, but at least one or two had had promotions or left for better jobs. But, as he dug deeper, something more sinister came to the surface too: of those who seemed to have furthered their careers, several had subsequently disappeared—just dropped out of sight—and at least one had died.

And when he tried to interview those who were still with the company—in dead end positions, he could not help noting—he struck a brick wall. Not one would speak further the moment he mentioned Belinda Carmichael.

It was then that he remembered the book the panhandler had pointed at, the Bible, and also recalled that his own name was in it. Matthew, author of one of the Gospels. In Hebrew, the name meant "Gift of Jehovah."

And that was when he discovered his mission.

Meanwhile, the dinners together progressed, as well as after hours work in the office. He was, if nothing else, creative, and he brought his whole talent into the project, while she, on the surface more practical-minded, helped mold his ideas into final form.

He kept his guard up. He loathed this woman—he kept reminding himself of this fact—he was only pretending to get close to her to gain information. "Matthew," she would say, "you don't mind me using your first name, do you?" He would nod, the company being informal in such matters, but at the same time, when he could not avoid addressing her directly, he made sure to stick to "Ms. Carmichael."

And always he kept his mind on his mission, which was simply this: to betray the betrayer. He knew who she was now—at least metaphorically—having started to reacquaint himself with the Bible, the Book of Genesis, and with the one who had betrayed all mankind. Not Satan as such, but Satan's handmaiden, the Serpent in the Tree—while he was Matthew, the bringer of Good News, come to staunch Satan's power. To spread counter-rumors that, in time, would show the truth.

But he knew also that he must move carefully. He had to be sure, and, as he delved deeper—as he got closer—as, weekends, he would rent a car to avoid her recognizing his own and scout the area that she lived in—he found the truth slippery, hard to grasp hold of.

As if the truth itself were a serpent.

He put his vacation off, even though he would have liked to just get away, to retreat to a cabin he owned in the woods down South—one of the luxuries he, as a bachelor, was able to afford—and spend two weeks fishing. To play, as it were, the role of Peter, the one Jesus Himself had appointed a "fisher of men." But he realized he could not, at least not for now, because he, too, was fishing, but for something deeper.

Something more sinister.

And so his research went on, he getting close to one of the women in Personnel so he could see records that should be closed to him, hiring detectives to check other companies where some of Ms. Carmichael's victims had moved to—finding more turning up missing, or else deceased—spending the evenings, too, when they were not working late together, tracing her footsteps. Following her movements.

Then one night, at one of their weekly dinners, after she had finished her steak, Belinda smiled at him. "Matthew," she said, "I want you to come home with me."

"I, uh, it's late," he stammered, but she placed a finger across his lips.

"It's important, Matthew. It's something I've worked on that I need to show you, but—you'll see what I mean—it's something I can't bring in to the office. It needn't take long . . ."

He acquiesced—he felt he had no choice—although something within him screamed out danger. He drove her in his car, scarcely listening to her directions since, after all, he already knew the way. He parked the car in a lot he knew of, and walked with her to her basement apartment—snake-like, underground, what he already thought of as her burrow. He went with her into the living room where, as he already knew, she spent her weekends as well as evenings as if the difference between day or night meant nothing to her.

This time, however, she turned the lights on, then turned on the TV.

"Just watch, Matthew," she said as she rammed a tape into the VCR.

Standing, aghast, he watched himself as seen from her thinly curtained window. He watched himself driving up in his rental car, but with the picture clear enough that he could be recognized. He watched himself walking past on the sidewalk, sometimes taking notes, sometimes approaching even closer. And other pictures, too: him stopping in at a detective agency. Even, in one sequence, at the office, talking to Mary in Personnel, whispering to her and holding her hand as she reached in the file cabinet to take a folder. . . .

"You see what I mean, Matthew," Belinda whispered, "about not showing you this at work?" She turned to face him, and, as she did, the musk of her perfume made him dizzy.

"I, uh, I-I can explain," he said, but once more she placed her finger across his lips.

She smiled at him again. "I could, of course, have you arrested for stalking, Matthew. Except I understand. I've known men before, even shy ones like you."

She started to unbutton her blouse. "I know what it means for a person to desire—one might say almost to become obsessed with—something he thinks he can't have. To so fear failure he can't bring himself even to ask, and so, instead, tries to content himself with only watching . . ."

"I-I . . ." Matthew did watch, in spite of himself, as if at a distance where he could see both of them. She reaching forward, taking his hand and placing it on her breast. He acquiescing.

He saw himself kiss her.

He felt a dark spiral, himself spinning helplessly, she coiled around him as they fell to the couch, her hands loosening his belt. His easing her bra off. Feeling the hardness there, then slipping downward.

"Belinda," he murmured.

And then all was darkness.

That morning he felt like hell. Not remembering how he had gotten home, how he had gotten into his own bed. He looked at himself in his bathroom mirror.

The fisher become bait.

He cut himself shaving, then thought of Belinda's steaks—always ordered rare—as he dabbed at the blood. Then, in the shower, of the scent of musk perfume.

Then, at work, of what he felt were the stares of his co-workers, though, when he stared back, he always found them looking elsewhere.

Then, after lunch, he saw a new beggar shaking a paper cup on the sidewalk outside the lobby.

But as for Belinda—Ms. Carmichael, he tried to correct himself—when she stopped by his cubicle later, she seemed as fresh and crisp as always. Her teeth white and shiny, her hair brushed back just so. Her pants suit freshly pressed.

"Matthew," she said, "I brought the boss up to date on our project. You know, the parts we discussed last Friday. He liked what I showed him."

Matthew winced.

"He thinks we should follow that line of pursuit." She paused and smiled. "Not the very latest, of course, but you know what I mean. In any event, do you think we could get together again tonight?"

Matthew shook his head. "I'm, uh, I'm pretty tired."

Belinda smiled again. "I understand, Matthew. Let's let it go one night. Then, tomorrow, perhaps again dinner?"

They settled at first into a routine of three-nights-a-week at Belinda's apartment, plus a fourth night when they just had dinner. Snakes did not need to eat much, he learned, even the largest consuming scarcely more than their own weight in an entire year—how many small filets mignons would that be? he wondered—as, taking advantage of his "nights off," he continued his studies. Belinda disgusted him, yet at the same time he lusted for her, whipsawed back and forth much like a snake himself, facing a snake charmer. Realizing also that she was no true serpent, not anatomically, but all too human—all too much the seductive houri as she lay within his arms, legs coiled about him, and yet with her flesh at night still exuding what seemed to him a peculiar coolness.

As if she were cold-blooded. Which, as he knew, she was metaphorically, but only—only, he prayed—metaphorically.

But then he realized one more truth about her.

He knew already she was a metaphorical vampire. She sucked the creativeness from his soul, transforming it into something of her own which she presented to their project leader. Letting him have credit too, for now, though always with her stamp. Physically she remained fresh, young, sprightly, while, day by day, he looked and felt older.

He asked her once. He showed her a gray hair. She laughed, a tinkling laugh, saying between breaths, "Matthew, Matthew, am I too much for you? Do I make you older?"

Older, yes, he thought. He nearly answered her. Older and weaker.

But then she smiled her little smile, with just a tiny pout, showing her pointed teeth. "Or is it only that I make you wiser?"

And then he remembered. The Serpent in the Tree—that of Knowledge of Good and Evil. That which the beggar had tried to warn him of. Snakes could be arboreal, including members of some of the most dangerous of the snake families—cobras—boas—but there were others, too. Lamias—Lilith—the first wife of Adam. She who abandoned man for Satan and became a serpent too, half-reptile, half-woman.

And then her sisters—the Greeks knew of them. Lamiae, as they were called in Latin, who sucked out the youth from the souls of their boy-lovers. Succubi as they were later known in the Middle Ages.

And there were more than just one.

This he learned also. The Tree of Knowledge—the memory of it, of having read of it in the beggar's Book—reminded him once again of his quest: as Matthew, to seek truth, exposing false knowledge. He considered, momentarily, that he might be going mad. But then, that night, in Belinda's arms—they long since had altered their nights together, planning ahead for a change of clothes, an overnight suitcase, so he could lie with her until it was morning—he had to get up to pee. Turning the light on, he glanced at her eyes, and saw they were open. Not blinking, not even seeing—he waved a hand in front of her face and they did not track it—but just staring, open.

And that wasn't all of it. Now, further, he began to observe other women, seeing the way that some of them acted. Mary in Personnel, that afternoon when Belinda had taped her, not just placing her hand in his, but, after she found the folder, rubbing against him. Body to body.

But now practically ignoring him the few times his work still brought him to her office, as if she knew, by Belinda's scent on him, that he was now taken.

And other women, even teenagers he saw in the park. Girls he might have thought too young, but now, as he watched them, he saw the ways they languidly swung their legs to the music from their boyfriends' boom-boxes. Their flutters of eyelashes—false ones, of course, since snakes did not have eyelids.

Pointed tongues licking lips.

This was the very same park—the memory suddenly came back!—that the panhandler had died in so long ago.

Of poisoning, so the newspaper said.

And he was overwhelmed. So many lamiae. So many false women, half-serpent, half-human. Each a seductress, each in her way a snake, cold-blooded, ruthless—yet insatiable, too, for the warmth of men. Sucking men's virtue, their heat of virility—their very strength—and making it their own.

Belinda found him two mornings later, when he had failed to come into the office, sitting alone in the park on a bench. His suit was rumpled. He had not shaved, he had been there all night. She took him home with her.

He realized then he could not fight all of them. Nor was he meant to: "For every man shall bear his own burden," Saint Paul had written in his Epistles. If he could crush more than one, just as a man might destroy baby serpents just hatched from their eggs, before they could mature to full-venomed reptiles, that would at least be a start. But that was not for now.

For now his burden, alone, was Belinda.

Belinda, who said that he should stay nights with her every night now. That he should move in to be with her always.

Yet how could she be killed? Once more his mind cast back to the words the beggar had spoken, about how, if you chopped a snake in two, you just ended up with two new serpents. Alive with new poisons. And which one had he, the beggar, tried to crush? Which one had turned on him?

The following week the boss suggested he take a vacation. "Just for a rest, you know. You skipped yours earlier, but there's a reason for taking vacations. You can't work forever."

He said he'd consider it. Then, that weekend, telling Belinda he still felt shaky and needed some time alone, he took a plane to Atlanta, then rented a car and drove south to his cabin. He aired it out and fixed a few things, then flew back north in time for work Monday.

When Belinda asked, he just told her he had a surprise for her. Then he suggested perhaps they might take their vacations together, that she had mentioned hers was coming up. And that the boss had said that he was due one.

"A wonderful idea," Belinda exclaimed, then brought her voice down. "But back in the office, don't you think they'll suspect we've become lovers?"

Both of them giggled, but Matthew's laughter came from something different, something he had remembered the night he had sat on the park bench. He had been thinking about his youth, and his memory had turned to a merit badge he had earned in the Boy Scouts, studying woodlore, as a sort of incipient snake-hunter. Just as the teen-aged girls in the park were incipient lamiae.

He nodded, finally. "Here's my idea. I have a cabin—it's almost a small house—on the St. Mary's River in Florida that I bought for fishing. It's really pretty, the scenery there, just across from the Georgia border. Near the Okefenokee Swamp, but on dry ground, of course. Nothing dangerous. And maybe, I thought, just the two of us, out in the woods together alone, with nothing to bother us—we'd rent a car in Atlanta or Jacksonville, lay in some fresh steaks, wood for the fireplace since it's already nearly September and nights can get chilly . . ."

"Good for snuggling, you mean?" Belinda asked.

"Mm-hmmm," he answered.

The merit badge he had earned in the Scouts had been in herpetology. And, in the work that he had done for it, he had at least learned how to catch serpents.

Again he bought plane tickets to Atlanta and rented a car, but this time he drove with her east to Savannah. "For a romantic evening," he told her. "One night in a hotel."

And then the next morning, a new rental car. To cover his tracks—although what he told her, as they continued south along the coast, was just that it was a more practical make for where they were going.

They turned back west and south, passing briefly through Woodbine and Folkston, picking up supplies, then across the border to Boulogne. And into the woodlands.

He had prepared well, the weekend before. He carried her, as if a bride, across his cabin's threshold—he knew from his Boy Scout days that a serpent's head must be immobilized, either by pinning it under a forked stick or catching it in a noose—and, she not resisting until it was already too late, he thrust Belinda's head into the coil of hemp he had suspended behind the cabin door. Dropping her suddenly, slamming the door shut, he watched the noose tighten around her throat, pulling her upward.

He grabbed the rope's free end and, loosing it from the door, hauled it through a system of pulleys, lifting her higher until she just dangled, seemingly lifelessly, slowly swinging back and forth while he retied the end to a cleat in the far wall.

And then he just left her. He unpacked the car, bringing in the steaks and champagne, and cooked his own supper—making a point of eating his steak rare.

He slept alone, finally, feeling his strength come back. Not all at once, of course.

But, even as he slept, little by little.

The following morning he still felt giddy. As he shaved, though, he still felt exhausted. He started to make breakfast, fixing coffee and eggs and bacon—men's food, to bring his virility back to him—when, from the corner of his eye, he saw her shadow twitch.

No! he thought. She could not be still alive. But then, again, he thought back to his scouting days.

Snakes could not be just hanged. Serpents' musculatures were among the most powerful of all Earth's creatures, pound for pound and inch for inch, and especially their throat muscles. What one must do next, when one had managed to trap a serpent, was simple, if gruesome.

One must cut its head off.

But where, precisely, did a snake's head begin? Where did the body end? Woman-formed, yes, the distinction seemed obvious, but if, within, the muscles were snake muscles . . . ?

And, if one cut wrong, would not one still get two snakes? Or, if one released the noose prematurely—to get at the head's base—might not the reptile revive itself suddenly, whipping its tail back to coil around him? To crush him, anaconda-like, even as he tried to kill it?

He cut her down, finally, but not before making sure that the twitching had been nothing more than an unconscious reflex. And not before tying her hand and foot, pinning her wrists and arms against her body. Thus bound, he carried her, still unconscious, down the stairs to the

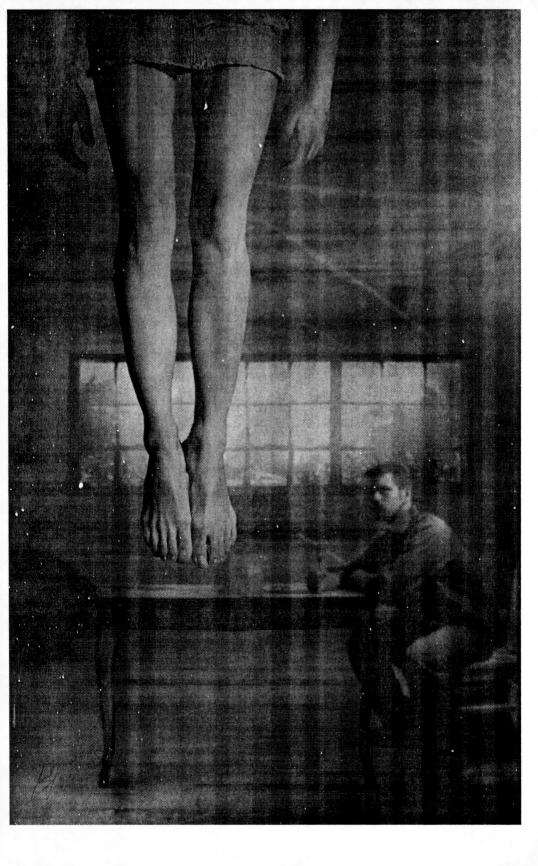

cabin's basement where, finding a strong chair, he took more rope and tied her fast to that.

Then, at last, convinced it was safe, he went back upstairs and, latching the basement door behind him, out to the shed behind the cabin to find a machete.

When he returned, it was nearly dark. He had spent the afternoon sharpening the steel blade on a grindstone, realizing that as soon as he struck, if he did not kill it, the serpent would strike back. He would have just one chance.

But then, as he re-descended the basement stairs, he realized that he had already missed it.

"Is that you, Matthew?" a plaintive voice called. He nearly dropped the blade. Turning the lights on, he saw that Belinda had awakened.

"I—uh," he spluttered, then suddenly stopped. He felt his strength already draining, and knew that to answer would give her more power. Would weaken him further.

Gritting his teeth he raised the blade, but then her eyes met his.

"I-I love you, Matthew," the woman—the woman part of her—simpered. "I-I don't know why you're doing this, Matthew"—her eyes seductive, moist, deep, almost crying, yet still pulling to him—"but I know you must have some reason. Something you could tell me."

He tried once more to raise the blade, but could not. He found himself trapped, like a bird by a snake, by the depth of her stare.

The machete fell to the floor, startling them both with the clang it made, causing her gaze to break just for a moment.

Her eyes almost welling tears—but not quite crying!

Because, he remembered, snakes don't only lack eyelids. They also lack tear ducts.

"No!" he shouted. He could not quite reach the machete again. He could not quite pick it up—it was too late for that. One part of him cried out to rush to her, to untie the ropes, to let her wrap herself around him, her arms, her legs, the moistness between her thighs. While yet another part screamed back, no!

Exhausted, he turned away. Circling behind her, avoiding her eyes, he, as quietly as he could, tore a strip from his shirt. Then, still quietly, he blindfolded her with it.

Her body arched, straining against the ropes.

"Bastard!" she hissed. Then, just as quickly, she softened. "Matthew," she purred. "I-I'm sorry, Matthew. You know I don't mean it. I j-just love you so much . . ."

He took other pieces of cloth and stuffed them into his ears. He shook his head—no, he would not release her!

But also he knew he could no longer kill her, and so he just pulled up an overturned box and sat across the basement to watch her. Neither one moved. Until she spoke one more time.

"M-Matthew? I'm hungry."

He brought her steak that night, feeding her bite-sized pieces with a long-handled barbecue fork. He cooked it rare, until she signed with her head one evening that, if he wished, he need not cook it at all. Then, when the steak ran out, he drove back to the nearest town, but, passing a slaughterhouse on the highway just outside it, he remembered another thing he had learned in the Scouts about snakes.

And so that night he fed her pig's blood, congealed in a pail, set in her lap so she could reach it to lick it with her tongue, like the beast that she was, he no longer even needing to touch her now. But, as with the steak before, he never gave her much—even anacondas, he knew, the largest, most voracious of serpents, could go ninety days or more between feedings, so what he did give her was more just a means to keep her quiet. To stop her complaining.

While he, each night sitting on his crate in the basement across from her, racked his brains to try to find some end to their stalemate.

Thus the weeks mounted—both their vacations were over by now, but that no longer mattered. Jobs no longer mattered. Daytimes he fished, catching food for his own meals. Twice weekly he drove his truck to town—he had long since returned the rental car and bought the beat-up Subaru pickup to take its place—to refill her bucket, making an excuse about using it for fertilizer to build up a garden he planned for the next spring. Once weekly he cleaned her, sating her first with blood—snake-like, she tended to get logy after she filled herself, not even swearing at him as he passed her. Not even trying again to seduce him, although she did that, too, during the times when she was more active. Then, toward the mid-part of October, he noticed something else. He himself had long since started to feel young once again, especially now as the evenings got cold, the days more rainy, just like he had before the first time he had had sex with her, while she—she had taken to moaning and rubbing against her ropes whenever he came near, like an animal in heat. And now her skin was becoming wrinkled.

As if she were aging.

Then he realized, of course, it was working. The "spell," as it were, was reversing itself, giving him back the mind and the spirit she had stolen from him all that summer, while she—deprived of the lust that she hungered for—the couplings she needed—was finding, in turn, her own strength being drained.

And that was how it would end! "They don't die like we do," the bearded panhandler had told him. That among other things. Things about skins and poisons and killing and how, if you cut a snake, new serpents grew from its sundered pieces. But the machete had rusted by now in the damp Florida air, and, in any event, he no longer had need to cut her.

He found she had gone mad—how long had it been, the thought came to him, since that one long, terrible night in Belinda's apartment when he had thought that it might have been he who was going insane? But she, she now rolled her eyes, bulging them even beneath the blindfold he still kept on her, flicking her tongue in and out like a serpent's, moaning, hissing. . . .

Writhing against the ropes he nightly tightened.

Fascinating him! So much so that he scarcely noticed the sound of the wind as he completed his vigil one morning until, back upstairs, he turned on the radio. That was when he heard, for the first time, that a late-season hurricane was approaching Jacksonville.

Pulling on fresh clothes, he ran to his pickup. He knew he was not in immediate danger—the worst wind would likely not reach this far inland, but, even if it did, his cabin was soundly constructed. Rain, however, was another matter. Low-lying roads could easily flood and he had neglected to get new supplies.

He made good time, reaching the town well before noon, finding a store open where he was able to get what he needed. As for Belinda, she no longer even seemed to want her blood, so listless had she become in her madness.

He hurried the trip back—to no avail, though, as roads now were flooding, and as often as not he was forced to make detours. But it occurred to him that, even though the cabin was sound, as near the river as it was, the basement could flood.

Some snakes could, of course, swim. They lived half in the water. In fact, as he drove the final few miles home, as the afternoon darkened into evening, he saw, it seemed to him, hundreds of serpents—moccasins chiefly, the cotton-white of their mouths gleaming up at him from the road as his headlights caught them—writhing, twisting, fleeing somewhere.

To higher ground, likely.

While, in his basement, Belinda could not flee. He did not know why, but he worried for her now—some last vestige, possibly, of the power she once had held over him? For a brief moment he thought he might faint. That the weakness had come back!

He shook it off. To help himself keep his concentration, he made a point of running over any snake he saw in the roadway. All the while driving as fast as he could, still not sure why.

Why, if he did find the basement filled, Belinda's drowned body, should he not be happy?

Unless . . . unless, it suddenly hit him, it was he who had been wrong all along. Belinda Carmichael was, perhaps, an oversexed woman. And, yes, she was pushy. Perhaps she was the kind of woman that he should never have become involved with, not even just at work. But, nonetheless, innocent. . . .

He saw, for a moment, a gray shadow cross the road. A larger shadow, larger than those the cottonmouths cast when his truck's lights pinned them—an alligator, perhaps, but too far in the distance to quite make out. In any event, it had long disappeared when he fishtailed around the next curve and, slamming his brakes, onto the trail that led down to his cabin.

He jumped from the cab, running, telling himself no, he had to stop. To bring the supplies in the cabin with him, not leave them in the truck's bed to be soaked. But some part of his mind still pushed him empty-handed inside, pausing only to snatch up a lantern as he unlatched the basement door. And then down the steps to the basement itself.

"Belinda!" he called as he flicked on the lantern, and noticed, first, that the floor was still dry. He reached for the light switch—the cabin still had power! He blinked as the basement ceiling light came on.

He saw on the chair in the basement's center, the ropes still coiled in loose bights around it, the empty, wrinkled, shed skin of a woman.

Midnight Snack
Ken Brady

The monster was not hiding in its usual corner when Morris walked through the living room to get his midnight snack. He tightened his grip on the baseball bat. Nothing put him in a worse mood than having to look for the monster, and he knew things were not going to go smoothly tonight.

"Where the hell are you?" Morris whispered. He didn't want to wake his wife. In ten years, she had only awoken once during his evening foray to the kitchen. Three years had passed, and she still wouldn't go near the dishwasher. The monster's fault, not his. The only thing that annoyed Morris more than having to look for the monster was having to do dishes. For the last three years, he'd done them every night.

Morris crept around in the near-darkness of the living room. He squinted, trying to use the light that filtered through the curtains from the front porch to his advantage. He reached under the sofa, and came up with a long-lost issue of *Field & Stream*, but nothing else. No monster.

"This is not helping the situation," he said.

He poked his head into the fireplace, and glanced up into the darkness of the chimney. Nothing. Then he heard footsteps. Or, maybe the padding of heavy paws on linoleum. He pulled out of the fireplace and jog-walked into the kitchen.

It was completely dark.

Morris reached for the light switch, then thought better of it. The monster would be expecting that. It loved attacking light. Best case scenario, it would dive at him the moment the circuit closed, right as the light dazzled his eyes. Worst case, it would be *in* the light bulb, and closing the circuit would splatter entrails throughout the kitchen. He didn't want to clean up that kind of mess ever again. Besides, the noise would surely wake Kathi, he wouldn't get his snack, and he'd have to cook up an explanation. He was too tired for that.

Not to mention hungry.

The recycling bin rattled. Morris made a bee-line to the plastic tub and yanked off the top. He thrust his hands in, shuffling through several folded cardboard boxes and a litany of soda cans and beer bottles. No monster.

Morris opened a cabinet, rifled through some of Kathi's dull oat-based gruel, pushed aside boxes of Wheat Thins and some things that vaguely resembled rice cakes. He couldn't see any of it, but knew it was there. Exactly where it should be. He was looking for something—anything—that was out of place.

Another rattle. He couldn't finger its origin, though. He opened the fridge, and realized, a moment too late, his mistake. The light from the refrigerator blared into the darkness, dazzled his eyes, and sent a single cockroach skittering across the floor for cover. Morris almost followed the cockroach's lead.

But the monster didn't attack. Morris let his eyes adjust, looked around the kitchen. Nothing out of the ordinary. Nothing. Perhaps the monster was in the living room after all. Maybe even the garage. That would be a pain, as there was an infinite amount of crap out there that Morris would have to dig through just to find the damn thing.

His stomach growled.

He searched the fridge, looking for something that might tide him over until he took care of the monster, and could then sit down to a proper snack. Some grapes sat in their plastic bag, untouched since last weekend. An entire shelf was dedicated to Kathi's rice drinks and healthy, enriched soy products. But no meat.

No meat.

It irritated him. He was a meat-eater. Always had been, anyway. It was entirely against his better judgment that he was with a vegetarian. But there she was, and she was beautiful. Not just physically, as in "My, do you realize you look like Claudia Schiffer with more cleavage?" beautiful. Mentally beautiful, able to comprehend everything from his littlest, basic fears to his most intricate and interwoven fantasies, usually better than he could himself. He hadn't really had a choice in the matter; it was marry her or spend the rest of his life fantasizing, maybe alone.

And it *was* a great marriage. With one exception. Kathi would not, under any circumstances, allow him to eat meat. Especially in their house. He was cool with vegetables, didn't have an aversion to them, but he needed meat.

He even suffered through Kathi's experimental "life bread" phases. Every week, she would bake a loaf of bread packed full of every nutrient in the books. There were always ten different grains, the names of which Morris had never heard previous to that loaf's unveiling. Nine times out of ten, the bread was rock hard and took three glasses of milk just to get down a single, heavy, stomach-anchoring slice.

Morris looked around the kitchen, in the wash of refrigerator light, and spotted the latest loaf of bread on the counter.

"This is better for you than meat," Kathi always said.

And he ate it and smiled. If he smiled widely enough, Kathi would let him have a frozen Twinkie for desert.

But there was something primal, something so very decadent about meat.

In his formative years, hunting deer for meat was a sacred rite within his family. It was a time when the men of the Great Suburban Tribe went out to the Vast Mountains and killed Bambi. Somehow, the need for that ritual had stayed with him, and he felt empty without the meat.

So, he sneaked it, from time to time. Okay, every night. And if Kathi ever found out . . . he hated to even think about the consequences.

His stomach growled again.

"All right, all right."

Morris was about to close the fridge when he spotted a hidden surprise. A sealed, translucent plastic container. He could see a vague shape inside but could not quite identify it. Pushing a head of lettuce out of the way, he pulled the container into the light.

It was heavy, the substance inside thick, almost solid. Morris tried to make out what it was, looking through the side. He swore it was stew. It had the consistency stew attains after a day in the fridge, when the white fat congeals to the sides and surface, carrots and other helpless items stuck half-submerged like vegetable icebergs. And suspended within, wonderful chunks of solid, pressure-cooked, mouth-watering meat.

He didn't think to be cautious.

He cracked the seal and pulled the lid up about a quarter of an inch before the monster swirled out of the container in a blast of carrots and gravy. Morris yelped and dropped it. The monster took on its most impressive form there in front of him, and he forgot about the mess that clattered to the linoleum.

The monster stood seven feet tall. Its sinewy body pulsed with its heartbeat, dark maroon flesh folding around its roughly humanoid frame. Its head was a mass of scar tissue, two beady black eyes set close over a ragged tear of a mouth. It had no nose. Morris had never seen a nose in this incarnation, one of the monster's dozen forms. This was the all-out fighting model. The tank. The beast.

Morris swung the baseball bat, but the monster reached out a muscled arm and deflected the blow. It grabbed the bat, then backhanded Morris across the kitchen. Morris thudded hard on the linoleum, almost hitting his head on the counter. He stood quickly as the monster devoured the bat in two bites. Morris searched for the nearest item he could use as a weapon.

The monster turned its back on Morris and regarded the fridge. The door still stood wide open, and the light spilled out across the monster's flesh. A glint in its eyes reflected the light with hunger. The monster reached into the fridge, its hand going for the single seventy-watt bulb behind the shelf of soy products.

Morris knew this was his only chance. Whether the monster needed light, or simply thought it was pretty to look at, he didn't know. He only knew that the moment during which the monster went for a light source was his only moment in which to act.

He lunged toward the monster, letting loose with an unexpected battle cry. There was no time to worry he might wake Kathi. Right now, it was kill or be killed. Devour or be devoured.

Morris slammed the loaf of "life bread" across the back of the monster's head, and heard the sickening crunch of bones breaking. The monster hitched once or twice, and Morris bludgeoned it again with the bread. Then he held the loaf over his head like a mighty battle axe.

The monster buckled forward, slid to the floor, and was silent.

Morris wasted no time. He dropped the bread, dragged the monster's carcass through the door to the garage, then hurried back into the kitchen to clean up the mess.

He stopped short. Kathi stood in a delicate nightgown, staring sleepily at her loaf of bread lying on the floor, quite smashed, unceremoniously soaking up the remains of monster stew.

"S-s-sorry, honey. I'll clean it up."

"What happened?"

"I dropped the, uh, bread, honey. And some jam."

Kathi regarded the mess on the floor. She squinted.

"It looks like gravy. Or stew."

Morris panicked, then realized Kathi didn't have her contacts in. It was a good thing she was nearsighted.

"Kath, I didn't want to say anything . . . bad . . . about your bread. It just needed a little something more. I used some of your soy milk to soften it up."

Kathi didn't look convinced, but was too sleepy to fight it much. In the morning she'd have forgotten. Morris led her toward the bedroom, away from the mess.

"I heard you scream," Kathi said. "It wasn't the monster?"

"Monster?" Morris replied. "No. Haven't seen the monster since the—"

"Dishwasher."

"Right."

This closed the subject. Kathi stopped talking about it, and probably stopped thinking about it. She went back to bed wordlessly.

Morris went to get a skinning knife, a bone saw, an axe, and a long-handled spatula.

He dragged the monster's corpse into the small back yard, and began the relatively simple process of skinning and cutting from its flesh those bits which were fit to eat. It was very little, in the end. Morris stuffed the rest into three Hefty sacks, then carried the sacks to the dumpster at the neighboring apartment complex. He threw them in, next to the corpse of Monday's monster.

Thirty minutes later, courtesy of the community barbecue in the apartment courtyard, Morris walked back to his house and into the kitchen with two large, steaming steaks. He cut two slices of bread, made much more bearable and moist by the stew-soaking.

He sat down, applied some salt and pepper, put his sandwich together, and consumed his usual midnight snack.

Pavlov's Breast
Steve Verge

The breast pump lay on Katy's lap, her thumb switching it on, then off, then on again. Her engorged breasts ached for relief, but her aching heart fought against the urge to comply. She raised the pump, her hand incidentally brushing the terry cloth robe from her leg. Such a waste, she thought. If only. . . .

She returned the pump to her lap where it vibrated against her exposed thigh. She found a moment of solace, losing herself in the gentle vibration of the pump, drifting away as she was mesmerized by its uneven hum. Then an unholy snort from the next room snatched that moment away and brought her back to the overwhelming grief of the here and now. She wondered how Mark could sleep so soon after—why he would want to.

Her eyes squinted through puffed lids. Illuminated only by the seashell nightlight in the corner, the room made a vain attempt to protect her from its lore, but the memories were too fresh. Indistinct photos loomed over the shadowy dresser top like tombstones in an overcrowded cemetery. Dark stains muddied the crib sheet—dotted the carpet—spattered the curtains. In the concurrent view of her mind's eye, framed angelic faces taunted her with reminders of shared occasions that would never happen, futures that could never be; the stains bled crimson, damp and glistening in the sunlight of that unforgettable morning.

She didn't have to be there. She could've been in a hotel room as the police had suggested—as Mark had urged. But what purpose would that serve? Mark thought it would be good for her to stay away until they had a chance to have the room cleaned and emptied out. He thought she needed time to heal, thought she could forget in record time like he apparently had. What did he know? What did the police know? Well, there was one thing she did know. Neither one of them would be too happy to find out that she had crossed the magical, yellow police barrier. She might taint some evidence while she was busy not forgetting.

But forgetting was not an option. How could she forget the loss of her own child? Why would she want to? A clean room wouldn't help. Checking into a different hotel every night from now until the day she died wouldn't help. Burning every photo and eradicating all evidence that a child ever existed wouldn't help. Ethan's face would remain in her memory, just as the murder scene would.

Of course, officially it couldn't be called a murder without a body. But she knew. Everyone knew. She didn't need an expert to tell her that a four-month-old child can't lose that amount of blood and live.

Even though her mind knew that Ethan was gone, her body didn't. It had been conditioned to respond at this same time every night. The body woke up. The body slipped out of bed without waking Mark. The body tiptoed into Ethan's room. The body sat in the corner, awaiting the hunger—the feeding. Until now, she hadn't realized how much she'd become a slave to her body—her breast. Somehow, she'd lost her identity. She was no longer Katy, no longer Mark's wife, no longer Ethan's mother. She'd become Pavlov's breast. She needed to be weaned and it would take more than a breast pump to accomplish it.

Another snort ripped through the silence separating the two bedrooms. Damn him, she thought. How does he sleep? How did he sleep two nights ago with God knows what happening in the next room? More importantly, how did she stay sleeping right along side of him? Part of it may have been the conditioning. After feeding, Katy would return Ethan to his crib, creep back to her own bed, and both mother and son would sleep soundly through the rest of the night. Another part of it may have been the unexpected sex that awaited her return to bed that night. Exhausting sex that perhaps induced a slumber deeper than usual. Damn him for that too! And damn her as well!

Katy switched off the breast pump and raised her arm, preparing to hurl it against the floor. She wanted to see if something as insignificant as a shattered hand-held appliance would wake up Mark. She expected it would.

From the corner of her eye, she detected movement. Great, she thought, Mark wouldn't even give her the satisfaction of being woken up. She turned her head toward the doorway, expecting to see him, arms akimbo, giving her a "why are you doing this to yourself?" look. Instead he was hunched over, a blanket shrouding his head and body.

Katy lowered her arm and set the breast pump on the floor. She opened her mouth to request that he leave her alone, but sucked back the unspoken words when he lifted his head.

A pair of glowing, yellow eyes peered out at her. Their gaze probed her, frightened her, excited her. A small amount of milk trickled from her left nipple, dampening the terry cloth. She shuddered, unable to scream—no, not unable, not wanting to scream.

The cloaked figure sniffed the air and then trudged toward her. Its mouth hung open, revealing a set of unevenly spaced, spiked teeth. A thick froth bubbled through the gaps in the lower row and ran down its chin onto the worn blanket that proudly displayed the same dark stains that defiled Ethan's room.

As much as she wanted, Katy could summon no anger for this beast. She had used that all up on Mark. Instead, she welcomed it. In its bite she saw closure. In its belly she saw escape. It would wean her of the guilt, the grief, the longing, the love. It would take away her life as it had her son's. More than anything it would punish her for failing to save him.

The beast stopped in front of Katy and dropped its blanket, exposing its true nature. Clumps of wispy gray hair dappled its scalp. Withered flesh and muscle sagged loosely on its bones. Its unthreatening manhood shriveled up into its crotch. It was not so much a beast as it was an old man masquerading as a beast. It even exuded the stale odor of old man from its pores. The beast was more human than inhuman—more him than it.

With open mouth he leaned toward her. She squeezed her eyelids shut, waiting for the teeth to rip into her flesh, hoping she'd be able to hold back the screams like Ethan had, not wanting to wake Mark and perhaps allow him to intervene. Calloused fingertips brushed against her neck and dragged the robe down over her shoulders. She clutched the arms of the chair, bracing herself for the initial strike. "God help me," she whispered.

Katy felt his lips push against her left breast, encircling the areola. The engorged breast instinctively spurted milk into his mouth. It gushed forth in a steady flow as he gulped it down. Guilt, grief, longing, and love streamed out of her and into the beast. Whether this was right or wrong didn't matter. It was natural, necessary. Pavlov's breast had responded to the beast's need and rekindled the maternal instincts that were still smoldering in her soul. It was what she was born to do—what she had given birth to do.

With each swallow, the beast was giving back a portion of what he had taken away. Katy opened her eyes, cupped the back of his head with her hand, and pulled it tightly against her. One of his teeth pricked her nipple. The fine hairs on her arms sprang up in response. She exhaled softly, trembling.

The beast pulled his head back. Katy's hand yielded its resistance, her nipple popping out of his mouth and recoiling toward her spent breast. He tilted his head upward and gazed into her eyes. The glow had dissipated so that his eyes looked more humanlike. Its skin looked smoother, younger. The old man smell was gone, a new, fresher scent replacing it.

Overwhelmed with a euphoria that combined maternal satisfaction and lust, Katy returned pressure to the back of the beast's head, urging him toward her other breast. "More," she moaned.

The beast removed her hand from his head and placed it on her knee. A single word spoken in answer, dry, barely audible: "Wait." He sank to the floor, coiled into a ball and gathered the blanket around himself, tucking his head inside the folds like a sheltering turtle.

Katy breathed hard, almost panting. How could he stop when there was more milk to give, more pleasure to receive? She needed him now. Her breast needed him now. Waiting was not an option.

She slid off the chair, dropped onto her knees, and placed her hand upon the blanket. Through the fabric, she felt his body spasm and then begin to vibrate. As the vibration increased, the shape under the blanket condensed. Katy felt her hand sinking toward the floor. Her heartbeat accelerated. Part of her wanted to yank away the blanket to see what was happening underneath, but her hand wouldn't respond. She lost herself in the gentle vibration, drifting away as she softly hummed Brahms' Lullaby to herself. The vibration stopped.

The tiny lump shifted underneath the blanket, followed by a muffled whimper. With newly restored control of her senses, Katy threw back the blanket, exposing a naked infant roughly the size of Ethan. He rolled onto his back, kicking his feet in the air. His golden eyes twinkled. He opened his mouth, revealing a set of tiny, spiked teeth. A soft coo escaped from his mouth, eliciting tears from Katy's eyes. Milk dribbled from her nipple. She scooped him up with shaky hands and drew him into her breast to finish feeding.

Golden Rule
DONNA MUNRO

"Just a few more hours and we'll be home," Mommy said as the cloud-capped hills rolled past their tightly packed mini-van.

Sissy sighed and wrapped her ballerina fleece tighter around her legs. Mommy tried not to notice how her little girl was looking more and more like a woman. The girl's bronze shoulders peeked out of her yellow tank with angular grace. In another year or so, Sissy would be just as tall as her mother and the feistiness Mommy had always treasured in her daughter was sure to turn into the sullen gravity of teen angst.

"Yay! Almost home! My fingers are twitching for my Xbox," Junior said from the back seat, surrounded by his books and cards.

Mommy smiled at him through the rearview. He was still her baby . . . huge blue eyes and sloppy hair. His roly-poly body and round baby face still mystified her. In one moment, like this moment, he could be so young—like Peter Pan but a bit nerdier. Sometimes he would age in the space of a breath, usually at a point in an adult conversation when the ideas being bandied had worn thin, he would express some potent bit of poetry or recite some obscure fact. In those moments, she could almost see what he would grow into in the next few years.

"Jeez, Junior, can't you think of anything else?" Sissy hissed over her shoulder. "We haven't seen Daddy in a week. What about him?"

"Yeah, I wanna see him too," Junior said, with a skip in his voice.

"We all do, baby," Mommy said quietly.

Between the hills and dips, the road unwound like a kite string. They played the ABC game to pass time, though Sissy kept changing the rules as they went. One moment, when Junior was in the lead, Sissy would announce that trucks were fair game. She'd pull letters from their hulking steel trailers while Junior squawked, "No fair, no fair." Mommy tried to play referee, but she enjoyed their little squabbles as much as the moments when they were quiet and loving with each other. Her two were tight as an over-stretched belt and tight was the same as love.

"Oh, mom. Look . . . look there," Sissy said, pressing her face against the glass.

Coming up on the side of the road was a VW bus, painted in swirling blues and hitching greens. The psychedelic swirls nearly obscured the overly thin, mop-headed young man sitting near the rear right tire, head down and knees hugged in an instant of woe. The tire was flat and the van tilted under the folded appendage comically.

"That's so sad," Sissy said. "We should help him."

"Daddy says that strangers are dangerous, Sis. He could be a crazy or something."

Mommy nodded as they passed the bus, splashing through a puddle of gray water that must have drenched the young man. In her mind, she could see his shoulders slump just a bit more. It was a moment in life she recognized well. In his mind, the mind of the young adult, everything was a struggle. This moment was probably a moment of despair for him—perhaps testing his will to be independent or worse, testing his will to keep living. She'd had moments like that when she and Daddy had first married. Moments so hard that she felt cessation of breath would make everything better.

The clouds broke, peppering their windshield with fat drops of rain. A streak of lighting cracked the deepening melancholy of the sky and she glanced to her daughter's face. A tear of pity clung to Sissy's jaw, though the girl's breath hadn't quickened into the gasping sobs she tried to use to get her way. A genuine tear from her often silly, self-absorbed preteen! She glanced back at her son, usually too mired in his own world to even respond to easy questions until Mommy scolded him into a guttural response. He was twisted in his seat belt, looking back in the direction of the van, though he couldn't possibly see it through the hill they'd crested.

Charity, kindness and decency . . . they'd worked so hard to instill those values into Sissy and Junior's heads. Treat others as you wish to be treated. How often had she told them how to live their lives? How often had she tried to teach them the golden rule? She worried for a moment about safety, then decided that living your values was a risk. Sometimes, risk was the greatest value of all.

She checked for traffic, then slowed and cut the van across the lanes and through the grassy divide between the highway. The kids cheered as she drove back and whipped around again, stopping behind the van where the young man still sat, clutching his knees though he was soaked to drowning from the torrential rain.

Mommy tooted her horn and the young man's head bobbed up, though his eyes still held the misery of youth. Sissy squealed with glee as he jumped up and rummaged in his van, pulling a backpack free. Junior threw open the side sliding door and cleared a spot on his long bench seat in the back.

"Thanks folks," the young man said as he stepped into the back. "Thanks for saving me."

Mommy smiled at that, knowing she'd made the right decision.

Sissy handed him her fleece blanket to dry off on.

Mommy pulled out onto the open road again, as Junior handed the man a juice box and a pack of blueberry mini-muffins.

"I'm Zach," the young man said in a haunted voice. "Where are you heading?"

"St. Louis, but we can stop at a gas station so you can get your car towed."

The young man's eyes widened and narrowed quickly. "Nah, it's not worth it. That piece of junk won't get me to Chi-Town. Let the highway patrol have my van. Can I hitch with you for a while?"

"Sure," Mommy said. "We go right past 57 on our route and that'll put you five hours out of Chicago. Just settle back . . . it's a good three hours yet."

Sissy smiled at the man and reached out to squeeze Mommy's hand. The girl was proud. Mommy could feel it in the stretch of her fingers and the tight warmth of her daughter's rough palm. Yes, she'd done the right thing.

They drove on in the silence that traveling weaves. Junior was engrossed in his book, while Sissy's fingers tapped out the rhythm pouring mutely into her ears from the back-angled headphones she wore. Mommy glanced at the young man through the rearview, expecting to see him drowsing or staring off at the scenery. Instead, she found he was staring back at her with a hardened expression. Their eyes locked for a long second, then his gaze shifted to the passing treeline.

The stare or something in his eyes had unlocked the fear she'd pushed away earlier and it rose again, clenching her belly in knots. Zach, she noticed, clutched his backpack to his chest tightly, as if it were a ward or a charm. The pack itself was as expected—dirty and worn, but the shape of whatever he had in it wasn't right. It looked too lumpy to be clothing and too big to be books. It almost looked like he was hugging a bowling ball.

Stop it, she thought, *now you're just scaring yourself.*

She focused on the road, watching the signs that ticked off the miles as they sped by. St. Louis 257 miles. St. Louis 200 miles. St. Louis 187 miles. She checked the rearview again for the stare, but found that Junior was staring instead. She shifted in her seat, so she could see what it was that the boy was watching with such intent.

The backpack. It was dripping.

Darkness had enveloped them and the flashing lightning didn't illuminate the van's interior enough for her to confirm what she feared the liquid was. However, Junior's nose was twitching. She wished that her sense of smell was as sharp as his. Maybe then she'd be able to smell shampoo or some other harmless thing she hoped was leaking out of the pack. Zach's gaze shifted from the window, slowly rounding to catch Junior's eyes. He looked down at the backpack and gasped, tilting it on its side.

Here it is, Mommy thought, *if you are normal, you will open the pack and fix whatever is leaking. Please be normal.*

Zach's eyes shifted to Junior and back to the pack. He picked up Sissy's fleece blanket and began frantically wiping at the wet corner. The blanket absorbed the liquid in a widening stain.

"Junior," Mommy said, hoping to find some control of the situation before it turned, "it isn't polite to stare."

"Yeah mom, but his—"

"What did I just say?"

"But—"

"No buts, mister. Now say you're sorry," Mommy demanded, hardening her voice to cut off his protests.

Junior tore his gaze away from the backpack and found his mother's. "I'm sorry."

"Not to me, to Zach."

Junior turned and whispered his apology to the stony-faced young man still swabbing the bottom of the backpack with the blanket. Mommy was glad that Sissy was so involved in her music, because she would be the first to react emotionally to the tension that was rising between Junior and the guest.

"Daddy was right," Junior said, almost under his breath.

"Not another word, young man," Mommy said, struggling to keep the 'I am not amused' mom face firmly planted over the face that threatened to break through—the 'I'm scared shitless' face.

Junior, with the courage only a ten year old can muster, stuck his tongue out at Zack and returned to his book. The young man smiled a feral grin and turned his attention back to his leaky pack.

Sissy's CD stopped spinning and she leaned down to retrieve another.

"Look lady," Zach said as he continued to wipe the pack slowly, "you are going to keep driving. You are going to drive me to Chicago or I will have to hurt your children. I may hurt them a little anyway, but if you do what I say, I may let you live."

Sissy looked up at her, the fear and anger crushing her innocent features into a quizzical mess.

"Okay, just don't hurt them." Mommy glanced from the rearview back to the road. All she had to do was drive until the van ran low on gas. Then she could stop at a gas station and—but if she tried to get help, she was sure he'd hurt one of her babies.

"You are a bad man," Junior said. His eyes flashed with anger. "Daddy would make you get out for saying those things."

"Well, you little shit—your Daddy's not here is he?" Zach seemed to be loosening up, as if threats and viciousness were his natural element. "In fact, if your Daddy was here, he'd be in little pieces like the man in my bag. But you are hardly worth the effort. I think when I kill you, I will just cut your throat and leave you by the side of the road for the coyotes to fight over."

Junior gasped. "Mommy?"

"Look here, we took you in and I agreed to drive you, but don't threaten my boy. Just stay calm and let me drive you," Mommy said. Her hands were gripping the steering wheel so hard, she worried for a second that she might rip it off the column. She took a deep, calming breath and continued. "We'll get you where you need to go, just don't do anything rash. Okay?"

Sissy whimpered and balled up in her seat. It looked like she hoped that the villain in the back seat would just forget her.

"I think you should shut up lady," Zach said. "Shut up and drive."

He stood and stumbled forward as the van hitched over a pothole. He reached over and grabbed Sissy by the arm. He dragged her into the back seat with a rough jerk.

"No," Sissy screamed. "Leave me alone. Get your hands off of me."

"Shut up girlie," Zach said. "You'd be more fun to kill. I'd cut off all your clothes and then strip off your skin. Maybe I'd even eat your soft flesh. Your mom is so old that she'd be like jerky, but you . . . you'd be delicious."

Sissy's sob deepened into a wail. "Mama, he's pinching me. Can't you make him stop?"

Mommy's mind spun. If only Daddy were with them. If only she hadn't fooled herself into trusting this monster in their car.

"Mister, you better stop" Junior said, using his best man voice. "You gotta treat others as you want to be treated. That's what made mommy pick you up."

"Keep driving lady or your baby girl's going to get hurt," Zach said. When she glanced back, she saw him run his long, white fingers down her cheek. Her daughter's eyes were wide and watery, but her mouth was set hard like stone.

She focused on the driving rain and the slick road in front of her, cursing herself for being a fool.

"If you hurt them, I'll make you suffer," she muttered, "like you've never suffered before."

Zach laughed and pulled Sissy toward him. He put his arm around her, like they were on a first date, and smiled. He leaned in and whispered something and moved his other hand toward her.

Mommy saw a reflected flash as light hit something metal he held in his hand. A knife. Steel, she hoped. Yes, just sharpened steel. She smiled, but hid it behind a cupped hand.

"Don't worry Mommy," Sissy said through her tears. Her lilting voice cut the tension with a razored edge. "Just keep driving."

Mommy's eyes darted to Junior who watched the knife's flirty ballet with interest. Her son's eyes flashed as the edge of the blade spun in the man's hand, leapt to Sissy's exposed shoulders, scraped down her arm without a cut, and floated back into the air in front of the girl's flushed face.

"Zach, the turn off to Chicago is ten miles from here. There's a rest stop. Please let us use the facilities there. Chicago is such a long drive and we promise not to do anything rash. Right, kids?"

The children nodded their agreement, though Sissy's nod was jerky.

The man waved the knife at her in what she assumed was an assent and continued its flirtation with Sissy's skin. The smell of blood, Sissy's, made Mommy's nose twitch. Through the rearview, she could see two crimson cuts on Sissy's forearm.

A jolt of fear tightened her knuckles on the steering wheel again, jerking the car onto the rumble strips on the roadside. The growl of the wheels didn't stop the maniac from cutting the girl. He pressed the blade into the joint of Sissy's slim pinky.

Sissy's tears and hissing gasps had become almost unbearable. Mommy's body fought with her mind. She wanted to jerk the car off the road, ram it into a tree, and destroy them all if it would stop him from hurting Sissy. It occurred to her that he wouldn't stop, even then. She kept driving, hoping that some solution would come to her. There had to be a way to keep them safe, safe from all harm.

"Mister, you are a monster," Junior said as his sister began to scream.

The knife paused for a second as the man turned and punched Junior in his face. The impact flattened the boy's nose with a crunch Mommy felt in her bones.

"You bastard," she swore. The car swerved as she watched her son fall away from the fist, blood running down his face in twin streams. Junior wasn't unconscious, but his mumbles were incoherent. They said 'pain' and nothing else.

"Keep driving, Mommy," Zach said, returning to Sissy's finger.

Mommy could hear the metal biting bone with short scraping sounds. The rest area sign that flew past announced the turn off was only one mile away. She pressed the pedal to the floor, lurching the mini-van into overdrive. She hoped that at the rest area there would be truckers or vacationers or mounties with steaming coffee mugs in their hands and sharp eyes that could end this for her. She had to save the family, but she hoped that she could find a decent way to do it. Her values were at stake.

Junior fell forward as she spun her van into a parking spot in the deserted rest area. There was no cavalry in flannel shirts and dirty blue jeans waiting to save them. Only the empty restrooms with white tile and motion-activated lights witnessed her terror. Only vending machines would stand guard as they fought for their lives.

"Okay lady. You're going to take your boy and clean him up. I'll stay here with your girl and if you do anything funny, I'm going to drive away with her. I promise, what you've seen here ain't nothing. I'm just playing with her a little. You don't want me to get serious, do you?"

Mommy shook her head and reached for her purse.

"Leave it and the keys . . . just so you know I mean business," Zach said.

Mommy nodded and jumped out of the driver's seat. She hurried around the van and opened the sliding door. Zach grabbed Junior by the arm and shoved him out the door. Mommy caught her boy by the hand and pulled him to her in a hug. Zach began to pull the van door shut, slowly, softening the sounds of Sissy's screams.

Junior pulled Mommy toward him. "He's going to try to kill us all Mommy. He's hurting Sissy." Mommy nodded.

"Daddy says that monsters look like everyone else. They were never ugly or hairy like in the storybooks. Daddy says real monsters are people that don't live by the golden rule."

The knife glinted in the light that shone through the side windows of the mini-van. Sissy scrambled back away from the man's clumsy grasp, her eyes flashing back and forth. Mommy threw herself against the sliding door. Zack's fist clutched the short blade as he moved.

"Mommy?" Sissy begged. "Please?"

He reached her with a lurch and plunged the blade into her abdomen. Once, twice. Mommy couldn't watch anymore.

"Daddy says if people break the golden rule they deserve what they get," Junior said. "Please, mom?"

"Go ahead then, just make sure you follow the rule," Mommy said. If only Daddy were there to help them. They were too young to have to do this.

Junior pulled open the door as Zach's knife fell again, plunging into Sissy's stomach. Zach looked up, rising out of his murderous haze slowly.

"Sissy, follow the rule," Junior said.

His voice descended down the scale from the musical prepubescent soprano Mommy so loved into a low growl. Sissy drew herself up and flung the monster off of her and out onto the wet blacktop. The girl winced as she stepped out of the car, though Mommy knew the pain was not from the knife wounds. It was from her feet and her spine stretching.

Zach flipped from his back to his stomach and pushed himself up, the knife flashing.

"You little bitch, I'll . . ." He froze as Junior turned toward him, his lengthening snout pulled back into a canine grin.

"The rule . . ." Junior growled as his vocal cords changed. "The rule . . ."

"Wha . . ." Zack stumbled back, dropping onto his elbow with a thud. The impact loosened the knife in his hand and he scrambled to find it. "What rule?"

Mommy knew her little ones weren't capable of explaining anymore, so she spoke for them.

"We believe that being human means to treat others with respect," she said, laying her hand on her daughter's furry ear. Junior tore his jeans with his white, cavity-free canines. The pants fell away in shreds. "We live by the golden rule—treat others as you would be treated. We hoped to avoid this . . . nastiness, but you insisted on treating my family like beasts. You have shown us how you want to be treated and now . . . my children will treat you that way."

Zach's wide eyes watched the children as they circled, snouts flecked with foamy saliva. He scrambled to his feet and grabbed for Mommy as they closed in. His arm caught her neck in its crook and held her.

"I don't know . . . I . . . you animals stay back or I'll cut your mommy's head off," the Zach monster said.

Junior yipped in fear and slunk back, but Sissy held her ground, growling.

"That's right. Me and Mommy are going to get in the car and leave you little . . . freaks here. Be good and Mommy's head stays on her neck."

Mommy felt his grip tighten on her as he pulled her back towards the car with slow steps. The knife lay hard against her neck, but the edge hadn't caught her skin. She spoke, trying to calm him.

"You can't get away with this. Just let us go before this gets any worse." she said.

"Who's going to stop me? Your little monsters?" he asked.

Mommy felt her anger and fear solidify in her belly like a stone. Her muscles were tensing against the wash of emotion and soon she wouldn't be able to hold it back.

"Stop calling them monsters," she said, mentally counting to hold her temper. "They are only following the golden rule."

Zack laughed and let his blade cut her skin. The searing pain tore into her reserve and stole her patience. She felt her body begin to rip as she changed into the other. Her back lengthened and her joints popped as she wrenched free of his grip. In the seconds of blinding change, she pounced, swatting him to the ground.

"You are the monster!" She howled. Her jaws snapped, gripping his neck, heedless of the knife he swung in useless arcs, hacking at her barreled, furry torso. She held him down, canines sunk deep into his windpipe and murmured to her babies to come teach him about rules.

The two pups eagerly dug in, pulling strips of flesh from him as he gurgled around the ruined mess that once was his throat. After a while, he dropped the knife.

Once Mommy was satisfied that Zach's bones and shredded clothes were well hidden in the deep woods behind the rest stop along with his last victim's fragmented remains, she loaded her cubs back into the mini-van. They didn't speak much, since most of their energy was focused on healing the nasty wounds the monster had inflicted. Sissy's new tank absorbed the final drops of blood escaping from the closing knife wounds in her stomach and Junior's nose had a new angle that made him look more boyish somehow. She watched through the rear view as they cleaned their retracting claws and licked each other's faces clean. She was happy that they'd proven themselves to be virtuous humans.

"Daddy will be so proud," she said finally and turned back toward the break in the clouds and the red moon that lit their way home.

Junior nodded, happily patting his stretched belly. "Now we don't have to stop for dinner."

The Undead

If you could communicate with the dead, or even bring back a loved one, would you? What would be the consequences of those actions? If things go wrong, are you prepared to perform an exorcism or to fight off a hoard of flesh-craving zombies?

Wishbone
ERIN MACKAY

Sharon had tried to move on. So many people had told her it would be the best thing, just to move on. Remember the good times, remember the love, remember him, but don't dwell in the past. Don't look back.

So she tried, she really did. When the alarm went off every morning, she woke up even when she would have preferred to stay asleep. She got dressed and fixed her hair in the still silence of the house. She drank her coffee and read the paper and resisted the urge to recount a particularly annoying letter to the editor to the empty space on the other side of the table.

She went to work, where things were almost normal except that some people still didn't know what to say to her. Nine hours later, she came home to the same silent house she had left. Unable to bring herself to cook yet, she microwaved frozen meals and ate them in front of the television. Sometimes she watched sitcoms all night, the remote control dangling idly in her hand, until she fell asleep on the couch. Other times, she read books, or crocheted, or just sat in his armchair staring up at the ceiling as the quiet house sank deeper into night.

Moving on, though, was much harder than Sharon's well-meaning advisors made it sound. One night, when the voice of the evening news anchor had become a dull buzz in her ears, and swirls of leftover marinara sauce were drying to the sides of a flimsy plastic dish, she decided not to.

Not to move on, that is. Why should she? The flickering blue light of the television screen illuminated her revelation: Why shouldn't she long for things she could not have? Whose business was it if she did?

So she stopped trying to move on. She immersed herself, instead, in the anger and grief that had been lurking in the dusty corners of her heart. She wallowed openly in how unfair it was that he had been taken from her so quickly—an accident, a phone call, a funeral, and it was done. Too sudden, too random. Six years of marriage they'd had, with nothing but possessions to show for it. Six years of formless memories were all that was left to her; a six-year stretch of empty road in her rearview mirror. Too unfair. Too much left to do that could never now be done.

Nobody knew Sharon had given up trying to move on. She still woke up every morning and drank her coffee and studiously did not read any part of the paper out loud. She still went to work and typed and filed, still came home and fed herself from a frosty cardboard box. She still held the remote control and ran her fingers over the rubbery buttons even when she didn't feel like changing the channel.

But Sharon had a plan, one that did not require anyone else knowing: she wished. Wishing worked, if you did it right. She wished for the way things had been before, she wished to have him back alive and whole and just as he had been on the day before he died. With every heartbeat, with every inhalation and exhalation, every sip of coffee and letter to the editor, with every blind courtesy copy, every *peel plastic back at corner to vent during cooking*, she wished.

She wished on stray eyelashes and on her necklace clasp when it worked its way around to the front. She crossed her fingers so much she did it unconsciously, and at the firm's Thanksgiving potluck she pushed the managing partner's secretary out of the way so she could be the one to pull the wishbone. At night, she stood outside in the cold to wish on the evening star.

Days passed, then weeks, with no result. Maybe death was too much for the simple home remedy of wishing. After all, a lot of things needed undoing to bring him back, alive and whole and just as he had been on the day before he died. Sharon finally admitted that this was beyond grammar school magicks. She needed a professional.

At work the next day, Sharon closed her office door and took out the phone book. Sliding her finger down the brittle yellow page, she muttered the headings under her breath: Sorcerers and Wizards-Alchemy; Sorcerers and Wizards-Conjuration and Transmutation; Sorcerers and Wizards-Divination . . ." Sharon sighed. None of these looked promising. ". . . Elementals; Egyptian; Enchantments and Charms; Illusions; Indian (American); Indian (Eastern); Invocation (Cosmic); Invocation (Extradimensional) . . ." Wow. That sounded dire. But what she wanted was dire, wasn't it?

She picked a likely looking advertisement for one Magus Theophrastus Nelson, Ph.D., M.D., D.Div., *Board Certified in all aspects of Extradimensional Invocation, including Spirits, Demons and assorted minor Sheydim. Free Consultation.* Sharon picked up the telephone and dialed.

"Good morning, Magus Nelson's office," said the pert voice on the other end of the line.

"Good morning." Faced with the professional confidence of the other woman, Sharon was suddenly unsure of herself. "Um . . . I'm not sure I'm calling the right place . . ."

"I'll be happy to help you with that," the receptionist chirped. "Tell me about your case."

"Well, I have a wish."

"I see. And the traditional applications have not succeeded?"

"No. And believe me, I've tried."

"I'm sure you have." The woman's voice now dripped well-rehearsed sympathy. "Do you feel comfortable sharing with me the nature of your unfulfilled need?"

Sharon hesitated, licking her lips. "Well, you see, my husband died recently—"

"Oh, no." It was not a sympathetic exclamation. It was abrupt, flat, cold. "No, I can't discuss wishes involving the dead."

"But—"

"No, I'm sorry. Magus holds no commerce with necromancy. Thank you for calling."

Sharon tried not to feel personally insulted by the click as the receptionist hung up. Necromancy was, of course, illegal, the only crime still punishable by the stake. Naïvely, she had hoped that some other branch of the magickal arts might encompass what she needed. But the woman's reaction told Sharon everything she needed to know about the exact sort of professional required in this situation.

She closed the telephone book and put it back in the drawer, trying to decide what to do next.

A few nights later, Sharon shivered as the wind blew between her ankles and up her skirt. The peculiar silence of midnight, the stillness of chilled moonlight and sleeping humanity, enveloped the deserted street. Her own footsteps jarred her ears, the sound bouncing off cracked concrete, broken glass and dented metal like a scattering of pebbles. Not for the first time, she wondered if she were really this desperate. Every sane human being in this place was safely indoors right now.

Searching for the house numbers was arduous work in the haphazard street light; and she couldn't look for long without her nervous gaze being drawn away by some imagined movement in the shadows. This part of town was just the sort of place where imps and elves and yellow-eyed vampires preyed upon the unwary. Or upon the cold and alone, like her. She huddled farther into her coat. She had taken off anything that sparkled to keep from attracting elves, and she carried pepper spray against the imps. She had forgotten about the vampires in this neighborhood, though, and the only defense she had was to try to look unappetizing.

The necromancer's hovel, when she finally found it, was as dreadful as she had feared. The address was a second-floor flat in a building with boarded-up windows and a creaking fire escape, every available surface covered in imp and elf graffiti. When the necromancer answered the door, she turned out to be a woman perhaps in her mid-forties, her short-cropped hair brushed with gray. Her mysterious magickal ensemble consisted of faded blue jeans and a crookedly buttoned oxford shirt. She beckoned Sharon closer so they could speak without their voices carrying into the street.

"You're Sharon?" she asked in a cigarette-husky whisper. "Willy says you wanna raise your husband?"

"Yes." Unsure what else would be appropriate to say, Sharon left it at that.

The woman straightened and stepped back into the entryway. "Come on in."

Sharon followed her inside, grateful for the warmth of the place, if nothing else. "Thank you, Magus."

The woman barked out a laugh. "I ain't a magus. Call me Pauline."

Pauline led Sharon to her base of operations, a dirty kitchen with a shaky, paint-splattered table. "Coffee?"

"No, thank you. I'd really rather just . . . get on with it."

Pauline peered at her. "You sure you ain't a cop? You kinda smell like one."

Sharon shook her head. "I'm not a cop. Here." She dug into her coat pocket and produced the envelope that held a few strands of his hair. "Is this enough?"

Pauline opened the envelope and frowned at the contents, the sum total of what Sharon had been able to glean from the bristles of his hairbrush. "I guess it'll do. Have a seat."

Sharon did as she was told while Pauline went to the counter and began assembling the tools of her trade—a teapot, a volumetric flask, a Büchner funnel, a feather duster. Sharon lost track of the odd objects pulled out of the cluttered cabinets and drawers. "Where did you learn to do . . . this?" she ventured.

"Prison," Pauline said, leaving the rest of the story to Sharon's imagination. "Tell me, Missy." Pauline paused in her activity to look at Sharon. "Why the hell you going to all this bother to start again with this one? You're young; you give it time, you'll get over him. Easier than putting yourself through all of it again someday." She snorted. "And a helluva lot cheaper than me."

Sharon returned Pauline's gaze without blinking, then told her everything. She poured out her anger, her grief, her *longing, longing, longing* for just one more day with him; for things undone, for words unsaid, for six years of empty road.

"I can't do it without him," she said near the end. "I can't move on."

Pauline listened, and nodded, and went to work.

Pauline had warned her that the spell might take some time to work. As Pauline's livelihood and continued uncharred existence depended upon satisfied customers, Sharon was willing to take her word for it, and to wait. She waited. She lost track of the days and of the endless nights of waiting. Then one night, hours into a heavy, dreamless sleep, the doorbell rang.

The abrupt sound bludgeoned through the stillness of the house and made her heart lurch through several sickening beats. Awake too suddenly to think clearly, Sharon lay frozen for a long time, adrenaline whitening her mind around the edges. Finally, her brain and her limbs arrived at the conclusion to get up and answer the door.

When she was halfway down the hall, the bell rang again, jerking her breath down her throat and sending her hand to the wall for balance. Sweat gathered beneath her cotton nightgown. Clenching her jaw in resolve, she reminded herself that she had wanted this, she had wished for it, she had paid good money for it. She told herself sharply that it might be nothing, just a drunk neighbor at the wrong house. Anything to get herself to the door. By the time she put her eye to the peephole, standing up on straining toes to reach it, she was shivering.

It was him.

She jerked back from the door, blinking as though she could clear the flash of vision from her eyes. Her lungs drew in a barrelful of air and she moved without really meaning to, whirling until she was against the wall.

She didn't know why she was so afraid. The yellow porchlight showed him alive and unmistakably whole. Pauline had delivered; Sharon hadn't woken up in a zombie movie or a cautionary tale. He just looked . . . tired. In fact, he was so normal, so unchanged, Sharon began to think that maybe she was the crazy one. Maybe the accident and the phone call, the funeral and all the weeks after had been her hallucination, her delusion.

The doorbell rang again, and he called to her, called her name, just as he had so many times before. "I think I lost my key, baby." He sounded a little confused. But, of course, he would be. If this was real.

Nothing, though, could make Sharon move. She was safe against the wall; she was asleep and would wake up any moment to her comforting routine of anger and wanting and wishing.

Then he got mad at her. "Dammit, Sharon, open the door, right now. This isn't funny."

And Sharon didn't have to think anymore about what to do. She snapped into automatic, into movement without motive, reaction without meaning. She twisted the deadbolt, turned the knob and pulled open the door.

He smiled at her, that charming smile she had missed so much, for so long. For so, so long.

"Hey, baby. Forgot my key. Can't for the life of me remember where I left it."

She stared up at him with eyes dampened by relieved, unbelieving tears. She had gotten her wish. He was here, alive and whole and just as he had been the day before he died. He was even wearing the same shirt, the one she had ironed for him that morning, clean and lightly starched the way he liked it. She buried her face in the cotton weave, and he was real. He was solid and warm and he smelled like himself, like shampoo and aftershave and the airport. It was like he'd never been gone.

He wanted to sleep, and Sharon couldn't blame him. But she stayed close as she followed him to the bedroom, touching him whenever she could. She needed to reassure herself that he was here, that he was real, and that he wasn't going to disappear. More than anything, she was terrified that this magnificent, miraculous gift might be taken away from her.

"It's good to be home," he told her, before he lay down on the bed and let his eyes sink shut.

She waited until he was asleep. She sat on the edge of the bed, watching him as she used to do before . . . before. The diluted moonlight through the window shade turned his face sallow, and his eyelashes cast dark shadows against his cheek. He breathed in and out in the slow rhythm of perfect peace, that marvel he had always been able to achieve every night. *Every single night.*

She was shaking with incredulous joy. Sometimes, you get your wish, she finally realized, reaching out carefully to brush her trembling fingers over his sandy curls. Sometimes, the evening star and a well-timed wishbone and a little cash under the table could get together and grant you your heart's desire. She didn't care anymore how or why it had happened, she only knew that he was here. Just the way she needed him to be.

A wry smile crossed her face as she watched his chest rise and fall. This, she thought, was why necromancy was illegal.

She counted each one out loud, just as she had done on her fingers every night since he had died. Through the expensive weave of his shirt and into the flesh of his chest she plunged the knife, once for the blonde in New York, once for the brunette in Atlanta, once for the petite Asian in Los Angeles, and once for his lying secretary who helped him hide the credit card bills; once for the excuses she gave her friends, once for the excuses she gave her mother, once for every dinner party her humiliation had provided gossip for; and once for his never agreeing with her about the letters to the editor.

When she finished counting, she wiped the knife on the tail of his lightly starched shirt and laid it down beside him. She could already feel the changing within herself, the mending, the dissolution of all the unfairness and anger. True magick, that. Pauline had earned herself a bonus.

There. Now she could move on.

No Worries, Partner

Jim C. Hines

My ticket printer was haunted again.

I yanked the power cord out of the wall, and the printer died midway through an obscene parody of "Home on the Range."

My desk lamp promptly blew its bulb. I couldn't tell if it was the ghost again or simply another quirk of the building. The El Rito Western Cultural Museum had begun its life as a two-story hotel, back at the start of the twentieth century. My office came complete with its own bathroom and shower, along with plush beige carpet and red and gold wallpaper.

The downside: the mildew irritated my allergies, the carpet gave me electrical shocks every time I touched anything metal, and the window-mounted air conditioner rattled so badly I expected it to fall onto a passing patron any day now. Still, my office was better than some. The room next door was abandoned, ever since termites crumbled part of the ceiling a few years back.

The tickets I had managed to print began to stand on end, climbing into an impossibly steep tower of cards. In seconds, the tower touched the water-stained plaster of the ceiling.

"Stop that!"

Seventy-four tickets shot into the air and began to circle the office, slaloming between my chair legs and doing loop-de-loops in the breeze from the AC.

I didn't have time for this. The New Mexico WestFest, the museum's annual Cowboy Poetry Gathering, was just over a week away, and I had to do the jobs of three people.

I reached for my desk. The ghost might be leashed to the building by magic, but it could be driven from my office. The instant I touched the drawer handle, the tickets shot back into a perfectly neat pile on my desk. The ghost knew as well as I did what was in that drawer.

"Now get the hell out of here."

"Hell of a greeting," came a voice from the doorway. "What's got you all a-twitter this morning?"

I stared, trying to figure out why the woman in the doorway looked familiar and hoping she hadn't seen the possessed tickets. My boss would kill me if anyone outside the theater learned about our paranormal problems.

The woman wore a leather cowboy hat—an Akubra, which I wouldn't have recognized before I started here six months ago. A sheepskin vest covered a red shirt from last year's West-Fest. Black hair hung down her shoulder in a rope-like braid. She grunted softly as she pushed her wheelchair farther into my office. The wheels sank in the carpet like it was mud.

"Can I help you?" I asked.

"Sure thing." She offered her hand. Her grip was stronger than mine. "Rhian Black."

"Ted Pendelton," I said. Then the name clicked. Rhian Black, winner of Australia's Waltzing Matilda Bush Poetry contest a few years back. "You're one of the performers. You're not supposed to arrive until . . ." I scrambled for my Palm Pilot. "Your hotel reservation is for next Tuesday, not—"

"No worries. I'm crashing with T. J. for a few days." She winked when she saw my expression. "It's not like that. I'm not having a naughty with him or anything."

She glanced around the office, grimacing at the scattered paperwork that blanketed my desk, the file cabinets, even the bathroom counter.

I cleared my throat. "I hate to be rude, but I've got a meeting in five minutes, and—"

"I know. Things are always crazy this time of year, and you're swamped. Literally, if that plumbing problem gets any worse."

"What?" I slipped past her to peer into the bathroom. The faucet was on, but the water wasn't dripping into the sink. Instead, the stream curved upward into a bubble the size of a beach ball . . . and it was rippling into my office.

"I warned you!" I grabbed a ruler from my desk and slipped into the bathroom, ducking beneath the undulating sphere. A flick of the ruler popped the oversized bubble, and several gallons of water crashed to the ground, soaking my shoes and trousers. I turned off the faucet and headed for my desk.

"Watch it, mate." Rhian grabbed my arm and pulled me down as my music collection—mostly new age, none of that western stuff—shot over our heads. "This sort of thing happen a lot around here?"

"Unfortunately, yes." I gritted my teeth as my CDs gouged the wall. T. J. had warned us time and again not to say anything about the various "eccentricities" of the museum. We got enough bad press from our annual conflict with the Blue Devils motorcycle gang. If the public learned about the supernatural creatures the Blue Devils left behind each year, it could put us out of business.

Of course, T. J. had never said what to do if one of his precious cowboys barged in on a phantasmal tantrum.

"Better duck again," Rhian said. My CD rack was empty, so the ghost had moved on, pulling the thumbtacks from my bulletin board. Phone messages and schedules fluttered to the ground. The thumbtacks aligned with the points toward us. Rhian spun her chair and pulled me down as the rainbow-colored barrage launched through the air.

Most of the tacks wedged into the back of her chair. They sounded like raindrops on a tent. A few stuck into my shoe, and two pricked my leg through my trousers.

"I hate this job," I muttered as I crawled toward the desk. I got the drawer open as Casper popped my stapler and prepared for another assault. I pulled out a small, metal-bottomed cylinder, which made a rattling noise as I shook it.

"Magic rattle?" Rhian asked.

A gray ball of feline fury scrambled into the room, claws digging into the carpet. Alley, the museum's cat, pounced onto my desk, spilling tickets onto the floor as he leapt and batted at the air. His paws flailed like something out of a Bruce Lee movie. He hopped down to the floor and reared again, continuing to bat the air as he herded his invisible opponent toward the door. Then, tail still lashing, he pranced back to me.

"Cat treats," I explained, opening the lid and handing Alley his reward.

Rhian nodded. "Your ghost's afraid of cats then, is it?"

"Right." I cringed. "I mean, there's no such thing as ghosts."

"Must have been those kamikaze thumbtacks that threw me off." She twisted in her chair and began to pluck the tacks from her wheelchair. "Hey, you mind giving me a hand?"

"Look, I'm not supposed to tell anyone about the ghost." I knelt down to get the ones she couldn't reach. "T. J. says we've got enough problems without the public thinking the place is haunted."

"No worries. I won't say a word." She glanced about the chaos that was my office. "Does it have a name?"

I rolled my eyes. "Casper."

"Is he normally this much of a devil?"

"He's been getting worse all week. I think he knows WestFest is coming." She looked confused, so I tried to summarize as I sorted through the tickets. "You know the museum has a history with the Blue Devils, right?"

She nodded.

"They didn't tell me about it until after I took the job," I grumbled, mostly to myself. "It started about five years ago, when the convention center double-booked WestFest and the Blue Devils' motorcycle rally. The museum won, and the Blue Devils rode in to protest.

"It got ugly, and then one of their riders, a guy named Flame, decided to crash the rodeo. People then didn't know Flame was a necromancer, but they could tell he was strange." I had seen pictures in the archives. Calling Flame strange was like calling the Sahara a mite dry. "He's got an animal spine running up his helmet like a bone mohawk, and his bike is trimmed with deerhide and fringe. Dangling silver skulls on the handlebars, skull for the gas cap, and bull horns mounted in front.

"I guess he drove right out in the middle of the bull riding event. He wound up playing chicken with an eighteen-hundred pound Charbray bull, trying to scare it off. Bad idea.

"The cowboy jumped off. The bull and the motorcycle both wiped out. Flame crawled away, and the bull . . . um . . . well, he got a bit over-affectionate with the man's bike."

Rhian smirked. "Didn't take too kindly to that, did he?"

"No. The next year, I'm told he turned a skeletal rattlesnake loose in the vents. The year after that it was termites that refused to die." I had seen the doctored records that concealed thousands of dollars spent on termite bait. "Last year he turned the ghosts loose. Alley chased the others off, but this one seems to be stuck here."

Rhian scratched Alley behind his ears. He rubbed his gray-striped body against her wheelchair, then reared up for more attention. Rhian grinned, then glanced back at me. "No wonder T. J. suggested I stay out of the museum this week."

T. J.

I dropped the tickets and glanced at the clock and swore. "I was supposed to be downstairs fifteen minutes ago."

Rhian tagged along as I hurried toward the elevator, berating myself all the while. T. J. hated to be kept waiting. I wondered how many snide remarks they would gift me with this time. Lisa would say something, even if nobody else did. They all knew I didn't fit in, but Lisa was the only one willing to come out and say it. I didn't know if that made her more honest or more obnoxious.

I was so busy worrying, I almost didn't notice the music. Repetitive, quick-strummed chords on an acoustic six-string, coming from the gift-shop. Hadn't Lisa locked up for the meeting? I turned away from the conference room and headed back up the hallway. Another minute wouldn't make a difference, late as I was.

It wouldn't have mattered anyway. Nobody had made it to the conference room.

T. J. and Lisa were dancing together in front of the counter. They had overturned several shelves, but they danced on, stomping on postcards, bolo ties, and those leather Y2K keychains Lisa was still trying to sell. Dave, the archivist, was dancing by himself next to the music rack. His face was red, and his round body was dark with sweat. One hand clutched the wall as the other slapped his leg in time with the music.

"Over there, by the register," Rhian said.

The music came from a blue guitar, polished to such a perfect finish that I could see the dancers reflected on its surface. The strings were like silver tinsel, shivering with each note. I had seen it before, in one of the displays. It was Bobby Redcliff's guitar, and it was being played by Bobby Redcliff himself.

As far as I knew, Bobby Redcliff had died three years ago of lung cancer.

He looked good for a dead man. Unlike the intangible Casper, Redcliff looked as solid as any other cowboy. His skin was gray, and his eyes were filmed over, but his long fingers strummed without missing a beat. He had white hair, a blue bandana looped around his neck, and a tan cowboy hat on his head.

I knew who was responsible, even without glancing through the huge windows to see the leather-clad crowd outside. At the forefront, a needle-thin man in black and blue leather stood with his hands pressed against the window. Tiny skulls decorated the fringe of his vest. Flame, the Blue Devils' necromancer.

I grabbed a horseshoe-shaped picture frame and hurled it at Bobby Redcliff's head. It bounced off his skull and crashed into the souvenir plates behind him.

"That ain't your ordinary ghost, mate," Rhian said, tugging my shirt. "That's a bloody walking corpse. Time to back off."

I wasn't ready. All of the damage would eventually come back to my office when we had to fix the budget and file the insurance claims. More paperwork to pile up on my desk. I didn't have time for this!

I grabbed an oversized pewter belt buckle and threw it at the window. An instant later, I recalled T. J. explaining that they had replaced all the windows with shatter-proof glass as a precaution against vandalism. The buckle took a frosted chip from the window, but Flame simply grimaced and started wiggling his hands.

Bobby Redcliff walked toward us. My foot tapped nervously as I hunted for some other weapon.

"Now, Ted!" Rhian was already backing down the hall.

"I can't." I might not like my coworkers, but I couldn't just abandon them. "I've got to—"

"Dead fiddler coming up fast," she snapped.

I realized two things then. The same song was also coming from farther down the hallway, getting louder every second. And my foot was tapping in rhythm to the music. My whole body trembled with the urge to dance. I forced myself to break away and retreat after Rhian, all the while muttering how much I hated this job.

We made it as far as the branding dioramas, quarter-scale models of actual New Mexico cattle ranches. A third musician waited for us there, a woman armed with a harmonica. She played the same melody as the others. I reached for Rhian's chair, hoping we could squeeze past the rack of branding irons to escape.

I wasn't fast enough.

The music of the dead had perfect rhythm. I watched my body move, unable to control

even the muscles of my fingers or toes. I sensed that if ever a single note was delayed even an instant, it would open a gap in the music, a crack through which I could break free.

A part of me didn't want to. For the first time in months, I wasn't feeling overwhelmed and stressed about hotel bookings or missing credit card orders or arguments with the technical people about how to get our computers down to the convention center. My thoughts were slow and dreamlike. My entire body was warm, like I was relaxing in the summer sun.

The museum fragmented and reformed around me, and colors sparked in time with the music. It was like watching fireworks through a kaleidoscope. Sweat burned my eyes, since I couldn't blink more than once per measure of the music.

I began to hallucinate, thinking about the day I first came to the museum, almost a year after losing my job at the bank. All because one of the mining hot-shots couldn't balance his checkbook, then blamed it on me when his check bounced and the creditors threatened to repossess his Lamborghini.

He had fancied himself a cowboy too, with the big hat, the oversized buckle, and rattlesnake boots that looked like they were swallowing his legs.

The first few days, the museum people had tried to include me in their little group. They invited me along for margaritas one evening, then sat around talking about people I had never heard of, events I couldn't care less about, and town gossip I couldn't follow, having only lived in El Rito a couple of weeks. The few times I tried to contribute were met with awkward silence and looks I could only describe as pitying.

They didn't invite me along again, and I didn't ask.

The colors faded, and the beat of the music died, replaced by my pulse throbbing in my head. Strong hands grabbed my waist and lowered me to the floor.

"Shake it off, mate. Easy there."

"Rhian?" My body was trembling. I couldn't feel my legs. "What happened?"

She held up a battered brass harmonica and a fiddle with a broken neck. "I took their toys, and they rotted away on the spot. Made a hell of a mess, too."

I grabbed the arm of her wheelchair and pulled myself into a sitting position. "But the music. I couldn't move. How did you—"

"How do you think?" She tapped her legs with her free hand. Even the heavy jeans weren't enough to hide their frailness. "Never been much of a dancer, even back when these still worked."

"Then we can stop them. All we need to do is get you back to the gift shop, and—"

"Whoa. First off, I'm not too eager to face the music a second time, if you know what I mean. Second, I can't imagine your friend the necromancer would just sit around while we nicked his guitar."

I struggled to my feet, still holding her chair for support. "At least we're not helpless if he sends more musicians after us."

She shoved her wheels, pushing away and nearly costing me my balance. "You think part of me wouldn't rather be dancing?"

"What?"

Her hat shielded her face as she glanced back. "Come on, let's figure out how to get rid of this last fellow before he dances your mates to death."

"Bloody hell," Rhian said as she leaned back from my window. We had retreated to my office to plan and regroup.

"My thoughts exactly." I still didn't know how long it had taken Rhian to break the spell and free me, but it had been enough time for the rest of the Blue Devils to arrive. Motorcycles lined the street, all legally parked. I'd bet they even kept the meters fed. Others circled the block, turn signals winking at every turn. Nothing to justify police intervention.

I sat down. Some time while we were downstairs, Casper had returned and stapled the West-Fest tickets into a two-foot high, very phallic structure. Grabbing the staple remover, I began taking it apart. One by one, I flipped the tickets at the trash can. It didn't look like we would need them after all.

"Stop that," Rhian said.

"Why? You think they're going to just turn around and go home when they're through? You actually think they're going to let us hold your damned gathering?"

"I don't expect them to 'let' us do anything. Or are you planning to sit on your ass while they kill your friends?"

I flexed the rest of the tickets, showering them onto the carpet. "T. J. said they've never killed anyone before."

"Tell you what. You want to leave, you go right ahead." She backed away until her chair blocked the doorway. "But you're going to have to get past me, and I'll beat your ass from here to Queensland and back if you try."

I had no doubt she would do it. I had felt the strength in those arms. "What do you want me to do?"

She spat on my nice plush carpeting. "I want you to help me save this place and teach those bastards a lesson."

"Right. The accountant and the poet are going to rumble with the Blue Devils." Even if I wanted to fight, the numbers were plain. Twenty-plus gang members against a middle-aged man and a woman in a wheelchair.

"You still don't get it, do you?" She twisted her braid through her fingers as she talked. "Ever wonder why you've got hundreds of reservations, some going back as far as last year? Why folks come thousands of miles year after year? The people who bought those tickets, they're my family. We all are. For me, this is the one place I can be a cowgirl again. These folks don't see the chair, they see the woman I used to be before I went and got my spine crushed in a car wreck. And I'll be damned if I'm gonna let your bikers take that away from me."

I wanted to yell at her, to make her see how hopeless it was.

I also wanted to forget the way she had faced down two dead musicians to save me, a man she barely knew. I tried to tell myself it was because she needed my help to rescue her *real* friends in the gift shop—her "mates"—but I didn't buy it.

"Do you have any idea how to fight them?"

"Not a clue, mate. But it'd better be quick. They weren't looking so good, especially Dave."

Her easy forgiveness only made me feel more ashamed. Ashamed, and . . . envious. I had heard that same passion from people on the phone as I took their reservations, but I had never understood. I had never belonged to a family like that. Not as a kid growing up out east, not at the bank, and certainly not here at the museum.

"We can't fight them," I said. Before she could argue, I added, "So here's what we're going to do . . ."

I left Rhian behind as I crept down the stairs to check on the others in the gift shop. With my fingers jammed in my ears to muffle the music, I hurried through the hall and peeked in the glass door.

No Worries, Partner

Everyone was still alive. Except for Bobby Redcliff, of course. Dave was slumped against the wall, but his feet were still tapping, and that was a good sign. Even through the door, I could feel the music beating through my veins, and I had to fight to keep my feet still.

I crept closer, and something tugged my leg. I yelped and hopped away. My hands brushed against a leather bullwhip coiled about my thigh, the lash flicking like a tongue. That damned ghost!

"Casper!" I ripped the whip away and threw it where I thought the ghost might be. I would have gone looking for Alley, but at that moment I realized my frantic hop had landed me square in front of the door, in plain view to anyone who happened to glance through the windows.

I looked out. Flame and several other gang members stared back at me. We started running at the same time. I made it six steps before the whip slithered around my legs again. Casper was going to get me killed! The bikers needed to circle around to the front of the building to get in, but by the time I scrambled free, I could already hear them kicking through the old velvet ropes at the vacant admission booth.

I ducked into the janitor's closet, pulled the door shut, and was immediately assaulted by a still-damp mop. Water dripped down my face and shirt, and a lemon scent filled my nostrils.

"Is Flame making you worse than usual, or are you just mad at me for turning Alley loose on you this morning?"

Casper dumped a bottle of glass cleaner onto my trousers. I could hear the Blue Devils coming, checking doors and singing, "Where did you go, little man?"

"Do you really want to do this?" I whispered. "If so, that's fine. You win. I'll let them have the museum. I'll surrender, quit my job, and go home."

I lowered my voice still further as the bikers neared my hiding spot.

"But before I leave, I'll crush Meow Mix into every doorway and window. I'll crawl through the ceiling and scatter it between the walls. I'll plant catnip in each crack of earth for a block. I'll dump dried catnip into the vents and the air conditioners. I'll buy every unspayed cat at the pound and bring them *here* when they go into heat. You thought Alley was bad? Do you have any idea how many stray cats there are in El Rito? If you don't help me, you're going to find out."

I waited to see what he would choose. I wasn't assaulted by any more cleaning supplies, which I took as agreement. I cracked the door and peeked out. "Do exactly what I say. If we get out of this, I'll find a way to keep Alley off your back."

The bikers were a few doors down, checking the restrooms. I took a deep breath, slipped into the hallway, told Casper what to do, and took off.

The first biker was surprisingly easy. Casper slipped the bullwhip around his legs as he chased me back into the displays of the museum proper. He tripped and clobbered his head against a wooden display horse wearing a custom English saddle with silver and turquoise accents.

The next room was a history of cattle rustling. Many of the displays included some of the tricks and gimmicks used by local rustlers. I grabbed a wood and iron contraption, a pair of "shoes" that fit over a man's boots and allowed him to leave cow tracks when he walked. I threw them at the first biker to follow me into the room.

It looked like I was going to miss completely, but the shoes changed trajectory in mid-air. Casper aimed a bit lower than I would have, but it was effective.

Unfortunately, we still had Flame to deal with. He scanned the air, ignoring me as he hunted his renegade ghost. He grabbed a trinket from his belt, a bit of braided hair and animal bones, then waved his arms and shouted in a language I didn't recognize.

I looked around for another weapon, something to distract the necromancer, when another gang member plowed into me from behind. Stunned and bruised, I lay there and waited to be pummeled or killed.

Nothing happened. I rolled over to find a tarnished Colt revolver floating in mid-air. The man who had tackled me was now backing into the wall as fast as he could scoot.

I reached for the gun, changed my mind, and fled before they could figure out that any gun kept in a museum was unlikely to be loaded.

I made it. I stopped at the fire exit, and I heard no sounds of pursuit. I could slip free. Even if the alarm went off, the bikers outside wouldn't want to cause a public commotion by chasing me. I could escape!

Escape, and abandon Rhian here, alone. Abandon T. J. and the others to Flame's mercy.

I glanced at my watch. Only ten minutes since I had left Rhian upstairs. I didn't know how long I could keep running.

My hand wavered on the steel bar of the fire door, then slipped down to my side.

I knew the museum better than the Blue Devils. I managed to avoid them for nearly an hour. They finally found me hiding behind a player piano, sweat drenching my shirt as I massaged my cramped legs.

Flame's attire was even more disturbing up close. He still wore his helmet, spine and all. Several ribs hugged the side like insect legs. The rat skulls on his fringe rattled like beads as he walked. He smelled like gas and, strangely enough, chocolate.

"How'd ya do it?" he demanded. His friend kept my wrists bent as they marched me back to the gift shop. "How'd ya make my ghost act up like that?"

The longer I kept them busy, the more time I bought for Rhian. I fought to keep my voice steady. "Call it a hostile buyout."

"Don't give me no lip, boy." He grabbed my tie and smiled. "Else I'll slice the lips right off your face and feed 'em to my pets back home."

His companion never spoke. I could barely see his face, but the glimpse I got when I craned my neck revealed a man who appeared almost as uncomfortable as I felt. Could it be that Flame wasn't that popular even in his own gang? Who could blame them, really? The man talked to ghosts and walked around with dead animals hanging off of his jacket.

"You cowboys are so damn stubborn," Flame said. He ripped the wrapper off of a Kit Kat and jammed the first piece into his mouth. "Blue Devils never forget an insult. You people didn't even apologize for pushing us off of our turf."

"I wasn't here when that happened," I snapped. Then, either because I was too tired and angry to care, or else because Rhian's bluntness had rubbed off, I added, "Can I help it if you had to take it up the tailpipe?"

The biker holding my wrists snorted.

Flame turned red. He grabbed my face and squeezed. With his other hand, he pulled out a bone-handled knife. "I don't like folks talking crap about me or my boys. How about I fix it so you keep what we call a 'respectful silence' from here on?"

He moved the blade in front of my eyes like a cobra preparing to strike. My mouth went dry as the desert, and in the midst of my panic, I found myself wondering if losing my tongue on the job would be covered by workman's comp.

"G'day, Flame." Rhian waved as a tall man pushed her chair up the hall. To judge from the blue guitar on her lap, she had come straight from the gift shop.

"How'd you get that guitar?" Flame snapped. I wondered the same thing, since I knew Flame had left at least a dozen Blue Devils guarding the gift shop.

"This here is Dell Johnson," she said, pointing to the man pushing her chair. "Three-time state champion roper. He plucked this thing out of Redcliff's hands as slick as a whistle."

Dell touched his hat in greeting.

Flame scowled and grabbed one of his skulls.

"Wouldn't do that, if I were you," Dell said softly. He cocked a thumb at the gift shop, then backed away, allowing us room to see.

Dell wasn't the only stranger in the building. Four more people stood in the shop, helping the gasping museum staff to recover. One of the gang members was using a grease-stained rag to wipe up the puddle that had been Bobby Redcliff.

Outside, the rest of the Blue Devils were surrounded by another thirty or so men and women, most of whom wore cowboy hats. Pickup trucks, Jeeps, and even a yellow topless Corvette were parked throughout the street.

"My mates weren't too happy when they found out about your little game," Rhian said. "We figured we'd have a word with you blokes, see if we couldn't work things out."

Behind her, Dell smiled and played with a Bowie knife, the blade of which was longer than Flame's entire knife.

"Your friends decided to play nice," Rhian said. "How about you?"

Flame played nice. By the time the police arrived to investigate why Fifth Street was blocked off, he and the rest of the Blue Devils had already left, with the understanding that next time would be far less pleasant.

"Think they'll be back?" Rhian asked.

I was bent over my computer, trying to get the blasted WestFest tickets formatted again. I had been working fourteen-hour days since the Blue Devils left three days ago. But so had the rest of the staff, as well as a few of the cowboys who had stuck around to guard the place and found themselves making copies, returning phone calls, and driving equipment to the convention center.

"I doubt it," I said. "You had almost forty local cowboys here in an hour. Think what we could do with more time."

It still amazed me that so many had come. Of those forty, not one had breathed a word to the newspapers or TV reporters. But I guess families were always the best at keeping secrets.

"What about Casper? I haven't seen him around lately."

The ghost had survived Flame's magic, if "survived" was the right word for a ghost. He had fled to T. J.'s office, where he ripped the keys off the keyboard and arranged them on the desk to spell "BIKRS GO H0ME."

"I gave him an office," I said. "The empty one next door. The door's always closed, so it keeps Alley away. T. J. wasn't too happy about it, but he didn't argue much. His exact words were, 'I reckon I owe you one.'"

She laughed. "That just leaves you then. Are you gonna join us for WestFest, or were you planning to stay holed up in here the whole time?"

I gestured at the disaster that was my office. "I still need to get this mess sorted out. Ticket receipts are missing, the gift shop inventory needs to be redone, and—"

"You need a break, mate. You should at least come by my reading on Saturday. I've got a new poem you'll like. I call it 'The Bean Counter and the Blue Devil.'"

I flushed, pleased and annoyed at the same time. "If I'm just a bean counter, don't you think I'd be a bit out of place?"

"Hell, mate. You stood up to those dipsticks long enough for me to round up the gang. You've got as much right to be there as anyone. If folks say otherwise, they can answer to me."

I grinned. "It's a cowboy gathering. I can't even ride a horse!"

"And I can?"

Before I could answer, she took off her hat and tossed it to me. I caught it automatically. "Take it." She laughed again. "It's better than that cheap tourist crap Lisa sells in the gift shop." Despite everything I had been through in the past week, I laughed right along with her. Rhian winked and backed toward the door. "See you around, cowboy."

Pentacle on His Forehead, Lizard on His Breath

JAMES MAXEY

I ran three red lights trying to reach David before the cops did. I steered with one hand and had the cell phone in the other, trying to talk him down. Five minutes had passed since David called me for help, whispering, sounding paranoid, which was good, paranoid was good. Paranoid might keep him cautious. With luck, he hadn't given anyone a reason to call 911. What worried me was that he'd stopped responding. I was pretty sure he'd dropped his phone. I kept yelling, "It's okay! I'm almost there!" but the only reply was distant shouting, something about keys. Or maybe monkeys.

I slowed to a less noticeable speed before reaching Adam's Art Supplies. I was relieved that only a few passersby stared at David as he waved his arms and shouted at the open door of his van. Probably the cops weren't on their way, but I decided to assume they were. This scene was the worst nightmare of every friendly neighborhood drug dealer. Acid was developed as a truth serum. Who knew what David might tell the cops about me?

"David," I said as I got out of the car, two parking spaces behind him. He looked up, then down, and stopped shouting. He reached to the asphalt and picked up his cell phone.

"Buzz?" he asked into it.

I kept my voice calm and steady. "I'm right behind you, David. You don't need the phone."

"Okay," he said into the phone.

I switched from calm to condescending. "David, man, I'm disappointed. You know what I told you about set and setting."

He twisted his torso and neck around to look at me, as if his shoes were nailed to the ground. He stood in the middle of a messy smear of paint. He'd dropped his bag of art supplies and had been stepping on the tubes, bursting them. Muddy, flesh-toned sneaker prints showed evidence of his pointless meandering around the van.

"Buzz! Thank God you're here."

"How you doing, David?" I noticed that he'd drawn an upside-down pentacle on his forehead in ballpoint pen. "Looks like you might be having a little bit of a bad trip."

"No, no. I was doing fine until they took my keys."

"Who?" I asked, worried that some conscientious citizens had already tried to intervene.

"The monkeys."

"What monkeys, David?"

He rolled his eyes and pointed at the van. He stammered, plainly frustrated at explaining the obvious. "The *monkeys* in the *van*."

"I don't see any monkeys," I said. "It's okay. I think they've gone."

He ran his hand through his hair, leaving a wet red streak. I thought he was bleeding, until I realized it was paint. He stared at me, looking nervous. "No," he said, dropping his voice to a raspy whisper. "They're invisible monkeys."

I nodded. "Makes sense. I can't see them."

"They've taken my keys and locked the doors."

I looked into the open vehicle. The keys were in the ignition. I leaned in and grabbed them. He snatched my arm and yanked me back.

"Are you crazy?" he asked. "They crush skulls with those jaws. They eat brains, Buzz. It's their *Jell*-O. Don't you know anything?"

I pushed the van door shut with my free arm.

"It's okay," I said, jiggling the keys so he'd notice them. "They're trapped now."

David loosened his grip on my arm. I could see him trying to fit this turn of events into the fractured dream-story in his head. I carefully, cautiously placed my arms around him and hugged him. "It's okay," I whispered. "You're safe now."

Some people think pushers don't give a damn about their clients. But this is a business like any other, and the secret of any long-term relationship is customer service. I sold him the acid. I'd help get him down. David was my favorite customer. His money/sense ratio was heavily skewed toward money. He spent in a weekend what other clients spend in a year. It would break my heart to see him go to jail.

David swayed in my arms for several long seconds, then pushed me away, shaking his head.

"I'm cool," he said.

"You're cool?" I asked.

"Cool. It's cool."

I looked around. Everyone watching turned away. My appearance on the scene had released them from the potential responsibility of dealing with the psychotic screamer in their midst. They could now stay uninvolved without guilt. But the sooner we got out of the open, the better.

"Why don't I take you back to your place?" I said. "We can come back for the van later."

He nodded.

"Why'd you come out anyway? You know what I told you. It's set and setting. You've got to have the right mindset, and you've got to be in a place with positive energies. You definitely shouldn't be out driving around."

"Ran out of ghost juice," he said. "Decided to make a mayonnaise run."

I nodded, figuring it made sense to him, and wasn't important to me. I knelt down to gather up the scattered tubes. A large tube of white had somehow escaped trampling. David dropped to his knees. I winced at the sound of his kneecaps hitting the asphalt.

"My God," he said, staring at the smeared and swirled paints that coated the parking space. "*My God.*"

"What?" I asked.

"Don't you see?" He opened his arms before him, encompassing the scene, a look of serenity upon his face.

"What?" I tried to control my impatience.

"It's him," he said, contemplating the muddy smear. "It's my father's face."

I rubbed my temples. *Of course.* David has this *thing* about his father.

Luckily, David fell quiet after that. I was able to guide him into my car. I noted the paint he was getting on the seats and floor mat. I would add the cleaning cost to his tab. He wouldn't mind. David had a nearly bottomless well of money from some kind of trust fund. As I closed my door I heard sirens, still a few blocks away. I drove off calmly, merging into traffic as a black and white pulled into the parking lot. No problem. Everything was good. No harm except for a little mess from spilled paints. The cops wouldn't waste time on this.

"Teakettle," David said.

I nodded in agreement. Occasionally, acid will make you pull the wrong words down from the little shelves in your head. No sense in trying to puzzle it out.

"We'll get you home in a jiffy," I said. "Get you to bed. You look tired."

"I haven't slept in three days."

"Really?" I asked, forgetting the question was useless.

"Three or seven." He held up four fingers. "The ecstasy keeps me boiling."

"Right." Whatever was keeping him going wasn't ecstasy, though, since the E he'd bought from me was just generic Sudafed.

Fortunately, David didn't live far, just down by the campus. He lived in the attic of this old Victorian house. The whole floor was his, a huge space, which he used as a studio for his paintings. David's stuff was pretty good, but he was nowhere as famous as his father. Of course, his father hadn't gotten famous until after he was dead. I guided David up the stairs. His body was trembling, his face pale and sweaty. The drugs were still riding him hard. But once I got him into his apartment, I could turn him over to his girlfriend Celia and be done with this.

Except, of course, Celia wasn't home. Or at least she wasn't answering the knocks. The only sound from inside was a steady, shrill whistle.

"Where's Celia, David?"

"Oh. She left. We had a fight."

"Too bad."

"She was trying to hide all the knives."

"Hmm," I said.

"So I had to do the ritual with a toenail clipper."

"Ah," I said.

Fortunately, I still had his keys, so getting in wasn't a problem.

The place was a mess. Books and canvases were scattered everywhere, and black plastic bags had been hung over the windows. Squat candles guttered at two points of a pentacle that had been laid out on the floor with duct tape. The other candles were extinguished, reduced to shapeless pools of wax. A horrible odor filled the air, like something burning. A cloud of steam rolled from the little curtained off area at the back of the studio that served as the kitchen.

"Teakettle," David said, moving toward the kitchen. He took the shrieking kettle off the tiny electric stove. He opened the top, and all but vanished in the steam cloud that issued forth. The stench gagged me.

"My herbalist recommended this lizard," he said. "Reconnect with the dinosaur within. Mainline to the oblongata." I assumed he was grabbing the wrong words again until I noticed a baggie of dried reptile parts on the counter, labeled with a Chinese script.

"Sure," I said, picking up the baggie, staring at the recognizable heads and eyes looking back at me, "*my* stuff is illegal. Jesus, David, you'll put anything in your mouth, won't you?"

"At least once," he said, pouring himself a cup of the tea, which trickled from the spout with the speed and thickness of jet-black honey. "Want any?"

"Pass," I said. I headed away from the kitchen before he actually drank the stuff. I pride myself on a strong stomach, but hey. I looked at the canvases propped up around the room. This was stuff I hadn't seen before. David had abandoned his realistic style and was painting very dark shapes now, geometric, almost architectural, like shadowy rooms and halls, but off somehow, sinister.

As David relieved himself in the bathroom, I stooped to take a closer look at his reading material. There were a dozen books propped open on the floor. All his books were stained. The corners of LeVay's *Book of the Living* were smudged with mustard. Saint Germaine's *The Door Beyond Death* had been dropped into the tub at some point, and was now brown and warped. Crowley's *Magic and Mind* had paint-smeared pages ripped out and tacked against the legs of the easel. I got a closer look at the painting on the easel. From across the room, the canvas looked blank. Now, I could see it was glazed with brush-stroked mayonnaise that was starting to turn a little yellow.

Perched on a small table near the easel was the only pristine book in the room. It was a copy of *Into Madness*. I'd heard about it, of course. It was the book that had just been published about David's father, Alex Cambion. I skimmed over the excerpt on the back cover. Alex had been an illustrator for magazines in the seventies, before David was born. Some people said he painted like Norman Rockwell then, but that wasn't the work that made him famous.

David came out of the bathroom, naked.

"You going to stick around?" he asked.

"You still tripping?"

"How can I tell?" he asked. "Maybe. I've been asleep for three days now."

"Awake," I said.

"Whatever. I don't think the acid had any effect. I still feel too grounded."

"I think it had more effect than you might be noticing, man." I studied his face. It was hard to tell if he was fully back. Acid can be surprisingly subtle. Its effects can ebb and flow. "It was good stuff. I play straight with you."

He nodded. "You might be the only friend I have left, Buzz. Did you know Celia left me?"

"I heard."

"She thinks I'm crazy," he said, a sweep of his hand directing my gaze to the duct-tape pentacle. "I've been trying to talk to my father."

"Nothing crazy there," I said. "Lot's of people miss their folks when they pass on."

"I can't remember him," said David. "He killed himself when I was seven. He was schizophrenic. He'd been living in an asylum since I was five."

"Bad break," I said.

"Was it? Last week my grandmother auctioned one of Father's asylum paintings for nine million, and that's not a record for his work. His suffering has paid for everything I own."

"Huh," I said. "Kind of his gift to you, maybe."

"No," said David. "I've been trying to get inside his mind. I've been trying to get into his world with the drugs and the sleep and the rituals." He shook his head. "I've gotten on the edge, I think. I keep getting close. But I'm too *sane*. Father didn't know his own name at the end. Words were just a maze to him. All he understood by the end was how to put paint onto canvas. Some people say they find a language in his final paintings. I've never understood the vocabulary."

He seemed lucid now, as lucid as a sweaty naked man with a pentacle on his forehead and lizard on his breath is ever likely to be. I edged my way to the door as I said, "You seem to be feeling better."

"Better is so relative," he said, bending over to place new candles at the points of the pentacle. "Ever since that book came out, I've just been so . . ."

After a moment, I realized he wasn't going to finish the sentence. He began to light the candles.

He stood in the middle of the pentacle, his eyes closed, his hands folded before him in a prayer, his paintbrush pointing toward heaven. The way he held his arms, I could see for the first time the deep scratches along the insides of his wrist.

Wonderful. No wonder Celia had hidden the knives. I decided to stick around until David fell asleep. If he'd really been awake three days, I wouldn't have to wait long. Acid and lizard tea couldn't keep a person going forever.

I snatched a beer from his fridge and plopped onto the couch. David was saying a prayer, mumbling most of the words. I tuned him out. A lot of addicts are into this mystic mumbo jumbo. They use the acid to try to "rend the veil of reality" as David put it once. They are convinced that there's something more than their physical body and the world they can see with their eyes. I have no financial incentive to argue. But my years in the business have led me to one pretty solid conclusion. People are nothing but chemistry. There's no soul or spirit separate from our bodies. We're just big, walking pots of brain fluid soup. We can change the way we think and feel by adding the right spices, a little acid here, a little pot there, simmer in some beer, and hey, you get happy stew if you don't set the heat too high and wind up scorched. All the occult bullshit, the prayers, the candles, were harmless, but pointless.

At last, David finished his prayers, opened his eyes, and focused on the canvas. But he knew I was still there.

He said, "My grandmother says that the first real sign that something was wrong was when Dad began having problems with insomnia. Just after I was born. He was twenty-three. And now I'm twenty-three."

He dipped the brush into dark blue paint and began to work. I watched him for a while. I broke into a second beer, then a third. He seemed very calm. The way he painted was almost like a dance. His whole body swayed and dipped as his brush swirled across the canvas. Night fell and the little light that seeped around the trash bags dimmed. The candles cast strange shadows. On the walls, it was almost like two people stood before the canvas, moving independently, one slow and deliberate, the other manic. The air was stuffy and warm. At some point, I must have fallen asleep.

It was David who woke me.

"See what I have done," he said.

I looked at my watch. He'd been at this all night. I was stiff and dry-mouthed. Blearily, I allowed myself to be led to the canvas. My eyes popped open, wide-awake. I'd seen plenty of David's work. He was talented, sure, but this was something else. It was rendered with near photographic detail. It seemed like it should have taken days to paint. David must have worked like a demon to finish it in a single night. And from his twisted, drug-altered mind, had sprung . . . tranquility.

The painting was reminiscent of a *Saturday Evening Post* cover. A painter sat before his canvas, and his toddler son was in his lap. The painter looked down, beaming with pride, at his son with a brush in his hand and paint all over his clothes. And the canvas they sat before was like a mirror, with a boy and his father painting from the other side, and behind them sat a mirror, in which the larger painting was recreated, and within this was a canvas recreating the scene, and so on. The detail was amazing, but even more impressive were the expressions on the faces. There was so much happiness captured here. And yeah, corny as it sounds, even love.

"Whoa," I said. "This is really good. Really, really good. The faces . . . whoa."

"He doesn't remember this," said David. "My son was only two at the time. But he used to sit with me for hours. He loved to watch me work. He would fall asleep in my lap."

I sighed. He was still tripping. David didn't have kids.

"David," I said, "you're wearing me thin, man."

"He thinks you're his friend," said David. "You have to tell him something important for me. He'll believe you."

"Forget it," I said, rubbing my eyes. I was tired of this trip, tired of puzzling out drug logic. Would this weird mother never crash? "Write yourself a note or something. I'm going home."

David grabbed me by the shoulders and pulled us face to face. His grip was unbelievable, the kind of strength you get with PCP or something.

"Listen to me, punk," said David. "You know who I am. Don't play with me."

"I know who you think you are," I said, in the most soothing voice I could muster. "You're tripping. You're not Alex Cambion. Snap out of this."

"My time remaining is short. I would as soon spit on you as speak to you. You're a detestable poisoner of souls, but you're the only one within reach. I pray you have one tiny shred of decency within you."

"Dude," I said. "Chill out. I'm your friend. You know you can trust me."

"Then tell him," said David, his voice trembling on the edge of tears. "Tell him I loved him."

"Sure, no problem, I'll tell him. Trust me."

Finally, his eyes closed, and he collapsed in my arms. I dragged him to the couch. He felt light as a skeleton.

At last I was free to leave. I'd been around enough to know that a crash this hard wouldn't be over any time soon. He was out at least the next 12 hours, maybe more.

I went back to my life, happy that the worst of the ordeal was over. I swung back that night to check on him, expecting him to be zonked out, and found him awake. He was sitting on the floor in front of the canvas, his cheeks sunken, dark, heavy bags beneath his eyes.

"You okay?" I asked.

"This painting is still wet," he said, staring at his paint-covered fingertips.

"You painted it last night. No big surprise. Don't oils take a while to dry?"

"Oils need a lot of time to dry. It takes weeks to paint some things because of this. Even with a month I couldn't have painted this," said David. "I've never had his skill."

"You never know what you have in you," I said.

"It's signed by him. Alex Cambion."

"Huh," I said, looking at the signature. "Sorry dude, I was here. Watched you work on it. It's yours. Maybe that acid did you good. Better art through chemistry."

"It's like a message from him," said David, his voice cracking. "But I was never with him when he painted. This is like something to taunt me, something to remind me of a life I never had."

"Maybe you just didn't get close enough to understand him, man. You still need to do more inner work to touch the space he was in."

"Yeah," said David. "I guess so."

"Look, you tripped pretty hard these last few days. If you need it, I got some stuff that will help you sleep. You drink plenty of water, get some rest, and maybe in a week or so you'll be ready to try again."

"I don't know."

"It's worth a shot. I sold you Sunshine last time. But a shipment of Hearts is coming down next week. It's pricier, but should give you a little more control, and let you go deeper than your last trip. All you need is the right set and setting."

"Maybe," said David, scratching the scabs along his wrist, his voice distant and tired. "Maybe. I just want to connect with him, you know. I want to know if he even knew I was alive. That's all I'm asking. Just, maybe, if, you know, he loved me."

I nodded, then said, "David . . . maybe next time you'll find out."

Pentacle on His Forehead, Lizard on His Breath

I talked a little longer to make sure he was okay. I left him only after I was sure he wasn't a danger to himself, and with the promise that he would get some sleep. As for what he'd said to me the night before, I guess David is brain-fried enough that he might believe that his father's ghost borrowed his body. But I know what's best. David is the sort who can take almost anything and twist it around until it tortures him. What kind of guy would I be if I didn't watch out for my best customer?

Undead Air
JOHN PASSARELLA

Philadelphia morning show DJ Preston Elliot sat in front of his adjustable microphone and said, "Oh, man, this is fucked up."

Fortunately, he wasn't speaking on air at the time. A glimpse at the Scott System LCD screen countdown timer showed 1:57 left to play in U2's "Sunday Bloody Sunday." In hindsight, probably not the best song choice. He hadn't bothered to check the queue, but who could blame him after the early morning attacks on L.A., Boston, New York, Chicago, and right there in Philly.

Preston had dressed for comfort in a black and tan long sleeved T-shirt, jeans and sneakers, although funeral attire would have been more appropriate on this morning.

"What now?" his co-host, Steve Morrison, asked from his usual standing position in front of his iMac at the far corner of the U-shaped workstation. Long enough to accommodate the five show regulars plus an in-studio guest or two during normal broadcasts, the table seemed much too large for just the two of them. Wearing a black T-shirt, jeans and work boots, Steve shrugged in frustration. "Do we leave? Stay? I mean, what the fuck? Does anybody even give a shit if we stick around? Unless they're stuck out there"—he jerked his thumb toward the soundproof layers of glass overlooking the early morning darkness of Riverside Drive—"you can bet your ass they're glued to CNN."

After urging the rest of their morning show crew to head home and join their families and loved ones, Preston and Steve were alone in the studio. They recognized a duty to their listeners, to keep the lines of communication open during the crisis. "Might as well stay," Preston said with a shrug. "At least up here we're not breathing that red mist shit."

"According to these reports out of Homeland Security, the red mist has no apparent effect on the living," Steve said, looking up grimly from the Web browser display on his iMac. "Only the dead."

"Forget bioterrorism talk," Preston said, shaking his head with lingering disbelief. "No one saw this weird shit coming."

They had been less than ten minutes into their high-energy morning drive-time radio show when Kathy, their traffic reporter, received an update through Metro Networks about a multi-car pileup on the Schuylkill Expressway. Forty cars, maybe more. Horrible accident, they'd assumed. But it hadn't been an accident. A terrorist group calling themselves the Counterstrike Liberation Front had soon claimed responsibility for the planning and execution of the early morning tragedy. A scenario which had played out with frightening similarity in five different cities across the United States.

Near as they could ascertain from scattered reports, an oil slick on the Schuylkill had caused motorists to lose control of their vehicles, resulting in a multi-car pile-up. While the dazed and injured had climbed out of their cars, pickups, SUVs and minivans, a tanker truck abandoned—or positioned—nearby released an ominous red mist moments before erupting in a staccato series of explosions designed to hurl deadly shrapnel at and through the accident survivors.

No one at Homeland Security could have predicted what happened next.

The strange red mist had settled on the dead, as well as the maimed and dying, a chemical determined to be a nerve agent, though some were calling it a nerve *re-agent* since its sole effect seemed to be reanimation of the dead.

"Who the hell are these guys?" Preston asked. "I've never heard of the Counterstrike Liberation Front."

Steve leaned over the iMac, bracing himself on the fists of both hands as he skimmed a relevant website. "Been flying under the radar," he said. "Says here they're mercenary terrorists."

"Terrorists for hire?"

"Terrorists hired by other terrorists."

"What the hell happened to martyrdom? Dying for their cause?"

"Gets old fast," Steve said acerbically.

"Anonymous terrorists," Preston said as he picked up his headphones. "What's the point?"

"Fear of the unknown," Steve guessed. "Make us second-guess every national and international policy."

"Thirty seconds," Preston said. He was coming out of a song with no idea what to say to the frightened masses out in the predawn darkness. Queued up next on the Scott System was a "Preston and Steve" sweeper, which Preston cancelled. Airing a show promo announcement would have been inappropriate. Hell, everything seemed inappropriate at the moment.

With twenty seconds left of the song, Preston fielded a call on the station's private line and knew he had to put it on the air.

"Preston, it's me," said a familiar and frantic voice. "I'm here. On the Schuylkill. Right in the middle of it."

"Aaron?"

"Yes." Aaron Murphy, the station's overnight disc jockey, had become ill and left the station early, after setting up about a half-hour of automated programming to finish his show. "Hey, on second thought, my stomach flu wasn't so bad."

"Listen, Aaron, I'm about to go on air. You up for it?"

"Why I called in, man."

Preston reached over to the Scott System LCD and tapped the toggle to switch the system from automatic to manual. When the song finished, there would be nothing but dead air, waiting on what Preston would do next.

With practiced hands, Preston worked the large console, potting up the sliders for his and Steve's microphones. Above the studio clock, the red ON AIR sign lit up. Preston leaned toward his microphone and said, "Hey, gang, this is Preston back with Steve. You know what? This morning gets crazier by the minute. We have Aaron Murphy on the phone with us and he's at the accident scene." Preston pushed up a third slider. "Aaron, tell us what's happening there."

"It's a living nightmare here, Preston."

"Are you injured?"

"No, but . . ." A hiss of static replaced his voice for a moment. ". . . trapped within the barricaded section of the Schuylkill. It's dark and my windshield is cracked—a mess really—with that red junk all over it, but I can see the flashing police lights at either end."

Steve spoke into his own microphone. "Is it true? The stuff we're hearing?"

"Depends on what you're hearing," Aaron replied. "But, yes, the dead are walking, if that's what you mean. They—they gotta be dead. Some of them. Big holes in them, but not bleeding, not really. Dripping . . . oozing, but not bleeding." He heaved a sigh. "Worst part is, they're attacking anyone who survived the explosions and all that shrapnel."

"Attacking . . . how?" Steve said.

"With their teeth, like rabid dogs."

"They're not—are they . . . ?"

"Eating the living?" Aaron said. "Don't think so. They stop as soon as the living become the dead—or undead."

"What about your position? Are you safe?" Preston said.

"Well, they haven't noticed me yet."

"Can you reach the police perimeter?" Steve asked.

"Not a good idea. The police are shooting anything that moves," Aaron said grimly. "Right now, I'm hiding in my car, trying not to move."

"What the hell? That's nuts!"

"Must figure we're all contaminated."

Over the connection, in the background, pops and bursts of gunfire were punctuated by indiscernible, guttural announcements over bullhorns intermingled with moans and screaming.

"Oh, no!"

"Aaron?" Preston said. "What's up?"

"Twice as many police cruisers now. . . . Something's happening. Lot of cops gathering at the barricades, lining up," Aaron was breathing rapidly. "Think they're planning a sweep. To, um, to clean it all out."

"Listen, Aaron," Steve said. "Stay below the dash. Behind the engine block. You'll be safe there."

"Not for long, I'm afraid . . ."

The bursts of gunfire became almost continuous, like violent white noise, along with amplified shouting, bloodcurdling screams and—growling.

"Aaron? What the hell's happening?"

"They're coming," Aaron said. "Rushing the area. Shooting everyone! Gas masks." A forced exhalation. "This is it."

"Stay down, Aaron," Preston said. "Keep your head down, man!"

"Preston, the weirdest part is being just across the river from the studio—so close—and yet it's like I'm on another world. With the gas masks, the humans look like aliens. And the dead—the undead . . ."

"What? What about the undead?"

"They're running—staggering really—toward the river," Aaron said. "They—they're jumping—jumping right into the Schuylkill!"

Preston sighed. "Maybe that's the end of it," he said. "Stay low, Aaron. Wait it out."

Steve glanced at the dark sky through the multiple layers of glass enclosing the fourth floor radio studio. "Preston, if they're dead," he said with a note of alarm in his voice, "they can't drown."

"So—what? They'll swim?"

"Across the river," Steve said, nodding. "Or, hell, walk across the bottom, like a scene out of Harryhausen. And—"

"We're across the river." Preston finished. The sounds relayed through Aaron's cell phone connection had subsided. "Aaron? You there?"

"Yes," Aaron whispered. "I think . . . they're all gone. All the undead and—no! It saw me—the windshield—!"

Preston and Steve heard a muffled crash, followed by the sounds of an intense struggle and enraged, bestial growling, punctuated by an all-too-human shriek.

Aaron screamed, "Oh, Christ! Somebody, help—HELP!"

The cell connection receded. Aaron had probably dropped the phone during the struggle. The crisp report of two gunshots made Preston flinch in his chair. "They . . . they shot them. Cops shot both of them."

Steve passed a trembling hand over his shaved head and swallowed hard. "We don't know that, Preston," he said. "Maybe they needed two shots to put down the dead guy. Maybe Aaron . . ."

They heard several moments of crackling and hissing from the dropped cell phone, then a single click and the stark silence of a lost connection. Out of habit, Preston slid the potameter down. Hopeful speculation aside, he didn't expect another sound to emanate from Aaron's phone.

Steve walked to the window and looked down four floors at the parking lot, awash in islands of cold gray illumination from street lights. Then his gaze swept up and across the dark, hulking expanse of trees blocking the view of the Schuylkill River. "Can't see a damn thing," he whispered.

They arose from the murky depths of the Schuylkill, a ragtag army of the walking undead. As they scrambled up the embankment, river water gushed from their sopping clothes and gaping wounds. They were an eclectic representation of the early morning workforce. Some wore tailored or off-the-rack business suits. Others sported T-shirts imprinted with various silk-screened endorsements paired with jeans, while a few wore drab work uniforms or jumpsuits complete with embroidered nametags. Many of the previously well-dressed women had already lost, broken or cast aside their high heels. Whatever the former quality of their attire, the indiscriminate abuses of shrapnel, blood, and river water had leveled the sartorial playing field for the undead assemblage.

Bespattered with blood and viscera, some of it their own, they clambered up the uneven slope, cracked fingernails clawing for purchase. Shambling shadows, they lurched through the undergrowth to emerge at the tree line along Riverside Drive. Their undead faces were driven but deranged, filled with a base human instinct for violence. And they expressed their hostility solely against the living. The red mist's overriding imperative was rage against those who had escaped its fallout.

The road was curved, dark and deserted, but ascended to a series of lighted parking lots fronting an illuminated office building. With a string of anticipatory moans and struggling groans, they encouraged one another forward, toward the light and the living. Toward those they must destroy.

Jeff Richards alarmed his Mazda Tribute and walked toward the entrance of 100 Riverside Drive, a Conshohocken four-story brick office building his marketing firm shared with several other companies, including a prominent Philadelphia radio station. Because the station broadcasted around the clock, the parking lot was never deserted. Several cars, along with the colorfully painted radio station vans, always claimed the best spots, even though he was, without fail, the first to arrive at Richards and Cole, LLC. Though the cluster of cars that greeted his arrival seemed sparse for a Monday, he shrugged it off as an anomaly.

Undead Air

Per his morning routine, Jeff had listened to an assortment of classic rock CDs in his 6-CD changer throughout his commute. Far as he was concerned, this was an ordinary Monday.

He stopped at the empty, glass-enclosed first floor lobby entrance. As part of his morning routine, he held his aluminum travel mug filled with black coffee, a rolled up *Philadelphia Inquirer* tucked under the arm, and the tan leather briefcase his wife Lisa had gifted him Christmas before last. He set the briefcase down to punch his five-digit code into the door's security keypad. After the security mechanism clicked its release, he swung the door wide and held it with his foot. He reached down to scoop up his briefcase and, at that moment, heard scraping and shuffling sounds behind him.

Before he could react, a wet and slimy hand clamped over his face and wrenched his neck back. Something dark and fetid, growling inhumanly, leaned over him and teeth ripped into his throat. He struggled, screamed, and tried to break free, but there were more of them, wet and heavy bodies, clawing hands, surging over and past him in reeking waves, grabbing and stomping and biting, dragging him down and pulling him apart, until everything went mercifully dark—

—and then he awoke as one of them.

No longer alive, but undead. Chunks of flesh missing from arms and legs and a substantial portion of his throat, he no longer felt pain . . . only rage.

Amid the scattered newspaper and spilled coffee, his fallen body had propped open the door for the others.

Though he followed them into the familiar office building, his morning routine was forgotten. Any ideas or inspiration he may have had during the forty minute commute to Richards and Cole, LLC were likewise gone.

He now had a darker purpose.

"Fifteen seconds," Preston announced. "Anything?"

Piped through the station's hanging speakers, Evanescence's "Bring Me To Life" began to fade as Steve glanced out the window one more time. "Couple more cars in the lot. That's about it."

By mutual agreement, they had begun to alternate between playing a song and five or so minutes of on-air discussion. Any listeners wanting all news all the time would have already switched to an AM news station or turned to the television or Internet. The DJs would comment on the morning's events and take listener calls, but also throw in an occasional song for those who wanted to escape the madness for a few minutes.

"Maybe they swam downstream," Preston said as he flipped through some news updates and checked the latest from Metro Networks. "Cops reporting the closed section of the Schuylkill under control, but they're not opening it yet. Probably checking cars for survivors."

"And killing anything that moves out there."

Preston sighed. "Yeah, my gut says that's exactly what's happening. And they don't want the press in there until after the purge." Preston's eye caught a line of type on a news bulletin. "Shit!"

"What?"

"Oh, wait. Five seconds."

They slipped on their headphones.

Preston switched the Scott System to manual. As the song concluded, he potted up their mikes. The "On Air" light burned red. Preston first reported the Schuylkill Expressway update, but then turned his attention to the news bulletin. "Listen, gang, if you needed another reason to stay locked in your house, here you go. We're getting reports of the infection spreading. From the undead to the living. Recently living, that is."

Steve leaned toward his own mike. "What's going on?"

"Cop's gun jammed. The undead attacked and killed him. And then—"

"—he arose from the dead. Crap!"

"Says the cop was nowhere near the initial explosion and mist fallout."

"So it's propagating like some kind of undead virus."

"Through blood or saliva," Preston said. "They're not sure what happens if you actually survive the undead attack."

"Makes sense," Steve said. "Mortal wounds. You can't become undead without dying first."

"They haven't ruled out the possibility that a single bite could trigger a fatal infection?"

"Any evidence of that?"

"Too soon to tell," Preston said. "On a positive note, they caught one of the CLF bastards. Right here in Philly."

"How about a listener contest, Preston?" Steve suggested. "Winner gets to toss the scumbag into a wood chipper."

Preston smiled. "I don't have a problem with—what the hell?"

"What?"

Eyes wide, Preston was staring beyond Steve's shoulder at the heavy wooden door that opened on the hallway. Rather, he was looking through the narrow, vertical window pane, inset with safety mesh, which ran almost the full length of the door.

"What is it? I don't see anything."

"Someone's out there," Preston said nervously. "More than one someone."

"Who?" Steve asked. "We sent everyone home. Unless . . ." He cleared his throat. "This building's secure. Right?"

Preston stood, craning his neck. "Is it?"

"Okay, I'm starting to get a Murphy's Law vibe here," Steve said. Even tethered to his headphones, he could walk to within three feet of the locked hallway door, which was several paces nearer than the door leading into the offices. "Still don't see—"

A man's face slammed into the glass.

Steve had a split-second to note the man's face had been damaged before the impact. Swollen eye, missing teeth, gleaming white bone exposed through one lacerated cheek. The next moment, the glass pane was webbed with cracks and smeared with fresh blood. Despite the mess, Steve could see what was behind the man.

"Preston," Steve said grimly. "They're here. Lots of—"

A hand partially stripped of flesh smashed through the damaged window and strained to reach Steve's throat.

He jumped back reflexively. "Whoa! That was close." Close enough for him to notice the man's broken and bloody fingernails. Steve grabbed one of the studio's cushioned chairs and thrust it at the undead man who was forcing his body through the shattered window pane. Absurdly, Steve felt like a lion tamer. All he needed was a whip.

More of the undead piled up behind the first man, pushing him unmercifully through the narrow gap, and pounding on the door with their fists and feet.

"Preston," Steve said, lurching forward as several hands grabbed the chair leg and attempted to wrest control of it. "We'd better get out of here. While we can."

Preston nodded and spoke urgently into the microphone. "Listen, gang, this isn't a prank.

The radio station's been invaded. Any cops listening, haul ass to 100 Riverside Drive! We're counting on you! Hope we're back soon, people, but if not . . ." He took a deep breath to steady his voice. "Rage on!" He silenced the studio mikes, put the Scott System on automatic and wondered how long the station would run unattended before the undead destroyed the equipment. Peter Gabriel's "Red Rain" began to play.

Steve tugged off his headphones and released the chair, but had to duck as the undead man hurled it at him. Sailing over his head, the chair smashed the stack of plastic trays holding interoffice mail, timesheets, and scrap paper.

Preston whipped off his headphones, pushed the chair out of his way and hopped over the paper and plastic debris on the floor. Steve waited for him at the office door.

Some of the undead had picked up the short round table from the fourth floor lobby and were using it as a battering ram to break through the hallway door. The first undead man was almost all the way through the shattered window. His business suit was in tatters and smeared with blood. He was taking the brunt of the damage from the battering-table, but hardly seemed to notice or care as he clawed his way into the studio. Bloody drool looped down from his chin as he growled at them.

Preston shook his head.

"You're not thinking of going down with the ship."

"No," Preston said. "It's just weird how they don't feel any pain." He exhaled forcefully. "Okay, let's go. I have a plan. Assuming we can reach our office before them."

"Am I gonna like this plan?"

"Of course," Preston said with a grin. "It involves weapons."

Once through the door into the office area, Steve said, "Give me a hand."

They couldn't lock the door from outside the studio, so they did the next best thing. They barricaded it. After pushing an intern's desk against the door, they grabbed four chairs and piled them on top. "Should slow them down. For a couple minutes, anyway."

Steve nodded and they ran down the hallway to their office. They'd taken no more than a dozen steps when they heard the undead—probably several undead—slam into the barricaded door. A chair crashed to the ground, its impact muffled by the thin carpeting but still as startling as a cannon shot. "Hurry!"

They turned down the hall and ducked into their office, which served several of their on-air staff. Preston entered first. Right behind him, Steve closed the door softly and engaged the lock. Though large, the office was cluttered and windowless. Covering the walls were black and white Preston & Steve "Camp Out For Hunger" banners and more than a few life-sized posters of scantily clad starlets who had, invariably, graced the covers of numerous men's magazines.

Preston's left corner workstation featured a computer and three shelves packed with assorted collectibles. In the center of the office, a round walnut table functioned as an informal conference table. To the right, beyond their mounted dry erase idea board, was another desk, this one with a thirteen-inch color television that somebody—probably Casey, their producer—had left on, tuned to a cable news station running updates, expert analyst interviews, looped video and streaming news crawls without providing much new information. In the back right corner was Steve's inner office, packed with his Pro Tools digital audio editing workstation, a TiVo, VCR, DVD player, and a phalanx of action figures and spaceship models from various cult films and television shows. Between Preston's workstation and Steve's office stood two black four-drawer filing cabinets decorated with elliptical radio station bumper stickers. Atop these cabinets, Preston found the specific collectibles he hoped would be their salvation: his replica swords.

Over the years, he'd acquired full-sized replica swords from various movies, including *Highlander*, *Conan the Barbarian*, *Lord of the Rings* and *Kill Bill*. While most lacked the precise cutting edge of true weaponry, these swords had the potential to be lethal in their own right. Preston hefted two. "Do you want the Hattori Hanzo?" he asked, referring to the katana crafted by the fictional sword maker in *Kill Bill*. "Or Narsil?" The latter was a replica of the sword of Aragorn, warrior king of *Lord of the Rings*.

Before Steve could decide, the drop ceiling exploded.

An undead man wearing a blood-spattered gray T-shirt, jeans and work boots crashed to his hands and knees on the round conference table and blinked rapidly, as if startled by his failed attempt at stealth.

Steve reached for the nearest weapon, leaning against the file cabinets, which happened to be a baseball bat—a genuine Louisville Slugger—left as a souvenir by visiting members of the University of Delaware Blue Hens baseball team. He took a double-handed grip and swung for the fences.

The undead man growled—before his face disintegrated. Moreover, the force of the impact whipped the man's head around so violently that his neck snapped. Amid scattered papers and CDs, he toppled to the floor, truly dead.

Steve hefted the bat and gave a satisfied nod. "I'm good."

Preston shrugged. "Chick's dig the long ball." But he remained ambivalent about his own weapon choice. While Narsil had an epic pedigree, the blade of the Hattori Hanzo katana, at thirty-eight and a half inches, was two inches shorter and would probably work better in close quarters. Preston slid the Hanzo from the glossy black scabbard. The deciding factor was the much sharper edge of the katana. "Shorter, sharper," he said, nodding. "Let's go to work."

"Hack and bash?"

"What else?" With a meaningful glance at the breached ceiling, Preston said, "I'm not real keen on sitting here waiting for drop-in guests. How about you?"

Steve shook his head. "It's an extremely local problem. Let's work our way down to the parking lot and hit the road."

"Sounds good."

As Steve reached for the doorknob, Preston positioned himself in front of the door, sword raised and ready for a downward strike. He was about to tell Steve to open the door when the voice on the TV caught his attention. Something about breaking news. "Wait a minute."

"We don't have a—" Steve stopped mid-sentence, his attention following Preston's gaze to the small color television.

"—word of hope from Philadelphia. The alleged Counterstrike Liberation Front member captured by police has revealed under interrogation that the effects of the red mist are apparently temporary. If what we are being told is true, the reanimation of the dead will last approximately one hundred and forty minutes from the initial deployment of the red mist, after which time all those affected by the red mist, directly or through undead attacks will, collectively, cease to . . . to function. Obviously, we have no way to confirm the accuracy of this information until the necessary time elapses, but we thought it important to apprise you, our viewers of the latest—"

"About two and a half hours," Preston said. "Since this began."

"Not even."

"Of course, that won't help much if we become infected and undead before then."

"Humor me, Preston," Steve said. "Let's pretend this glass is half-full."

"Why not?" Preston said with an agreeable shrug. "Let's go!"

Steve unlocked the door and flung it open.

The hallway was empty.

Preston sighed. "So far—"

They heard a thunderous crash followed by the tumultuous roar of a couple dozen undead.

"Not so good." Steve said. "This way."

They ran down the hall away from the sound of charging undead, toward the hallway that fronted the station's business office. From there, they could run to the stairs or, if the lobby was clear, take the elevator down to the ground floor.

Steve opened the door and Preston rushed through, wielding his sword high over his shoulder. At first he thought the hallway was deserted, but then he spotted a woman standing near the corner as she turned to face him. Stepping up beside Preston, Steve said, "Is she . . . ?"

She was a definite looker, with long flowing blond hair and a classic hourglass figure, wearing a black dress with a plunging neckline and a hemline several inches above her knees. Perfect, if not for the streaks of mud on her arms and legs. Plus, she was barefoot. Not a good sign. Eerily calm, she began to walk toward them with a seductive smile and a broad sway to her hips.

That's when Preston noticed the tear in her dress and the deep horizontal gash in her abdomen, above the bikini line. "Too bad."

"Hand's down," Steve said with a shake of his head, "Philly's Hottest Undead Babe." He cleared his throat. "If we ever had such a contest."

"Right."

"She's not like the others," Steve said. "We could slip by and let her—"

The smiling undead woman stopped about three feet from them, opened her mouth as if she were about to ask for their autographs—and shrieked like a fucking banshee.

Startled, Preston reacted reflexively to quiet her. He swung the Hattori Hanzo in a blurred horizontal arc and felt a moment of resistance surge up his arms a moment before the blade came free. Apparently, it was sharp enough. The woman's detached head spun through the air with a pronounced backspin and a swirling fan of natural blond hair before thudding against the wall and dropping to the floor. Seconds later, the headless body pitched forward, causing Preston and Steve to jump aside as it thumped to the carpet.

"Always liked that sword," Steve said.

Preston eyed the frosted edge appreciatively. "Not bad."

Something banged into the door behind them. The doorknob rattled under fumbling hands. Down the hall, four undead burst through the stairwell door. "Business office or elevator?"

The business office was tempting, but Preston realized it would be a short term solution. They had no idea how many undead were roaming the halls. If they hoped to survive the next few hours, they needed to leave the building. "Too many of them," Preston said. "We need to get out."

"If some of them came up on the elevator—"

"—it might still be on this floor."

They ran down the hall and turned the corner where they had first noticed the undead woman in the black dress. Straight ahead they saw the ruin of the door into the studio. Even with the broken table lodged in the narrow window, Preston thought he glimpsed a figure or two milling around inside. Might have been his imagination, but he wasn't taking any chances. Halfway along the hallway were two side by side elevators. Preston jabbed the down arrow several times, hoping he could impart his urgency to the automated machinery by sheer will. "C'mon, c'mon!" he whispered.

The studio door swung wide, revealing a balding undead man in a dark blue canvas jumpsuit with the name Henry embroidered in red letters on a white nametag. From the opposite direction, several undead men lumbered around the corner, growling and drooling.

The left elevator dinged.

The double doors parted.

Preston and Steve lunged inside—

—but they weren't alone.

A man in a ravaged charcoal gray suit glared at them with insane, red-rimmed eyes. A substantial chunk of his neck was missing. And his shirt and necktie were soaked with blood. Something about him seemed familiar. "I know this guy," Preston said. "Works in this building. Joe—no, Jeff something."

With a slobbery snarl, the man launched himself at Preston.

At the same moment, balding Henry caught the edges of the closing elevator doors and began to force them open.

Preston tried to swing his sword at Jeff, but his elbow slammed into the side of the elevator. Then, because of the bad angle, the tip of the blade gouged into the metal wall. Preston leaned away from the man's snapping jaws, keeping him at bay with his left forearm.

While Henry struggled with the doors, Steve leapt to Preston's defense with a furious attack. He slammed the broad end of the bat into the back of Jeff's right knee, staggering him, then caught his shoulder and spun him around, off-balance. Employing his superior upper body strength, Steve lowered his shoulder and rammed the smaller man's chest, just as the elevator doors slid open.

Jeff would have staggered through the elevator doorway if Henry hadn't, at that moment, lunged forward. The two undead men collided, offsetting their individual momentum, and clutched the elevator doors for support. As they attempted to regain their balance and renew their assault, Preston pivoted to face them. He raised his katana in front of him and thrust it forward, spearing Jeff's throat, driving the tip of the blade out through his spine and right through Henry's neck.

Gurgling in tandem, the undead men clutched feebly at the blade.

Behind them, more of the undead were arriving.

Preston had no choice. He shoved both men back into the gathering crowd, knocking down a few of the new arrivals in a frenzied pile. And lost his grip on the embedded sword in the process. The elevator doors closed silently. Preston turned to Steve and said, "Undead-kebob."

Steve grinned, nodded. "You're unarmed."

"Yeah," Preston said. Nervously, he rubbed his empty hands together before shoving them into his jeans pockets. Nodding solemnly, he whispered, "Shit."

"Don't worry," Steve said. "We'll make it."

When the elevator doors opened on the ground floor lobby, Steve took the vanguard, baseball bat resting on his shoulder. "All clear," he said. They hurried across the deserted lobby, now littered with loose newspaper pages, and strode through the enclosed foyer out into the early morning.

"Damn it!" Preston said. "Should have looked for a fire axe."

"Let's not go back and tempt fate."

Reluctantly, Preston nodded.

Though the sun had risen, the sky was apocalyptically dark. Plumes of black smoke were spreading across the city like a funeral shroud. In the distance, military helicopters made slow sweeps over what was presumably the location of the initial terrorist attack, their spotlights knifing down through the gloom. Every few seconds, muffled explosions sounded. Easy to imagine the end of the world had arrived.

"Look," Steve said, pointing with the tip of his bat. "Cop."

A police cruiser sat two lanes over in the long parking lot, partially blocked by the radio station's black van. A uniformed police officer stood beside the patrol car. "Hey! Officer!" Preston called, waving his arms back and forth over his head.

"Wait," Steve cautioned. "Something's wrong."

The cop took a nervous step backward, away from something beyond their line of sight. His semi-automatic was out of its holster. "Freeze!" he shouted, firing a warning shot for emphasis. Then he proceeded to empty his handgun in a methodical sweeping motion, directing shots at several targets. Punctuating the sharp crack of each round was a series of inhuman growls and snarls and, once, the shattering of a car window. After emptying his sidearm, the cop didn't waste time reloading. He retreated to the back of his cruiser and appeared to be fumbling with the trunk lock.

That's when Preston saw them, rising from between parked cars and SUVs. Sensing an advantage, a dozen or more of the undead closed ranks around the police officer.

"Cop probably came to help us," Steve said, hoisting his bat. "Let's go."

"Uh—yeah, but what if he thinks we're undead?"

"What?"

"Look at us," Preston said. "We're disheveled, spattered with blood. We could be undead for all he knows."

"Well, whatever you do," Steve said before sprinting to help the police officer, "don't growl at him."

Preston sighed, shrugged and ran after Steve, wishing he had something—anything!—that could serve as a weapon. At the moment, all he had was an impressive arsenal of harsh language, which was unlikely to deter or offend the undead. Unless, of course, they worked for the FCC.

Despite Steve's best intentions, they were too late.

The police officer had managed to open both the trunk of his police cruiser and the long black case sitting on the spare wheel well, but as he removed the black Remington 870 pump action shotgun from the case, four of the undead pounced on him. Somehow he managed to disengage the safety and pump a round into the chamber, but he struggled to bring the barrel to bear on any of his assailants. The bloody hands of the undead fought for control of the black polymer stock of the shotgun while their teeth sank into the officer's face, neck and wrists with the snarling aggression of rabid dogs.

The cop pulled the barrel of the shotgun close to his chest to retain control of the weapon, and the muzzle wavered precariously under his chin.

By the time Steve arrived with a mighty swing of his bat, three more of the undead had besieged the overwhelmed cop. A moment after Steve connected with an unsuspecting undead skull, the shotgun roared.

The undead staggered away from the blast, away from the cop—

—who swayed back and forth for a moment—

—most of his face gone.

"Ah, Christ," Preston moaned.

The shotgun slipped from lifeless fingers and clattered to the ground.

The cop—Vasquez, according to his brass nametag—crumpled beside it.

Dead—with no chance of undead reanimation—the cop held no more interest for his undead attackers. Their red-rimmed gazes turned toward Steve. And Preston. "Now what?" Preston asked.

"Get over here!"

"Are you freakin' nuts?"

Steve swung the Louisville Slugger in wide arcs, keeping the circle of undead at bay, at least for the moment. "The shotgun!"

"Ah—right!" But first he had to cross the circle of undead to reach Steve, who stood behind the police cruiser in a fighting stance, beside the body of the cop, daring any of the undead to get within reach of the bat. With a yell—an improvised battle cry—Preston rushed forward, grabbing the nearest undead man by the back of his scalp and slamming his face into the passenger side window of a Honda Element.

Slipping through the momentary gap in the undead circle, Preston scooped up the shotgun and joined Steve who said, "Stand behind me. Boxes of ammo in the trunk. Load up, partner."

Steve continued to make threatening sweeps of the bat while Preston opened several boxes of 2¾" shells, 00 buck, federal tactical loads, medium brass—according to the label—and stuffed them in the pockets of his jeans. Each shell packed the firepower of nine 9mm rounds. He'd need all he could get before the morning of the undead was over.

The Remington 870 held one shell in the chamber and four in the magazine. In addition, the polymer stock was molded with a spring-loaded depression on each side designed to hold two extra shells front to back for easy reloading.

Without warning, one of the undead charged Steve, arms flailing, jaws snapping in anticipation.

He had been expecting one of them to make a move. The undead were nothing if not impatient. He swung the baseball bat over and down, in a wood chopping motion, splattering the man's ear like an overripe piece of fruit and crushing the side of his skull. The man staggered, fell to one knee. One more overhead swing brought him down.

"Got that thing loaded yet?" Steve said over his shoulder.

His mouth dry, Preston said, "Working on it."

Keeping the muzzle to the side, he pulled the fore-end back to eject the empty casing, pushed it forward to chamber another shell, and fed two replacement shells through the carrier into the magazine. "Locked and loaded," Preston said, stepping out from behind Steve. "Let's do some damage."

Two undead men rushed forward, one wearing a shirt, necktie and slacks, the other a hooded gray sweatshirt and jeans. The latter had a jagged chunk of a green and white highway sign lodged in his ribs. Preston swung the barrel of the Remington at Sweatshirt Guy and blasted a hole through his abdomen, cycled the action, then swiveled his hips and shot White Collar Guy in the chest. Both men staggered backward from the impact, but soon lurched forward again.

"Head shots!" Steve said. "Or cervical vertebrae. C7 and up. Better make it C5 and up. Just to be safe."

"I'm impressed that you know that," Preston said. "Scared, but impressed."

Steve shrugged. "Watch enough zombie movies, you learn a few things."

Preston raised the barrel of the Remington and blasted White Collar Guy in the face. The man dropped to his knees, fell forward and stayed down. The next blast, at even closer range, caught Sweatshirt Guy in the throat, beheading him. His detached head plopped into the hood of the sweatshirt a moment before the man toppled over backward.

"Crude," Steve said, "but effective."

"This is a shotgun," Preston said, "not a laser-sighted rifle."

"Fine. Anything from the neck up is good."

A large undead man leapt at them from the roof of a Chevy Suburban.

Preston swiveled, raised the barrel of the shotgun but managed only a chest shot. The man collapsed to the blacktop briefly but climbed to his feet, snarling and drooling. Preston ejected the last shell. "Sorry. Gotta reload."

"Gotcha covered."

Preston stepped back again, fished loose shells out of his pockets and began to reload the chamber and magazine. He planned to save the spring-loaded shells in the molded stock for an emergency. One of them as a personal exit strategy, if it came to that. Better than being eaten alive.

Steve swung the baseball and connected with the undead man's raised forearm, breaking one, possibly both bones. Another chopping swing caught the man with his guard down and smashed his cheek bone. The undead man spat out several teeth, but had plenty left as evidenced by his snarling grimace. One more blow to the head dropped him, but cracked the bat.

Another two undead, a casually dressed man and a woman in a business suit, rushed forward. Steve swung the bat at the man, breaking his face and the bat at the same time. Then he swept his right leg out to trip the undead woman. What was left of the bat resembled a short spear, or a wooden stake. When another undead man grabbed Steve's shoulder, he whirled around and drove the jagged point through the man's right eye.

Hurried footfalls thumped across the roof of the police cruiser as Preston finished reloading. The charging undead man launched himself at Preston who, despite the urgency of the situation, waited a fraction of a second longer than he would have liked to get a bead on the man's head. He couldn't afford to waste any more shells. Fortunately, he scored a direct hit; unfortunately, the man's momentum continued to carry him forward. He plowed into the DJ, who rolled with the impact, an awkward reverse somersault.

"Trouble!" Steve exclaimed.

Preston's skull whacked against the blacktop, but he shook it off as he came out of his roll into an unsteady crouch. He rose with the Remington clutched in his hands.

Believing Preston's fall would nullify the advantage of his shotgun, the remaining undead had charged en masse, growling, snarling and drooling with a wicked light in their eyes.

Standing back to back, Preston and Steve fought them off with grim determination. Steve held his shattered Louisville Slugger in a double-handed grip and, with short but forceful stabbing motions, impaled throats and eyes. Meanwhile Preston aimed high and fired round after round into the relentless tide of undead. Soon the corpses stacked up around them, a macabre pile of ruined flesh, twice killed, hemming them in, but also serving to slow the undead onslaught.

Whenever Preston needed to reload, Steve feinted and jabbed with his split bat to keep the undead at bay. Ultimately, their consuming rage overruled any lingering sense of self-preservation retained from their natural lives. Oblivious to pain and indifferent to mutilation, they were emboldened in their un-death.

When the multitude of undead had dwindled to less than a half dozen, Steve allowed himself a ragged smile. Panting from exertion, he said, "We're gonna make it."

Preston loaded the chamber and magazine one last time. His pockets were empty. Five ready to fire, plus the four spring-loaded in the stock. Would have been enough, but then he noticed ragged and bloody people streaming out of 100 Riverside Drive. The undead they'd left behind in the office building had finally found their way back outside. A dozen of them. Maybe more. And every one of them veered toward the heart of the struggle. "We've got company."

Steve's head whipped around. His shoulders drooped. "Crap!"

"Yep."

"Preston," Steve said, then paused to clear his throat. "Just in case, you know . . . save a shell for me."

"Last two are for us," Preston said grimly.

"So, uh," Steve said as he impaled the throat of a former office supplies salesman, "how many you got left?"

"Not enough for them."

"Didn't think so."

"Any ideas?"

"Let's go out blazing."

Preston took a bead on the head of a former paralegal. "Rage on!" he shouted as he fired point blank. His shoulder had begun to ache from the repeated kick of the shotgun. By now, each time he pulled the trigger, he braced himself with an anticipatory grimace of pain. Nevertheless, he made each shot count. This late in the battle, Steve and he had been scratched, bitten and clawed on their legs and forearms and hands, superficially, but deep enough to draw blood. If they went down without a bullet to the brain, they were sure as hell coming back as undead disc jockeys.

Preston ejected his last shell. "Down to four," he said, as he popped the last four shells from the dual depressions in the polymer stock. "Two for them; two for us."

"Slight problem."

"Yeah," Preston said. "I count nine of them."

"Ten," Steve corrected. "You missed the one skulking behind the red Jetta."

"Ten or two hundred. What's the difference?" Preston said as he loaded the last four shells. "Too many is too many."

Steve dropped one with a throat strike.

Preston drilled one between the eyes.

Steve spun around, drove the tip of his bat into a graying former banker's eye, lost his balance amid the haphazard pile of bodies, and then lost his grip on the bat's handle, which was slick with blood. The banker teetered and toppled sideways, tumbling far down the pile with Steve's diminished weapon embedded in his eye.

Taking careful aim, Preston fired his last "them" bullet and eliminated a former stock analyst from the bloodthirsty horde.

Exhausted, Preston and Steve stood back to back, surrounded by the last six undead. Those six growled and snarled and snapped their jaws. Hands and necks twitched as they salivated in anticipation. They scrambled over the pile of bodies like a pack of wolves confident of an easy kill.

Between deep breaths, Steve said, "This is it."

"Looks like."

"We could try . . . to haul ass out of here."

At that moment, several stragglers lumbered out of the office building, saw what was happening and rushed to join their undead confederates.

"I'm wiped out," Preston said with a quick head shake. "And they never seem to get tired. No, man, there's too many left. Can't risk getting caught."

"Figured as much," Steve said.

"We had a great run."

"You know it," Steve said. "Let's go out on our terms."

Preston swung the shotgun barrel toward Steve's head and hesitated.

"Sure you can go through with this?" Steve asked.

Considering the alternative, Preston nodded.

"Do it," Steve said. As he gazed down the muzzle of the shotgun, the black ring seemed to expand before his eyes, blotting out everything. Unnerved by the implacable stare of imminent death, he decided to look away at the last instant. "Wait!"

One of the stragglers never it made it to the ring of six. He toppled over, fell flat on his face and lay there motionless. One by one the others fell. Then each of the six made one last weak lunge at the two living men before collapsing.

"What just happened?" Preston asked.

Steve snapped his fingers as realization dawned. "What time is it?"

Preston checked his wristwatch. "Eight-thirty."

"One forty!" Steve exclaimed, laughing. "One hundred and forty minutes."

"We made it," Preston said, smiling as he shook his head in disbelief. Against incredible odds, they'd outlasted the red mist effect. He glanced at the shotgun in his hands and his expression sobered. "To think, I almost . . ."

"Forget it," Steve said, a bit shaken by what had almost happened, even if he didn't want to admit it aloud. He surveyed the mangled pile of bodies. "You know, I'd hate to think we killed our own listeners."

"Bad as it was," Preston said, "we did them a favor."

"How so?"

"Saved them from killing the living," Preston said. "Doubt they'd want that."

"Always looking on the bright side."

"You know," Preston said, "we have another hour and a half of show left."

"Assuming they haven't demolished the studio."

"Worst case," Preston said with a shrug, "we take the rest of the day off."

Epilogue

The Woman Who Walked with Dogs
MARY ROSENBLUM

"You be in this house by dark."

Mama's words were always the same, a parting benediction as she left for her job at the nursing home. "I don't work for no daughter of mine to be out on the street at night. I'll call you."

The street at night. . . . "Yes, Mama," Mari June would say. "I got homework to do." Sometimes she wondered if Mama really knew.

"Good girl, you do that." And then Mama would close the door firmly, with a bang of decision, as if by that single definite slam she could seal the door airtight against the dark seductive dangers of nighttime on the streets of their crummy city neighborhood.

Nah, Mari June thought. Mama didn't know. Mostly, she was afraid of boys.

Don't you have any boys in this house while I'm out workin' my fingers to the bone for you, she'd say. *I find out you actin' slutty, you hav'n boys droppin' in like you're trash, and you'll be out on the street so fast your ears'll flap.*

She didn't know about the street.

Silly, too, because Mari June didn't like boys. They stared at her in school, but their stares stopped short at her skin, sliding over her like sticky fingers. They looked at her breasts— those strange and uncontrollable twin magics that swelled and itched and sometimes seemed like alien flesh, changing the sleek way she slid through the grimy city air, making her clumsy. Sometimes her nipples hurt and when they did, a strange creature moved deep in her belly. It was dark and furry and lived between her hips and when it moved, it made her breathless, her skin cold and hot at the same time.

Mari June let Mama's slam keep the door tight shut against boys and did her homework because she had a 4.0 this year again, so far, and she was going to keep it. But Mama didn't have a cell, which meant she had to wait for her breaks to call home on the pay phone in the lobby. Because of Miz Bellamy, the Supervisor from Hell, Mama called her. And her break came at 6 and she didn't get off until 11 PM. So there was plenty of time to do her homework and answer Mama's 6 PM call. If she was careful, she could still get out and back in by 11:30, the earliest Mama could get home, even if the busses were running on time. Mari June locked the front door and took her English book and Alegebra to the dining room table to finish the stupid story problems (a snap, she had done them all in sixth grade) and work on her report on Romeo and Juliet.

It's not really about them falling in love and dying, like most people think, she wrote in her long narrow handwriting. *It's about families and how stupid they are, how they only see what they want to see, instead of what's really in front of them.* Then she stopped and chewed on the end of her number two pencil, thinking about that. Might not be a good thing to turn in.

She'd already gotten in trouble with Mrs. Roberts when she had written about Columbus landing for Columbus Day. Mrs. Roberts didn't like her title—'There Goes the Neighborhood'—to start with. "We're celebrating our history," she had scolded Mari June in front of the class, handing back the pages marked with a big, red C-. "We're proud of our country and our heritage in this class."

Mari June erased those first sentences about Romeo and Juliet and changed the title to "Young Love." *Romeo and Juliet is a classic tale of tragic and unrequited love,* she wrote. The 'unrequited' alone should get her an A, she figured. Mari June bent over her notebook, looping her p's and f's carefully, because she only planned on writing this crap once, thank you. Timed it perfectly. The phone rang just as she finished the last syrupy sentence with a flourish, poked that final period into place.

She picked it up, said "Hi, Mama," as she gathered the pages with the other hand. "Still working on it. Won't finish before bedtime. No, I'll get done. I'll be asleep by the time you get home." Well, she'd be in bed, at least. "Too bad Lori called in sick. Maybe you could make Dragon Lady empty a few for a change? Sorry, Mom." Mari June rolled her eyes. "I didn't mean to be rude about Ms. Bellamy . . . I was kidding. Yeah. 'Night, Mom.'" And she hung up thinking that if she had to work for Ms. Bellamy, Dragon Lady, she'd starve first. And Dragon Lady wasn't what she'd call her, either.

She put her books in her backpack for the morning, mussed up her bed and left the toothbrush, wet, beside the soap dish in the bathroom and dampened the towel, just in case she had to race Mom into the house (had happened). Mom noticed those kinds of details.

Safeguards in place, she went out.

The moon floated overhead in the darkening sky, almost full, a pale, lopsided sphere like an orange fallen out of Mr. Schwartz's wire shopping cart when he bumped it up and over the curb. School had started four weeks ago. New friendships had been forged, boundaries freshly drawn between the gangs, teachers tried and tested. Everyone knew what was what. Summer was a nostalgic memory, routines as familiar now as the cicadas' end-of-summery monotony.

But tonight, a hint of fall edged the air, a tiny tweak of chill, a promise of red leaves, pumpkins, Halloween, a gorge of candy, never mind Mama's threats every year to drag her off to the Halloween Party at Saint Sebastian's where you had to wear costumes of the Virgin Mary or Cinderella (who should have sold the stupid carriage for a good price and caught a plane to one of those white sandy islands you saw in the magazines), and only got lame treats like stale oatmeal cookies with bright orange icing and plastic-wrapped popcorn balls that stuck to your teeth and pulled out fillings.

Halloween, that chill breath promised. *The real thing, with good candy, and scary things in the dark that want to suck your breath. Then Christmas, then Easter eggs, and pretty soon it will be summer again.* The nightair tickled her and she giggled, pausing on the sidewalk in the streetlight's yellow pool to check the watch Mama gave her for First Communion. It was only 6:20. Plenty of time. She stepped off the white sidewalk, out of the nice safe pool of streetlight yellow and into . . . the night.

By day the street was safe, boring, a sunny reality defined and bounded by the iron rules of the known—stop signs, neatly painted siding, mowed lawns, and the mail man. *A good neighborhood,* Mama always said when she whined about the bills. *It's worth whatever it costs so you can grow up in a good neighborhood.* And she would level a hard, accusing stare at Mari June. *Even if I have to go without new clothes or those cute shoes I saw at Kaufmann's, it's worth it to give you a good place to grow up. You listenin', girl?*

Yes, ma'am. Why adults seemed to equate *good* with *boring,* Mari June had never been able to figure out.

The Woman Who Walked with Dogs

But by night. . . .

By night, Elm Street was another world, with different rules.

By night, Mr. Kingston, who yelled at you if you stepped off the sidewalk onto his perfect lawn, wore a red ball gown and a blonde wig and sometimes spit champagne at his image in the full-length mirrors that lined one wall of his downstairs rec room. Mrs. Silvano, who swept her sidewalk every day and always asked you if you had said your rosary sang to her dead husband at her big black piano that took up her living room. He sat right next to her on the piano bench with his hand on her butt. In between numbers she told him about her day, laughing, answering him, and tossing her head, really young and sexy, not all shriveled up and old.

Ms. Johnson, who was really a vampire, waited for the young men who arrived every night, parking their cars around the corner on Maple Street, across from the empty lot where the boys rode their bikes. She would greet them at the door all dressed in black and usher them inside, pausing to peer past the screen door, eyes searching the night street like laser beams before closing the door. Once or twice, up early with the sun, Mari June had seen them stumble out again, white as the grubs you find under the bark on dead trees, or maybe something that lives in a cave. Then there was Miz Willows who walked her invisible dogs, chirping at them, babytalking to them, commanding them to get off that lawn right now, don't you pee on that nice lily plant you big lunks. Her yard was all beaten dust and scraggly old rhododendrons with burnt up drooping leaves and straggling weeds that struggled and sometimes bloomed along the rusty chain link fence that bordered the sidewalk. Muddy brown rawhide bones and old sun-bleached rubber toys lay here and there. No dogs. Some of the boys threw stones into her yard and pretended to hit them. Then Miz Willows would come out the front door, yelling and waving a broom, threatening to call the cops, threatening to let her dogs loose to chew on their butts, her gray hair standing up all over her head, her Hawaii print dress as faded as the rubber toys in the dusty yard and about ten sizes too large. The boys would run away laughing and she would babytalk to her invisible pets, hushing their inaudible barking, telling them it was okay, not to kill the boys 'cause they were just babies, before retreating to the house again.

Mari June liked Miz Willows. Mom wouldn't let her have a dog and so she pretended—something she wouldn't admit to if they tore her tongue out, like Sister Martha described when she read to them in Sunday School from the really cool, gross book about all the things people did to the saints. She'd created Shep when she was little, scared of the dark, and Mom wouldn't let her have a night light because everybody knew that they were a fire danger. Shep was a big German Shepherd that slept on the foot of her bed and would tear out the throat of anybody who tried to hurt her. So she felt a certain kinship with Miz Willows, even though her hair was pretty awful. But she was old anyway, so it didn't matter.

And besides, Miz Willows was the only one on the street who was the same in the daytime as she was at night. Mari June slipped across the street in the narrow crevice of shadow between the streetlights in the middle of the block. If Mrs. Silvano or Ms. Johnson saw her, they'd tell Mama, and then she'd send Mari June to stay nights with Aunt Susanna over in Lents who had ten kids and lived in a house with three bedrooms. So she slipped across the narrow crack of shadow like a ghost and onto the sidewalk in front of Mr. Kingston's house. Sure enough, there he was, down in his rec room, back arched, head tilted like the old pictures of Marilyn Monroe in the history books, right down to the blonde wig and the black spot (that was supposed to be pretty but just looked just like a black spot to Mari June) by his mouth. His breasts were about the same size as the movie star's, too, which really made her curious. She hoped to run into him on the sidewalk one day—literally—see if they were padding or if they might be real.

He had a thick green bottle with a long neck tonight, and he tossed his head back, tilted the bottle to his lips, then faced the mirror. Liquid sprayed out, spattering the glass, running down in long streaks. Fascinated, Mari June crouched by the blooming Rose of Sharon, peering raptly between the branches. Maybe he filled the bottles with ginger ale, she thought. Mom said champagne cost a lot. But he sold cars. Mrs. Silvano had said something about that once, how that was why he always drove a shiny new car, that's why he parked it in the back yard, inside the tall board fence with the big padlock on the gate. Because it didn't really belong to him. He was just putting on airs, she had said and sniffed.

She watched him for a little while, but that hint of fall breathed on the back of her neck and filled her with a winey, cidery tingle of excitement. Mr. Kingston with his jowly, Marilyn Monroe face and stained dress was . . . old. Mari June drifted across the limp fall grass, letting the beams from the squashed-orange moon push her along, restless as the first fall leaves skittering along the sidewalk. Mrs. Silvano's high, shrill soprano seeped through her cracked-open windows. *Beautiful dreamer, dream of my heeaartt. . . .* Ms. Johnson leaned against the front door of her house, watching for her next victim, her eyes reflecting the red glow of her cigarette.

All old tonight. All boring. Mari June crossed the street, cut through the vacant lot with the bags of garbage and lawn clippings burst and spilling on the rough clay like cut-open stomachs she thought, like scenes from the book on the saints Sister Martha read. The yard on the far side didn't have a fence and Mari June crossed it, navigating around flowerbeds, the grass a weird washed out gray in the squashed-orange moonlight. Across the street, barricaded by a fence of nose-to-tail beater cars loomed . . . The Park.

Mari June always thought of it in capitals, the way her mother spoke of it. *Don't you set a foot in The Park, girl. You-know-who hangs out there! You know what They'll do to you!* And when Mari June had once said that no, she didn't know, and asked for clarification, Mama had delivered a stinging slap and a sharp admonition to *watch your mouth, girl, don't you get smart with me.* Adult speak for "I don't know."

But she paused at the sidewalk, eyeing the dark bulk of the cars, an occasional bit of chrome reflecting the moonlight like animal eyes. Waiting. She imagined them snapping their hoods like cartoon alligator jaws as she squeezed between them, lunging at her with sharp chrome teeth and glaring headlight eyes. Enough time? She checked her watch and hesitated.

The moon laughed at her and Fall tweaked her hair, teasing her, daring her.

Mari June lifted her chin and marched across the empty street, I'm not scared of you, you're just empty metal like old oil drums and that's all. She stared at the wide dark snouts of the cars, teeth hidden behind painted bumper lips. They stared back at her, eyes dull and smug. *We choose to let you pass*, they whispered in the hiss and skitter of the dry leaves on the blank black asphalt. *This time we choose to let you passss.*

She walked between them, head still high, the skin on her thighs quivering, hairs erect, wary of movement, aware of the soft scrape of jeans against metal, faint heat leaking from the car-snout like dragon breath.

They let her pass and she didn't run as she stepped up onto the curb, didn't change the rhythm of her walk one beat as she stepped into the grass on the far side, hairs prickling on the backs of her legs, tiny antennae trained on the sleeping cars. . . .

Maybe next time . . . they whispered behind her.

The air changed as she stepped off the sidewalk, as if she had passed through an invisible door. The chill in the air intensified, breathing down her neck, making her nipples hurt. She crossed her arms on her chest, squeezing those swollen not-quite-part-of-her breasts against her ribcage until they ached. Leaves swirled around her feet like puppies and she hesitated, back to the streetlight glow, facing darkness beneath the trees. A deeper darkness than the darkness in her back yard, it pooled like a brooding creature between the trees. Ordinary maples by day, in the dark their branches stretched out, gathering the darkness to them, whispering together beneath that squashed moon.

For just a moment, Mari June hesitated. Behind her, the cars tittered. Then she put her arms down at her sides and walked resolutely into the pooled darkness. It swallowed her and then parted like a curtain. Ahead she saw the swingset and jungle gym, bright with graffiti like Christmas lights in glowing red, green, blue, empty and strange in the moonlight, like the ruins of a civilization that had flourished and died right here in the city and nobody ever noticed. Beyond it lurked the benches, not the benches that old men sat on by day, drowsing and staring at the squirrels, or hard, tired-eyed women yelling at kids on the swingset not to pull Jamie's hair, or stop throwing sand. Nobody had ever sat on *these* benches and Mari June edged around them, sheltered by the thick darkness, not willing to step into the empty space beneath the moon's stare. A bird called, a hollow questioning sound and the trees answered, whispering their answer in a rustle of leaves.

Time to go home, she told herself. Got to be there for sure when Mama gets back, let the empty-oil-drum-cars giggle and laugh! But as she turned, she heard them. Loud voices hard and bruising, not-caring. The darkness thickened and retreated, leaving behind the kind of darkness you saw at the edges of the streetlights, tame darkness, submissive.

Yah, you wish, dude. Boobie's asking a dime, the slut. And then she did me and. . . .

Mari June shrank back into the darkness of the night maples, wanting to pull it around her, hide in it. But instead, she felt the darkness pulled from around her the way someone might pull the blanket off you in the middle of the night, leaving you cold and naked. Visible. They drifted into the squashed-orange moonlight, tall and gray, dodging, pushing each other, laughing. One of them leaped to catch the top arch of the jungle gym, swinging out, feet arcing down to a perfect landing, spinning to punch another's shoulder.

She wanted to run, but her body had frozen, stiff as one of the mannequins in the Nordstrom's windows downtown, body hard plastic, her shirt hanging on its hard ridges and curves, jeans slack around her rooted legs. Not thinking. Frozen.

They danced closer, walking weird, legs almost stiff, every pelvis thrust out, going first. Leading. She tried to swallow but her throat was dry and they heard it . . . the rasping of it. All looked.

"Hey." Tallest one moved forward, bending a little at the knees now, his eyes on her like the headlight glare of the tittering cars. "What have we here?" The others were moving now, spreading out, making a fence between her and the cars, street, home. The playground wall crowded her back. Strange yards beyond it with fences to stop her, clotheslines to catch her.

"It's a chick."

"Whatcha doin' out here, little girl?"

"I got what you need, honey."

They moved closer, lithe, sinuous shadows, their faces blurred by orange moonlight, hair black as night, clothes baggy, gang uniform. She'd know them, if it was morning. If they were lounging here, laughing and spitting, hassling the younger boys, hitting them up for their lunch money, CDs—yeah she'd know them. Put a name to them, a street, a family. Littl Big, his dad's in jail for dealing crack, mom's a hooker, that's Brushy, been kicked out twice, this time's his last chance, Spell Boy, he was maybe the one who let the oil out of Principal's car, wrecked the engine. . . .

Not tonight. Tonight they had no names.

They were staring at her. Like the boys at school.

Only . . . hungry. Like the kids who got free lunch at school. Staring at the gray meat loaf and drooling.

She backed up one step, two. They moved with her, faces sharp and feral in the orangy moon-glow. Their eyes gleamed like cats' eyes in the dark, and the thing in her belly moved, like a cat waking up, full of hunger. She hated them for waking it.

Hated it for waking for them.

Hard cold bumped her back. The wall, the brick wall layered with grafitti and white paint like some kind of urban lasagna. The thing in her belly clawed at her, and heat and cold buzzed in her ears.

"Hey, baby," one of them said. "Don't be scared, baby."

The others laughed, the sounds sawing at her brain. They moved closer, faces identical, shark-grinning, feral eyes speaking to the thing in her belly, calling it by name.

"Now don't you go peein' on those bushes, you hear? You mind your manners, you dogs." The voice cut through the moon glow and they all looked, faces turning in perfect unison.

Miz Willows stepped out from nowhere, wearing the darkness like a hem of black cats, prowling feral around her feet as she stepped into the orange moonlight, walking straight up to Mari June as if *they* weren't there at all, as if it was just the two of them in the park. *They* didn't really move aside for her. But somehow she walked through them. "You're out late, Mari June." She smiled, her face as clear as if it was noon, like a private spotlight shone down to illuminate it. "You go out late, don't you leave Shep home. You bring him with you."

"Hey, old woman. Get the hell out of here."

"Not your bizness, bitch."

The tallest one reached for her, grabbed for her arm, like you'd reach for a left-behind newspaper on the daytime benches, toss it on the ground before you sat down. Mari June cringed.

Miz Willows turned around, a look of mild surprise on her face. She didn't say anything, but all around them, the hem of darkness grew, rising up like ebony fog, taking shape—legs and wide chests, thick necks, blunt, wide muzzles. White teeth gleamed and the growl seemed to come from the ground, the trees, the thick darkness itself. A cloud slid across the squashed moon like someone covering their eyes with both hands.

"Hey." Tallest one stepped back. "What the hell . . . ?"

Black as the dark, they edged forward, heads low, white gleam of teeth like exposed bone. Mari June tried to count them, but when she looked straight at them, she saw nothing but darkness and the shape of benches, trees, the colorless poles of the play structure. *They* took a step back, but not all together, not in unison, not any more. "Bitch," the tallest one hissed, but behind him, one of them broke. Ran.

The dark surged forward, razored with teeth, and the night growled.

They all ran, not yelling, silent as the torrent of shadow surging at their heels, toward the street, toward the cars, toward the safety of the yellow street-lamp glow beyond.

A metallic banging like car hoods and trunks slamming echoed through the night. A car alarm went off, shrill shrieking and beeping, splitting the night like an axe blade.

It stopped.

The cloud slid timidly away and the squashed orange moon peeked out. Miz Willow smiled at Mari June, her hair tufted, dry and ugly, her eyes bright, brighter than the orange moon's feeble glow. The breeze frisked around her and Mari June rubbed her arms, goosebumps speckling her skin. The shadows were slinking back, sliding silently across the moon-washed grass, glints of white light like splinters of razor blades here and there. Grinning. Licking shadow chops.

"You shouldn't be out here without Shep." Miz Willow wagged a finger at her. "Don't you go leavin' him home. Bad things out here in the night. You need your dog."

"Yes, Miz Willow." Mari June could only whisper.

"That's better. You promise?"

"Yes, Miz Willow." And Mari June squeaked as something cold poked her hand. She looked down. Shadow streaked the ground, but right there, by her left knee, it kind of lifted, almost like a low bank of black fog with the shape of a dog. A big dog, maybe a German Shepherd. The cold poked her again, moist, like a dog's nose. "Shep?" She whispered it, felt Miz Willow's eyes on her, felt the night tapping an inky toe, waiting. "Good boy." She swallowed, what the hell, said it out *loud*. "Good boy, Shep, good boy for coming. I won't leave you home again. I promise."

When she looked up again, Miz Willows was clear across the park, striding along like a man, like she always did, the shadows swirling around her legs. And if she looked at them sideways, didn't really *look*, you know, she could almost, almost see Rottweilers and furry Malamutes, Boxers, German Shepherds, and even a Border Collie or two. They melted into the line of scrawny elms at the far edge of the park and . . . vanished.

"Good boy, Shep." She almost-looked at him, admired the upright ears, the fine head. "You're really handsome, you know? Let's go home. Quick before Mama gets home."

She walked straight back, right between the cars who looked at the asphalt with their bright, headlight eyes. *You can pass,* the night breeze whispered in their grilles. *You can pass with him.* And she wasn't afraid.

They just made it.

She stripped off her clothes as Mama's key turned in the locks, pulled the covers up as her footsteps creaked down the hall, breathed slow and even as Mama peeked in the door. "You're a good girl, baby," Mama murmured low and soft. "You sleep well, honey." At the foot of the bed, Shep watched her and didn't growl, but after Mama closed the door, his bright golden eyes filled the room with a dim, warm light.

All kinds of rumors went around in the next few days. . . . Littl Big, Brushy, Spell Boy, Breaker, Fireball, they got busted for dealing, got offed by the Ninth Street Knights, were robbing banks in Philly. Mari June listened to the "I heard they . . ." whispers and nodded and didn't tell anybody that she'd heard anything at all. And her mom threw a fit because some punk had gone down the line of cars parked on the block and had banged up every one. "You tell me what the cops want a raise for when they can't even catch a bunch of hoodlums out smashing up cars with a hammer, huh? You wanna tell me?"

And Mari June didn't tell her it wasn't a hammer that made those dents. Shep went everywhere with her, just like she'd promised. He curled up under her chair and stared at Tim Pollack when he stared at her and he stopped. He slipped through the lunchtime crush in the halls by her side, and not one person stuck her with a pin or tried to grope her. He lay under the table at lunch while she ate her peanut butter sandwich and one day Emiline Jackson and Sheraline Brown came over to sit down, and they were pretty nice, and popular, too, not cheerleader popular but pretty cool. They were nice. Shep thumped his tail at them.

She took Shep out for a walk every night after Mama made her check up call, even if she wasn't done with her homework. They watched Mr. Kingston dance in his prom dress and listened to Mrs. Silvano sing with Mr. Silvano, which made Shep put his head back and howl like a wolf. Mari June howled with him, and they both ran away, her giggling, Shep panting, as Ms. Johnson came out of her house looking thoughtful, looking after them as she lit her cigarette and settled down to wait.

Then they went to the park and the cars looked down at the asphalt and not at Mari June, and they walked through the darkness and the moon said polite nothings in the vault of its sky and nobody bothered them. And sometimes they saw Miz Willow and Mari June always waved.

Politely.

About the Contributors

Kelley Armstrong is the author of the Otherworld paranormal suspense series. She's currently at work on book seven, plus the first novel of a crime series to be published in early 2007. Armstrong lives in Ontario with her family. For more information, check out her website at www.kelleyarmstrong.com

David Seidman was born on January 20th, 1979 in Southeastern Pennsylvania. Growing up, David's love for both the horror genre and painting helped shape his creativity, but what defined his art, was the discovery of film noir, silent films, and photography.

While attending college at the University of the Arts in Philadelphia, David experimented with his artistic style by combining traditional art with photography by way of the computer. He graduated in 2001 with a B.F.A. in Illustration, top honors in his class, and a hunger to release his work on the masses.

Since beginning his freelance career David's artwork has garnered much attention, winning him several awards and being displayed nationwide. David's illustrations have been published around the world and can be seen on everything from cd covers and comics to advertisements and apparel. He has illustrated book covers for authors such as Alan Dean Foster and Jim Butcher and has worked for clients such as the Philadelphia Eagles, the band Phish, and *Amazing Stories* magazine. For more about David and his work, please visit www.lunarlightstudios.com.

Sarah A. Hoyt is the author of a fantasy trilogy—*Ill Met By Moonlight, All Night Awake*, and *Any Man So Daring*—detailing a magical reconstruction of Shakespeare's life. She has also published over three dozen short stories in magazines that include *Analog, Asimov's* and *Amazing*. Her novel *Draw One in the Dark* is coming November from Baen books. At the same time Prime Crime Books will be releasing the first of her Three Musketeer Mysteries (written as Sarah D'Almeida). An upcoming trilogy from Bantam books takes place in the far-flung reaches of a magical British Empire.

Sarah lives in Colorado and is furiously at work on her next dozen books.

Alexa Grave's love of writing started when she was fourteen, induced by the fantasy daydreams she created in her mind since she was a child. In 2005 she received her Master of Arts degree in Writing Popular Fiction. She currently lives in Wisconsin with her husband, three cats, two turtles, and a twelve-year-old goldfish (a fish that was around when she first started writing). If you wish to learn more about her, please visit her website: http://www.sff.net/people/alexagrave.

P. Kirby grew up in El Paso, Texas and is a graduate of New Mexico State University. Though an avid reader, Patricia only started writing fiction in 2003. Recently, deciding the price—one soul—was too high, she quit her secure but mind-numbing government job to concentrate on writing.

She prefers to recast familiar villainous archetypes—dark elves, vampires—in a more heroic light and avoids traditional "big-bad out to destroy the world" storylines. Her writing can be found at *Neverary, Lost in the Dark*, and in the upcoming anthology *Beyond the Blackened Mirror*.

Home is a tiny house in the desert, shared with her long-suffering husband. Patricia is co-owned by an uppity Arabian horse, a sanity-impaired greyhound, and a brilliant little mutt. She has never owned or been owned by a cat. When not writing, she spends her days thinking up Ramen-noodle-based recipes and trying to convince her horse he is not a dog.

Ron Horsley is a writer/artist from Columbus, Ohio. He has written numerous short stories and edited/published the 2001 critically-acclaimed collection *The Midnighters Club*. He currently is pursuing a degree in Graphic Design and living in Las Vegas, NV.

He likes cats, Katherine Dunn novels, and was not guilty of the Lindbergh Kidnapping (though photographic evidence seems to suggest otherwise).

Eugie Foster calls home a mildly-haunted, fey-infested house in Metro Atlanta that she shares with her husband, Matthew, and her pet skunk, Hobkin. She is an active member of the SFWA, winner of the Phobos Award, Managing Editor of *Tangent*, and Submissions Editor for *The Town Drunk*. Her fiction has been translated into Greek, Hungarian, Polish, and French, and her publication credits include stories in *Realms of Fantasy*, *The Third Alternative*, *Paradox*, *Apex Digest*, *Fantasy Magazine*, *Cricket*, *Cicada*, and anthologies *Hitting the Skids in Pixeltown*, edited by Orson Scott Card; *Sages & Swords*, edited by Daniel E. Blackston; and *Writers for Relief: An Anthology to Benefit the Survivors of Katrina*, edited by Davey Beauchamp.

Visit her online at www.eugiefoster.com.

Kelly Hale has been writing short stories for thirty-eight years. This is the first to appear on the printed page, which is a testament to sheer bloody-mindedness if there ever was one.

She is the author of a novel, *Erasing Sherlock*, and co-author of another, *Grimm Reality* (with Simon Bucher-Jones.) She has written and produced plays, attempted spec scripts for television, and performed at poetry jams in the beautiful Pacific Northwest where she lives, happily surrounded by coffee houses, friends, and family.

Stephen D. Rogers has had over three hundred stories and poems selected to appear in more than a hundred publications. His website, www.stephendrogers.com, includes a list of new and upcoming titles as well as other timely information.

Joy Marchand holds a B.A. in Classical Studies from the University of the Pacific and currently resides in Salem, Massachusetts where real magic is in the air all year round, but especially in October, during Salem's month-long Halloween celebration. Joy's short stories have been featured in *Writers of the Future Volume XX*, the *Elastic Book of Numbers*, and *Polyphony 5*. She is currently at work on a novel about angels and demons set in Central Texas. Visit Joy's website at www.joymarchand.com.

Jon Sprunk lives in Harrisburg, Pennsylvania with his wife, Jenny, and their three enormous cats. Between his day job as a juvenile detention specialist and evenings spent with his family, he tries to squeeze in some time for writing. Among his inspirations are the works of fantasy giants J.R.R. Tolkien, Robert E. Howard, and Gene Wolfe. When not working on his latest novel, he enjoys traveling, collecting medieval weaponry, and long Sunday afternoons of watching football.

"Office Magic" is his third fantasy story in publication.

Elaine Cunningham has written twenty-odd fantasy books, some odder than others, and about three dozen short stories. *The New York Times* bestselling author has written in several shared-world settings, most notably Star Wars and the Forgotten Realms, and recently made a foray into the world of EverQuest with *The Blood-Red Harp*, to be released later this year. *Shadows in the Starlight*, the second book in the urban fantasy series Changeling Detective Agency, hit bookstores in February 2006. A former history and music teacher, she is hard at work on a historical novel set in 16th century Scotland.

Melissa Frederick wrote and illustrated her first fantasy novel at age seven, a story of mysterious islands and mountains made of ice cream and a teenaged girl driving around the world in a blue, cigar-shaped Winnebago. By age ten, after failing to finish several notebooks' worth of fantasy-adventure novels, she decided she was all washed up as an author. Since then, she has more or less gotten over her writer's block and managed to complete a Master's degree in creative writing at Iowa State University. Her poetry and short fiction have appeared in journals such as the *Timber Creek Review*, *The Macguffin*, *RE:AL*, *Kalliope*, and the *Crab Orchard Review*. She was also a featured author in the 2003-2004 season of Writing Aloud, a short-story reading series produced by the InterAct Theatre Company in Philadelphia. Currently, she teaches literature and creative writing at Rosemont College and is inching her way toward a Ph.D. in Renaissance literature at Temple University. In the course of her studies, she has become intimately acquainted with Philip Sidney's *Arcadia* and Edmund Spenser's *Faerie Queene*, to the detriment of her sanity.

Michael A. Pignatella lives in Connecticut with his wife and two children. He left high school thinking he would be the next Stephen King, and instead somehow found himself an attorney. After fourteen years of stifling his creative impulses, he finally listened to his muse and returned to writing in 2001, and he hasn't looked back. He is working toward his Master's Degree in English, although he is not quite sure what use he will be able to make of it when he is finished. While he still makes his living as a lawyer, he enjoys thinking of himself as an author. His work has appeared in *Aoife's Kiss*, *Black Petals*, *Dark Corners*, *nanobison*, *Wicked Hollow*, and *Wondrous Web Worlds vol. 4*, and he is currently working on a novel.

Christe M. Callabro grew up in an undisclosed region of SouthEastern Pennsylvania. She received her Bachelor's degree in English from Penn State University and now uses English every day. English helped her earn her M.A. in Writing Popular Fiction from Seton Hill University in 2005. Currently, she works at making other people sound swell, while writing here and there and sending out her novel. Her short story "Blood and Ambrosia" appeared in the anthology *Cloaked in Shadow: Dark Tales of Elves* in 2004. If you see her, be nice to her. She doesn't bite, unless you ask her to. Politely.
Contact Christe at cmcallabro@gmail.com

Robert Guffey is a graduate of the Master of Fine Arts Program at California State University at Long Beach. He is also a graduate of the Clarion writer's workshop in Seattle, WA. His first published short story "The Infant Kiss" received an Honorable Mention in the 2001 edition of *The Year's Best Fantasy & Horror* (Vol. #14). His short stories, articles and interviews have appeared in such magazines and anthologies as *After Shocks*, *The Chiron Review*, *Like Water Burning*, *Mysteries*, *New Dawn*, *The New York Review of Science Fiction*, *Paranoia*, *The Pedestal*, *Riprap*, *Steamshovel Press*, and *The Third Alternative*. He is currently teaching English at CSU Long Beach. He can be contacted at rguffey@hotmail.com.

Richard Parks is a former paint chemist. When he got tired of coming home a different color every day he switched to computers and is now a network administrator. He lives in Mississippi with his wife and three cats. His stories have appeared in *Asimov's SF*, *Realms of Fantasy*, *SF Age*, *Amazing Stories*, *Weird Tales*, *Fantasy Magazine*, and Lady Churchill's Rosebud Wristlet, as well as anthologies such as *Not of Woman Born*, *Robert Bloch's Psychos*, and *Year's Best Fantasy*. PS Publishing will bring out his novella, *Hereafter and After*, as a signed limited edition in late 2006. His first story collection, *The Ogre's Wife*, was nominated for the World Fantasy Award. His second collection, *Worshiping Small Gods*, is due out from Prime Books in mid 2006.

Rhonda Mason has a Masters degree in Writing Popular Fiction from Seton Hill University and a B.S. in Environmental Geoscience from Umass Lowell. While writing is her first love, she loves to talk about her second: rocks. Well, minerals, to be more precise. She'd be hard pressed to pick a favorite, but corundum, beryl, and ilmenite are right up there. She also loves dragons, swords, castles . . . well, basically anything fantasy related. Except chain mail bikinis. Those are definitely out. Someone go hurt her if she ever writes a book with such ridiculous armor in it. However, capes and mage robes as "armor?" Totally acceptable. If she could be any animal she'd be a dragon, of course. If forced to pick a "real" animal she'd argue that dragons are real, and then grudgingly pick a falcon. Her weapon of choice is a kris dagger—or a sword. Her favorite magical power is, without a doubt, call lighting. But you can't beat the classic fireball. Or a simple shield spell. She credits William Horner, the wonderful and dedicated editor/creator of this anthology, with broadening her horizons as a writer. Without him she might never have ventured into the realm of modern dark fantasy or short fiction. Her words of wisdom (borrowed from George Eliot) are: "It is never late to be what you might have been."

Jill Knowles writes dark fantasy, horror, and paranormal romantica. She can still count her short story sales using both hands, but the number is creeping steadily up. Soon, she'll have to use her toes as well. Currently, her work can be found in *Tales of the Talisman* magazine, and "Abyss and Apex" online magazine.

James S. Dorr's new book, *Darker Loves: Tales of Mystery and Regret*, is due out from Dark Regions Press (www.darkregions.com) as a companion to his current collection, *Strange Mistresses: Tales of Wonder and Romance*, while other work has appeared in such venues as *Alfred Hitchcock's Mystery Magazine*, *New Mystery*, *Aboriginal SF*, *Fantastic*, *Terminal Fright*, *Future Orbits*, *Shadows of Saturn*, *Gothic.net*, *Chi-Zine*, *Marsdust*, *Lenox Avenue*, *Enigmatic Tales* (UK), *Faeries* (France), *Redsine* (Australia), and numerous anthologies. Dorr is an active member of the SFWA and HWA, a semi-professional musician, an Anthony (mystery) and Darrell (fiction set in the US Mid-South) finalist, winner of Best of the Web 1998, a Pushcart Prize nominee, keeper of a gray and black cat named Wednesday (after Wednesday Addams of *The Addams Family* and whose favorite toy is a plastic fake spider), and has had work listed in *The Year's Best Fantasy and Horror* eleven of the past fourteen years.

Ken Brady is a writer, actor, and filmmaker. His short fiction has appeared in or is forthcoming from publications including *Analog*, *Weird Tales*, *Writers of the Future*, *Strange Horizons*, *Rosebud*, *The William and Mary Review*, *The Fortean Bureau*, *Black October*, *Exquisite Corpuscle*, *Midnight Street*, *Science Fiction World*, and *Talebones*. His fiction has also been reprinted in seven languages worldwide. In addition, he has sold stage plays to Playscripts, a screenplay to Miramax, produced an award-winning feature film, and worked on an interactive CD-rom with Alan M. Clark. He currently lives in Portland, Oregon. For more information, check out his website at www.sff.net/people/kennethbrady.

Steve Verge plays a married man with two children in real life. He lives in Michigan where he coaches little league, takes the kids fishing, plays baseball on weekends, mows the lawn, and participates in any number of other activities enjoyed by mainstream society. In his writing life, however, he likes to play on the darker side. Although he's never engaged in a seesaw massacre or been killed by a giant, mummified egg, some of his characters have. His early fiction appeared in classic small press publications such as *Haunts* and *After Hours*. He's a former winner of *Scavenger's Newsletter*'s Killer Frog Award, captured third place in the *Twilight Tales* Flash Fiction Contest at the 2004 World Horror Convention, and has earned honorable mention in *The Year's Best Fantasy And Horror*. He has even rubbed off on his children, both of whom have been published in the local library's annual *Write For Fright* booklet. His recent work has been featured online at deathlings.com, *The Dream People*, and *Flashshot*. Look for more in the anthologies *Travel A Time Historic*, *Goremet Cuisine*, and *Mind Scraps*. His story "Pavlov's Breast" hasn't been endorsed by the La Leche League, but he's still hoping.

Donna Munro usually writes her horror and fantasy stories between teaching history to teenagers, her daughter's soccer games, and her son's cello lessons. Her stories have appeared in *Playgirl*, *Crossroads*, and *Litmag* where she won first place for her prose. She credits her success to the wonderful training she received from Seton Hill University's Writing Popular Fiction Program. The mentors and writing community there, she says, create the best environment for producing memorable stories (be sure to check out the chapel at night). "Golden Rule" was inspired by her daughter during a long road trip from the East Coast to St. Louis. Enjoy!

Erin MacKay was born in Mobile, Alabama and raised all over the Southeastern United States. She lives in Atlanta with her husband and two dogs, and works downtown as a legal assistant. Her interests include history, gourmet beer, football, and anime, not necessarily in that order.

Look for Erin's short fiction in *Corpse Blossoms* from Creeping Hemlock Press; Fantasist Enterprises's *Cloaked in Shadow: Dark Tales of Elves*; and *Surreal* magazine.

Jim C. Hines has been writing for over a decade now, though he tries not to think about that. His work has appeared in such places as *Realms of Fantasy*, *Turn the Other Chick*, *Sword & Sorceress*, and numerous other magazines and anthologies. Jim lives in Michigan, where he spends as much time as possible with his wife and children, all the while waiting for fame and fortune to arrive. They haven't shown up yet, but Jim remains hopeful. He suspects they took a wrong turn in Albuquerque. If you see them, please direct them to www.jimchines.com, so they can get in touch. Jim would like to dedicate "No Worries, Partner" to Teddi in Elko. She knows why.

James Maxey's stories have appeared in *Asimov's*, *Abyss and Apex*, and several anthologies. His debut novel *Nobody Gets the Girl* is still available from Amazon. He is currently working out a deal with a publisher interested in his second novel, an epic fantasy entitled *Bitterwood*. Fans of sporadic, rambling essays about angels, comic books, politicians and circus freaks should check out his blog at jamesmaxey.blogspot.com.

John Passarella won the Horror Writer Association's Bram Stoker Award for his co-authored first novel, *Wither*. Columbia Pictures purchased the film rights to *Wither* in a preemptive, pre-publication bid, though the film has yet to be made. As part of his Wendy Ward series, Passarella has written two stand-alone sequels to *Wither*, *Wither's Rain* and *Wither's Legacy*. He authored original media tie-in novels *Buffy the Vampire Slayer: Ghoul Trouble*, *Angel: Avatar* and *Angel: Monolith*. Scheduled for June 2006 publication is his supernatural thriller *Kindred Spirit*.

Passarella is a member of the Author's Guild, the Horror Writers Association (HWA), the Science Fiction and Fantasy Writers of America (SFWA), and the Garden State Horror Writers (GSHW). A former Treasurer and current mentor of the HWA, he is also the current webmaster for the GSHW. Through his AuthorPromo.com business, he hosts, designs and/or maintains websites for various authors. He is the webmaster for *New York Times* bestselling authors Harlan Coben and Nicholas Sparks.

Passarella lives in southern New Jersey with his wife, three children, and assorted pets. He maintains his official web site at www.passarella.com.

Mary Rosenblum first published in *Asimov's Magazine* in 1990 with "For A Price," a Clarion West story. Since that first publication, she has published more than 60 short stories in SF, mystery, and mainstream fiction, as well as three SF novels, *The Drylands*, *Chimera*, and *Stone Garden*. Her SF stories have been published in *Asimov's*, *The Magazine of Fantasy and Science Fiction*, *SciFiction*, and *Analog*, among others. She won the Compton Crook award for Best First Novel, The Asimov's Readers Award, and has been a Hugo Award finalist. She has also published a mystery series and short stories as Mary Freeman. Her next novel, *Horizon*, set on Earth's orbital platforms, will be out from Tor in November 2006.

Mary lives in the Pacific Northwest. When she is not writing, she trains dogs in tracking, sheep herding, and obedience work and grows all her fruits and vegetables on country acreage. You can find more information at her website: www.maryrosenblum.com

W. H. Horner is the Publisher and Editor-in-Chief of Fantasist Enterprises. A resident of Wilmington, DE, William enjoys Yoga and Tai Chi when he is not reading, writing, or editing. He earned a Master's in Writing Popular Fiction in January 2006, and is currently finalizing edits on his first novel, a high fantasy adventure. You can visit his (all-too) quiet corner of the web at www.whhorner.com. Rumor has it, he's looking for clients for his freelance editing gig.

Coming Soon

the Art of MODERN MAGIC

$25.00 • 80 Pages
ISBN 13: 978-0-9713608-9-1
ISBN 10: 0-9713608-9-8
Fall 2006

The Art of Modern Magic contains all thirty-five illustrations, a full-color spread of the cover, sketches, and excerpts from the *Modern Magic* anthology that inspired the dark visions that Seidman created with cameras, computers, and a steady hand.

The MODERN MAGIC Soundtrack

Coming Soon

From industrial to country, from ambient to metal, *Modern Magic: The Soundtrack* is a musical journey across the modern soundscape, inspired by the twenty-six tales of fantasy and horror found in the pages of the anthology.

Coming Soon

Bash Down the Door and Slice Open the Badguy:
Humorous Tales of Swords & Sorcery

Evil emperors. Powerful curses. Bananna peels of death. It's a veritable chorus line of thick-skulled warriors, worthless wizards, and hapless henchmen.

$17.00 • 35 Illustrations
Trade Paperback • 6" x 9"
ISBN 13: 978-0-9713608-5-3
ISBN 10: 0-9713608-5-5
Fall 2006

Blood and Devotion
Epic Tales of Fantasy

The clash of steel.
The scent of blood.
The heat of fire from heaven.
The cries of the dying and of the dead.

Brave warriors and devotees to the gods follow the path their faith has put before them, and when religious fervor meets skill of arms and magic, kings will fall, armies will collide, and men and women will perish.

$17.00 • Illustrated
Trade Paperback • 6" x 9"
ISBN 13: 978-0-9713608-8-4
ISBN 10: 0-9713608-8-X
Fall 2006

The Dark Illustrations of
David Seidman

The haunting photo-illustrations by David Seidman are available as 8½" x 11" prints on 80#, white, acid-free cover stock.

Order prints at http://art.fantasistent.com, or photocopy of the order form.

Art From Modern Magic

Page # of Illustration	Qty.	Price Each	Extended Price
Cover (signed & numbered)	_____	$20.00	_____
_____	_____	$12.00	_____
_____	_____	$12.00	_____
_____	_____	$12.00	_____
_____	_____	$12.00	_____
_____	_____	$12.00	_____
_____	_____	$12.00	_____
_____	_____	$12.00	_____
_____	_____	$12.00	_____
_____	_____	$12.00	_____
_____	_____	$12.00	_____
_____	_____	$12.00	_____

Add $3.00 shipping for each print.   Shipping: _____

                                                                                   Total: _____

Please **print** the following:
Name: _____

Address: _____

City: _____ State: _____ Zip: _____

Do Not Send Cash.
Make checks or money orders out to Fantasist Enterprises at
PO Box 9381, Wilmington, DE 19809, USA

Printed in the United States
50553LVS00004B/37